To Pip

Mary Victoria was born in 1973 in Turner's Falls, Massachusetts in the United States. Despite this she managed to live most of her life in other places, including Cyprus, Canada, Sierra Leone, France and the UK. She studied animation and worked for ten years in the film industry before turning to full time writing. She now lives in Wellington, New Zealand with her husband and daughter.

Lovely to meet you!

M. Victoria

BOOKS BY MARY VICTORIA

CHRONICLES OF THE TREE

Tymon's Flight (1)

TYMON'S FLIGHT

CHRONICLES *of the* TREE — BOOK ONE

MARY VICTORIA

HARPER
Voyager

Harper*Voyager*
An imprint of HarperCollins*Publishers*

First published in Australia in 2010
by HarperCollins*Publishers* Australia Pty Limited
ABN 36 009 913 517
harpercollins.com.au

HarperCollins*Publishers*
25 Ryde Road, Pymble, Sydney, NSW 2073, Australia
31 View Road, Glenfield, Auckland 0627, New Zealand
A 53, Sector 57, Noida, UP, India
77–85 Fulham Palace Road, London, W6 8JB, United Kingdom
2 Bloor Street East, 20th floor, Toronto, Ontario M4W 1A8, Canada
10 East 53rd Street, New York NY 10022, USA

National Library of Australia Cataloguing-in-Publication data:

Victoria, Mary.
   Tymon's flight / Mary Victoria.
   ISBN: 978 0 7322 9098 6 (pbk.)
   Victoria, Mary. Chronicles of the tree ; bk. 1.
NZ823.3

Cover design by Darren Holt, HarperCollins Design Studio
Cover illustration by Frank Victoria
Map by Frank Victoria
Typeset in Goudy 10.5/13pt by Kirby Jones
Printed and bound in Australia by Griffin Press
50gsm Bulky News used by HarperCollins*Publishers* is a natural,
recyclable product made from wood grown in sustainable plantation
forests. The manufacturing processes conform to the environmental
regulations in the country of origin, New Zealand.

5 4 3 2 1   10 11 12 13

For Faith

TYMON'S FLIGHT

PROLOGUE

I saw the shape of God
Like to a mighty Tree:
Of fire were Her branches made,
Fearful Her symmetry ...
— Saint Loa of the Leaves

The body of the pilgrim, bound to a hastily constructed bier and wrapped in cheap bark-fibre, slid almost too easily over the dirigible's deck-rail and plunged without a sound into the depths. Father Adelard Ferny leaned over the rail and peered after it. The tiny human bundle dipped and spiralled as it fell between the gigantic leaves of the World Tree, glancing once, briefly, against an outcrop in the sheer wall of the trunk before spinning to oblivion. The priest winced then shrugged as he drew back from the rail. At least there had been no cause for scandal. At least they had been rid of the corpse before they arrived in Argos city air-harbour, and were subjected to unwelcome questions and tedious procedures from the quarantine guards. In the end the sick man had been as self-effacing in death as he had been in life: invisible, emaciated by the fever that took him, no more than a husk of parched skin and

I

dried bone. It was a mercy, thought Father Ferny. A heavier man would have been knocked off his bier during the fall and gone to his rest in ignominious bits.

The priest turned his attention to the group of foreign pilgrims huddled on the deck of the ship. He was glad to see that they, too, found no cause for criticism in the funeral service. They were not mumbling to each other in their wretched language for once, murmuring the Tree knew what behind his back.

'Nothing is free,' he declared to his bedraggled flock. 'The Tree does not give Her blessings for free. One must die so that others may live, so that the canopy may continue to flourish, the rains to fall and the sap to flow.'

His sermon was interrupted as the dirigible's ether sacks released a tremendous hiss of gas and the ship resumed its descent towards Argos city. Father Ferny coughed in annoyance and waited for the drawn-out sound to cease. His audience took advantage of the lull to shuffle to the railing themselves, blinking in the updraft.

A magnificent vista opened before them. The dirigible greatship with its teeming mass of sails and ether sacks was a tiny dot against the western marches of the Tree trunk, a mote on the vertical face of the world. To starboard of the vessel, in front of the pilgrims, stretched a vast and furrowed mountain of bark, so wide that its curvature was almost invisible and so high that both its summit and its base were lost to view. The immensity of the wall was broken by a profusion of spoke-like limbs, the largest many miles in length. Several hundred feet above the dirigible the trunk culminated in the gently rising plateau of branches and twigs that made up the Central Canopy's crown. Its summit lay more than seven leagues to the north and east of Argos city, and five miles higher, in the frozen Upper Fringes. The greatship had spent the better part of its recent journey in warmer latitudes, skimming in a wide arc about the southern marches of the Tree, just above the leaf-tips. But now as it made its approach to Argos city it sank beneath the green billows — slipped between mottled twig shafts and towers of alternating leaves, taking several minutes to pass each burnished blade. The dramatic Treescapes of Argos were said to be among the loveliest in the world.

The foreign pilgrims did not appear to appreciate the beauty of the Central Canopy for its own sake, however. They gaped over the railing after their departed colleague as if they were searching the trailing mists for some sign — as if they were expecting him to rise up again, like a saint in rapture. They wore matching tunics of grey. Their faces were ugly and grey, too, thought the priest: dirt-pale and lined with fatigue and privation. They were silent but they smelled. He could not help but shudder as he shrank back from the unwashed bodies crowded next to him at the rail. At last the hiss of ether faded and he was able to speak again.

'Death is a consequence of life. Violence is the price of peace,' he announced irritably, raising his voice to draw his listeners away from the gulf. 'It has always been so. Because of our terrible sins, we must buy God's grace at a price.'

For two years Father Ferny had faithfully served the Priests' Council, recruiting these young Nurians from the drought-infested colonies for the annual tribute to Argos. He had travelled the Four Canopies, visiting regions undreamt-of by his colleagues: places where the barbarous natives had never practised proper Tree-worship, never heard of God's green grace. He had put up with impious pilgrims, insufferable colonists, an impossible climate, all in the hopes of making a name for himself at the seminary. And still he could not get used to that smell, that dirty, thirsty, Godless smell of the Eastern Canopy. It was the smell of slavery, the smell of poverty. The foreigners carried it with them even here in Argos, in the lush green hub of the world. The whiff of drought followed them about like a curse. Look at them, gulping in the wind like fools, he thought. The Dean will be lucky to get a specimen for the Rites out of this lot.

The Nurian tithe-pilgrims were ostensibly volunteers, though young Adelard had experienced many and varied interpretations of that word during his travels. The eastern colonies, twenty leagues and four weeks' voyage by dirigible from Argos city, might have been another universe entirely. The Eastern Canopy grew on its own vast outcrop of the Tree, separated from the rest of the world by a gap as much spiritual as physical. The closest branches broke the clouds a day's journey from the Central Canopy. They were bare and grey, shorn of their green glory, for the East had been leafless for generations. No life-giving sap flowed through its branches; no Tree-water rose in its dry wells. The colonies were truly a Tree-forsaken place. There, a man might fall into bad company and wake up after a night of revelry to find himself bound in service on a tithe-ship. He might find that his own family had volunteered him for pilgrimage after a particularly disappointing vine-harvest. Father Ferny did not ask too many questions of the youths he herded aboard his ship at the height of the dry season. In any event, there always seemed to be enough of the poverty-stricken Nurians willing to sell their freedom — or that of their children — for a few barrels of water. The tribute never went unpaid, and the tithe-ships never returned to Argos empty of cargo.

And when the foreigners arrived at the site of their pilgrimage the miracles continued. Every year, despite Father Ferny's private misgivings, one among the group of Nurians invariably offered himself up during the spring Sacrifice. Every year this unlikely volunteer would throw himself into a Tree-rift, eagerly and of his own accord. It was, as the missionary never tired of repeating to his flock, this act of willing martyrdom that appeased the wrath of the Tree and banished the Storm-demons back beneath the clouds at Her feet. For Ferny, like most of his colleagues, believed the world was hemmed in by a godless Void. The Storm clouds that enveloped the base of the Tree were full of legendary horrors. Though it was not possible to see the roiling vapours from the vantage point of the dirigible, no one on the ship could forget what lay hidden below, under the softly stirring leaves of the Central Canopy. No one could forget where the dead man's journey would end.

'The weight of sin pulls us all downwards, my children! This is the law that drags all bodies into the Storm!' intoned the priest, rolling his 'r's' magnificently. The majority of the pilgrims glanced nervously away from the chasm in reaction to his words. He smiled; they were so predictable. 'We are all sinners, otherwise we would not fall. We are dependent on God's green grace. No other can save us from the Storm. No other can deliver us from darkness and chaos and carry us up to the light.'

He squinted up at the sun glancing through the towering columns of leaves. Too high, already — the morning hours were slipping away. The sermon had gone on too long. The funeral ought to be over before they docked in Argos city. If the officials at the air-harbour knew there had been a fever death aboard, the crew would be quarantined for three whole days. And that would cut Ferny's rest and recreation period down. Besides, the damned Nurry had simply been a weakling. He had been sick during the whole journey, probably sick before he signed on, and had perversely chosen this very morning to give up his pale little ghost. A dud, damn him, root and stock.

'We must mortify the flesh, mortify the heavy, sinful body and become sublime,' the priest gabbled on, in an effort to finish his homily before they arrived. 'We must turn our thoughts to Sacrifice, to giving up the body and the things of the body. Only thus do we save our fellow men and earn the right to soar to the highest heavens. The Tree might withdraw Her blessings at any time. Did wrong belief not offend Her in the East and cause the leaf-forests to wither away? Did She not allow the Storm to rise up and whip away the Old Empire in order to punish the heretics and disbelievers? Beware, beware the wrath of God, for Hers is the power to decide —'

This time he was interrupted by a half-articulated word, an inadvertent sound from one of the pilgrims at the rail. A moment later a cry went up from the ship's lookout that caused a chill to pass through Father Ferny, a confused terror.

'Ha-ven!'

The foreigners jostled each other, leaning eagerly over the side of the ship. Below them, perhaps half a mile from the ship, the towers and turrets of Argos city could just be seen through the thinning mist. The celebrated capital was built in the crux of a branch extending at an angle from the trunk-wall. Four of the town's five tiers clung to the slope of the limb, spreading down in ever widening circles to a valley-like trench where the branch joined the trunk. As if in answer to the sun, bells pealed out from the peaked roofs of the seminary in the topmost tier, sending another shiver through Adelard Ferny. He assumed it was nostalgia. He was home.

The sailors bellowed and whistled to each other in the dirigible's rigging, and the prow swung round in a stately arc as the ship made its final approach to the air-harbour. The foreigners stood agog at the rail, straining to see the object of their journey, the sacred centre of their pilgrimage. At last, half hidden behind an obscuring outcrop in the trunk, a cleft became visible. The Tree-face above the city was split by a narrow rift, a black hole plunging to unseen, inner depths. It was the holiest of holies, the Divine Mouth! Thirty-nine pairs of eyes searched out a winding thread along the bark wall, the ledge that led from the docks to the lip of the hole. The Argosian priests might have been concerned with their Rites and with preserving the world as they knew it, but the Nurians had a marked preference for apocalypse.

'The King will come,' the foreigners whispered to each other in their own language, as Father Ferny gave up his battle for their souls and hurried back to the Captain's cabin, his ears plugged against that confounded murmuring. 'He will die and rise again out of the Mouth. One day, the King will come. We will be free.'

One had to die so that others might live. It had always been so.

PART ONE
SEEDS

In the seed, the tree. In the boy, the man.
— Argosian saying

I

On a clear spring morning the sound of bells from Argos seminary carried for miles. The shrill voice of the carillon called the priests to temple ritual, marked the saints' days and holy days and echoed out at regular intervals to proclaim the hours. The first peals issued from the bell-tower at dawn. They tumbled through the Priests' Quarter and into the terraced town like rain, and rang out almost directly above the novices' dormitories, serving to rouse the sleepy students for prayers.

The boy woke that day, as every day, to the familiar sound. The bells were part of the natural order of things: it never occurred to him to imagine a morning without them. He rolled out of his narrow hammock and into his breeches in one practised, fluid motion, coming to a halt by a table on which stood a washbasin and a polished hardwood mirror. The black disc reflected his wiry shadow. He stuck out his chin and peered into the dim image in a fruitless search for stubble. The dormitory was just beginning to come to life and several more figures sat up in the hammocks, groaning and cursing at the bells. The boy made a face in the mirror.

'Give it up, Tymon,' remarked a voice. A heavy-set youth emerged from one of the hammocks, yawning. 'You won't grow leaves till the root gets planted!'

His comment provoked a smattering of laughter among his fellows, but the lad named Tymon did not allow himself to be bested. He left off searching his chin and grabbed a white tunic, the standard dress for novices, out of a clean pile on the floor.

'Bolas thinks he's quite the man,' he observed to the room in general, pulling the tunic over his head. 'But the only planting he does is in the temple gardens.'

His answer drew a few appreciative whistles. The hammocks were disgorging their blinking, dishevelled occupants and the students loitered by the two speakers, relishing the debate. Tymon filled the washbasin by the mirror with water from a hardwood jug.

Bolas grinned tolerantly, tucking a prefect's green sash over his ordinary white tunic. 'At least my Rites-duties are over and done with, which is more than can be said for you, bound-boy,' he said. 'Where are you off to today in such a hurry? Lentils need sorting in the kitchen? Anyone would think you like doing slaves' and women's work.'

Another round of snickers. Tymon's back stiffened. The taunts were familiar but never failed to find their mark. To be 'bound' or indentured to the priests was one thing. To be a slave, a foreign tithe-pilgrim, was quite another.

'I'm no one's property,' he snapped as he splashed water over his hot neck. 'Besides, what's wrong with the kitchen? Don't you enjoy the company of women?'

He smiled through gritted teeth, dipped his fingers into the basin, and flicked a handful of water at the other boy.

'I have seven sisters,' muttered Bolas, wiping the droplets from his cheek, with a grimace. 'I know more about women than you'd ever dream of. Anyway, they're Impure. Do you want to go to the Guild Fair, or not? Or have you already been barred, you fool?'

A ripple of agreement ran through the room at his mention of the Fair. The students in the dormitory were all in their Green Year, the time of a young man's maturity in Argos, and due to celebrate their initiation rites at the spring Sacrifice. The 'Green Rites' conferred the advantages and responsibilities of full citizenship, a status available to only a few in the city. One reward of initiation was admittance to the Guild Fair that took place after the Festival. The novices were indifferent to the duties, the laws of Purity and Impurity, and solemn sacraments which accompanied the Rites. But all were agog to attend the Fair. Tymon was no exception.

'Of course I'm going,' he exclaimed, stung. 'I don't kiss the priests' robes, but it doesn't mean I'm barred.'

'Well then, be careful,' shrugged his comrade. 'You'll have time enough to play at being a man after Rites.'

'Boys play, men do,' declared Tymon. 'And I don't mind what I'm doing so long as Nell's around. You'll have to excuse me — I have an appointment this morning. Cover for me at prayers!'

Without waiting for a reply, he dodged past the slow-moving students and out of the dormitory doors.

The novices' sleeping quarters were accessible only by ladder. Tymon swung through a hatch in the floor of the exterior balcony, skipping down the narrow rungs with the ease of long practice, his body as taut and tight as a spring. He was now on the cusp of the growth spurt that turns a youth into a man, full of pent-up possibilities. He had few close companions, for his indenture set him apart from the other novices. But he could be trusted to amuse his fellows with his schemes and dreams and had acquired a reputation for high jinks at the seminary. He had other plans that morning besides the supposed aim of lovemaking. The mention of Nell, a kitchen maid, was only a diversion. He might have confided his true motives to his friend Wick, who slept in another dorm, but did not feel like explaining himself further to Bolas. He felt no urge to win the prefect's pleasure, to confide more fully in the son of a common carpenter. The wider divisions of Argosian society persisted among the students under a thin veneer of equality. A bound-boy could not afford to be too generous.

'Don't forget your apron,' Bolas yelled after him in annoyance. 'And garden duty. Hoi! Tymon! Garden duty! Don't forget!'

But by the time the prefect strode out onto the balcony his quarry had disappeared, lost in the tangle of ramps and ladders under the building. Bells continued to peal out over the seminary. Morning light flooded the dormitory building and drenched the slope of the branch behind it in startling yellow. Below, the rooftops of Argos city glistened in the rising sun.

Halfway down one of the ladders, Tymon paused. The dormitories were at the summit of the seminary, or 'Priests' Quarter', and commanded a sweeping view of the town. Gleaming bark roofs and thatched turrets tumbled higgledy-piggledy down the steep incline of the branch that supported the city, only to come up short against the wall of the trunk. High in that sheer face, the sacred Mouth lurked hidden behind its outcrop, a brooding hollow presence over the town. He did not lift his eyes to the enigmatic cavity. His gaze flitted over the streets, to alight eagerly on the wide-open curve of the air-harbour. The quays inscribed an arc on the southern side of the city, spanning the trench between the supporting branch and the trunk. The West Chasm yawned beyond.

Tymon chewed his lip in a reverie. To him the arc of the air-harbour seemed full of hazy promise; the dirigibles that lined its quays bore all his hopes and dreams. Bulky freights and farm barges, sleek government vessels and imposing merchant ships creaked on their moorings, ether sacks billowing in the wind. He searched out the space reserved for the largest merchant craft. There, tethered on its own quay in magnificent isolation from the other dirigibles, hovered a triple-masted greatship, the word *Stargazer* painted in bright blue letters on its hull. It had just returned from a season voyage to the Eastern Canopy. He could see the small figures of the crew climbing high in the rigging, tying up the sails. His heart soared. A dirigible was the key to freedom as far as he was concerned. His ambition was to one day possess such an instrument of liberty, to study the fine art of navigation and make his name as an adventurer in foreign parts. His understanding of what that work might entail was limited and highly romantic. He watched the activity on the quays for a few minutes, a wistful expression on his face. Then, roused by the sound of voices overhead and the tug of hunger, he slid down the remaining rungs of the ladder and dropped into the cloistered courtyard below.

The last bell notes were tolling out over the seminary. Priests in their dark green robes herded younger students up the back stairs to the temple in time for morning prayers, winding up the side of the steep buttress of bark that divided the seminary in two. On one side lay the monastery, student dormitories and classrooms: on the other, the Priests' College, library and main doors to the outside world. The temple Hall with its bell-tower stood high on the central ridge, presiding in pomp over the entire city. The young truant gave both the stairs and the hurrying figures a wide berth and darted down a dark corridor through the heart of the buttress, emerging a few moments later in the sunny College quadrangle. He made for the main doors on the east side. Halfway across the quadrangle, however, he abruptly changed his mind and turned to his right, entering a small compound under the shadow of the seminary walls. From the low building at its heart came the sound of laughter and the smell of pancakes.

The kitchens were the only section of the College that employed women. The din of breakfast preparations had already invaded the compound and as the boy drew near the building a tight-knit group of cooks and serving girls spilled out of the doorway to meet him. They had brought lentils and beans into the courtyard to sort for chaff, and bore their trays and folding stools like ammunition, setting them down with a clatter and clash of finality. One of them, a large, kindly-looking matron in a red headscarf, nodded to Tymon with a customary blessing.

'In the beauty, my sprout.'

'In the beauty, Amu Masha,' he replied. He gallantly offered her his arm, helping to install her bulk on one of the precarious folding seats; he called her 'Amu', or 'mother', as much out of affection as respect. 'Feeling well this morning, I hope?' he asked.

Masha beamed. 'Better than usual. The Dean is leaving on his retreat.'

'Which means he won't miss you at first prayers,' put in a young brown-haired woman, sitting nearby. She did not look at Tymon or mark his dashing pose, picking diligently through her lentils. 'Hurry and you might still get there on time.'

'Charity doesn't wait for prayer, Nell. I have to visit Galliano,' he said airily.

'He has to visit Galliano,' echoed several of the kitchen sisterhood, exchanging knowing glances.

'I suppose you'll be wanting to take the poor lost soul some charitable gifts,' observed Masha. 'See what you can find in the pantry, Nell.'

Though a novice in his Green Year had no right to associate with females outside the bonds of kin, some customary leeway did exist in Tymon's case. The kitchen matriarchy was his adoptive family. It was Masha, the head cook, who had found the little babe lying in a woven basket by the seminary gates some fifteen summers ago; he had grown up among the pots and pans, by turns petted or scolded by a fleet of serving maids. His kitchen sisters may have been limited in their sphere, but they ruled their small realm completely. The brown-haired woman laid aside her tray with pursed lips. She did not bother to motion to Tymon to follow her: she knew he would. A novice's only alternative to the lack of female presence in the seminary was an active imagination and Nell, the youngest and prettiest of the maids, was the subject of much energetic discussion among the boys. Tymon experienced a distinct sense of gratification as he pursued her through the kitchen door. He wished his dormitory mates could see him now, Guild Fair or no Guild Fair. The position of bound-boy had its own advantages.

Inside the kitchen, trestles had been brought out in preparation for breakfast and the air was sweet with the smell of pancakes and frogapple sauce. Three serving apprentices were busy at the grill, turning the golden pancakes and filling a stack of plates. Tymon's belly grumbled. His attention wandered from Nell to the plates, then back to Nell again. He tried a winning smile and the formula the older boys at the seminary had assured him worked miracles.

'You're looking beautiful today, Nell. Did you change your hair?'

The serving girl was evidently less impressed with the lad than he was with himself. She fetched a cold roast bird from the pantry and slapped it down on a counter without ceremony, along with a stick of barley-bread.

'That's all you're getting,' she announced.

'Ah, come on. Have a bit of mercy. Just one kiss.'

'Green Mother, give me patience.' She pushed past him and out towards the door. 'Mind your Rites, Tymon. And wipe that look off your face.'

Tymon grabbed the victuals and pursued her, dancing between tables. 'Alright. How about a pancake?' he called.

Without waiting for an answer, he lifted one neatly off a plate and stuffed it into his mouth. She shrieked in indignation, but he was past her and into the garden in an instant, his cheeks bulging, choking with laughter. He was about to quit the compound when Masha's voice rang out across the garden.

'Young sprout.'

He hung back, an edge of impatience in his answer. 'Yes, Amu?'

The older woman beckoned to him from the other side of the compound. 'Give me just a moment of your precious time. I have something to show you.'

He followed the old cook's round and homely form with far less alacrity than he had Nell's. He suspected she was going to give him a moral lecture, to remind him to complete his Rites-duties in time for the Festival. Tymon resented the seemingly endless requirements heaped on him by the seminary in order to be eligible for the ceremony; he had put off carrying out the least palatable of the duties until now, and consequently faced several weeks of grinding tedium.

Masha led him to a small shed at the far end of the kitchen building, a linen press stacked with drying laundry. From one of the shelves she took down a package wrapped in rough strawpaper which she turned over lovingly in her large hands.

'You'll be going to your Rites soon,' she sighed. 'It's a special time. Oh, I know all you fine young things don't give a gnat's tooth for the Green Rites. But they're very important. Are you listening to me?'

'Yes, Amu.'

'You'll be a man. Better still, you'll be an educated man, a superior man, and you'll have options. I want you to do well for yourself, my sprout.'

'I know. Thank you, Amu.' He fidgeted with impatience.

'Remember,' she continued, fixing him with an earnest eye, 'that you're an indentured orphan. It won't be as easy for you as for the others. You must take the Purity laws seriously. Don't give those tight-nailed priests a scrap of a reason to bar you, understand?'

'I understand.'

She raised an eyebrow at his glib answer.

'Really, I do,' he protested. 'There's no reason to worry.'

She maintained an eloquent silence, opened the package and shook out a length of fine cloth the colour of new leaves. Tymon leaned closer, his interest piqued.

'These were my son's Green robes,' she said, softly. 'I made them myself, a good many years ago. I've decided they will be yours. I'm not going to give them to you now — you'll only drag them through the dust, heaven knows where. But I wanted you to know.'

The boy reached out involuntarily to touch the soft folds. 'Thank you, Amu,' he mumbled, unable to think of what else to say. Masha's son was long dead, taken by fly-fever at a youthful age. Dimly, Tymon realised that he was, to all intents and purposes, the old cook's only surviving family.

She held the cloth protectively against her bosom. 'Promise me,' she pleaded. 'Do your duties. Keep the laws. Be good for just a little while. They'll be watching you. Remember you have privy duty every day next week, as you haven't done it for a month. And you're assigned to help out at the Bread-Giving this year. Don't miss it.'

'I won't. I promise.'

'Get on with you then.' She folded the green robes into their package again. 'Remember these will be waiting for you on the day of the Festival. I know you'll have earned them.'

He turned to leave, but she had not finished with him. 'And don't keep fussing around Nell,' she chided. 'You're like a shillee-pup in heat. It's ridiculous.'

Tymon ducked away from her fond embrace, waving his farewell. Masha's expression as she watched him hurry out of the compound hovered somewhere between a laugh and a worried frown. She spoiled him out of pity, for to be indentured to the College was hardly an enviable fate. An orphan's lack of family or patronage meant he owed his livelihood to the Priests' Council. The debt would be collected promptly at the end of his schooling through a period of service, unless by dint of good fortune and diligence he was apprenticed to a Guild Master who would pay off the bill. Masha had tempered this chilly arrangement with real mother's love. She gave Tymon his moment in the sun before life caught up with him. Even Nell had a soft spot for the boy. He would have been mortified to learn that she thought of him as no more than an endearing, if tiresome, younger brother.

Tymon, however, was largely unaware of the thoughts and feelings of those around him. Outside the compound he tucked the bread and meat under his arm and made straight for the doors on the east wall of the quadrangle. They were open, their carved façades inscribed with the seminary motto: *Knowledge is All*. An old man sat on a stool just under the shadow of the archway, preoccupied by a large, convoluted jar-pipe. The boy halted at his side.

'In the beauty, warden. I'm on charity duty.'

The warden wrestled with the snarled tubes of his pipe. When he had finally untangled the mouthpiece, he took a deep draw and wheezed, 'Pass, please.'

Tymon proffered a disc of bark from the pocket of his tunic. The warden's cataract-filled eyes could hardly see the marker, but he rubbed the disc through expert fingers before handing it back.

'Do you have permission to leave the seminary this morning, boy?' he asked, breathing a cloud of blue smoke through his nostrils.

'Yes, sir.'

Tymon banished the twinge of worry that accompanied this half-truth. He had no specific mandate to leave the seminary at that hour, and was stretching the definition of charity duty to its limit. But he calculated that the priests might overlook his absence at first prayers. The Dean, after all, was on holiday.

The warden nodded and waved him on, blinking with milky eyes. As Tymon passed him by he took the pipe out of his mouth and observed: 'I see them hanging over your head in a cloud, child.'

'Who, Apu?'

'The little demons. They buzz about like flies.'

'Yes, Apu.' Tymon smiled at the old man's madness, and set off down the steep ramp away from the College.

'You grow backwards,' shrilled the warden. 'Roots over branches. Beware fire!'

He peered blearily at the receding figure of the novice, then hunched his bony shoulders, and clamped the pipe firmly between his teeth.

Argos city was a wonderful sight in spring. The night rains had made the leaf-thatch sparkle, and the creamy lightwood and russet bark-brick of the houses seemed scrubbed clean in the morning sun. The five tiers of the town were a shining tumult of platforms, narrow causeways, alleys and courtyards, with more stairwells than boulevards and more ramps and ladders than arcades. Flat space was at a premium in the city. Tymon took the main causeway that zigzagged down to the docks, weaving through a maze of shop-fronts and street stalls, past bleating herds of shillees being driven to market, vendors burdened with crates of vegetables and floridly cursing cart-drivers. The causeway was crammed with people. Some smiled at the sight of Tymon's white tunic. But the faces that turned in his direction were not always kind. A novice was supposed to be in the temple at this hour, and not everyone took an indulgent view of missing prayers.

The thoroughfare came to a congested end in the lowest tier. The boy elbowed his way through the crowded market towards the city gates. Access to the docks and the principal road out of the town was by means of a tunnel through a fortified tower, closed off at one end by a pair of massive hardwood doors. The great portals were thrown wide on special occasions to permit large gatherings on the quays, but the usual method of exit and entry was a small postern gate cut into one side. Today this was open, a rectangle of light at the far end of the vaulted passage. He hurried into the cool gloom of the tunnel. The contrast with the sunlight outside was blinding. He was so intent on reaching the gate that in his headlong rush, he collided with someone in the vault.

A white face loomed out of the darkness.

O Ever-Green, o giver of life …

Tymon recoiled from the man in front of him. The sound of chanting rose in the tunnel, a ghostly echo. In his haste he had not seen the white foreigners filing in the opposite direction through the gatehouse. He had forgotten that the *Stargazer*, vessel of his dreams, also transported Nurian tithe-pilgrims to the city. This year's consignment had arrived that very morning, and they were singing psalms.

Green Thy heart, green Thy face.

The faces of the easterners were wan and grimy from their long journey. *Dirty Nurries*, the townsfolk called their annual visitors contemptuously. *White lice.* The logic was explained to every Argosian child at an early age. If the Nurians were forced to live in drought and misery, to barter away their freedom for simple necessities, it was entirely their own fault. God had passed Her judgment on the heathen. They were Impure as a race. The spectacle of the submissive convoy triggered emotions Tymon found hard to untangle. Recovering from his shock, he drew back stiffly to the tunnel wall and allowed the foreigners to pass. He cursed his luck under his breath. Association with pilgrims was forbidden to novices in their Green Year. Even touching their ugly white skin might incur a penalty, a special rite of cleansing or an added duty on the service roster. But it was not only fear of censure, or even a squeamish dislike of what was different that caused the boy to scowl at his toes and avoid looking at the strangers as they shuffled by. He was reminded uncomfortably of the taunts in the dormitory. The step between indenture and slavery was a crucial one: Tymon's whole future hinged on that definition. The presence of the tithe-pilgrims stirred up a lurking fear that the all-important step was not wide enough.

All things in their proper place, sang the pilgrims.

The foreigners' piety was unfathomable to Tymon. They appeared to accept their fate with dismal composure. They filed obediently off towards the city jail, where they would be confined, apart from specific outings, until the Rites. After that they would be sent off to work on a vine plantation. As each one set foot on the main causeway he bowed devoutly in the direction of the Mouth. Tymon felt a vague sense of disgust.

'Watch out!'

The command had an unquestionable authority and brought his steps to a halt. He had been about to turn away from the miserable spectacle, to continue on to the postern gate, when the voice rang out. The last of the foreigners had left the tunnel. There was no one else nearby. The only object in the vicinity was a covered wagon of particular design, stationed at the market end of the vault, near a small door leading to the guards' quarters. The canvas awning pinned over its roof had been pushed aside, showing the sturdy hardwood bars within. The Purity laws extended to cleaning the streets of vagrants and undesirables before the festival, all those who could neither claim an occupation in the city, nor consented to go to the poorhouse. A pair of mournful pack-beasts stood yoked in front of the prison cart, pestered by flies. But no one sat in the cage. Tymon glanced anxiously back towards the guards who accompanied the pilgrims. Had one of them shouted the order?

And then he saw it. It was no more than a fleeting image, a brief glimpse in the milling crowd. One of the pilgrims was different. One of the foreigners neither bowed nor prayed, and seemed in no way intimidated by his surroundings. A slight youth walked at the rear of the procession, gazing fearlessly about him. Wisps of reddish hair strayed out from under his grey skullcap. He surveyed the people in the market with a calm smile, unconcerned with rules of Purity or propriety — or even, apparently, his own safety. The vision lasted an instant. A guard burst through the crowd and laid hold of the youth's shoulder with a loud curse, thrusting him after the others. The pilgrims moved on and the red-haired youth was gone.

'They aren't all the same, you know.'

The hairs prickled on Tymon's neck. The mysterious voice had spoken again. He searched the gloom of the tunnel; the darkness seemed to be articulating his own, unspoken thoughts. This time he pinpointed the source of the remark. The prison transport was occupied, after all. In a corner of the cage, shadowed by the canvas covering, sat a beggar. The man's weather-beaten face was hidden beneath a battered, wide-brimmed hat; he was draped in an ancient travelling cloak of indeterminate hue. Only his eyes gleamed brightly under the hat. They were an unusual, clear green and fixed Tymon with piercing intensity.

'Sometimes,' said the man, nodding in the direction of the pilgrims, 'appearances can be deceiving.'

The boy was unnerved. He salvaged his pride with a shrug. It was bad enough to be confronted with the tribute workers. He was not about to allow himself to be sermonised on the subject by a vagabond.

'What's it to you?' he muttered.

'I speak only as a fellow traveller,' replied the tramp with gentle courtesy. 'We all have need of a friend in strange places.'

Tymon squinted at him in the dim light of the tunnel. The vagrant's manner was gracious, at odds with his rags. He wondered if this was some trick to solicit money.

'That's true, I suppose,' he allowed, cautiously. 'I have to go now. Good luck to you.' He moved towards the postern gate.

'Wait a moment, if you please.'

The mild request was irresistible. Tymon hesitated.

'It's a pity to leave without being introduced.' The prisoner smiled at him through the bars, a flash of white teeth. 'Who are you, young sir?'

'I'm — I'm a novice at the seminary,' stammered Tymon. He was reluctant to give his name to a vagrant.

'In this case the clothes really do make the man,' laughed the other. 'I knew that from the cut of your tunic. But it doesn't answer my question. Who are you?'

'My name is Tymon,' the boy answered warily.

'Again, I did not ask your name, though I thank you for the confidence,' said the man. 'I asked who you were.'

Tymon stared at him. He felt unable to speak. The beggar leaned forward eagerly, as if the answer to that one question were the most important thing in the world. His face caught a ray of light from the mouth of the tunnel; the boy saw that his right cheek was disfigured by an angry red scar. He shivered. He was spared the embarrassment of response, however. Just then, soldiers emerged from the guards' quarters in a blast of raucous merriment, slamming the door behind them.

'You. choir-rat,' cried one of them. 'You're in the way. Get out of there!'

Tymon stepped hastily away from the wagon. A soldier vaulted into the driver's seat and sent his long whip curling over the backs of the pack-beasts. He ignored the prisoner. The vehicle began creaking through the tunnel towards the gate and the docks. The remaining soldiers marched before it and unlocked one of the great doors to the air-harbour; it swung open, groaning on its hinges. The vaulted passage filled with a sudden wash of sunlight. As the cavalcade rattled through the opening the stranger lifted his hand to Tymon, a silent gesture of farewell. The boy did not wave back. At that very moment he had been gripped by the distinct, unpleasant sensation that someone else was watching him from behind. He spun around towards the market end of the tunnel. There, to his alarm, he made out an imposing figure dressed in green.

The Dean! Tymon shrank back against the wall of the vault for the second time, his heart beating. He could see Father Fallow and several members of his retinue approaching down the main causeway, accompanied by a bowing, scraping young priest in missionary robes. The Head of the College kept his colleagues under strict control and his subordinates in a constant state of nervous anticipation; the last thing Tymon wanted was to be caught by him out in the city during morning prayers, and talking to a convicted felon, besides. The act would certainly be classed as Impure. Too late, Masha's warnings came flooding back. He hugged the long shadows of the tunnel and ducked through the air-harbour gate after the wagon, obsessed by a single thought. He must not be seen.

The covered cart turned to the right on the docks, rolling away along the boardwalk. The canvas awning had slipped over the bars. Tymon hastened in the opposite direction, eastwards, towards the trunk-face. Where the quays met the wall of bark, he followed a terraced ramp that wound up the Tree like a wriggling wormhole. Soon he had left the air-harbour far below. He climbed alone up the deserted road, an ant on the monstrous expanse of the trunk. The ramp doubled back on itself, angling back and forth along the wall. With each northward bend, a slit in the bark came further into prominence, revealing at last a gaping black hole. Whether out of long habit, or some instinct of self-preservation, the boy again avoided raising his eyes to the Mouth. He never stopped or looked behind him until he reached one of the minor branches sprouting above the city. Here the way divided. The ramp continued on, zigzagging upwards until it lost itself in the leaf-forests above. The lesser limb was about half a mile long and grew perpendicular to the trunk, extending almost horizontally to Tymon's right. A dusty track threaded along its upper ridge. He stopped at the intersection to catch his breath. The slopes of the branch were carved into neat terraces filled with loam, supporting rows of green barley vine. Birds wheeled in the dizzy space beyond.

Only then did he realise that he had failed to return the beggar's gesture. He had been too concerned with saving himself to say goodbye. The detail made him feel obscurely ashamed, as if he had insulted a saint instead of a nameless tramp. The whole encounter in the gate-tunnel — the arrival of the pilgrims, the conversation with the man in the cart — had left a sour aftertaste in his mouth. The sentiment was ridiculous, he reasoned: he had troubles of his own. He had been right to leave before the Dean noticed him. In any case, he had better things to do that morning than waste his time on slaves and vagrants. Having resolved the matter on a rational level, at least, he set off down the little used track along the branch ridge. The whispering green vines closed about him and he was completely hidden from view.

2

Tymon followed the track along the limb for about half a mile until it wound up a knot and left the barleyvine terraces behind. When he had climbed high enough over the green rows he stopped to look about him. There was no sign of movement on the main road up the trunk. The Tree seemed empty of life except for blackbirds, perched like sentinels along the vine-frames. To his right, the terraces ceased abruptly where the limb curved under and gave way to the gulf. The topmost tier of Argos city lay about two hundred feet below. The cry of merchants and vendors in the streets and the shouts of the sailors on the air-harbour quays carried upwards on the warm breeze. Tymon could see the roofs of the Priests' Quarter from where he stood. The polished hardwood dome of the temple Hall dominated the rest, shaped like the closed petals of a flower. Behind it rose the bell-tower, a thin, tapering construction like a needle, built in the more austere style of the founding fathers of Argos. The bells inside were said to be made of sacred hardwood, carved from the heart of the world. Certainly, no other carillon rang out as sweet, or could be heard as far away. As the boy lingered on the knot, the bells struck seven times, solemnly pronouncing the hour. Morning prayer would be under way in the Hall. Everything seemed pleasant, and busy, and right.

All things in their proper place.

The pilgrims' song grated in Tymon's memory. He exorcised the foreigners' ghostly white faces with an effort of will, and continued on up the knot. A tumbledown bark-brick wall now ran parallel to the path. Around a sharp bend he came within sight of a ramshackle windmill, half-ruined, its courtyard overgrown with creepers. But the sackcloth sails were still turning and the workshop was in use. In the yard lay a multitude of broken and unnameable objects, spare parts and half-finished gadgets. A continuous sound of whistling and various thumping and hooting noises came from inside the workshop, as if some huge, alien bird were kept prisoner there. The boy picked his way between the piles of debris towards the cacophony.

'Father Galliano!' he called out. 'I've come! It's Tymon. I have lunch!'

Immediately the thumping died down, though the whistling noise continued in the background. The bent brown figure of an old man appeared in the workshop doorway, wiping his hands on a sooty apron. His beard was also spotted with soot and he wore an ancient, mangled cap with flaps that hung down over his ears. Underneath the apron could still be seen what remained of a green robe, tucked into a pair of sackcloth breeches. He hurried towards Tymon, gesturing wildly in his excitement.

'I've done it!' he cried. 'Come and see, boy! This is a great day, a great day!'

Father Jonas Galliano was technically no longer a priest. He had been stripped of that title and position over ten years ago by the Priests' Council for espousing heretical beliefs; the College kept him on a meagre pension out of charity. He was considered mad by most people, though they still called him 'Father', or the more familiar 'Apu', out of habit. His ideas on cosmology were eccentric. He believed that the Void was divine, not the Tree: he proposed that the infinite universe contained other Trees, and that these worlds also supported life. To the dismay of the Argosians he maintained that gravity was a mathematical, not mystical force, and that Hell had a physical mass, attracting all bodies downwards. Such blasphemous notions had cost him his livelihood. To compound his disgrace, the old man made an obstinate pursuit of invention — 'As if,' concerned citizens lamented, 'the Saints and Fathers hadn't already provided us with everything we needed, and every device we could ever use.' Since this fault seemed incurable, Galliano had been left to court damnation in peace, at least until now.

Tymon's ostensible reason for visiting the workshop was to carry out his charity duty for the seminary. The scientist was not considered so far gone in heresy that contact with the wider community was denied him, and the visits were far more pleasurable than the other options available on the students' duty roster. The boy had been bringing lunch to Galliano several times a week for the past five years. Though he had no use for physics and understood nothing about cosmology, he found the old man's company refreshing. To a novice surrounded by rules and regulations, irreverence was a welcome break. Galliano's enthusiasm was infectious. This week he had been promised a surprise by his friend, something, the scientist claimed, that would be 'his inheritance'. Tymon speculated whether Galliano had somehow against all reason obtained an introduction for him at the Guild Fair.

He found himself being dragged into the workshop behind the inventor without further ado. He was barely able to shove his packet of food onto a nearby table before being propelled into the centre of a whirling cloud of soot, steam and heat. A makeshift furnace occupied the middle of the workshop. Over it hung several hardwood vats, their covers half-off, belching steam. A bevy of pipes connected the vats to a strange construction — a reinforced barrel equipped with a set of large pistons and a valve. It was from this that the continuous whistling came. Galliano set about covering the vats and using a pair of enormous bellows on the fire. The valve's whistle mounted in pitch and the pistons began to move. Faster and faster they pumped, till all movement was blurred and the valves screamed. The old man danced about, shouting to Tymon inaudibly through the din, his face ecstatic. The boy laughed back, more at his friend's antics than from any comprehension of his invention. At length the scientist uncovered the vats and allowed the pistons to slow down. His stream of talk gradually became audible as the thumping and whistling died away.

'... major breakthrough in science,' he cried, finishing his unheard speech with gusto, 'the likes of which has not been seen in Argos since we first harnessed Tree-ether! Aye, we'll do more than float the greatships now!' He stopped, beaming and sweating, and raised his hands to the heavens dramatically. 'Boy, we are no longer at the mercy of wind! We have entered the Age of Steam!'

Tymon looked at the squat contraption and its assortment of pipes with a cynical eye. Was this, then, to be his 'inheritance'? It seemed quite useless and he was at a loss as to how the noisy, belching artefact could ever replace a greatship. But he refrained from dampening the old man's joy.

'It's grand, Apu,' he said. 'What are we going to do with it?'

'Do? Do?! Haven't you been listening to anything I've said?' exclaimed Galliano. 'We're going to build a new kind of dirigible! An air-chariot — it'll go without wind and float without ether. You'll see!'

Tymon brushed this aside in disbelief. 'Surely a dirigible wouldn't float without ether?' he objected. 'How would it sail?'

'Like I say, the power of steam. The pistons will turn the propellers so fast that the craft will rise up into the air like a hummingbird. We'll fly faster and further than any wind-powered dirigible! This is the invention that sets us free!'

'But isn't it heresy to sail faster than the wind, Apu?' Tymon grinned. 'Aren't you worried Storm-demons will snatch you out of the air?'

'Aha! There we have the crux of the matter!' The scientist almost leaped into the air himself in his enthusiasm. 'What you call Storm-demons, I call gravity, boy. The force generated by the propellers will exactly counterbalance the pull of gravity. You don't still believe it's the weight of your sins making you fall, do you? It's time you grew out of such superstitions.'

'I never believed in that sort of thing, anyway.' Tymon bridled.

And it was close to being true. He was neither young enough to be frightened of fables nor old enough to be wary of reality. Religion was a matter of tradition and identity in Argos, rather than personal belief. There existed a gap between what was taught at the seminary and the practical reality accepted by Tymon's fellows, who were well aware that a literal Hell did not lie among the roots of the World Tree, just as the sun and moon did not hang on its branches. The students sneered in adolescent superiority at the Rites, but were eager to avail themselves of the benefits they would bring. It was a given that any boy with spirit would do his best to contravene the legion of petty rules imposed by the priests. Rebellion was accorded its own rigidly defined place. With Bolas' collusion, Tymon knew that he had three hours before he would be missed at the seminary; the time seemed long and the crumbs of liberty intoxicating.

'I'll do it,' he said. 'I'll help you build your heresy, Apu.'

'Good then,' replied Galliano. 'We start construction today. Where did I put my sketch-leaf?'

They decided to assemble the air-chariot in the workshop yard, as the weather was fine. The first hour of Tymon's freedom was spent cutting wood for the transverse beams on the craft. He breathed in the fresh air of the spring morning and thought with satisfaction of the other novices cramped inside the temple at prayers. By the second hour, as his classmates hoed the seminary gardens, the outline of the machine's barkwood skeleton had taken shape on the floor of the yard. Now that Galliano's creation was materialising before his eyes, he found himself won over to the old man's thinking. The fact of having access to a flying machine, however unusual its shape and method of propulsion, appealed greatly to him. The third hour of his liberty came and went and he forgot about the passage of time, about the students at the seminary collecting their readers and trudging off to class. He thought no more about his fellows, absorbed in his work with the scientist.

When hunger finally distracted the two of them from their task, Galliano permitted a break. They perched on the tumbledown wall and surveyed their creation through mouthfuls of Nell's roast bird. The machine would be clinker-built in the style of a light dirigible, with one important modification: in the place of ether sacks, it would have a hardwood propeller over the cockpit to lift it into the air. Later, they would add another propeller to the tail for steering. A thousand happy fantasies drifted through Tymon's mind. The air-chariot would allow him to realise his hopes. He would leave with Galliano to embark on a life of wild adventure. There would be no more rules, no rituals, no indentured service looming at the end of his schooling. He would return from his travels with boxes of costly Tree-spice, and pay off his debt to the College in one triumphant gesture. He pictured himself presenting a roll of delicate silk paper to the Dean, who forgave him everything. Nell would be impressed.

'Apu,' he asked presently, 'where do you want to go in the machine?'

Galliano eyed Tymon critically. Still more of a child than a man, despite all their Rites, he thought. 'Well,' he observed aloud, 'after initial tests are done, when it's fully safe, I suppose we could take it for a turn around the leaf-forests. Nothing to destroy when we fall down, eh?'

'No, I mean, once it's all tested and we know it flies perfectly, where do you want to travel to? Lantria?'

'Lantria? Why?' snorted Galliano. 'You could go there in an ordinary dirigible. No, I have something more interesting in mind, boy.'

'Like what?' Tymon was taken aback. He had always dreamed of visiting the great shipyards of Lantria, far away to the south, and had trouble conceiving of a more interesting destination.

'I spoke to you of an inheritance,' answered his friend. 'What we have here is the legacy of science,

Tymon. We're standing on the brink of a new age. I meant what I said: this air-chariot will set us free. All of us. Argosians, Nurians, everyone ... It doesn't necessarily need ether, though we'll add emergency sacks to the test model, just in case. With a few modifications it could run on vegetable or animal waste. Everyone will be able to use it. It'll mean a better world, mark my words ...'

One of the complaints brought against Galliano by the Priests' Council regarded his idealism. He subscribed to the flimsiest doctrines of social equality, none of which had ever been shown to work. Tymon did not attempt to follow the old man's reasoning. All he knew was that the mention of Nurians depressed him. He felt a twist of disappointment. The machine was not to be his personal inheritance after all, but another one of the inventor's grandiose and so far unsuccessful bids to save humanity. The boy could not have cared less for a 'legacy of science'. Galliano, however, was bubbling over with his new schemes.

'Imagine if everyone could travel and trade without restriction,' he continued excitedly. 'No need to sell one's life and labour for a few barrels of water. Better yet, imagine using the machine to find an inexhaustible source of water for everyone, once and for all! And where would we find that, you ask?'

He paused, his finger raised to the sky, waiting for a response. Tymon shook his head, silently protesting ignorance.

'Well, alright then,' resumed the scientist, deflated. 'If I asked you what the universe looked like as a whole, what would you say?'

The boy sensed that his friend's eccentric theories were about to make another appearance. Smiling, he gave the textbook answer on cosmology.

'The Tree roots go down into the Maelstrom of Hell below the Storm. The branches reach up to Heaven. We are in between.'

'Thankfully. But what about Hell? What really goes on under the Storm? We see the dome of the sky and the stars rising over the leaf-line. What do you imagine there is, down there, below us?'

The priests at the seminary had given graphic accounts of the Maelstrom to the younger novices. Tymon found the tales awkward to repeat.

'Well,' he sighed, 'The Fathers say there's a blasting inferno and eternal wind among the roots of the Tree, where demons ride about on the spirits of the dead, tormenting them with ... ah ... brooms ...'

'Brooms! What nonsense!' noted Galliano crisply. 'And an inferno? When all it does is rain under those clouds? Does that sound in any way probable to you?'

'No,' said Tymon with some relief. 'No, it doesn't.'

There was a pause. Tymon wondered what all this pointless conjecture could be leading up to. What did it matter if fire or water was at the bottom of the world, so long as the world existed? But Galliano's eyes were shining. He had left ordinary common sense behind, and would have been happy to debate existence itself if it furthered his ideas.

'Rain!' he whispered, exultant. 'All it does is rain down there, boy. And all we have to do is find a way to collect that rain. Gallons of free water.'

'Yes, in theory, but it's impossible —'

'Obviously!' crowed the inventor, deaf to anything but the first half of his reply. 'We now have the opportunity of a lifetime to benefit humanity! Finally, the science of exploration has caught up with our dreams. If we don't use the machine for the greater good, what kind of explorers are we?'

The boy glanced up in alarm. In the course of Galliano's rhetoric, he had put two and two together.

'No one can enter the Storm,' he cried. 'It's too dangerous!'

'If the machine is built solidly, I'm reasonably confident of my chances. I wouldn't use ether, as the sacks would be ripped apart by the wind. That's why the propellers come in handy. They would weather the Storm — use the wind, instead of being at its mercy.'

Tymon stirred uneasily. This was further down the road to heresy than he had ever known his old friend to go, and insanity to boot. To send a vehicle on a fool's errand into the Storm would invite censure in this life and damnation in the next. It was sacrilege to tempt the wind in such a manner.

'It's impossible,' he repeated. 'You can't do it, Apu.'

'Why not?' The scientist stared at him quizzically.

'Because it's unnatural!'

Galliano burst out laughing at this. '*All things in their proper place*, eh? Humans above, the children of the Tree, and demons below in the infernal Void! I didn't think you'd be one to trot out that drivel, Tymon. Really, you should know better. Does it strike you as feasible that we were meant to live in the Tree, that we'd always been here and that we'd be here forever? Wouldn't we have wings to fly like the birds in that case, or claws to grip the bark, or be able to wind about branches like snakes? What nonsense!'

'I don't think that,' Tymon stammered, hot-faced and flustered. 'The point is, no one survives the Storm. If we tried to go there, we'd never come back.'

'I'm going alone,' emphasised Galliano. 'There is no "we" about it.'

The boy gave up the argument in despair. Surely his mentor had read descriptions of the doomed Storm Ventures, logged on countless leaves in the College library? As a novice Tymon had never been granted access to the library stacks, but Galliano would have studied the texts for many years. Did he not remember the crimes of the mad Explorer Sect which sent innocent navigators to their deaths by the hundreds, all for the sake of so-called progress? They, too, had wanted to see what lay below the clouds, to map the shape of Hell. Their science had proven in the end to be demon-worship. Progress was given a bad name. Dimly, Tymon began to guess at the sort of charges that had cost Galliano his priesthood.

'There is one more thing,' said the old man, after getting nothing but stubborn silence from his auditor. 'You're right — the Storm is formidable. Normally I would not risk even my own life in it. But I have reason to believe that the Maelstrom is growing weaker. It should be possible to go in, collect the rainwater, and come out.'

Tymon shook his head again. The conversation had taken a turn for the ludicrous. A vision of demons beating the hull of the machine with broom-handles came to him. Why waste this wonderful invention on a mad heresy, debunked over a century ago?

'Every year,' continued Galliano, softly, 'I measure the wind speed and precipitation during the winter season. I have been doing this for almost fifty years. It was one of the first experiments I began when I was a student at the seminary, like you.'

'They threw you out of the College for doing experiments, Apu. Maybe they were right. You're going to your death if you enter the Storm.'

'For fifty years, I compared measurements,' persisted his companion, ignoring him. 'The results are inescapable. The rains in the Central Canopy are abating. The rain-wells are never more than half full nowadays, and the drought in the Eastern Canopy only gets worse. We'll probably be next.' He struck the top of the wall with the flat of his palm. 'I'm sure it worries the Council. Why else would they insist on the Sacrifice every year? Why else convince those poor fools to throw themselves into a rift? Staving off the anger of the Tree — a paltry superstition! But it distracts from the real problem.'

Tymon stared sullenly at the skeleton of the machine lying on the dusty flags of the courtyard. The invention might have been a means to a better world for the scientist, but for the boy, a dirigible was an end in itself. Why anyone would want to throw one away on a voyage to the Storm was beyond him. He did not seek to change his world, only to escape from it. He had no patience with the pilgrims, or with their Sacrifice; he told himself that if he had to watch a man die, it was only because he was given no other choice. Glumly, he wished that they would all, priests and pilgrims both, jump into the Mouth and disappear forever.

'If they want to do it, let them,' he shrugged. 'Maybe they really believe it'll cure the drought.'

'And what do you believe?' asked Galliano.

Tymon was as tongue-tied in the face of this question as he had been earlier that morning, confronted by the beggar. With the memory of the episode by the gates came a realisation of the time he had spent away from the seminary. His reprieve had long since run out. Bolas would be able to do nothing more for him. As if on cue, the faraway bells took up the call to afternoon prayer. Tymon jumped up from the wall in a panic. He had already shirked one temple ritual that day; two would be inexcusable.

'I have to go, Apu,' he cried. 'I can't miss afternoon prayers. Even Father Mossing would object.'

The old man glanced at him sharply. 'I wouldn't mention what you've been doing here today to any of your tutors,' he cautioned. 'They may not understand.'

'What do you take me for?' Tymon protested. 'A snivelling first-year?'

He jogged off down the path from the workshop. 'Don't fly away without me, Apu!' he called over his shoulder. 'I'll be back tomorrow, after lunch.'

He did not wait for an answer for he knew well enough that the old man would go nowhere without him. By Galliano's own very optimistic calculations, there remained at least three weeks' work before the machine would be air-worthy.

The scientist smiled as he gazed after his young friend. 'No chance of that,' he murmured. 'Without hope, what use is there in flying?'

He rose from his seat with a sigh, and shuffled back to the half-formed carcass of the machine.

3

The main stairs to the temple stretched in an unbroken line from the city streets to the Hall at the summit of its buttress. The bells had finished tolling by the time the boy reached the top of the steep incline, puffing and sweating from his run. He took off his sandals and thrust them behind a pillar, the last in a long line of abandoned footwear trailing along the portico. Like all Argosian shrines, the temple Hall had eight sides. Its doors faced east. The fluted columns and arcades that adorned its exterior were cunningly anchored to the supporting branch, and appeared to rise seamlessly out of the bark, as if the Tree had simply grown them to order. A bird could fly from the summit of the dome across five hundred feet of open air to alight on the ledge outside the Divine Mouth. From where Tymon stood the Tree-rift was just visible. This time the boy's eyes flicked towards it. He raised his hand to his forehead in an automatic gesture of piety — then stopped, and dropped his arm with an angry shrug. The rituals of devotion he had grown up with seemed suddenly childish and unnecessary. He hurried through the open doors of the temple, into the fragrant shadows beyond.

Inside the Hall, the atmosphere was dim and hazy. The only natural light came from eight high arched windows, one in each facet of the dome. The dusty rays filtered down into the central nave through layers of smoke and incense. Dozens of small beeswax candles blurred the heavy air with a haze of flames and sap-burners sent thick curls of vapour up to icons of the saints. Priests were ranged in tiered seating along six of the eight walls: the rows of students sat cross-legged on the carpeted floor below. One of the Fathers stood at a raised lectern on the northern end of the Hall, leading the gathering in prayer. Tymon joined the row of youthful worshippers nearest the doors. His contemporaries might have been there all morning, he thought to himself wryly; he had left them as they were going up to the temple and found them still firmly ensconced when he returned. They were chanting the First Liturgy of the Tree. He added his voice belatedly to the chorus.

… And from Her flowed the Sap of life
That causes all to be.

Father Mossing, the priest at the lectern, was a comic favourite among the novices. When Tymon's eyes had become accustomed to the low light, he was able to make out his tutor's round face beaming over the gathering. Mossing rarely scolded a latecomer to prayers. He continued the service after Tymon's tardy entrance without missing a beat, leaning his plump arms on the lectern.

'The Tree is the Beginning.'

'The Tree is the Beginning,' his audience dutifully repeated.

'The Tree is the End.'

'The Tree is the End,' muttered the congregation.

'The Tree is Life.'

'The Tree is Life.' The boys' voices straggled out of time with each other.

'She lifted us up from darkness into the light, from death to life. She bore us up in Her arms that we might behold Her beauty. In the beauty we walk.'

'In the beauty.'

'Today's lesson is Saint Usala the Green, chapter nine, verses three to twelve.'

There was a rustle of cracked leaves as the congregation turned to the appropriate place in their psalm books. Mossing read out the passage in singsong tones.

'*And the divines accused Saint Usala of perverting the youth of the city, saying:*

"You teach the young ones sorcery. You bring together Focal groups and claim to see the future. This is blasphemy. Prophecy came to an end with Saint Loa. The Sap is silent and shall be so until the End Days.'

"On the contrary, the Sap speaks all the time, if you would only listen," replied Saint Usala. "But I do not teach sorcery. A sorcerer meddles with forces he does not understand. A Grafter knows those forces are meddling with him."

The sweat dried on Tymon's neck. The echoes of the Hall threw back the words of the reading in sudden gusts and unrecognisable fragments, as if

50

the building itself were speaking, denying the official version, telling a different story. The past seemed still to breathe in the place. The Hall doubled as an ecclesiastical court and many of the saints and martyrs of Argosian history, as well as its most notorious heretics, had at one time passed through these doors. Saint Loa himself had stood there as he cursed and cast out the Seven Hypocrites of Mung; there, the twin seers, Pesh and Amran, had prophesised the fall of the Nurian Empire. The infamous Sorceress of Nur had ended her career in this very spot. Even the Saint Usala of the reading had been brought to trial in the Hall, arraigned by the Council on charges of heresy and sorcery. She was only canonised a century after her death when many of her predictions were found, embarrassingly, to have come true.

The priests in Argos were wary of those claiming to see the future. Only one official canon of prophecy was admitted by the seminary. Only that art of Grafting, the sacred Sight accorded by the Tree to Her chosen emissaries, was still considered a mark of sainthood. Grafters were said to be able to speak with the Sap: no mere fluid running in the heartwood, but the mystic life-force of the Tree. The prophets of old did not only predict the future. They cultivated it, trained and pruned it, until it conformed to a certain ideal and was 'as it should be'. They had powers equal to their task. They could speak with the dead, bend a man's will to their own, or conjure up false visions to confuse their enemies. These powers of illusion, or Seemings, became reality if those watching believed strongly enough in them. But none were left with the faith to merit a Grafter's power. The priests taught that direct communication with the Tree was now impossible. Only annotation, discussion and endless commentary on what had already been Seen was acceptable. The line of prophecy had come to an end and the authorised canon was complete. The art of Grafting belonged to legend.

Tymon, for his part, was uninterested in legends. He paid little heed to the temple reading and less to his history lessons. Across the Hall he distinguished the figure of his friend Wick, stretching backwards out of a row in an attempt to capture his attention. His classmate clutched his throat and made a gagging face, the attitude of a hanged man, then pointed merrily in his direction. Tymon shrugged back in a show of indifference. He could guess what Wick had to say: he had probably been missed at Treeology class that morning, and was in trouble with one of the tutors. A habitual truant, he hardly considered skipping class a crime worth mentioning. He pretended not to notice the other boy's continuing contortions and allowed his gaze to wander over the Hall, as it had a thousand times before. Mossing droned on.

'And Saint Usala asked the divines, "Do you believe in the End Times?"

"Naturally," they said. "The righteous shall be divided from the wicked. The Mouth shall speak. It has been prophesised."

"As simple as all that?" said the saint, and she laughed.

Her reply displeased them. "And what do you believe?" they retorted.

The repetition of Galliano's question jarred in Tymon's ears. He frowned at the temple ceiling. Colourful scenes from the life of Saint Loa, founding Father of Argos, adorned the eight archways holding up the dome. They showed the prophet performing the deeds for which he was celebrated. Despite having seen those same pictures since his childhood, he noticed for the first time, with distaste, that one of the carvings portrayed a group of eastern pilgrims visiting Argos. Though no Nurian, free or tithe, had arrived in the city until centuries after the saint's death, the image appeared to anticipate the glory and power of the Argosian Empire. The foreigners were immediately recognisable, dressed in matching caps and gowns with their pale painted faces angled up at the temple in attitudes of adoration.

Father Mossing's book snapped shut, jolting Tymon from his thoughts.

'Sacrifice is the deepest mystery,' the priest warbled happily, as if he were announcing a wedding. 'The death of one brings life to the many. Physical death brings spiritual life. We must all bear in mind Saint Usala's story in the coming days, for she walked the Path of Sacrifice like many of the saints. She gave herself up to the Tree, became Eaten, that we might receive God's green grace. Those who walk the Path die so that we might truly live. They fall to darkness that we might see the light ...'

Wick was now leaning out of the row at a dangerous angle, his grimaces extreme. Tymon remembered with a sudden stab of anxiety that he did not yet know if he had been spotted with the tramp that morning. Wick's paroxysms might signify more trouble than he had at first thought. Mossing's sermon ground on unheard as he considered this new and unpleasant possibility. The Dean had already departed on his retreat, but he might well have communicated Tymon's transgression to someone else and left instructions regarding his punishment. He threw his classmate a look of wide-eyed innocence. Wick indicated a cut throat with his hand, a stage beyond hanging. *You're dead*, he signalled.

Tymon was obliged to wait, squirming with frustration, until the service was over to obtain any further information. At last Father Mossing ground to a halt and the novices belted out the closing hymn in a babble of impatience, pouring out of the doors before the echoes had faded from the Hall. Tymon made out Wick's grinning face in the crowd on the outside portico and pushed his way towards him. When he arrived at his side the other boy clapped a hand on his shoulder with a show of mock severity.

'You'd better have a good excuse, young man!' he pronounced, in a plausible imitation of one of the seminary Fathers. He spun Tymon about on his heel and marched him along the portico. 'You missed morning prayers and garden duty, and Rede was furious you skipped Treeology! Out with it — which demon of the flesh tempted you to sin?'

Wick was a smooth-faced, smiling boy, full of confident exuberance. The only son of a well-respected trader, he had no financial debt towards the seminary and might ape the priests with impunity. He was no snob in his associations, either. Few students objected to being called his friend — even if that honour came with the attendant duty of playing class clown. Tymon preened a little as he was shoved ahead of Wick like a gardener's barrow. His anxiety dissipated. His crime, as he suspected, had been the ordinary one of absenteeism.

'Rede's always furious,' he answered, breaking free of Wick to retrieve his shoes from the jumble at the end of the balcony. 'What difference does it make?'

'Ah, but he was angrier than usual today.' Wick lowered his voice as they fell into step with the other novices, filing down the back stairs that connected the buttress to the cloistered courtyard below. 'He decided to make an example of you. He gave us a long lecture on "the dissipations of youth". Prissy old white-neck.'

Father Rede, the Treeology professor, was an Argosian colonial, born and bred in the Eastern Domains. He still carried the stigma of his origins despite all attempts at re-assimilation. Tymon might have sympathised with another victim of social prejudice. But Rede was a tyrannical character, universally despised.

'He was just waiting for an opportunity, I'm sure,' he shrugged.

'Oh, yes. And what an opportunity. *The body is a temple, to be kept immaculate and free from sin.*' Wick's voice imitated to perfection the nasal tones of the hated professor. '*He whom the Impure touch of Woman hath caused to sully that temple shall stand shamefaced at the hour of death!*'

Tymon chortled appreciatively. 'Pompous old fart. I can just see him — in the beauty, Father!'

The last part of this response was a hasty acknowledgement of Father Mossing, who had overtaken them on the steps. The priest seemed not to have heard their exchange and only smiled vaguely at Tymon as he hurried down to the courtyard, making no reference whatever to his absence at morning ritual. The boy had almost decided that his truancy had been forgiven, or at least forgotten, when he heard the priest calling to him from the bottom of the steps.

'Ah, Tymon. Before it slips my mind. A word.'

Mossing smiled genially up at him. Tymon's mood of satisfaction faded. He obeyed the summons unenthusiastically, descending the last few steps shadowed by Wick.

'You were seen outside the seminary this morning, during first prayer,' admonished the priest. 'You know perfectly well that all outside duty must wait till after ritual. I'm not one to be too much of a stickler for rules, but we have standards to maintain here. Please be conscious that your actions are noted and judged by the people of this city.'

The boy nodded with a sinking heart. So the Dean had spotted him in the tunnel, after all. He was sure that he would now be chastised for speaking to the tramp.

'Another thing,' purred the priest. He nudged Tymon a little further from the students trooping down the steps, and turned his back on the loitering Wick. 'I understand the fascination of the — ah — military life to young men of your age. It's a healthy passion and I don't mind it. But a novice in his Green Year should not be socialising with common soldiers, do you understand? It's demeaning to the seminary.'

Tymon nodded more slowly, and with mounting perplexity. He had hardly spoken with the soldiers at all. It was odd that Mossing made no mention of the tramp.

'Anyway, remember your position here. Don't let it happen again.' Mossing winked at him, his small eyes almost lost in the folds of his cheeks. He sauntered away in the direction of the monastery gardens. Tymon was left gazing after him in bewilderment. It seemed impossible that he had not been seen with the beggar.

'You got off light!' drawled Wick, at his elbow. 'Rede won't be so easy on you!'

'Rede, Rede. There's more to life than Rede,' said Tymon meditatively. 'I'll take whatever he has to give.'

The two boys joined the other novices bound for their afternoon study session, a daily rite of tedium taking place in long drab classrooms on the east side of the Priests' Quarter. As they marched across the courtyard, Wick pursued his theme.

'What were you up to this morning, anyway? What's all this about soldiers?'

'Mossing made a mistake,' replied Tymon. 'I went to visit Galliano.'

'What? Doesn't that make three times in a week? What's so great about the old heretic?' Wick spoke with emphasis on every other word, his conversation lively to the point of exaggeration.

'We're building a dirigible.'

Tymon's declaration was tinged with a smug note of triumph. He had only briefly considered keeping Galliano's project a secret: the scientist had warned him not to speak to the professors, but surely there was no harm in telling his best friend?

'The old man invented one that flies without the wind,' he continued, lowering his voice in the crowded halls of the seminary. 'I think it'll work, too.'

'No!' Wick gave a disbelieving guffaw. 'Where would he go, anyway? He's a bit creaky for a tour of the canopy!'

'Well, that's the problem,' Tymon sighed. 'I wish he would go somewhere in the canopy. He's got other ideas.'

'Where else is there to go?'

This time the boy hesitated before answering. He did not know whether to betray the full extent of Galliano's eccentricities to Wick and mention the awkward plan of entering the Storm. He thought with a pang of the scientist's vulnerability, his childlike enthusiasm for questionable ideas. But he was also keen to impress his friend. He told himself that he was still abiding by the spirit of his promise. Wick could keep a secret.

'He wants to see what's under the Storm,' he whispered in his companion's ear.

'How —?'

Wick was unable to finish his question. They had reached their assigned classroom and the babble of student voices was dying down. But his interest was evidently hooked. His eyes goggled inquisitively, much to Tymon's satisfaction.

'Later,' murmured the boy, with a conspiratorial smile, writing with his finger across his palm.

The study session was the time for note-passing. The novices would remain in the dreary, grey-walled classroom all afternoon, seated on straw mats and chanting their lessons in a loud cacophony. There was one desk and chair in the room, reserved for the use of supervising professors. A stream of written communication between the students made the hours of rote-learning more bearable. Tymon and Wick retrieved their psalm books and pens from a pile on the desk and took their places on the floor as the tutor in charge of the session entered the room. To Tymon's discomfiture it was Rede himself who stalked through the door that day, his dark robes flapping like the feathers of some mournful bird. But instead of calling out the psalm number to be copied and committed to memory, the priest stood silent at the head of the room, a curl of disgust on his lips.

The Treeology professor was a small, sallow individual distinguished by an air of permanent exhaustion. He fixed the world with a heavy-lidded stare, the look of a man unappreciated by the vulgar mass of his fellow beings. He always carried a light barkwood switch, which he held behind his back and tapped between his fingers as a deterrent to the wayward. He had a disturbing habit of picking his teeth with the tip of the switch. This afternoon he was particularly sour, allowing the novices to wait in silent suspense for at least a minute before he spoke.

'It has been brought to my attention,' he announced, finally, 'that there are those within these walls who prefer a life of debauchery to honourable duty, and who care nothing for the kindness already lavished upon them.' He paused and leaned forward on his toes, surveying the students as if they were rats upon a garbage heap. 'There are those who think the seminary is a cheap inn, a place to eat and sleep and come and go from at will, with no higher purpose. I am here to tell you this is not the case.'

Rede's telltale colonial accent, the slight flatness of his vowels, was discernible even after all these years. Tymon glanced surreptitiously up at his professor, wondering if he had no other means of amusing himself than to lecture his charges. He seemed entirely lost in his homily. Turning half away from his tutor, the boy carefully tore a corner off his exercise leaf and scrawled with his pen on the scrap of paper. G. *thinks he can survive the Storm*, he wrote. *He wants to explore under the clouds using the machine*. He crumpled the note into a ball and sent it rolling along the mat to Wick. A few moments later his friend flicked an answering scrap towards him.

'This is a place of beauty,' continued Rede sententiously. 'A temple of learning. We are all here to learn, even your tutors.'

His gaze swivelled about to rest on Tymon, who had been on the verge of collecting Wick's note. The boy hurriedly camouflaged the movement by adjusting the psalm book on his knees. A smile as thin as a lizard's crossed the professor's features.

'Master Tymon,' he observed, dryly. Tymon found himself the focus of a roomful of eyes. 'It is a real pleasure to be granted the privilege of your company. We were disappointed you refused us that honour today in Treeology class.'

Nervous titters ran through the assembly. The boy put on his best apologetic face.

'I'm truly sorry, Father,' he replied. 'I was completing my charity duty this morning and lost track of time. It won't happen again.'

Rede's reptilian smile widened. 'Ah yes. It is true that charity is the essence of all Treeology, and far more important than any paltry little class of mine.' Tymon waited for the priest's sarcasm to exhaust itself, but his tutor was on a roll. 'I have also learned,' he rasped, 'that you gave up ritual for the third time this week, to complete the same august duty! Truly, your self-sacrifice knows no bounds. If we could all treat our fellow man with such compassion! If we could all have such clear priorities!'

Rede strode up and down the line of mats, borne away by his own oration. Tymon stretched a furtive hand towards Wick's note. It was just out of reach.

'We must give generously to all in need! For there but for *Her green grace*, go we,' sang the professor, quoting scripture. '*All things in Her sweet embrace, all depend on Her green grace ...*'

He spun abruptly around, causing Tymon to jump. His smile was now an open sneer. 'Of course, Master Tymon, considering your origins, I imagine you'd have plenty of sympathy for the lowlifes in this city,' he snapped. 'Like attracts like. I know perfectly well you haven't been carrying out your charity duty, unless charity includes a visit to the brothel. Don't lie to me, and stand up while speaking to your betters. I won't have a bound student giving me such cheek.'

Tymon scrambled to his feet in surprise and hot embarrassment. It was the second time that day his motives and associations had been entirely misjudged by the priests. He did not mind that he was suspected of worse crimes than he had committed. It was the snide reference to his lack of family, his 'bound' status, that cut him to the quick. In Argos, a man's worth, even the state of his soul, was determined by lineage; a dearth of family was a dearth of virtue. The impression the Fathers had given him as a child was that his antecedents were shameful, a matter best forgotten. He had concluded that his parents must indeed have been reprobates to abandon their own flesh and blood so completely. He would have liked nothing more than to be allowed to forget them. Besides, his tutors were supposed to ignore social differences among the novices, treating all alike in the classroom. But Rede was given to humiliating displays of discipline. The boy stared at the scuffed mat between his toes, mortified.

'I'm sorry, sir,' he mumbled. He did not attempt to justify himself. He knew the exercise was pointless.

Rede ignored his reply. The switch appeared from behind his back, and he began using it on his teeth. There was an ominous pause. Stifled sniggers punctuated the silence. Some of the other boys leered insolently at Tymon. He wished the floor would open up and swallow him.

'I will not have you flout authority under my very nose, young man,' hissed the professor, at last. 'The seminary's charity is not to be taken for granted! If you miss one of my classes again, you may dispense with your Green Rites this year, as well as your place at the Guild Fair. Do I make myself understood?'

The hot blood rushed to Tymon's ears. To lose his chance to go to the Guild Fair over a crime as insipid as missing class was manifest injustice. It was clear that his indenture made him less of a man than the other students. He felt the discrimination keenly, all the more as the insult was delivered by the unpopular Rede.

'Yes, Father' he answered through gritted teeth.

'I want you promptly at my noon class tomorrow.'

'Yes, Father.'

'You may sit.' Rede released him curtly. 'Let this be a lesson to you all,' he spat, glaring over the rest of the room. 'The seminary will not tolerate laxity in morals. You are given fair warning.'

He turned on his heel and sauntered back to the desk. Tymon lumped down on the mat, breathing hard.

'Saint Dorit, chapter eight, verses four through seven,' snapped Rede. There was a general stirring of leaves as books were opened again and the novices went back to their copy work. Voices rose in a ragged chorus, chanting the lesson.

We are the same branch, the same leaf, the same blood ...

The words stuck in Tymon's throat. He burned with humiliation. He would rather have been struck with Rede's switch like a first-year novice than endure the little professor's bile. Furious tears pricked his eyes. As he sat there, hunched on the mat, his gaze fell on Wick's abandoned note, now within easy reach. He twitched the scrap into his fingers and waited, fuming, until he could safely glance at the brief message.

That's heresy! it said.

Dusk had fallen when the students re-emerged from their classrooms and trooped back to the cloistered courtyard. The smell of food greeted them from the refectory beneath the dormitories. After the scene with Rede, Wick had mollified Tymon's rage with a few eloquent looks cast over the edge of his copy-leaf; now, as the two boys entered the dining hall, safely out of earshot of the professors, he exclaimed: 'The brute! Imagine threatening to bar you from the

Rites like that, in front of everyone, when he's less than half a man himself — a white-neck, a louse-lover!'

Tymon contented himself with giving the refectory door a savage kick to express his feelings.

'It doesn't change anything,' he muttered. 'I just have to be more careful.'

The professors ate separately in the College and the refectory was the boisterous, vocal province of the novices. Tymon and Wick wound through the crowded tables and benches to their usual places at the back of the room, choosing a table occupied by Bolas and a scrawny, chinless novice in his fourth year.

'Long live Tymon the Disappeared!' called the scrawny boy as they sat down. 'You missed a sore day in Treeology.'

'And garden duty,' growled Bolas. 'I got your shift, but you're going to have to warn me in advance if you pull this kind of stunt again.'

'I'm sorry, Bolas,' Tymon replied penitently. 'It was important. Charity duty.'

The prefect waved the excuse away. 'Is that all you can cough up in the way of an explanation? Come on, Ty. I had to tell Mossing you weren't feeling right and I'd let you stay in the dorms. What did you do all morning?'

'He fell asleep in a vine-field,' put in Wick, as he helped himself to the pot of stew in the middle of the table. 'Cloud-head here dozed off on his charity run and forgot to come home on time. Believe me, I've already grilled him on the subject. I was hoping for a better story.'

'Is that all?' Bolas grumbled to Tymon. 'You made me hoe a double shift because you needed a morning snooze? Typical.'

Tymon only managed a pained smile in response. The explanation was unflattering, but as it was Wick who had come to his rescue he swallowed his objections and went along with the story. He gave his attention to the stew. Bolas turned to Wick.

'Did you get your Fair ticket yet?' he asked. 'Mine arrived this morning. Special courier and all. I wasn't expecting it so early. I thought, well, it'll be the families of Council members first, followed by the sons of important folk, like your father, Wick — meaning no disrespect — and us simple freemen last of the lot. But I was wrong.'

Wick shot Tymon a brief, conciliatory smile before responding to the prefect. It was on the subject of the Guild Fair that the greatest divide existed between a bound-boy and his fellows. Most of the novices had families or sponsors who bought them tickets, with or without the approval of the seminary: if their connections permitted such luxuries, the students might even attend the event before completing their Rites. Wick was younger than most of his friends and had not yet entered his Green Year, but his family would still be sending him to the Fair. The discrepancy rankled with Tymon. He tried not to listen to the rest of the exchange between Bolas and Wick and stabbed at the contents of his plate with his fork. The chinless lad craned forward to catch his eye.

'I for one don't believe you were on charity duty,' he gloated. 'So, tell us! Why was Rede so angry?'

'I made a pact with a demon,' mumbled Tymon. He did not care one way or another for the younger boy's interest, but felt somehow betrayed by the conversation taking place at the other end of the table. 'I can do whatever I want but I mustn't talk about it, not even to you, Piri.'

This answer drew a snort of frustration from the fourth-year student. 'Go on,' he wheedled. 'You owe us after leaving us to survive Rede on our own.'

'No.'

'Please?'

'No.'

'We know what the bound-boy was doing!' shouted a mocking voice from the next table, shattering Tymon's composure. 'Hoi, freak! Did you say hello to your Nurry friends in town today? Care to place bets on the fodder?'

Conniving snickers accompanied the remark. A shiver passed down Tymon's spine. Had news of his brush with the pilgrims reached ears at the seminary, or were the bullies at the next table simply teasing him, unaware that their remarks bore any relation to the truth? He recognised the leering youths from the study session. Their ringleader was a fat-cheeked and arrogant third-year named Fletch, the boorish son of a plantation owner, fat-cheeked and arrogant. Response was futile, and would only cost him further in taunts.

'What are they talking about?' he whispered to Piri, exasperated. 'What bets?'

But it was Bolas who answered, replenishing his plate from the communal pot at the centre of the table.

'Some people think it's intelligent to make wagers on which pilgrim will volunteer for the Sacrifice,' he observed scathingly. 'One of Fletch's bright ideas. Ignore him, Tymon.'

The boy frowned. This was new. He had not seen seminary students playing such games before. The idea perturbed him; it attracted and repelled him at the same time.

'What a perfect situation.' Wick rolled his eyes in disgust. 'One louse volunteers for the Sacrifice. The rest go to a vine plantation. Fletch makes a killing, either way ...'

'If they really volunteer at all,' piped up Piri. 'The bets could be rigged. I've heard —'

'What you hear is nonsense and what you say is worse, Piri.' Bolas cut him off impatiently.

'What have you heard?' asked Tymon. Morbid fascination with the subject was getting the better of him. 'Let him talk, Bolas.'

Piri flushed with excitement at being the centre of attention. 'I've heard,' he said, lowering his voice, 'that the priests help the ceremony along a bit. They choose a likely man beforehand. On the day of the Festival they get him drunk —'

'That's not true!' cried Wick. 'Shame on you, Piri, that's a dirty lie.'

'It's what people say,' protested the younger boy.

'Well, it's wrong. My uncle is one of the torchbearers for the Rites. He'd never take part in a murder,' said Bolas. He scowled disapprovingly at Piri. 'You shouldn't repeat vicious jokes.'

The chinless student crumpled with embarrassment. Tymon rallied to his defence.

'If we're talking about bad jokes, then the wagers are worse,' he pointed out. 'I'm surprised the Fathers allow it —'

He was interrupted by the jarring sound of Wick's laughter.

'I'm surprised you, for one, worry about what the Fathers allow,' his friend grinned knowingly. 'Relax, Ty. You're not the only one to disapprove of people like Fletch. We're not placing the bets, remember.'

Tymon would have liked to make a clever rejoinder, to dismiss the subject with a witticism, but his tongue felt heavy and useless and he could not find the right words. The memory of the red-haired pilgrim standing straight and proud in the marketplace rose unbidden in his mind. He found himself vaguely hoping that the unusual youth would not be the one volunteering, or being volunteered, for the Sacrifice. Although he did not really believe Piri's insinuations, he was not fool enough to suppose that dignity would be an acceptable quality in a slave. The mention of the tithe-pilgrims depressed him and he no longer participated in the conversation. After the meal he helped the others clear away the bowls and trestle tables, but when the work was done he let his friends return to the dormitories without him. He dawdled alone in the empty courtyard, watching the stars appear one by one between the great, stirring shadows of the leaf-forests overhead.

A great yearning took hold of him to leave the city, to be free of the priests, their Rites and his indenture in one stroke. It was unfair, he thought. If only Galliano's machine were not consigned to the Void, along with its mad inventor! If only the old man had dreamed of riches instead of science. They might have quit Argos when the air-chariot was built and sought out some haven of liberty together. He had heard that a man might find gainful work in Lantria, whatever his origins. He decided that he must convince Galliano to give up, or at least delay, the suicidal mission into the Storm. It seemed to him that night that unless the machine was saved, his life was a lost cause.

4

Tymon watched his fellows carefully in the weeks leading up to the Spring Festival. He noticed that unlike the other students in his class, he was not included in the process of Guild applications the took place in preparation for the Fair. Every boy his age was called to at least one meeting with prospective employers over the course of that month, except for him. The yearning that had filled his heart after his public humiliation by Rede hardened to cynicism, for he no longer believed that his guardians would allow him to be apprenticed to a reputable trade. He was just a bound-boy, incapable of more than physical labour, and certainly no candidate for an organisation such as the Navigators' Guild. He did not forget his dreams but began to consider other means of fulfilling them. He kept his head low and took care not to miss a single class. He carried out his Rites-duties without fail, baulking at no task, however menial. A plan to counter the priests had begun to form in his mind; it necessitated both time and discretion to come to fruition.

As the holiday approached, an atmosphere of giddy excitement took over the city. Inns were filled to bursting point and the odour of cooking invaded the streets and courtyards, for there would be celebrations after the Rites, a feast of indulgence after weeks of abstinence. The seminary was no exception. The preparations in the kitchens were enough to set the novices salivating days in advance: sweetbean pasties and bird pies by the dozen were left to cool on the windowsills, while a pile of rosy frogapples and three vats of Treesap wine lay in a corner of the compound garden, awaiting the revelry. They would be served up during the banquet that followed the Rites, in the private College pavilion by the air-harbour. The whole town would turn out on the quays that day to witness the famous ritual. The docks rang with the sound of hammers as stalls and stands were constructed to accommodate the crush.

The commotion provided a perfect cover for Tymon, who took advantage of the hustle and bustle at the seminary to disappear on errands of his own. He acquired a habit of rising before the dawn bells to slip out of the dormitory while it was still dark. His destination at that hour was, first and predictably, the kitchens, in quest of an early breakfast from Masha. His subsequent goal was more unusual, however. Every morning in the weeks prior to the Festival, he was to be seen mounting the steps to the College Library, entering the only section of it available to novices — the Prayer Room. It was baffling to his friends and frankly disturbing to the old cook, who marked the new tendency with alarm.

Masha was one of the few who cared to know about Tymon's comings and goings, regardless of whether he attended class or fulfilled his Rites-duties. Her instincts told her that something was up. It was not simply that the boy was glum and withdrawn. She put that down to his age and the sap of adolescence invading his body. It concerned her that he appeared to have caught religion. She had warned him to behave but had not expected her advice to be taken to such pedantic lengths. His visits to the Prayer Room were too good to be true. She noticed that he was making a point of avoiding Nell; purity laws notwithstanding, this sudden reversal of his natural leanings did not bode well, in her opinion. It was bad enough that he was indentured to the priests. He should not waste time trying to be one.

The day before the Festival, she was finally able to corner her charge and question him about his activities. Tymon had stopped by the kitchens that morning in order to beg for food and favours, as was his habit, and she took advantage of the opportunity to make him try on his green robes, which she had shortened to match his wiry frame.

'With the amount you eat you should be fatter than this,' she muttered, her mouth full of hardwood pins.

She added one carefully to Tymon's hem as he stood before her and squinted at the folds of the robe in the lamplight. Dawn was only just brightening the sky above the compound and the kitchen was quiet, not yet the centre of clatter and industry it would be in an hour or so.

'Two double-sized breakfasts a day for the past month,' she noted with asperity. 'And you're still as skinny as a piece of vine.' She straightened up from her work. 'Well, that's done. Now explain to me. What was it you were after again?' Her boy had come to her with a particularly strange request that morning.

'Ether oil, Amu. I know there's a store of it in the College cellars,' he pleaded. 'You can get it for me. Go on.'

Masha peered sharply at him. Tymon's eyes had the dusty, inward-turned look she knew too well, a mask for disobedience. He was up to no good, she decided. Ether oil was an expensive commodity, a distilled form of the volatile gas used to float dirigibles. It also produced hallucinations when taken with food. She snapped shut the sewing box with an impatient gesture.

'Planning a prank, I suppose?' she sighed.

'Yes, Amu,' he lied.

After weeks of stringent Purity laws, disorder and exuberance at the Festival were expected, a necessary finale. An old seminary tradition tolerated practical jokes after the Rites, an exercise simply referred to as 'the prank'. Any professor particularly reviled by the boys became the focus of a plot to ridicule him at the College banquet. Masha thought she knew now what Tymon had been planning all this time, in the library.

'Is it Rede this year?' she asked with a smile of relief. This was just what her boy should be preoccupied with at the moment, not books or religion. It was a reassuring return to form.

'Yes.' He tried to keep his voice neutral. She was wrong, of course. He wanted the ether oil for other purposes. But the prank was an expedient explanation.

'Well. Lord White-Neck has it coming to him,' she observed. 'Mind no one gets hurt and I'll find you a bottle. You can pick it up before Bread-Giving today.'

'Thank you, Amu. I really appreciate it.'

She narrowed her eyes at him, a work-roughened fist planted on her hip. 'You won't miss Bread-Giving, I hope.'

A breath of irritation escaped his lips. 'I'll be there. I've done all my duties up till now, Amu, haven't you noticed? I'm being good, like I said.'

'Green Mother, who bore us all,' snorted Masha. 'The day that's true will be a day of miracles. Now — off with those robes, before you dirty them. I'll have them ready for you tomorrow morning.'

A few minutes later Tymon hurried out of the kitchen compound, a bundle of Festival cakes in his hand and a gleam of triumph in his eye. The acquisition of the ether oil was a crowning achievement. He had no intention of wasting his prize on the students' prank, which he disdained in any case as an activity fit for mere children. Masha's suspicions were well founded: Tymon was indeed up to no good. His delinquency was of a more drastic variety than she supposed. He was still smarting from Rede's treatment and nothing would have pleased him better than to see his hated professor ridiculed at the Festival banquet.

But he was planning more than a prank, a schoolboy's revenge. He was not about to be barred from the Rites on a trumped-up charge, or beyond that, make do with the seminary's leavings. He wanted to be quit of the priests and their crippling indenture forever. He had decided to forestall the inevitable by running away.

As a novice, he had few personal belongings and no private space of his own. He overcame this problem by using the Prayer Room to organise his escape. The students' section was less an annex than a glorified stockroom for the library. Mildewed liturgies and moth-eaten psalms lay packed against the walls; there was barely space to manoeuvre between the towering columns of books on the floor. A stack of manuscripts near the back of the room served as a cache for Tymon. Quietly and steadily, he had been adding every extra breakfast to an accumulated hoard. Just as regularly, taking the utmost care not to infringe on seminary rules, he had continued to carry out his charity duty, visiting Galliano as often as his other responsibilities allowed. Some of the smuggled food went with him to the old man's workshop to fuel the construction of the scientist's flying machine. But much of the stash remained hidden in the Prayer Room, between the Nineteen Rain Chants and the Nonian Liturgies, in anticipation of a final getaway. The opportune moment for departure, the boy believed, was at hand. His hopes revolved around the air-chariot, and the air-chariot was ready.

He strode purposefully towards the Library, a three-storey building on the east side of the

College. The heavy doors swung wide at his touch and he plunged on without pause into the panelled corridor beyond. Tomorrow, he told himself, it would all come together. His patience would pay off. He had reason to feel elated: after weeks of construction, Galliano's machine sat in hulking black glory on the incline outside the workshop. It had been tested and found air-worthy. Twice they had watched the ungainly contraption rise ponderously into the sky, only to nose-dive back to the knot after a few seconds. Twice they had rebuilt the wooden body, throwing out excess weight. In the end the air-chariot had turned into a sleek, insect-like creation. It had a large hardwood propeller on its topside, trestle-legs and a steering propeller on its tail. The boiler was about the size of a wine barrel and devoured quantities of dehydrated sap, a thick, foul-smelling substance called Tree-gall. The craft was equipped with a single emergency ether sack. The day before, the old man and the boy had watched their creation lurch into the air without a hitch, tethered to a line. They had allowed it to hover noisily above the vine terraces for two minutes, defying gravity, before they killed the motor and watched it drift slowly back down to the knot unharmed. Tymon still had the taste of victory in his mouth. He had come to care as much about the success of the machine as Galliano, though for different reasons.

The scientist had promised him that they would conduct the first manned flight the day after the Festival. It was this expedition Tymon counted on to realise his escape. He imagined that he might persuade Galliano to drop him off in Lantria. In his enthusiasm he had not considered the fact that the South Fringes were at least three days' journey away, even in a flying machine. His notion of distances was that of a person who had never travelled more than a few hours from his doorstep. He lived in his dreams, and his dreams soared to far horizons that morning.

His step was jaunty as he pushed open the Prayer Room door. The musty tang of ancient leaves and slowly rotting parchments stung his nostrils; he blinked, blinded a moment by the gloom. The window shutters were still closed. He made his way fumblingly to the rear of the room and reached into the space behind one of the dusty stacks, retrieving a grass-weave bag. It smelled faintly of Festival cakes. He had just finished emptying his latest spoils into its depths, when an unexpected sound caused him to drop his booty and scramble to his feet in apprehension. A snort of quiet laughter echoed through the stacks as Wick's familiar form detached itself from the shadows.

'Well, well,' remarked the other boy, laconic. 'I didn't think you came here every morning just to pray. I was right, as usual.'

For an instant, Tymon felt cold. It was too dark in the room to make out much of his classmate's expression. Wick's face was a formless smudge.

'Have you been following me?' he blurted out, more anxiously than he intended.

'Following? Green grace, Ty, you're not that interesting,' laughed Wick. His teeth flashed in the dim light. 'I have a real job to do here. I'm library prefect, don't you remember? You know. Because of the Guild.'

Wick had announced to his friends a fortnight ago that he was to be considered for a bookmaker's apprentice. A place at the prestigious Scribes' Guild had been obtained for him on special introduction by his father, before he had even attended the Fair. He had spent much of his time lately closeted in meetings with his prospective employers. Tymon envied the ease with which his friend's future was being arranged, irrespective of age and the fact that he had not even entered his Green Year. He watched morosely as Wick squatted on his haunches beside the grass-weave bag, flipping it open with an appreciative whistle.

'Are these Festival cakes you're hoarding?' he exclaimed. 'You lucky beggar — no one gives me a second breakfast. You know you're not supposed to bring food to the library. You owe me.'

'Just take what you want and be quiet about it,' muttered Tymon.

Wick popped two of the little cakes into his mouth. 'That's quite a haul,' he commented shrewdly. 'Seems too much for one person.'

'You should be in a lawyers' guild, not doing a leaf-binding apprenticeship,' groaned Tymon in exasperation. 'It's a shame to waste such fabulous mental powers on parchment and glue.'

'So?' pressed the other, still grinning with impish insistence. 'You're not going to get out of this, you know. Who are the cakes for?' He waited pointedly for an explanation.

Tymon struggled with himself. He was tempted to confide completely in his friend, to tell him of his plan to run away from the seminary. He wanted to prove that he too had a promising, if unconventional future. It was with difficulty that he kept silent regarding the hopes he had nurtured over the past few weeks.

'You've caught me, oh brilliant one,' he conceded. 'The extra food is for Galliano. Satisfied?'

'I just enjoy being right,' returned Wick. 'I thought it might have something to do with the old man.' He glanced sidelong at Tymon. 'Is he still building that pointless heresy of his? The dirigible that goes without the wind?'

'It works.' The boy felt impelled to boast of his success, to defend his unorthodox pastime. 'We've made it fly.'

He was rewarded by the look of complete astonishment on Wick's face. 'So,' mused his classmate. 'Is he actually going to use it?'

'That's the idea.'

'Is the old fool still set on crossing the Storm?'

Tymon frowned uncomfortably. During the course of the machine's construction Galliano had often spoken of his aim of exploration. He had given up trying to dissuade the old man and set his sights upon his own goals. Wick's question upset his complacence — not only because it brought up the vexed subject of the Storm, but because it reminded him that despite all his preparations, he had as yet failed to discuss his getaway properly with Galliano. He feared that the scientist would see his request to go to Lantria as a form of treason, the abandonment of what, in his mind, was their shared objective. Time was running out before the test flight and still the matter remained unresolved. He planned to slip away the following evening during the College banquet and meet Galliano at the workshop. He told himself that he would speak with the old man then.

'I don't know,' he equivocated. 'Probably. Really, I just help him build it. Don't know what he's going to do with it in the end.'

'Is that so?'

Wick's voice contained a slightly mocking note, but his smile was as broad as ever. He plucked two more cakes from the bag and settled himself against one of the larger towers of books, patting the space on the floor beside him in an indication that Tymon should follow suit. The boy sank down, eyeing the dwindling bag of provisions with annoyance.

'Listen, Ty. I've been meaning to talk to you.' Wick wiped the crumbs from his mouth before lowering his voice. 'That crazy scientist is going to get you into trouble. No, don't shake your head, hear me out. His contraption works. Fine. But have you thought about what that actually means? A machine that flies without the wind, a plan to go into the Storm — that's grievous heresy. The Council could have you arrested and put on trial.'

Tymon only shrugged his contempt for the Council. 'I'm not afraid,' he declared. 'I'll be long gone before they come for me —'

He bit his lip, aware that he had betrayed his plan after all. The mistake was not lost on Wick.

He gazed at Tymon intently through the gloom of the stacks.

'The truth at last,' he chuckled. 'No wonder you were so keen on building a dirigible. The bound-boy is running away!'

Tymon did not feel that he could lie outright to a friend.

'It isn't all sorted out,' he said hurriedly. 'But yes. I've had it with this place: I'm leaving. I was going to ask Galliano to help me. I have everything prepared.' He nudged the bag with his toe.

'Where are you going?'

'Lantria.'

'The Fathers aren't easy on runaways, Ty. What if they catch you?'

'They won't, not if I leave during the banquet. I'll skip town during the Festival. No one will notice I'm gone till first prayers the day after.'

Wick sighed. 'Still. Are you sure it's a good idea to break indenture? It's only two more years —'

'I'm not going to sign my life over to the priests,' interrupted Tymon, with sudden vehemence. 'They don't own me.'

Wick recoiled slightly. There was a fire in his companion's delivery that surprised him. He opened his mouth to argue, then thought better of it.

'Well, you know best, I suppose,' he observed. 'Just be careful.'

'I mean to pay them back, of course,' added Tymon. 'Every wooden *talek* they've spent on me.'

This last statement was an exaggeration obvious to both boys.

'Of course,' Wick echoed tactfully. He grabbed a last cake from the bag and rose to his feet, brushing the crumbs from his tunic. 'I have to finish my rounds,' he said. 'Thanks for breakfast. Don't run off without saying goodbye, alright?'

He peered anxiously at Tymon, as if he expected him to abscond from the seminary as soon as his back was turned.

'I won't. It'll be the day after the Rites. There's plenty of time to say goodbye.' Tymon paused before sounding a belated word of caution. 'I can trust you to keep this quiet, can't I, Wick?'

The other boy laid a finger on his lips. 'As silent as the Mouth,' he swore. 'I'll leave you to your — ah — studies. Don't pray too long!'

He strolled out of the room. A moment later Tymon heard the sound of shutters being thrown back in the corridor, accompanied by his friend's unmelodious whistle. He kicked the reduced bag of provisions behind the stacks, his mood of buoyancy returning. He was glad he had taken Wick into his confidence. Now that he had articulated his plans to someone else they took on a more definite cast, a veneer of reality. Wick might prove an invaluable ally the night of his escape, covering for him when he left the banquet. He was undaunted at the prospect of travelling to the South Fringes with nothing but a bag of Festival cakes. Even the possibility of arrest held no dread for him. If the Priests' Council were going to formally accuse Galliano of heresy, he reasoned, they would have done so already. What he himself would do if all came to pass as he hoped, and how he would earn a living, he barely considered. He had a general notion that he would find work in the Lantrian shipyards. To this nebulous end he had accumulated his stock of food, a blanket and lantern smuggled from the dormitory, and some fire-sticks. His next acquisition, the ether oil, would complete the hoard.

A whole frustrating day remained before he would have the opportunity to show the old scientist his prize, however. That morning, all outside charity duty had been suspended. His time would be devoted to completing the last and least agreeable of his Rites-duties.

The sky was overcast as Tymon trudged down the front temple stairs in the company of Father Mossing, lugging a heavy basket of rusks. Though the Bread-Giving took place in the town at the foot of the public approach to the temple, tradition indicated that the seminary's largess was to come, like the Tree's green grace, from on high. Tymon was required to heave his oversized basket all the way up the back stairs from the College kitchen to the temple buttress, only to haul it down the main temple stairs into the street, an exercise in futility. The boy dragged his burden after Mossing, each step a reluctant scrape-and-bump. He loathed the seminary's annual, official act of charity with all his heart. But it was not the physical effort of the job that weighed on his spirits like a basket-load. The object of his discomfort lay in wait for him below. Grey forms sat crouched at the bottom of the staircase. Some had their hands already outstretched in supplication.

The tithe-pilgrims had joined the inmates of the city poorhouse to receive the seminary's blessing. They sat apart from the Argosians in the street, as if social strata existed even among beggars. To the left of the stairs, a motley collection of paupers called for alms, holding out their hands as the priest and the boy approached. Opposite them the foreigners waited in their own separate group, talking quietly among themselves. They seemed less enthusiastic, more wary than they had on their arrival in the city. It was one of the few occasions that the pilgrims would be allowed out of their holding cells before the Festival and their departure for their plantation homes. They were under escort, of course. Two guards stood over the grey-robed figures, leaning on their hardwood pikes. The local paupers clamoured for bread. Tymon could hear their shrill petitions already, drifting up on the breeze in strident expectation of generosity. But the tithe-workers waited in pointed silence. Most of them did not even glance in his direction.

The boy ground his teeth. He was certain his tutors had assigned him to bread-giving duty on purpose. It was a none-too-subtle reminder of his origins, of the life of degradation that might have been his but for the charity of the seminary. The presence of the pilgrims was an added vexation. The whole event encroached on his plans with dreary insistence and broke through his bubble of hope, mocking his attempts at escape. One thought kept him going. Hidden in the folds of his tunic was the hardwood flask of ether oil, Masha's gift to him. He wondered what she would say if she knew the real use he would make of it.

'God rewards Her loyal servants. Take Her grace, eat by Her grace, for this is the season of grace,' fluted Mossing.

The priest had reached the foot of the stairs and waded into the throng of Argosian supplicants, a jug of consecrated water in his hand. He dipped four dainty fingers in the tepid liquid and flicked drops over the heads of the people kneeling in the street. Their hands stretched impatiently towards Tymon, who followed at a slower pace. The smell of unwashed bodies gagged in his throat. As he thumped his basket down the final step the poor of the city pressed about him, pulling at the woven sides of the container, almost ripping it from his grasp. Voices rose in a confused babble of gratitude and recrimination.

'Take grace, eat grace,' breathed Mossing, in a shortened benediction, weaving through the crowd.

Tymon strove to haul the basket past the first and most aggressive row of people. The quantity of bread was fast reducing and there were still hands reaching out, questing fingers gripping the basket.

'One ... per ... person!' he panted, without any effect.

He gave up trying to control the basket and allowed the mob to shove him from side to side, harrying him until the last crusts were snatched away. With a sigh like the wind, the people pulled back. Once the bread was gone the paupers scattered with astonishing rapidity. Some lingered nearby, as if expecting another basket to be produced from thin air, but very quickly Tymon found himself abandoned at the bottom of the temple steps with the empty container. He eyed the crumbs rolling in the depths of the basket with vague embarrassment. The foreigners sat a little further down the street, patiently waiting their turn. The two bored guards by the pilgrims blinked sleepily. One picked his nostril, a slow, meditative process.

'Take grace, eat grace ...'

Mossing wobbled past the stairs towards the circle of grey forms, waving his wet fingers in the air. Tymon could see no way of discreetly attracting the priest's attention to show him the plundered basket, perhaps earning the relief of an early dismissal, without joining him there. He sighed and walked over to the pilgrim group, the empty container bouncing along the bark-brick paving behind him. On this officially sanctioned occasion he had nothing to fear from the foreigners' proximity. He allowed himself to scrutinise them more closely. Their pale, ugly faces were weary and dispirited. One young man rocked on his haunches at the edge of the circle, muttering unintelligibly. He appeared feeble-minded. Instinctively, without making a conscious decision to do so, Tymon searched out the slim figure with red hair.

The unusual youth was there, at the edge of the gathering. Once again, he distinguished himself by his difference. He did not converse with the others, but knelt on the dusty pavings with a curious stillness. His eyes were fixed on the priest, in breach of all custom. Tithe-pilgrims were supposed to show deference and lower their gaze in the presence of their revered masters. But the thin foreigner looked directly at Mossing, his peaked face tense with concentration. Tymon suddenly understood that he was about to speak. The youth was going to say something to the priest, to accost him in the street. It was an unheard-of violation. A second look confirmed that the Nurian had more than conversation on his mind, however. An object gleamed in the folds of his grey tunic. In a daze, Tymon saw the polished blade of a hardwood knife flash briefly in the youth's hand. The guards remained oblivious, their backs turned. The boy slowed his pace, mesmerised.

'... Eat grace ...' Mossing yawned, scattering bright drops of water over the heads of the people kneeling before him. He drew level with the thin youth.

Tymon shook the torpor from his limbs at last, opening his mouth to shout at Mossing, to warn him away. But before he could say a word — before the red-haired pilgrim could move or speak — a blurred shape leapt in front of them.

'Eat me!' A hoarse shout rang in the street. A figure jumped at Mossing, clawing on his arm, pulling his robes. 'Eat me!'

Tymon recognised the simpleton. The man's blank gaze was burning now, fixed on the priest with feverish intensity. Mossing fell back in surprise, the water from the benediction jug spilling all over his cassock. The lunatic opened his mouth and clamped his jaws down on the priest's rotund wrist. Mossing gave a strangled scream.

Tymon reached them before the guards did. He threw himself between the priest and the madman, laying hold of the pilgrim's sparse hair and wrenching his head loose from Mossing's arm. He grappled with the Nurian, pushing him down onto the dusty flags of the street. The fight was over almost the same instant it started. The emaciated foreigner was no match for Tymon and soon lay twitching in his grip, eyes rolling upwards in his head.

'Eat me,' he repeated in a husky whisper.

The guards skidded to the boy's side, brandishing their pikes and shouting abuse at the pilgrim. They grabbed the lunatic's collar and dragged him to his feet. He made no attempt to resist, staring stupidly ahead. When one of the guards struck him across the face, sending him sprawling in the dust, he only scrambled back to a sitting position and began rocking himself as before. His forehead was creased with perplexity. The guards cursed him, levelling kicks at his back. Tymon rose, shaken. He was more shocked by the reaction of the soldiers than by anything the crazed simpleton had done. He turned away from the dismal scene to where Mossing stood, cradling his hurt wrist.

It was then that he noticed the ether flask was no longer lodged in his belt-strap. It had slipped loose during the fight. Muttering an oath, he scanned the street, and within seconds caught sight of the precious object lying in a nearby gutter. The stopper was broken and the liquid had drained away. He bent over his treasure, bemoaning his loss. He was dimly aware of the soldiers sending the pilgrims back to their quarters with barked orders. The whole group moved away from the temple step. The simpleton was propelled bodily down the road by the guards. The foreigners stared over their shoulders in consternation at Mossing, or at the poor fool being kicked down the street between the soldiers. But as Tymon nursed his disappointment in the gutter, the broken flask in his hand, he saw that one face was turned in his direction. One pair of eyes bored into him, observing his dismay and preoccupation with the ether oil, as if nothing mattered but his own petty losses. The red-haired youth looked back at him with cool disdain.

5

That night Tymon dreamed of fire. In his dream he thought he heard the temple bells ringing, ringing the dreaded fire-watch, the signal that the town was burning. He ran down the narrow roads and lightless alleyways of the city, up ladders and down stairs, always on the lookout for a spiral of smoke or a treacherous flash of flame. He found himself hurrying through the dark and echoing gate-tunnel. The way was longer than it should have been and the tunnel had a number of twists and turns he did not remember; he wondered if he was on the wrong road. At last he glimpsed the bright rectangle of the postern gate. But just as he was about to burst through to light and safety, a tall figure in a cloak loomed in front of him.

'Who are you?' he cried in surprise.

'Who are you?' The echoes of the vault were full of mocking whispers. 'Who are you?'

'I'm Tymon!' he shouted at the figure. 'Let me go!'

He tried to push past the shadowy, faceless form towards the gate, but he could not find an opening. The cloaked figure seemed to take up the entire tunnel. Tymon beat aside the folds of the cloak, now as heavy and bulky as canvas, and clawed his way past endless swathes of dull green fabric in mounting frustration. Suddenly the last folds fell away in his hands and he was staring through hardwood bars. The cloaked figure had disappeared: in its place stood the familiar covered prison cart. In a corner of the cage, just as before, sat the beggar with green eyes. The man winked at Tymon from beneath his wide-brimmed hat.

'I've been waiting a long time for you,' he said.

'You can't wait here!' cried Tymon. 'There's a fire!' He glanced nervously over his shoulder in the direction of the city. It seemed to him that he could smell smoke.

'Call the guards!' he told the tramp. 'You've got to get out of here!'

'I have a message for you,' replied the man in the cage, ignoring his warning. He leaned forward now, as eager as he had been the first time they met. He grabbed hold of Tymon's arm through the bars.

'The key is in the bathhouse,' he whispered urgently.

'I don't understand.' Tymon shrank back in an attempt to disengage himself, but the tramp did not let go.

'You must tell Samiha,' he insisted. He gripped Tymon so tightly that the boy lost all feeling in his arm. 'Tell her it's time to come home. She has found what she is looking for.'

'Tell who?' Tymon frowned in bewilderment. 'Let me go! You're hurting me!'

The vagrant did not answer. His eyes were moss-deep, rainwater-deep. The tunnel wavered.

Nothing was real except those two eyes, and even they disappeared at last, as the world disintegrated and renewed itself, broke apart and was restored once more. Tymon blinked his own eyes and found himself staring at the dormitory ceiling. His arm was caught between the bedding and the weave of the hammock.

A dream! He sat up, extracted his arm and rubbed the life back into it. It was morning. The sky was already brightening outside the open windows and the breeze carried a scent of fresh baking into the dormitory. Then he remembered. It was the day of the festival, the day his life would change forever, for good or ill. No wonder he was having nightmares. He flopped down in his blankets again and closed his eyes, trying to relax, but sleep had fled. After some fruitless minutes listening to his companions snore, he swung his legs over the side of the hammock and slid to the floor with a grunt of resignation. Just as his feet touched the boards the seminary bells tolled out. The holiday had officially begun.

He had returned to the seminary the previous day, in the aftermath of the abortive Bread-Giving, supporting Mossing by his good arm and listening distractedly while the priest gasped out a diatribe against pilgrims, madmen and incompetent soldiers. Mossing, to his credit, did not blame the simpleton for the attack, but deplored the circumstances that allowed a lunatic into the city or onto a tithe-ship in the first place. He was touchingly grateful to Tymon for his intervention.

'You did me proud, boy,' he had repeated several times on their way to the infirmary. 'I've always said you would come out right in the end. Don't you worry about your Green Rites. I'll make sure you get through.'

Tymon could not help feeling gratified. Although he was still determined to leave the seminary, he permitted himself the luxury of hope. Organising his getaway would be that much easier if he had Mossing's good word and was free of the endless scrutiny of his professors. But after he left the priest on his hospital bed, he found himself brooding over the red-haired youth, and thinking of the attack that had not occurred rather than the one that had. He had meant to tell Mossing of the pilgrim's knife. Somehow, as the afternoon wore on, it became more difficult to do so, particularly since it was pleasant for once simply to be the object of praise. It was better to receive credit for an actual rescue rather than raise suspicions about one that had not taken place. Besides, how could he be sure that the red-haired youth had really been contemplating murder? How was he to know if he had been about to stab Mossing or use the knife in self-defence? Tymon had gone to bed that evening unsure of what he had actually seen, and uncertain of what, if anything, he should do about it.

The next day the question of a hypothetical attack seemed even more remote. The morning of the Festival dawned fine and warm. The boy could not resist sharing in the general excitement, the happy expectation that fired his schoolmates. His anxiety was forgotten, the problem of the pilgrim receded to the background and his own plans occupied all his attention. There were still many hours left until the College banquet: the last thing he wanted was to be thwarted by some petty run-in with authority and barred from the Rites, despite Mossing's assurances. He concentrated on getting through the Festival without incident.

The themes of his dream were easy enough to explain, in any case. Novices in their Green Year were required to spend the morning of the holy day preparing for the Rites ceremony, undergoing lengthy ablutions at the city bathhouse. Soon after breakfast Tymon and eighteen other students left the College in the company of two of the Fathers, bound for a large domed building in the second tier. They carried their official green robes folded neatly over their arms. Everywhere in the town preparations for the Festival were in evidence. Garlands of flowers decorated the house-fronts and woven cages filled with songbirds hung in the windows and doorways. The captives called through the bars with sweet, plaintive voices. It was considered good luck to buy a caged bird and set it free during the holiday; in a complete reversal of the object of the custom, more wild birds were caught, caged and killed at that time of year in Argos than any other. This irony was lost on the boys, however, and many of them stopped on the way to the bathhouse to buy the little cages from street peddlers. Once the vendors had pocketed the money, the birds were set free and the novices marched on, feeling grand, generous and kind.

Puffs of steam billowed out of the bathhouse as they pushed their way into the building. The air smelt of soap-fruit and wet wood. They jostled through the front lobby, craning their necks to see past a second set of double doors into the main bathing hall and deaf to the admonitions of the priests. The public section of the bathhouse, a domed vault partly sunk into the branch beneath the city, was equipped with a single long and murky pool divided into male and female halves, the slowly circulating water fed by sluices from the roof cistern. The hall rang with the shouts and laughter of the townsfolk readying themselves for the evening festivities. The novices were not permitted in the pool with the common dross of the city. The priests swept their charges on, continuing down the lobby until they reached a latticed door at the far end. Once a guard had opened the lock they passed into a private gallery, a covered walkway that ran along the north and west sides of the main pool hall. Many smaller rooms opened into the corridor, each one boasting two rainwater tubs and individual, heated cisterns. The seminary had rented out five of these private chambers for the use of the novices. The walkway was sheltered from outside eyes by a latticed partition, though those in the gallery could spy on the main pool with impunity.

The cleansing ceremony for the Rites followed a precise sequence that took the better part of the morning. The students removed their old clothing by cutting it off to mark the end of their childhood years. They bathed first in cold, then in hot water, with soap and without, to symbolise the ritual change of state. They chanted the Liturgy of Purity and chafed the skin on their backs, arms and legs with bundles of fireflax, the traditional symbol of spring, until their bodies were raw and tingling. As they rubbed off their old lives with their old skin, the priests lectured them, exhorting them to be honourable citizens, to be grateful for their privileges, to be men. They emerged from the vapour of the bathhouse three hours later arrayed in proud green and walked back to the seminary in silence, overtaken by a sense of solemnity. Dressed in their Festival finery, they were acutely conscious of the expectations hanging on their shoulders. The young men in green were the city's brightest hope. Not all the students were sons of rich merchants and plantation owners. Some, like Bolas, had families who had scrimped and saved a lifetime's earnings to give their boy a seminary education. It was the prefect who gave voice to this thought as they mounted the College ramp.

'Well, it looks like we actually came through,' he remarked. 'My old man would be proud to see it.' He grinned at Tymon. 'I lost money on you, bound-boy. I bet Wick you wouldn't finish your Rites-duties in time for the Festival. Happy to be proven wrong.'

Tymon adjusted the collar on the robe Masha had given him, enjoying the smooth pull of the material between his fingers. He was secretly pleased to have foiled the general assumption that he would not qualify for the Rites — all the more so because it appeared that Wick had taken his part. He told himself that he was only playing along, biding his time until he was able to escape. But he could not help feeling gratified.

'Glad to have cost you something,' he quipped.

As he spoke his gaze alighted on the old warden, sitting on his stool by the gates and beaming. At the sight of the blind man he stopped short and breathed a curse, allowing the others to push past him up the ramp.

'What's wrong?' Bolas waited impatiently for him. 'Come on. It's almost lunchtime.'

'My pass. I left it behind,' moaned Tymon. He had remembered that the treasured disc of bark, his ticket to freedom of movement, remained in the bathhouse among the shreds of his old novices' tunic. 'I have to get it before the Rites.'

'Green grace. Do you want me to come back with you?'

Tymon hesitated. It was a generous offer on the part of the other boy and one that he had not been expecting. Bolas would risk serious sanctions along with him if he did not return to the seminary in time for the midday meal. Tymon drew himself up: he wished to show that he needed no-one's help today.

'That's all right,' he said. 'I can get there and back quicker on my own.'

'Well, go on then,' Bolas laughed. 'And hurry. I should have held on to my money; there's life in the old wager yet.'

The remark was closer to being true than Tymon would have liked. When he begged his tutors to be allowed to return to the bathhouse, the priests greeted the news without surprise, as if they had been expecting an escapade of this sort. A certain skepticism coloured their response. It was clear they did not believe his story but had no reason to stop him, to keep him from making his final blunder. He was sent skidding down the ramp with the ultimatum that if he did not return to the seminary in time for the noonday meal, he would forfeit his place at the Rites and spend the remainder of the Festival sitting in the student dorms.

He ran back through the streets of the city with Bolas' shout of encouragement ringing in his ears. It was a humiliating retreat, a sharp contrast to the dignified march moments before. The idea that his whole plan might be spoiled by such a trivial mistake was intolerable. He arrived at the bathhouse out of breath and out of sorts, and barrelled down the damp lobby in a huff. After he waited for several excruciating minutes at the latticed door, a guard shambled up, yawning, to open it for him. At last he was through. The door to the gallery clicked shut behind him. The bathhouse was quiet; the rooms the boy hurried past were empty and even the main pool beyond the partition seemed unusually still, voided of its laughing crowds. He found his clothes piled on a bench and retrieved his pass with a sigh of relief. But just as he was about to leave the room, a slight movement, no more than a flitting shadow in the covered gallery outside, caught his eye. There was a faint scrape as someone lifted a loose section of the partition. A figure stepped noiselessly out of the pool hall and slipped across the walkway to one of the private rooms. Whoever he was, the person appeared not to have noticed anyone else in the corridor.

Tymon wavered. Part of his mind hammered, insisted, that he had no time for this. He had to return to the seminary before the noonday meal. But the shadowy figure roused his curiosity. The act of crossing from one side of the bathhouse to the other was so flagrantly illegal that he had to know more. He crept down the gallery after the intruder, peering cautiously around the open doorway into the room. The person had his back turned and was undressing with brisk efficiency. With a jolt, Tymon recognised the grey cast of the cloak on the floor, the slim form before him, the wisps of red hair under the trespasser's cap.

The tithe-pilgrims had been given time to bathe in deference to the holy day. The desertion of the public hall was explained: no one wanted to share a bath with the dirty foreigners. But no pilgrim should ever have ventured into the private section of the bathhouse. Tymon could not understand why the red-haired youth risked harsh punishment to bathe in the deserted room. Questions buzzed through his mind, multiplied and swelled as he watched the intruder take off his tight skullcap. One by one the youth removed the hairpins that had been holding a thick braid of hair in place, under the cap and out of sight. To Tymon's astonishment long, flame-coloured locks tumbled down on the stranger's shoulders. The youth undid the buttons on his tunic, his hands trembling with haste. The grey garment fell to the floor and revealed a length of cloth bound closely around his chest. The 'he' was a 'she.' A foreign girl had passed herself off as a man, as a pilgrim!

She was hardly older than a Green Year novice. Tymon caught sight of her delicate profile in the dim, filtered radiance from the skylight as she fumbled with the tie on her chest binding. He must have made an involuntary noise then, allowed a hiss of breath to escape his lips as he stood in the doorway, for she suddenly dropped what she was doing and spun around, gathering up the half-undone cloth to her chest. They glared at each other through the vapours of the bathhouse. Neither said a word.

After a while Tymon felt that he must speak or burst. The silence stretched between them unbearably. She simply looked at him, an indecipherable expression on her thin face, water droplets forming on her forehead and upper lip. The moisture in the air stuck strands of fiery hair to her cheek. Her body had a sharp scent, even from where he stood — the pilgrims could not have been allowed many baths — but the odour was not entirely unpleasant. She smelled of dust and spice and sweat. She was beautiful in her own way, he thought irrelevantly. Then he banished the notion. Slaves were not beautiful. The foreigners were ugly, white and ugly. He noticed with distaste that she had freckles on the skin of her shoulders. She was in the wrong place and in the wrong body: a woman's body. She had put him in an impossible position.

'What are you doing here?' he blurted, with an attempt at severity, though his voice broke embarrassingly as he said it, and the rebuke sounded more like a complaint. 'Don't you know this is a private room?' He could not bring himself to touch on the more conspicuous crime, the fact that she had been dressed up as a man.

Her stance relaxed as if she saw through his bluster. Deliberately, she waited a moment before answering. She tucked the cloth back around her waist. He noticed the hilt of the hardwood dagger she had concealed the day before poking out from beneath her belt. She obviously felt no need to use it now. She levelled her gaze at him.

'You're missing the point, novice.' Her voice was cool, almost cutting. Only a slight inflection gave her accent away as foreign. 'Or don't you find me feminine enough to attract attention in a public pool?'

Her mocking tone, her assurance, made him feel like a fool. It was clear that she had realised he was harmless and was not the least bit intimidated by him.

'Well, I was being polite,' he mumbled. Then he pulled himself together and retrieved a semblance of dignity. 'You'd better get out of here,' he warned her. 'I don't care what you do. But the guard may not be as understanding as I am.'

'Oh, I know all about your understanding.' Her manner was now openly sarcastic. 'I saw how much you understood yesterday when you struck down poor Juno at the temple.'

Tymon was indignant. 'Your Juno attacked a priest,' he retorted, irritated by the suggestion that he had acted without cause. 'What was I supposed to do, let a lunatic kill my tutor?'

'A lunatic?' She rounded on him, her eyes flashing. 'The man you beat off like an animal was an old friend of mine and a noble soul. He was no more a lunatic than you or I, a few weeks ago. Since we came here — your priests — your accursed tutors — have driven him mad. Ever since we set foot in your city he has become a stranger to us. Now he talks of nothing but the Mouth and sits in a trance. The priests have already eaten his mind. All that's left is a shell.'

'That's ridiculous,' Tymon snorted. He was furious at himself for being dragged into such a discussion, for arguing the point against his will. The circumstances were hardly conducive to a debate. 'Why would they do that? And how? You're talking nonsense.'

A smile twisted her thin lips. 'Don't you see? Are you blind and foolish, as well as cruel? They need a madman for their Sacrifice. Who else but a lunatic would throw himself into a Tree-rift? You don't think a pilgrim would volunteer for the job every year without being forced, do you, novice?'

Tymon was stung. Her question stirred up unpleasant echoes of the conversation in the students' refectory, the night of Fletch's wager. The coincidence disturbed him, undermined his confidence, and a niggling doubt that had remained after hearing Piri's claim resurfaced at her words. Something in the accusation rang true.

He gave an angry shrug and nodded towards the dagger. It was the only way he could retaliate.

'Is that why you wanted to attack Father Mossing?' he rejoined. 'Because you think he's responsible for what happened to your friend?'

'I had no intention of attacking. I only wanted to defend myself!' she protested. 'Do you think those soldiers would have allowed me to say anything to the priest without beating me down first? No, we can't have a dirty Nurry spewing filth on one of the Fathers and spouting lies about the seminary. Heaven forbid! After all, what's one foreigner against the good of the whole canopy? Next you'll be telling me not to worry, the rest of the pilgrims get a chance at a better life — and it all balances out in the end!'

Her voice was a whiplash. She was the most extraordinary sight the boy had ever seen, standing there half-dressed, her form as taut as a bowstring, hurling out her contempt for him and his kind. Her taunt was a mocking echo of the truisms spouted by the students.

'So. What if I were to say I might believe you about the Sacrifice?' he growled after a pause. 'How do the Fathers do it? Do they drug the food? Do you have proof?'

She frowned and looked away, her voice low, as if she was speaking to herself rather than to him. 'It isn't the food. We all eat the same food, when we get it. It's something else. A shadow on the heart ... No proof, no. That's partly why I —' She broke off, and stared at him in annoyance. 'Anyway, I don't see why I'm talking to you about it. Proof? You'd probably just shrug it off, even if you saw the whole thing happening under your nose. After all, you shrug off everything else. Tithes, slaves, colonies. What's a stranger's life to you? You prefer your ... your bottle of precious oil.'

She turned her back on him with that, and stalked over to one of the large round tubs in the room, her gait awkward and angry as she clasped the cloth to her chest.

'I had no idea this was going on,' grumbled Tymon. 'I'm not on their side, you know. I'm a bound student. I don't like the priests and I don't agree with them. I wouldn't be at all surprised if they lied about the Rites.'

It was a relief to admit the fact at last. His heart lightened even as he said it. She still had her back to him, however, and made no response to his explanations. He decided that a further concession was in order.

'And I'll have no part in it,' he added extravagantly. 'I'm leaving Argos soon. No dirty citizenship for me. I have a place on a dirigible — I'll seek my fortune elsewhere.'

He felt unable to tell the girl that he was simply running away. But the embroidered story of adventure seemed to make no impression on her either: she only retrieved a bucket of hot water from the floor by the side of the bath and added it to the contents of the tub. The recollection of his own plans made him realise that he had lingered far too long in the bathhouse already. He had to return to the seminary, to keep his privileges for one more day in order to pull off his escape. It was embarrassing to leave just as he was making his grand gesture of solidarity, but he had no choice. He moved towards the door.

'I have to go now,' he announced lamely. 'Good luck to you.'

She continued to ignore him, bent over the side of the tub, dipping her arm into the water to test its temperature. Her bony shoulders spoke volumes; her disapproving silence was deafening. He hung anxiously in the doorway, wishing that she would say something.

'What are you doing?' he asked at last. 'You should go back to the pool hall now, before someone finds you.'

Her answer was muffled, as if it came through clamped teeth. 'I meant to have a bath, and I will,' she said. Her back tensed. 'Are you going or not? Or do you feel like staying here and spying on me? That would be just like a priest.'

He turned and quit the room, piqued at her continued hostility. It was not as if he had personally done anything wrong. And he had apologised about the Rites. He felt misunderstood, maligned.

Her voice followed him out into the corridor, a hushed, angry murmur mixed with the sound of water sloshing against the sides of the tub.

'You say you don't know what's happening. You say you're leaving Argos. But you're a slaver, novice of Argos. Bound or not, you're a collaborator. That's as bad as murder. You kill our hope. People in the colonies sell their children for a bit of water, water like this that you bathe in and then throw out. If you can live with the knowledge of that, go ahead. Leave. Find your fortune.'

He fled, her reproach biting at his heels.

6

He made it back to the seminary with time to spare before the noonday meal, though he no longer laid much store by the feat and greeted the cheers from his friends when he arrived at the table with barely a nod of acknowledgement. He was spared their questions for the moment. To mark the occasion of the Festival the students would eat their lunch in the company of the professors, and as Tymon slid into his usual seat a hush fell over the rows of boys in the refectory. Eighteen priests, starched and collared in their holiday robes, filed through the doorway and took their places at the specially constructed high table to one side of the room. Father Fallow presided at the head of the party. Though the occasion was not as formal as the Rites banquet that evening, the students were still expected to behave with decorum. The boys waited in unaccustomed silence until the Dean was served. When he took up his fork the meal proceeded in a subdued murmur of conversation.

The good Festival food was wasted on Tymon. He had no appetite and could not concentrate on what was said at his table. None of the subjects that preoccupied his classmates — neither the Rites, nor the evening's festivities, nor even the Guild Fair — interested him any more. All he could think of was the red-haired pilgrim and what she had told him. Her fierce powerlessness haunted him throughout the meal. She seemed to stand over him as he ate, chiding him for every drop of water and every morsel of meat, making even the frogapple sauce tasteless. Worse still, her high moral tone was interspersed in his memory with the vision of her standing half-naked in the bathhouse. It was infuriating. He picked miserably at the contents of his plate, deaf to his friends. His budding pleasure in the holiday was obliterated.

The girl's last comments in particular had the sharp sting of truth. The term 'collaborator' pricked his conscience painfully. With that one word she had upset his careful calculations, sent his stratagems tumbling like a stack of cards. He almost hated her for it. He would have loved to mull over his getaway, to organise his escape the next day as if nothing had happened, but that illusion was shattered. She had called him a coward. She had condemned him for wanting to run away from his problems. He argued with himself that she must be a mad fanatic. He reasoned that he was only one person, that he could not remedy all the injustices of the world. But it was useless. His peace of mind was gone. He was old enough, and just wise enough, to understand that the girl had taken a terrible chance in coming to Argos. If a foreigner meant nothing to an Argosian then a foreign woman was less than nothing, an object to be used and abused. Despite his resentment, the idea of what would be done to her once she was discovered turned his stomach. What could she possibly hope to achieve in passing herself off as a pilgrim? Did she really believe she could take on the seminary, alone and unaided?

'Well, what are you going to do about it?'

Wick's eager whisper broke through his thoughts. Tymon realised that his four table companions were gazing at him expectantly.

'About what?' He frowned in confusion. 'Sorry, Wick, I wasn't listening.'

'I said,' breathed his friend, peering with exaggerated caution towards the professors' table, 'that you, of all of us, would have a decent plan ready for tonight. But now I'm not so sure. You've been spending far too many hours in the Prayer Room. It's affecting your mind!'

Piri sniggered and Bolas stifled a guffaw. Tymon shot a pleading glance at Wick, but the other boy only smiled innocently.

'Well?' he said. 'Do you have an idea for the prank or not? We're counting on you to come up with a surprise for our white-necked friend.' He jerked his chin towards Father Rede.

'The prank?' Tymon's relief was tinged with irritation. For once, schoolboy high-jinks left him cold. 'Surely that's for underclassmen?' he snorted contemptuously. 'Why are we still doing this?'

'We figured you'd be pleased to get your own back on Rede,' protested Bolas. 'He's been tough on you all year. I say give him what he deserves.'

'He isn't worth my time.'

'Oh, face up, Ty,' scoffed Wick. 'We all know you hate Rede. Now be a man and do something about it.'

'That's right,' put in Piri, huffily. Tymon's disparagement of younger students had not been lost on him. 'Don't play holy, bound-boy. We know what you're really thinking.'

'Make yourself feel better,' urged Bolas. 'Tell us how you'd like to make the old toad pay.'

Tymon had avoided looking directly at his tutors ever since they had arrived in the refectory. Now he lifted his reluctant gaze to the group at the high table. The pilgrim girl's accusations rang harsh in his memory. It proved surprisingly difficult to reconcile her story with the humdrum reality he had known since childhood, and imagine the stuffy, fussy professors capable of cold-blooded murder. The seminary Fathers were quite simply too dull for such intrigues. Even the members of the Priests' Council seemed incapable of ruthless action. The five old men sat only a score or so feet from Tymon, their frail shoulders bowed beneath bulky silk robes. With their scrawny necks and flounced green cowls they reminded the boy of a line of hunched, balding, green-feathered birds. They passed plates of food to each other and made shrill remarks about the weather, hardly a formula for the massacre of innocents. The reviled Rede sat some distance from that august company, at the foot of the priests' table, his low grade obvious even to the students. Father Mossing, by contrast, was seated in the place of honour, Tymon noticed — at the Dean's right side. The plump priest's bandaged wrist was conspicuous even under the puffed sleeve of his robe. He offered Fallow a tidbit from a bowl, taking care to expose his damaged hand as if to draw attention to the injury for his own advancement. The boy felt a surge of revulsion.

'Set that crazy pilgrim on him,' he muttered. 'See how he likes being the one who's Eaten for a change.'

The comment fell like a dead weight into the silence and his companions gawped at him in surprise. The impossibility of confiding in his friends, of telling them 'what he was really thinking' came home to him. He was as isolated as the pilgrim girl, in a certain sense. All he could do was smile feebly and shrug off the remark as a joke.

'Let's go for something a bit less lethal, shall we?' observed Bolas. 'How about barley-mushroom in his wine?'

Piri shook his head. 'He doesn't drink. No one drinks in the Eastern Canopy — they only pray.'

'They pray for something to drink,' Bolas pointed out, evenly.

'Jar-weed in his smokes, then,' suggested Wick.

'He gave up smoking last Tree Festival,' answered Piri, again. 'He gives up something or other every damned-to-root festival, to make up for the sins of his pale-face friends.' He darted a venomous glance at Tymon. 'Us poor little underclassmen already figured that out.'

Tymon made no response to the gibe. He felt a fool for his previous comment and had resolved not to be drawn into the discussion again. He shifted restlessly in his seat as the others, reiterated Rede's many shortcomings. The lunch was dragging on for an eternity. He stared at the green plumes dangling from the Dean's ornate hat. Could there not be a way to pursue his dreams and solve his moral dilemma at the same time?

When the idea dawned on him, he clenched his fists under the table in frustration, berating himself for not thinking of it before. He would take her with him, of course. He would liberate the prisoner, free the bird, unlock the cage. The new notion possessed him completely. He did not know what circumstances had compelled the Nurian girl to sign away her freedom, but he felt that his self-respect, his honour, even his manhood depended on giving it back. He would smuggle her out to the workshop that very night: Galliano would whisk them both to safety in his machine. In this wild burst of optimism, he had no difficulty imagining that the scientist would drop all his personal plans to deliver the foreign girl to a safe haven. Lantria would be a logical destination. The fact that his own private ambitions agreed so thoroughly with the mission of mercy did not strike him as questionable. He was more concerned with ways and means.

He fell to pondering how best to contact the pilgrim girl, how to separate her from her keepers and spirit her out of the city. He knew that the tithe-workers would be down on the air-harbour that day in their own special enclosure, to watch the Sacrifice. This was his chance to pull off an escape. He doubted whether the guard mounted on the pilgrims would last through the night's celebrations. There would be a moment, there must be, when all the townsfolk were eating and drinking and the Nurians were left to themselves on the quays. His eager ruminations soon spiralled into fantasy. He saw himself slipping wine to the inebriated guards. He considered disguises, filed down bars, mulled over forged offers to buy the pilgrim girl's freedom. He imagined leading her on a breathless getaway through the moonlit vine-fields to Galliano's workshop. The thought of her grateful smile as they whirled off at dawn in the air-chariot, just in time to evade capture, gave him a happy thrill. He had actually begun planning their subsequent itinerary when a remark from Bolas distracted him.

'Maybe Ty is right,' the prefect complained, rather too loudly. 'Set the crazy pilgrim on the old crank. There doesn't seem to be much else we can do.'

'Well,' said Piri, comfortably, 'it's too late for that, I'm afraid. I hear the lice are being shipped out straight after the Rites. No time for tricks.'

'What? Straight after? Where to?' Tymon started to life in a panic, his daydreams evaporating.

'The southern Tree-mines.' Piri gave a smug smile, pleased to display his greater knowledge. 'I suppose it won't be straight after, really, because of the holy day. But they'll be sent to the cooler tonight and packed off tomorrow, first thing. Remember that breakout a few years ago, after the Rites? They don't want that to happen again.

Fletch told me. His father leases a mine to the Council, so he's got all the facts.'

'He can keep them,' noted Bolas, 'if it doesn't help us with Rede —'

He was interrupted by the sound of scraping chairs at the high table. Fallow had risen from his place, followed by the rest of the Fathers. The ordeal of lunch was almost over. Silence descended once more on the dining hall as the students scrutinised the Dean's progress, eyeing him while he strolled unhurriedly across the room, conversing with Mossing. The boys would not be allowed out to join the celebrations on the quays until the Head of the College had retired. Several times Fallow stopped in his tracks and bent towards the other priest, nodding at this or that comment, as if he enjoyed deferring the moment of release. Each time he did so, the whole cavalcade came to a shuddering halt behind him.

Tymon could sense the mounting frustration of the students. If any member of the Council was capable of murder, he thought gloomily, it would have to be Fallow. Seldom had power in the city, both political and religious, been so concentrated in the hands of one man. The Dean had certainly put paid to his own fantasies of liberation with the early shipment of the pilgrims. Tymon had no doubt that it was his choice to send the tithe-workers away so soon; the decision bore Fallow's usual hallmark of ruthless practicality. When the Dean's lanky figure had finally passed through the doors, followed by the Fathers, a collective breath of relief escaped the youths in the room.

The time had come at last. The boys burst from the dining hall with a shout, barrelling through the Priests' Quarter and out into the city streets in an excess of high spirits. A giddy hour of independence stretched before them, an official amnesty before they would be required to return to the College pavilion on the quays in preparation for the Rites. They arrived at the level of the gates to find them thrown wide and festivities already well under way on the air-harbour. A tumult of voices rose from beyond the city walls. The gatehouse itself was a bottleneck for the Festival throng, and the students were forced to slow their pace, mashed uncomfortably close to each other in the oppressive vault. Peals of disembodied laughter and music drifted through the tunnel, accompanied by the sharp odour of grilled meat. It seemed to Tymon that the smell of burnt flesh emanated from the crowd itself, cooking in the confined space.

He chafed at this new delay. He had one chance, one opportunity to contact the pilgrim girl, and there was very little time left to accomplish his goal. He knew that he had to speak to her on the quays before the Rites, or not at all. He had to gain her confidence and work out a plan before she was herded back to her prison, then onto a dirigible the next morning. The whole affair was complicated by his status as a Green Year student. Today, of all days, contact with the foreigners was strictly forbidden him. The more he considered the problem of communication, the more insurmountable it seemed. Even his green robes worked against him, clamouring his identity to the world. He speculated whether he might slip the girl a written note, and realised that he had no idea whether she could read. No one else could be relied upon to act in his stead. The idea of asking Galliano to help him was out of the question. The old man's distaste for official ritual kept him away from public events and it was most unlikely that he would attend the Festival. Tymon briefly considered seeking Wick's assistance, but abandoned the notion when he remembered his friend's light-hearted attitude to the life-wagers. Wick would not understand. He had no recourse but to talk to the pilgrim girl himself. He had found no solution to his obstinate problem by the time he squeezed out of the tunnel and fought his way into the congested space beyond.

Chaos reigned on the city docks as the good citizens of Argos pushed, paid, harangued and bullied their way to the Festival stands. The east side of the air-harbour had been equipped with bleachers of plain lightwood to accommodate the common folk, while the wealthier spectators and certain institutions such as the seminary held private boxes and pavilions on the west end. Guild merchants and government officials rubbed shoulders with farmers and labourers in the scramble to find seating; Tymon saw high-born ladies hoisted into the air by their servants, lifted over the heads of the Festival-goers like ships' cargo. He dropped surreptitiously behind the rest of the seminary group, intending to give his friends the slip in the confusion, and scrutinised the heaving throng on the boardwalk for any sign of the pilgrims. He made out the official heralds for the Rites, a set of sombrely dressed individuals equipped with trumpets, hardwood gongs and drums of bound hide standing a short distance from the gates. But the tithe-workers were nowhere to be seen. The spot usually reserved for them, a slatted enclosure under the trunk-wall resembling a pen for animals, was an empty patch among the eastern bleachers. He would have to seat himself nearby, find some piece of sacking or cloth to throw over his bright robes, and wait for them to arrive.

He allowed the last of the chattering novices to disappear ahead of him into the crowd. But just as he was about to slink off towards the east quays, a hand took firm hold of his elbow and Wick's familiar enthusiasm crisped his ear.

'Here you are. Finally! I've been looking all over for you. Come on, we've got someplace to be.'

Despite his energetic protests, Tymon found himself being led inexorably towards the private booths and the wrong end of the air-harbour. His friend appeared to have a secret objective in mind, for he cautioned Tymon to silence with much in the way of theatrical flair, a finger at his lips. Finally he motioned him through a doorway to one of the stalls.

'I've never seen a fellow so reluctant to get a break,' he sniffed, aggrieved, as they stepped into the empty space under the booth.

'It's not a break if we're caught,' hissed Tymon. He glanced nervously at the stairs leading up to the viewing balcony.

'You'll thank me soon enough for bringing you

here,' replied Wick. His voice dropped to a conspiratorial whisper. 'First, I've been meaning to ask: are you going through with it tomorrow? Are you still leaving after the Rites?'

Tymon fidgeted with impatience. 'Nothing's changed,' he sighed. 'I'm not wasting two more years on the priests. Now can we go?'

Wick grinned. 'Calm down, you're flapping about like a girl. Yes, we'll go.'

Instead of exiting the booth, however, he made for the balcony steps, whistling loudly.

'Make sure you come and see me during the banquet. I have some important news for you,' he threw over his shoulder. 'It might change everything. We can't talk here, though. Come on, the others are waiting for us.'

'What, in a private box?' Tymon stared after him, aghast. 'Won't the owners be angry?'

'We are the owners, cloud-for-brains,' Wick answered. 'I told everyone at lunch, but you were in cloud-world and didn't hear me.'

With a twinge of jealousy, Tymon remembered that his friend had ready access to the world of privilege symbolised by the private booths. The stall probably belonged to Wick's family. There was nothing for it but to accept the invitation; the pilgrims were not yet in evidence on the quays. As he clattered up the narrow steps, he wondered what news the other boy had to tell him. He feared that circumstances would prevent him from ever finding out.

'My father, poor man,' continued Wick as they climbed, 'was invited to the Lord Mayor's pavilion at the last moment. Couldn't refuse, of course, even though the family box was already built. So it's ours. No one will bother us here.'

They ducked through the low doorway at the top of the stairs to the sound of a rousing cheer. Bolas, Piri and two other fourth-year students whom Tymon did not know were sprawled on benches at the back of the booth. In the short time since they had arrived the novices had broken out a forbidden gourd of Treesap wine. They were now passing the heady brew to one another, their mouths smeared with dark red juice. Though a special dispensation from the seminary waived the penalty for public drunkenness on the day of the Festival, most of the students were too young to avail themselves of the licence. They relied on subterfuge to enjoy the carnival atmosphere and a private booth, far from the prying eyes of the priests, was an undreamt-of luxury. Wick straddled a bench and accepted the proffered drink, tilting his head back to take a long swallow. Tymon imitated him more slowly.

'A stroke of luck,' commented Piri, his face hot with liquor, 'having this place of yours, Wick.'

Wick only gave a complacent smile.

'Three cheers for Wick's father's mayor's last-ditch invitation,' hiccupped one of the fourth-year students, sending the gourd around.

'Hear, hear. Now, let's get to business before we all fall asleep,' said Bolas. 'Do you have the stuff, Stel?'

The boy named Stel retrieved a small hardwood pot filled with a viscous fluid from the folds of his jacket.

'Fresh from the College stores,' he gloated. 'Sticks like a whore in heat.' He made an unpleasant smacking noise with his lips.

'Lizard skin glue,' Wick clarified, for Tymon's benefit. 'Piri thought of it. Has no smell, no colour, and it's quick acting. A layer on Rede's chair at the banquet — and watch what happens when Lord White-Neck tries to get up! Here's to the fourth years!'

He raised the communal gourd to Piri, whose thin face beamed with wine and happiness. Tymon also toasted the younger boy when his turn came around, but without conviction. He knew well enough from experience the feeling of pride when someone like Wick singled him out for praise. He told himself that he no longer cared for such honours, and that it was all the same to him if Piri took over his laurels as class clown. But the episode further dampened his mood. He left the other boys to hammer out the details of their plot at the back of the booth and moved his bench with a loud scrape towards the balcony railing, staring glumly over the sweep of the quays. The time before the Rites was slipping away, and still the pilgrims had not appeared on the air-harbour.

A gust of raucous laughter reached him from below. A knot of soldiers had gathered at the entrance to the next stall. The men were leaning in drunken camaraderie against the wall of the booth, listening to one among their number.

'... couldn't move him. Opened one eye. Said, "Love you too, Anna." Snoring again in a jiffy.'

'What did you do?'

'Covered him with a towel and left. He was still there when the lice went in.'

The guards roared with merriment. Tymon recognised two of them as having been present at the disastrous Bread-Giving, the sentries who had beaten down the madman. He shrank back from the edge of the balcony so as not to be seen, engrossed by the soldiers' talk.

'... can't say as I blame him,' one snorted through his laughter. 'Who'd want to watch a bunch of naked whiteys, anyway? Fleas and bones, the lot of 'em ...'

'I pity the lice,' another chuckled. 'Just pray that the towel stayed put. It's not decent to see that much of the captain, even for foreign tastes.'

The soldiers all howled in agreement. The group of boys behind Tymon hooted in a burst of simultaneous mirth, their voices drowning out the conversation below.

'He'll dance,' Piri exclaimed excitedly. 'With the chair stuck to his bony —'

His chatter was lost in a surge of competing voices.

'— just before the Fathers come back from the procession —'

'— if enough of us go, no one will ever know who —'

'— just make sure it's the right chair —'

Tymon leaned forward on the railing, a breath of frustration escaping his lips. He wanted to hear what the soldiers were saying, to gain an insight as to why the pilgrims were late on the quays. But the soldiers appeared to have dropped the subject of the foreigners altogether. The guard who had first spoken jangled a set of hardwood keys, reeling slightly as he tried to fit one after the other into the door of the next-door booth. The rest heckled him, making references to his inability to fit anything into anything, from keys, to locks, to women.

'You couldn't find a keyhole as big as the Mouth,' they jeered.

'No, no, no.' Bolas' voice rose in protest from the back of the booth at the same time. 'I've still got to find my way to the Mouth. You lot can drink yourselves under the benches without me.'

A heavy arm clapped across Tymon's shoulders, jolting him from his reverie. It was Piri's second classmate, still nameless to Tymon, a hulking fellow with a vacant smile. He thrust the wine-gourd irritatingly close to the boy's face.

'What about you, Greenie number two?' he slurred. 'Come and join us. What's so interesting down there?'

Tymon tried to push the gourd away but the other student only shoved it under his nose with vapid, grinning insistence. Beneath them at the foot of the next-door booth, the guards' banter had degenerated into a loud argument.

'Won't work. Damn things won't work.' The soldier with the keys gave the door a kick.

'Now, now, calm down, Ned. Are you sure you've got the right ones?' cried one of his fellows.

'Ty's in love,' Wick threw out from the back bench. 'It's the only explanation for his mooning around.'

'Course I do,' the soldier bellowed in a fit of drunken pique.

'What? Of course I'm not. Don't be silly,' Tymon protested.

'You muddled them with the Captain's set, you fool,' howled the voices of the guards.

'Oooo-ooh! Ty's in love!' sang the boys at the back of the booth.

'Who's your sweetheart, bound-boy?' called Bolas.

The fourth-year student continued to shove the gourd under Tymon's nose. He tried ineffectually to elbow him aside, but the other boy bore down on him with all his weight, still smiling, and turned the gourd upside down over his head, spattering him with bright red drops.

'What kind of fool are you?' Tymon exclaimed. 'I've got to go to the Rites in this robe!'

He searched his clothes angrily for the telltale dark stains. But the droplets of wine had only sprinkled his head. He ran his fingers through his hair, glaring at the younger student. The hulking boy simply shrugged.

'Leave him alone, Stumpy,' called Wick again. 'Can't you see he wants to be pretty for his sweetheart?'

'I am not in love!' cried Tymon, infuriated by his classmates' mockery. He wrested the wine-gourd away from the aptly named Stumpy and emptied the remaining dregs into his mouth, as if to prove his point. 'I'm not mooning around. I'm having a great time.'

'He's right, Ned.' A new voice joined the soldiers' debate at the foot of the stall, patient and slow, as if explaining to a child. 'The booth keys are on the prison ring. We have the warehouse ring. Look, see? It's yellow.'

'Is she down there on the quays?' goaded Wick maliciously. 'Is she waiting for you? Are you going to meet up with her later, Ty?'

Tymon frowned at him. His friend's teasing seemed innocent enough, but he found the accidental insight into his thoughts disturbing. He was not given a chance to reply, however. Just at that moment a strident note blared out over the air-harbour. The Rites heralds were sounding the preparatory signal for the procession. Tymon's eyes jerked towards the city gates as a line of grey figures emerged from the tunnel. The pilgrims had arrived at last.

'That's our cue.' Bolas jumped up. 'Best not to miss the drill. They take forever to warm up, but it's just as well. I need some air!'

Tymon wavered at his post on the balcony. He had forgotten in his excitement that he and Bolas would be expected at the seminary pavilion earlier than the rest of their companions to prepare for the Rites procession. It was during this solemn affair that the elect few actually participating in the ceremony — the Dean, high-ranking professors, Green Year students and processional guards, as well as the chosen Sacrificial pilgrim — would march the length of the air-harbour to the trunk before cheering crowds. There they would turn onto a narrow ledge that bypassed the main road, the so-called Path of Sacrifice, winding up the Tree-face towards the Mouth. It was the first and only occasion Tymon would join in that august pageant. Citizens lucky enough to have a seminary education witnessed the sacrament that took place in the rift only once in their lives. The other inhabitants of Argos, the unlettered working folk and the Impure, female half of the nation, never laid eyes on the Sacrifice at all. They waited for the Dean to reappear outside the Mouth holding aloft the pilgrim's ceremonial cloak, a flash of scarlet in the wind. It was the signal for general celebrations to begin.

All of Tymon's plans had come to naught. His time was up. He yearned to follow the foreigners and speak with the red-haired girl, but saw no way of justifying the move to his friends. He would be obliged to return to the seminary pavilion with all the other Green Year novices and wait idly for the procession to start.

'You're right, by the bells,' he heard the drunken guard concede outside, as he trailed reluctantly after Bolas. 'The keys are in the bathhouse. The keys are in the damned-to-root bathhouse.'

It was only then that Tymon recalled his dream. The soldiers had echoed almost word for word the bizarre message whispered by the vagrant in his nightmare: *The key is in the bathhouse.* And so, apparently, it was.

7

Tymon prided himself on not being a superstitious character. He laughed at auguries and prophecies, and had never allowed a backstreet fortune teller to paw his palm in quest of a few *taleks*. He did not believe that the story of his life might be traced in the stars, or in the veins of leaves that happened to fall at the time of his birth; he agreed with the priests at Argos seminary in one respect — that the arts of soothsaying and dream interpretation were either pointless nonsense or harmful charlatanry. He put his faith in real people, real places, the solid bark beneath his feet. The future was his to make. There was no such thing as fate. At best, the story of the keys was a coincidence, he decided. A bizarre but ultimately meaningless coincidence. He fidgeted in line behind the other waiting novices and stretched his neck from side to side in the tight collar of his robes. A curious sensation of heat had come over him, as if fiery sap had invaded his veins. His skin tingled under the constricting clothes. He had drunk too much of the students' wine, he thought. The dream was a coincidence. Nothing more.

'Come on, come on,' Bolas muttered beside him.

His friend's impatience was directed at the head of the queue. The priests and novices participating in the Rites stood in formation outside the College pavilion, waiting for the pageant to begin. The processional column was long enough to follow the curve of the quays, and the head of the line was visible, nosing to the right. Heralds occupied the first few rows, the streamers on their instruments fluttering in the breeze. The Dean stood behind them, accompanied by a squadron of the Council Guard. The members of this elite militia unit, splendidly attired in black and green, flanked the line at regular intervals, carrying unlit torches. The proceedings would begin on Fallow's command. The noise on the docks had already dropped to a steady hum in anticipation of his signal and there was a crackle of expectation in the air, a tangible surge of exhilaration. But the Dean was engaged in conversation with someone standing next to him, a man in a black surcoat. He had already kept the column waiting several interminable minutes. It was this delay that so incensed Bolas.

'I'd swear he enjoys dragging it out every time,' he fumed.

Tymon speculated grimly whether the protagonist for the Sacrifice had already been selected — primed and drugged, perhaps, well before the event — or whether the choice would be made during the ceremony itself. The pilgrim's supposed self-offering would coincide with the arrival of the procession at the eastern end of the quays and the foot of the trunk-wall. The boy could see the foreigners in their enclosure, a smear of grey amid the colourful bleachers. He could only hope that the pilgrims' return to the prison would not immediately follow the Rites.

'Five on Crazy.'

A whispered comment in the row of novices behind drew his attention. Out of the corner of his eye, he saw one of the students dropping five *taleks* into another's outstretched hand. With a rush of distaste, he identified Fletch as the receiving party.

'He's the favourite,' the fixer cautioned the other boy. 'You won't make anything. What about little Red? He's too scrawny for mine work. Proper runt.'

'Really?' The student making the bet seemed unsure. 'Crazy seems like the obvious choice.'

Tymon's disgust deepened. The fat-cheeked boy was still accepting life-wagers on the pilgrims. He could easily guess the identity of the man named 'Crazy'; his heart skipped a beat at the mention of 'little Red'.

'Sometimes obvious is wrong,' shrugged Fletch. 'But it's your call.'

'I don't know,' the first boy whined. 'Now you've thrown me off.'

'They're always together,' remarked Fletch, his voice syrupy. 'One's mad and the other's next to mad, as they say. Odds are more interesting on Red.'

'How interesting?' Tymon spun around to face the two players. He had not meant to speak, but a sudden fear gripped him, a panicky sense that he might be too late to help the pilgrim girl. Had she been chosen by the priests?

'What are the odds on Red?' he asked, gruffly.

'Who'd have thought,' Fletch smirked. 'Want to place a bet, bound-boy?'

'Leave it alone, Ty,' advised Bolas. Tymon ignored him.

'The red-haired one,' he pressed, searching Fletch's face. 'Thin, funny-looking fellow. I've seen him. He's the runt, right?'

'Maybe,' drawled the other. 'What are you willing to put on it?'

'Ty —' began Bolas once more.

'Tell me what the odds are, and I'll decide,' snapped Tymon.

'Oh no.' Fletch shook his head, grinning. 'That's not how it works, bound-boy. Show me the money first.'

Tymon made a pretence of rummaging under his Festival robes. He had no hardwood counters of Argosian money, but his College pass produced a convincing click in his pocket.

'I might give you five,' he answered.

'Ty!' Bolas tugged at his wrist. 'Don't be stupid —'

Tymon snatched his arm from his friend's grip. 'Well? What do you say?' he challenged Fletch. His voice had risen. 'Do you have the odds for me or not?'

The fixer smiled his unpleasant smile but said nothing. Tymon felt another surge of heat suffusing his face. He was aware that the liquor he had gulped down in the booth was having an effect on him, but his contempt swept all prudence aside. How dare the snot-nosed bully brush him off? He was about to lash out, to tell Fletch exactly what he thought of him, when he noticed a figure in dark green robes observing him from the end of the student row.

'The odds are very slight indeed of you going to the Rites, young fellow.'

Father Rede's bored tone sent a quiver through Tymon. How long had the professor had been standing there, listening to the discussion? He heard Bolas exhale with suppressed aggravation at his side. His friend had been trying to warn him, he realised with dismay. He hung his head under his tutor's scornful gaze. The priest's thin mouth twitched in a triumphant smile.

'Young man,' he began, as Tymon wilted before him, 'you have been given occasion to prove yourself worthy of taking the sacrament of the Rites and of joining this blessed company. I see no evidence, however, that you are aware of the high privilege you enjoy. No, you would throw it all away without a second thought. You have been warned and must reap the consequences. Therefore —'

'You will be given one more chance, and only one, to get it right,' interjected another voice.

Father Mossing stepped up beside Rede. Father Rede stole a sidelong look at him and bit his tongue, his frown deepening in surprise.

'A final warning,' Mossing continued. He did not smile but there was a gleam of humour in his eye. 'Because it is the Festival, and you are a Green student. But this is the last reprieve you'll get, young sir. Use it well.'

He turned on his heel and left, returning to the front of the column. The students exchanged glances.

'You are very, very fortunate to have such understanding friends, bound-boy,' hissed Rede. He extended his lizard-like neck towards Tymon, fairly spitting with impotent rage. 'If I again find you talking, making a spectacle of yourself or in any other way undermining the sanctity of this hallowed event, you will be sent back to your dormitory to await further sanctions. No more chances.'

He collected himself, gathering up his long robes like the shards of his dignity, and rolled his cynical gaze over the rest of the novices.

'You have all been given a priceless opportunity, though you don't seem to realise it,' he snarled. 'What you are about to embark on is an experience of deep spiritual importance. The Rites are no laughing matter, nor —' he glanced briefly towards Fletch '— are they an occasion for games or bets. You will show a proper amount of respect. Do not take your good fortune for granted —'

A shrill blast from the heralds' trumpets cut short the professor's diatribe once more. The Dean had given his signal. Rede glared furiously at Tymon, as if to impress upon him that there was much more to say and that he had escaped his deserts only through astounding good luck. Then he hurried off down the column. The drums rolled out a slow, solemn measure, and the procession shuffled forward.

'I've had enough,' Bolas muttered in Tymon's ear as the students swung into step with the beat of the drum. 'You really want to be barred, don't you? Well, go ahead. I won't try and stop you next time.'

Tymon could have laughed aloud. To be barred, expelled from the Rites, none of it held dread for him any longer. He almost welcomed the chance to break free of the whole wretched charade. It was ironic that Mossing had chosen this moment to fulfill his promise of protection, when the boy no longer cared for it. But he was grateful to the priest for one reason: he needed to stay on the quays. Rede would have sent him back to his dormitory and dashed all hope of speaking with the pilgrim girl. He murmured a clipped apology to Bolas as they marched, and lapsed into silence, his eye on the enclosure at the eastern end of the docks.

Before long it became impossible to talk to the other students, even if he had wanted to. Every few steps the heralds' trumpets emitted a piercing cacophony. The gongs clattered and crashed, obliterating all other noises. Tymon's ears rang. Between the horn blasts he could just make out the cheers of the crowd, as if from another world. The column moved more quickly than he had expected. In hardly any time at all they had passed the city gates and were skirting the first bleachers. The sound of cheering escalated. The townsfolk were chanting a refrain, a single word.

Go.

Tymon had shouted the same thing in previous years, bleated out the thoughtless directive with the rest of the audience in the stands. He knew all too well what would happen now. The procession would come to a halt at the pilgrims' enclosure, where the Dean would read aloud the Leaf of

Summoning, the sacred invitation to the Rites. He had watched every year, in awe as a child and with a degree of macabre fascination when he grew older, as a figure inevitably detached itself from the knot of foreigners and stumbled forward in answer to the summons. He both dreaded the crucial moment and longed for it to be over, for the affair to be done with.

Go, chanted the crowd. It was no hymn, no grand statement of belief — just a crude command, the collective desire of a group willing one person to death.

The head of the column approached the enclosure. Bands of sweat broke out on Tymon's chest and neck. He squinted beyond the ranks of green-robed novices, past the rough fence that separated the pilgrims' corral from the bleachers, seeking out the thin figure with red hair. At last he glimpsed the pilgrim girl sitting near the edge of the pen. As if to prove Fletch right, she accompanied the simpleton, who squatted at the base of the slatted fence. She had her arm about her friend's shoulders. She was infuriatingly close. If Tymon had stood a bare thirty feet further down the quays he would have been able to sign to her through the slats.

But the procession was slowing down already. The horns gave a final, jarring wail and the drums rolled once before falling silent. The top of the column halted beside the enclosure gate. An instant of disorder followed as the back rows stopped marching slightly too late and the students came up short against their tutors on the narrow boardwalk, caught between the bleachers and the gulf. They were forced pell-mell to reorganise themselves. Tymon found himself separated from Bolas in the resulting confusion, pushed farther up the column and to the left, almost to the beginning of the fence. His pulse quickened; he could do it now, he realised. If he could just work his way a little further forward, into the next row, he might be able to exchange a few words with the pilgrim girl during the invitation ceremony. He pushed his way through the line of novices, ignoring his schoolmates' protests.

And still it was not enough. He had arrived at the corner of the fence but he could not capture the girl's attention. She was looking the wrong way, her gaze trained on the Dean, like everyone else — everyone, that was, except the Nurian youth beside her, who stared at his toes. The heralds had stepped to one side leaving an empty space before Fallow at the enclosure gate. The Dean unrolled a long parchment. The cheering of the crowd died away.

'Nothing is free,' announced the Head of the College in the expectant hush. 'We receive life and grace from the Tree. Without Her, all things would cease to be. Should we not expect to give something in return for so great a favour?'

Fallow paused to allow his words to sink in. High above, dock birds wheeled and screamed mockingly in the silence, launching themselves from their nests in the trunk-wall.

'All things have a price,' resumed the Dean. 'The Tree is merciful. For the sake of all, She accepts only one. Here, on this blessed occasion, we repay our debt. *She giveth and She taketh away,*' he read from his scroll. '*Hath brought forth all, and will devour all again.*'

A sound like a faint sigh went up from the crowd. Tymon eased his way past yet another row of boys, the second to last before the professors' ranks. Someone swore at him in muted and colourful language. He squeezed beside the fence.

'*Kings She consumed, their pride to ashes blown …*'

He was barely five feet away from her now. Though the enclosure fence was the height of a man, it had been hastily built, the slats placed almost a hand-width apart. The pilgrim girl and her companion were clearly visible. He could catch the bubbling monologue of the lunatic, smell the acrid sweat coming off the young man's body. He decided to risk speech.

'Pilgrim!' he whispered through a gap in the boards.

'*Saints hath destroyed, and martyrs' bodies hewn.*'

She had not heard him. He tried again.

'Lady!'

The dangerous word finally caught her notice. He saw her eyes dart towards him, a slight frown appearing as she registered who he was. He beckoned to her through the gap. Slowly, unwillingly, she shifted position so that her head was nearer the fence, her face turned away from him. He leaned against the enclosure so that it seemed from the outside as if he was resting. Then he breathed:

'I can get you out of here.'

'*Who among us joins their ranks?*' continued the Dean.

'Must be going, must be going, must be going,' babbled the light-headed Nurian youth. The girl sat silent beside him, her head bowed. Tymon began to wonder whether she had heard him after all.

'What makes you think I want to get out of here?' she muttered at last.

The birds still circled in agitation over the main terraced road up the trunk, almost obliterating her words with their cries. Tymon leaned closer.

'Listen. I'm serious. We can work out a plan, escape together —'

She cut him off. 'I already have a plan of escape.'

'*Who among us walks the Path?*' Fallow's question rang out over the stands, imperative.

'You do?' Tymon stared at the girl, both relieved and nonplussed. 'Can you get out of the jailhouse tonight?

'Maybe. What's it to you?'

The birds, Tymon noticed distractedly, had increased in number. He scowled briefly up at the trunk-wall. They were wheeling over something on the main road: figures hurried along the ramp above the air-harbour, where it made its first zigzag turning up the trunk-wall. He could hear faint cries coming from overhead. He pushed the anomaly from his mind, concentrating on the affair at hand.

'The things you said last time. You were right,' he whispered through the slats. 'I want to stop being a collaborator. I want to help.'

'That's nice.' The girl's answers were terse, inattentive. She kept her eyes fixed on her friend. The simpleton seemed increasingly distressed.

'*Who will go and make the Sacrifice?*'

The air-harbour echoed with Fallow's call. Even the dock birds had subsided, quelled into submission by the hypnotic, recurring questions. Tymon's limbs twitched with the irrational urge to respond, to run to the front of the procession and offer himself up to the Dean. A great shout welled up from the crowd and ebbed away again.

'If you can get away, do it after the Rites,' he pleaded hoarsely through the din. 'The city postern should be open all hours for the Festival. Meet me on the main road, at the crossroads to the first branch, at midnight. I'll take you to someone who can fly you out of the canopy ...'

He glanced up again as he said it, towards Galliano's branch. There were still people on the main ramp; the birds circled over them silently. Whatever the altercation was that had originally attracted them, it had now ceased. The company on the road was dispersing. Most of the figures were making their way down towards the air-harbour. They were Council guards, Tymon saw suddenly. He recognised their long pikes. One figure was left on the road. It mounted the ramp slowly.

'*Who will go and feed the Grace?*' trumpeted the Dean.

'Must be going, must be going, must be going ...'

The Nurian youth's raving had mounted in pitch. Tymon was about to speak to the pilgrim

138

girl again, to ask her if she had understood his directions, when the simpleton moved. He half rose from the floor of the enclosure and remained in a crouched position, swaying on his haunches, his face anguished. The girl took hold of his arm in an attempt to calm him. She left the side of the fence to do so, murmuring in the youth's ear. Tymon seethed with annoyance at the interruption.

The scroll snapped shut in the Dean's hands. 'Who will go?' he challenged, sweeping the bleachers with his gaze.

The foreign youth was struggling to stand up now. The girl held on doggedly to his arm and reasoned with him in a breathless whisper.

'Who will go?' repeated Fallow, his voice thunder. He hardly spared a glance for the pilgrims. He was speaking to the townspeople, for their benefit. 'Who will be Eaten?'

The audience roared. Hairs prickled on the back of Tymon's neck.

'Must be going!' the madman cried. He leapt to his feet, almost knocking the girl over in his haste. She tried one last time, desperately, to catch hold of him, but he eluded her and hurried towards the enclosure gate. His voice was clear and bright, assured.

'I will go!' he called out.

There was an instant of dead calm. Then the crowd erupted, bellowing its approval. Screams, celebratory whistles and the din of hand-held clappers fed the fray. The pilgrim was allowed out of the enclosure by the Council Guards. He stood straight and smiling before the Dean, no trace of his former agitation showing in his face. The students beside Tymon craned forward to catch the conclusion of the ceremony. The pilgrim girl crouched at the foot of the fence, staring blankly at the spot where her friend had been.

'Did you hear me?' Tymon queried in an undertone. She gave no sign that she understood him.

'I accept your offer, on behalf of the people of Argos and of the faithful in the Four Canopies,' Fallow pronounced, at the head of the column.

There was a murmur of approval from the spectators on the bleachers. Tymon avoided looking in the same direction as his companions. The Dean would be anointing the pilgrim's forehead with sap, he knew, taking the crimson cloak from its special box and placing it on the man's shoulders reverently, as if he were a prince. A knot of distress twisted in his stomach. He did not want to watch the ritual taking place at the front of the procession. He did not want to see it, and he did not want to think about it.

'What's wrong with you?' he complained to the girl. 'Don't you understand what I said?'

She did look at him then.

'What's wrong with me?' she repeated, low and fierce. She brought her face close to the slats. He felt her hot breath on his hand. 'What's wrong with me? Maybe it bothers me that this whole town is sick with evil. You must be sick, or stupid. Why else would you think that I'd abandon my people and go with you just to save my own skin?'

Tymon was speechless. In all his planning and scheming, it had never occurred to him that the pilgrim girl would refuse his offer of help.

'It's incredible.' Her harsh whisper jarred in his ears. 'Don't you realise I might have my own business to attend to? I don't need you to save me, novice.'

'But,' he managed at last, 'you'll be sent away to the Tree-mines tomorrow. It's impossible to escape —'

'Maybe I don't want to escape,' she retorted, her voice ragged with emotion. 'I have a job to do here. If need be, I'll do it in a Tree-mine.'

Tymon bit his lip. The discussion was not going at all as he had intended. Dimly, he was aware that the Dean had finished his oration. The ranks of the procession were re-forming in anticipation of the second half of the journey to the Mouth. The pilgrim girl drew away, evidently considering that their exchange was over. But the boy lingered by the fence. He was unwilling to admit defeat, to simply go on about his business, no matter how little she seemed to need him. Despite the risk, he hung back in an attempt to convince her. It rankled his pride that she would not accept his help.

'Please,' he implored her. 'Just consider the offer. I'll be at the crossroads.'

She only shook her head at him. The heralds' horns blared out. The drums thundered to life again and the first rows of the procession swayed forward. She rose to her feet and dusted off her grey tunic.

'You have somewhere you need to be, I believe,' she said coldly.

He stared at her in dismay. His classmates were now marching on without him and his inactivity drew curious glances from the other students. He heard his name hissed through the ranks as the novices tried to recall him to the moving column. The girl began to weave her way through the seated pilgrims, towards the rear of the enclosure. Tymon pressed his forehead against the slats. She could not simply leave him there. It was unbearable. In a fit of exasperation, he blurted out the first thing that came to his mind. It was a word, a name, an act of desperation.

'Samiha!'

He barely distinguished her look of shock as she spun round. A hand clamped down on his own shoulder and he was forced about in turn, his back against the fence. Father Rede gloated over him a long moment before speaking.

'Well, Master Tymon,' he remarked. 'I believe that all your extra chances have run out.'

If a spectator on the stands had examined the air-harbour in the wake of the invitation ceremony, he might have seen two figures hurrying down the empty quays in the opposite direction from the Rites procession. One was a green-clad novice, the other a priest. The boy was forced into a humiliating trot every few paces, prodded on by the professor who strode behind him, his mouth compressed into a thin line of disapproval — or possibly satisfaction. Few people noticed the shameful exit, however. The procession had begun its ascent of the Path of Sacrifice and the attention of the audience was riveted on the line of priests winding along the high ledge. The crimson spark of the pilgrim marched proudly at its head. Shafts of late afternoon sun gleamed on the guards' polished pikes; their torches, now lit, were yellow flecks against the grey trunk-wall. The incessant din of horns and drums echoed over the air-harbour. Almost directly below the Path, the rest of the pilgrims sat in a huddle of identical attitudes, pale faces angled to the sky. They looked very much like their counterparts on the temple frieze.

As far as Tymon was concerned the eyes of the entire town were fixed on him in his disgrace. He jogged along the quays, jabbed periodically by Rede's bony index finger, his ears burning with embarrassment. But it was the ruin of his personal plans that was most bitter to him. Father Rede appeared to have every intention of accompanying him all the way to the College and making sure he stayed there. He would not be able to join Galliano for the test flight, let alone make his ultimate getaway, all because of one stubborn female. He had been a fool to want to help her, he thought. He berated himself for acting on impulse, for following the dictates of a dream. He told himself that he did not care if she was named Samiha, if she knew someone named Samiha, or if the preposterous coincidence would finally convince her to take him up on his offer. He would not be there, in any case, to assist her. He would be confined to his dormitory on the one night his hopes might have come true. Father Rede had already confiscated his College pass.

The priest said nothing as they climbed through the quiet streets of the city towards the seminary. He had not questioned Tymon as to why he had been speaking with a foreigner. It hardly seemed to matter to the professor what the boy's crime had been, so long as he was apprehended and the world was back to its familiar shape — tutor and delinquent in their time-honoured roles, all things as they should be. They mounted the ramp to the College in dreary silence. The warden was not at his usual post, but just as they were about to pass through the carved seminary doors, a stranger emerged from the shadows of the courtyard to meet them. He was an Argosian of middle age and middle build, dressed in a dull black surcoat that reached down to his knees, the uniform of a lay Father. His throat was swathed in a white kerchief. Tymon recognised the man who had stood at the head of the Rites procession with the Dean.

'Greetings, Father,' said the newcomer, acknowledging Rede with a calm nod. His facial features were coarse and unremarkable, yet the overall effect was one of sharp, supercilious intelligence. He gazed intently at Tymon. 'Bringing home a troublemaker, I see,' he said.

Rede's reaction was far less composed. He snapped to attention and his fingers gave a slight spasm on the boy's shoulder.

'My — my Lord Envoy,' he stammered. 'What a surprise! Are you not on the quays? But of course you come and go as you please, as you please —'

144

the priest stuttered with horror at his own indiscretion before rattling on '— Yes, a troublemaker. Indeed, a repeat offender. He has no respect for the law. I caught him attempting to communicate — for some immoral and degraded purpose, no doubt — with an unclean foreigner!'

'Is that so?'

The man in black stared unblinkingly at Tymon. The boy found that steady gaze hard to meet. His own eyes slid away in sullen embarrassment. He did not know who the Envoy was but Rede's reaction was a gauge of his importance. His tutor was almost tripping over himself to win the other man's approval, bobbing obsequiously as he spoke.

'Most assuredly, my Lord. I am accompanying the young felon to his dormitory, where I will personally confine him for the duration of the Festival.'

'Personally?' echoed the stranger. A note of dry humour crept into his voice.

'Yes — that is, if you think it — if you approve ...' Rede opened and shut his mouth several times in confusion, emitting no further sound. He looked very like a margoose chick begging for slops, Tymon thought. His elbows were raised like wings, and his oversized head on its scrawny neck twitched from side to side, mouth agape.

'I'm sure he can find his own way to the dormitories,' the Envoy interrupted smoothly. 'I must detain you, Father. I need your advice.'

The priest's chest puffed out visibly with pride, and not a little relief. He gestured imperiously to Tymon.

'Back to your quarters, boy. I do not wish to see your face until breakfast,' he announced. 'We shall determine what to do with you in the morning.' He propelled Tymon through the doors with a final shove between the shoulder blades.

As he stumbled into the College courtyard, the boy cast a furtive look behind him. The Envoy had his arm through Rede's and was steering the little priest down the ramp in the direction of the air-harbour. Tymon waited in a shadowed corner of the courtyard, his heart pounding, until the two were out of sight. Then he turned his back resolutely on the tunnel leading to the dormitories and hurried across the empty quadrangle towards the library building. A solitary messenger bird sounded a warning from the eaves as he mounted the steps.

Free. He was free. By a fluke, a marvellous chance. He hardly dared believe his good fortune. He padded down the plush carpet of the library corridor, his breath rasping in the stillness of the building. The place was deserted; even the most reserved and bookish of the priests had been bullied into joining the festivities. The Prayer Room was dim and quiet, its shutters closed. He picked his way between the piles of loose leaves to the Nonian liturgies. After taking a last stock of his provisions, he tied everything up in a bundle with a long cord, slung it over one shoulder and strode briskly out of the room. He hoped to take full advantage of the warden's absence from the College gates.

He almost bumped into Wick in the corridor.

'Stop — Ty — hullo,' panted his friend unintelligibly. He had evidently just arrived at a run and was out of breath. 'You were going to leave without saying goodbye,' he gasped. 'Lucky I knew about your stash here. I'd have missed you otherwise.'

Tymon felt a stab of compunction. 'I'm sorry, Wick. It was a last minute thing,' he said. 'Rede didn't give me much choice.'

Wick grimaced. 'I saw him poking you along the quays. I thought to myself, that's it, Ty's off. Why did he bar you?'

'Oh, for nothing, really,' lied Tymon. He did not wish to waste time relating the circumstances of his disgrace. He scuffed the floor with his heel, eager to be gone but reluctant to be brusque with Wick. 'I was talking to someone. Should have been more careful, I suppose.'

'I'm glad I caught you. I told you, I have news for you. You might change your mind about leaving, once you hear what I have to say.' Wick drew a deep breath. He moved closer to Tymon in the panelled darkness of the corridor. 'What if you had something to look forward to, Ty? Something good, right here, right now, in the city? Would you still risk everything to go with that crazy scientist?'

'Something to look forward to?' Tymon's gaze strayed to the end of the corridor and the main entrance lobby. He dreaded an early return of the warden or a reappearance of the mysterious Envoy. 'What do you mean?'

'I mean —' Wick spoke slowly, deliberately '— My father — now, I'm not guaranteeing anything

— but he might be able to work something out for you. Get you an introduction at the Fair. Would that convince you?'

Tymon's eyes snapped back to rest on his companion in consternation. It was one matter for a rich man's son to cultivate egalitarian habits while a student at the seminary. For such a blessed one to offer his less fortunate classmates real and tangible assistance was far more unusual. Tymon had simply never heard of it happening.

'You'd do that?' he gasped, with a rush of gratitude. 'You'd ask your father to introduce me to someone? That would be amazing, Wick — I never thought —'

He stopped abruptly. In the midst of his happy astonishment, the pilgrim girl's accusation tolled out in his memory, a death-knell to pleasure. *Collaborator.* His excitement drained away as if it had never been. How could he accept Wick's offer now?

'Well, no need to cry about it,' remarked his friend wryly, as Tymon's expression reflected a rapid succession of emotions. 'Just consider the idea. Maybe you don't have to go so far to get what you want. What do you say? Will you stay with me?'

Wick's smile was winsome. He watched Tymon with a curious intensity. There was a vulnerability to his expression, a chink in his usual shell of confidence, as if some personal choice of his own rested on Tymon's decision. It was with difficulty that the other boy finally dredged up an answer.

'I can't abandon the old man, Wick,' he replied sadly. 'I wish I could just call it quits. But I owe Galliano some help on the test flight, at least. We've been building up to this — he needs me.'

There was a moment of silence between the two young people.

'Well, the offer stands, if you change your mind,' said Wick with a shrug. His tone had grown distant.

'Don't get me wrong,' Tymon stumbled over himself in an effort to reassure his friend. 'It's a very generous thing you want to do for me. I just feel — I have responsibilities ...'

'Naturally. Do what you have to do,' answered Wick. The momentary openness was gone, replaced by his usual front of easy confidence. He smiled. 'You were sly to get away from Rede so quickly, anyway. How d'you do it?'

'There was a fellow at the gates. The Envoy. He wanted to speak with him. You should have seen Rede's face ...' Tymon shook his head, puzzled. 'Do you know who he is, Wick? I've never seen him in Argos city before.'

His classmate's eyebrows had risen at the mention of the Envoy. 'The Special Envoy of the Council,' he said. 'Their man in the colonies. Over and above the Colonial Board. He doesn't come here much — when he does, you can be sure something's up.'

'Well, he may be special, but I gave him the slip,' said Tymon rakishly. He still wished to impress Wick, even now. 'But he'll be back. I have to go while I can. Sorry to rush you.'

'Not at all.' Wick stepped aside to allow him room to pass.

'I'm glad we had the chance to say goodbye,' Tymon threw back at him, as he hurried down the corridor. 'Take care of yourself, guild-rat.'

'You too, bound-boy.'

Tymon paused at the end of the passage where it turned a corner to join the entrance lobby, and glanced over his shoulder. Wick's moon-like face glistened dimly in the shadows behind him.

'I'll be coming home one day,' he called to his schoolfellow softly. 'You'll see. I'll have a dirigible of my own, like I always said. What do you want me to bring you?'

Wick's laughter sounded hollow in the panelled corridor. 'Silesian bellweed,' he replied. 'Some of that in Rede's cup would make him dance till dawn. Better than gluing him to his chair, any day.'

As he watched Tymon disappear around the corner, the mirth faded from Wick's face. He waited in the dim corridor a few minutes longer, then abandoned his post and moved cautiously towards the lobby. It was empty. Tymon had slipped outside. Instead of leaving the building in his wake, however, Wick turned to the right and approached the imposing door to the main library. The stacks beyond were usually forbidden to novices. The carved black knob turned smoothly in his hand and the door swung open.

'Come in, master Wick,' said a voice. The man in black looked up from a table near the door, smiling his slight smile. 'I trust you have completed your task?'

Wick nodded, closing the heavy door behind him.

8

Tymon quit the College after his meeting with Wick, enveloped in his travelling cape, the bag of provisions and all-too-green holiday robes hidden beneath its folds. As he hurried through the deserted streets of the town, his eyes darted up to the trunk-wall in a constant, nervous reflex. The Path of Sacrifice was plainly visible above the rooftops of the lowest tier. Tymon's anxious gaze hovered near the summit of the dark, jagged line. He expected at any moment to see a flash of crimson against the grey trunk, the flame-like signature of the pilgrim's empty cloak held aloft by the Dean. The hum of the Festival reverberated in his ears, buzzing through the empty city. The noise would escalate to an exultant howl on Fallow's reappearance. The boy shivered and hunched his shoulders under his cloak. He avoided the major thoroughfares down to the air-harbour, passing through obscure alleys and by-ways to reach the lowest tier. He intended to take a back road out of the city, one that would keep him as far as possible from the Festival and the quays.

On the sleepy northern borders of the town, on the opposite side of the supporting branch to the air-harbour, a pedestrian gate opened onto a small footpath that wound up the trunk. It was used by local farmers to graze their herds of spotted, moss-eating shillees and amounted to little more than a shelf of crumbling bark, scarcely wide enough to allow two of those nimble animals to pass abreast. The trail gave the black slit of the Mouth a wide berth, meandering northwards up the trunk for two miles before doubling back in a long arc to join the main road at a point slightly higher than Galliano's branch. It was a time-consuming and indirect route to the old man's workshop, but the only one that enabled Tymon to leave the city unobserved.

He reached the small door at the end of its blind alley without incident. No guard occupied the abandoned post under the trunk-wall and he passed unchallenged onto the footpath. He was soon above the level of the closest rooftops and climbing steadily, a sheer drop to his left. Slivers of bark rolled away from his feet to spiral into the abyss. He walked quickly, his boots sliding and slipping on the ledge; he did not want to be near the city, near the Mouth, when the Rites procession re-emerged. Had the pilgrim already jumped? he wondered, gloomily. Did the madman have to be pushed over the edge of the Tree-rift in the end — thrust into that other, interior chasm? He tried to shut out the memory of the Nurian youth, his face shining with sudden clarity as he offered up his life to the Dean. He told himself that it was not his fault the stranger would die, that he should not waste time worrying about the inevitable. He had not had any part of it. He had not stood by as a man was thrown to oblivion. None of this was his fault, he told himself furiously.

He stumbled when he finally heard it, stubbed his toes on the uneven ledge and almost fell as the triumphant shout went up from the air-harbour. Screams and cheers echoed over the city, piercing the afternoon. The Dean's gesture had been sighted. The Rites were over. The boy regained his balance and steadied himself against the bark wall to his right, but did not pause to look over his shoulder. In any case, the mouth would be hidden now, obscured by a swelling ridge in the trunk. He felt rather than saw the procession returning to the quays. The distant drums filled his blood with throbbing repetition. He scrambled away from the pounding beat, lurched up the herdsmen's trail until the noise had diminished to a dim pulse beneath his feet and faded at last to nothingness. Sweating in his cloak and holiday robes, he climbed on one hot mile, then two. Despite the fact that he had left the Festival and the air-harbour behind, he was gripped by a sense of uneasiness. He reached the point at which the footpath doubled back on itself. The silence was complete: even the birds nesting in the trunk-face made no noise. He pressed on, dogged, his breath rasping in the stillness of the Tree.

The sun was sinking below the western leaf-line by the time he staggered onto the main road at last, his tired muscles aching from the climb. Over the side of the ramp, some distance below, he could see Galliano's branch, the track between the terraces a pale line wriggling along its upper ridge. The long shadow of the humped knot at its centre stretched back across the vine-frames to touch the crossroads. Although Argos city was obscured by the bulk of the limb, the faint sound of revelry reached his ears, a drifting echo of the festivities on the quays. It was not until he had almost reached the path to the workshop that he noticed the bowed form on the ramp ahead. A slight figure sat hunched on a gnarled twig-stump by the side of the road, its grey cloak almost blending into the bark.

For an instant he thought it was her — thought that the pilgrim girl had somehow, improbably, taken him up on his offer and arrived early at their meeting point. But a moment more of observation caused him to utter a cry of surprise and sprint the rest of the way down to the crossroads. There sat Galliano, immobile, his face bowed in his hands.

'What's going on, Apu? Are you alright?' blurted Tymon.

The scientist raised his head and nodded absently in greeting, but did not look directly at him. Tymon peered anxiously into his friend's face. He had noticed a suspicious purple swelling under Galliano's left eye.

'I'm paying the price,' murmured the scientist thoughtfully.

'The price for what?' The boy frowned. There was no doubt: the spreading stain of a bruise disfigured the old man's cheek. Had he taken a fall?

'I've been reminiscing,' sighed Galliano, glancing up at him at last. 'Fifty years ago today, I went to the Rites with the rest of my class. I was eager to be a priest.' He snorted derisively. 'And for what? Knowledge. Power. Ancient secrets. A pittance.'

The mention of secrets reminded Tymon of his plans for the next day. He still had to broach the subject of departure with his friend. He would enlist Galliano's help, he decided, whether the pilgrim girl came with them or not. There was still a chance she might change her mind.

'Apu, there's something I need to tell you —' he began.

'I wanted to speak to them again, you know,' the scientist continued, interrupting him. 'I rolled my old bones down to the air-harbour this afternoon. I had a few things to say to Fallow and his clique. But the Festival guards detained me on the road. It appears I've been declared "Impure" — a deviant, a sub-citizen, whatever you want to call it. I'm not fit to appear in the city on public occasions. In fact, I'm no longer welcome at all.'

Tymon gazed at him in consternation, his own concerns forgotten. This, then, had been the altercation he had seen from the air-harbour at the start of the Rites procession. The Council guards had beaten Galliano, bullied a defenceless old man. And he had not been there to help.

'They did that!' he exclaimed, pointing at Galliano's cheek. 'They roughed you up, Apu, like a common beggar!' He had never heard of an educated citizen, however eccentric, meeting the same fate as the vagabonds in the militia's cages.

'A senile old tramp, yes. An embarrassment. A non-citizen.' The scientist shook his head mournfully. 'Told me to move on, I wasn't wanted. It's all very neat. Half a century later I lose the last of the so-called privileges I was so eager to obtain during the Rites as a young fool. I'm no longer even a man.'

He looked so crestfallen that Tymon sat down beside him on the twig-stump. He felt too awkward to extend his gesture of sympathy any further, however, and could only answer with forced cheerfulness.

'Well, we don't care about them. We're getting out of here, aren't we? I've been meaning to ask — why not just leave tomorrow, once and for all? The machine is ready. I'm ready.' He smiled. 'We can even set sail for the Storm, if you like.'

The offer was only half in jest. Since his encounter with the pilgrim girl, he had ceased to worry about where he would go, so long as he was able to go at all.

'I'm not leaving,' replied Galliano quietly. 'I'll stay here and face the consequences of my actions.'

'Stay here?' the boy gulped in surprise. 'Don't you want to see what's below the Storm any more, Apu?'

'It was just a foolish dream. We pay the price for our dreams. We pay the price for everything. I have no right to dream. All this is my fault.' The scientist nodded towards Tymon's green robes, half-visible beneath his cloak. 'The Rites are my fault. The Sacrifice. One life for many and all that claptrap.'

Tymon burst into laughter. Nearby, a bird emerged from the vine-frames in a flurry of wings and raucous alarm, orange-bright in the last rays of the sun.

'Don't be silly, Apu,' he said, getting the better of his mirth. The old man's face was serious, however; he obviously believed himself guilty. 'The Rites aren't your fault. How could they be?'

'I told them.' Galliano's voice was small, miserable. 'Years ago — the year after my initiation, actually. The Tree is dying. I proved it. I was so eager to prove it, to make my second degree in Applied Treeology. Levels of Tree-water, sap-flow, leaf-growth. Graphs and measurements. Diagrams and core samples. Talked to all the brightest minds in the College. They listened. They took notes. They thanked me. A year later, they started bringing in the foreigners. I had no idea it would lead to that.'

'What, you mean ...' Tymon gaped at him in disbelief. 'There was never a Sacrifice before? No one jumped into the Mouth?'

'Never,' pronounced the scientist, solemnly. 'No one came to harm in the old days. Back when I was a young man, the Rites were symbolic. They were all about letting your former life go, about being born again, so to speak. It doesn't matter what actually happened during the ceremony. The point is, they changed it. By special order of the Council. They changed it because of my findings, my experiments.'

Tymon sat silent on the stump. Faint and merry, the sound of music rose from the invisible city, a raucous pipe and a sawing fiddle. His heart beat wildly. There was so much to take in, so many new ideas to absorb from what Galliano had said that he could not find the words to speak.

'Well, so that's it, then,' the old man murmured. 'You must despise me.' He rose from his seat. 'After all my high-minded talk about the pilgrims ... I don't suppose I'll be seeing you again.'

'What?' Tymon shook off his reverie, to find the scientist already tottering away down the track to the workshop. He jumped up after him. 'Of course I don't despise you! You only told the truth. It's not your fault —'

'I've tried to convince myself of that. It doesn't work. I am to blame. I should have known they would react with some damn fool piece of superstition.'

'Apu —' The boy quickened his pace on the dusty track. Galliano was surprisingly difficult to keep up with. 'Listen to me. It's not your fault. But you have to use the air-chariot. You will, once you hear this —'

'No, no, no.' The old scientist batted away Tymon's attempts to grab his sleeve and arrest his headlong progress. 'I've made up my mind. No more running away. I'll go down there again, tomorrow. I'll go down and pester them until they agree to see me. They can throw me in a jail cell —'

'Apu, you have to listen. I met someone today —'

'— till the whole world rots away,' continued Galliano extravagantly, deaf to his protestations. 'Someone has to stand up for what's right —'

'If you would just listen a minute,' panted Tymon. 'There's something more important you need to do. One of the pil —'

'That Storm business is all very well, but it can wait, boy!' declared his friend. He stabbed his finger excitedly in the air as he jogged down the track. 'We were being selfish. I told the Council once and I'll tell them again. The Sacrifice will not save us. The Tree is rotten to the core. Why, what is the Mouth but a symptom —'

He came to a skidding halt and turned to Tymon with an anxious expression. 'You didn't do it, did you? You didn't go to the Mouth?'

'They barred me,' growled Tymon, out of breath and exasperated at the old man's interruptions. 'For talking to a pilgrim. That's what I've been trying to say all this time, Apu. You won't want to bother with the Council when you hear my plan. We can help her escape — if she decides to join us, I mean — it's a girl, by the way, and no one knows — oh, it's a long story.'

'We won't fly too near the town, of course. No sense in drawing an audience at this point in the proceedings.' Galliano peered out from beneath the air-chariot, wielding a pair of oversized bellows, and cast a disparaging glance at Tymon's meagre bundle of provisions. 'You thought a basket-lantern and a dozen Festival cakes would get you all the way to Lantria? If you'd tried that, I'd have been dead of worry!'

Tymon only grinned in answer and slung his little bag into the air-chariot's cockpit. The machine cut a striking silhouette against the bright evening clouds. A spark of flame leapt in its belly and the pistons pumped and belched as the propellers beat with increasing fury. They had decided to do a short test flight that night after all, in order to be sure the air-chariot would be able to embark on a longer journey. As Galliano had noted dryly, it would be a shame to whisk their extraordinary fugitive from under the noses of the priests only to crash back down to the canopy a few seconds later.

The old man had listened to Tymon's description of the red-haired girl and her accusations against the Council with great interest, and taken to the idea of rescue as readily as the boy had hoped. He had promised Tymon that should the test be successful, they would leave the city together the very next morning — in the company of the unusual pilgrim if she turned up, and without her if she did not. He had even suggested, much to Tymon's amazement, that should she default on their arrangement, they might discreetly follow the tithe-transport and attempt to help her again at a later date. But he had also warned him that they would be fools to think the Council would turn a blind eye to their actions, particularly if they were suspected of helping a pilgrim.

'I was never privy to their lofty secrets,' he had admitted ruefully. 'A professor of Applied Treeology is useful only when you need his experiments to support your policy. My experiments do not support murder. But if what your friend says is true — and I have little doubt it is — then Fallow will do anything to keep the facts hidden. We won't be welcome in Argos city again. Alone, I don't care to go to the trouble of starting a new life. But together: that's something different.'

Now, as the air-chariot tugged at its moorings like an eager messenger bird, the scientist clambered out from under the machine, wiping his hands on a dirty cloth. He gestured proudly up at the belching, shuddering contraption.

'How do you like your inheritance, boy?'

'Inheritance?' Tymon repeated, dumbly over the thud of the propellers.

'This little beauty is going to be yours, I hope you realise,' noted Galliano. He sprang nimbly over the side of the machine and into the cockpit. 'We'll go to Lantria first, I think. Set you up with your runaway bride maybe.'

His inheritance. The boy felt ready to burst with excitement. This mad invention, this wonderful, absurd engine would be his after all. He was no longer trapped by the seminary. He had broken free of the cage.

'What about the Tree dying, and exploring the Storm?' he called back.

'We can always build another one for that,' Galliano yelled over his shoulder. 'Lantrians might help, actually. Nation of ship-builders. Cast off the ropes, boy, it's time to go!'

Tymon shook the tethers free, vaulting into the open cockpit after the old man. He could not stop smiling. The future was waiting for him, beckoning, just around the corner. He was obliged to clutch the sides of the air-chariot as it lurched into the air, spluttering and coughing. The vine-fields receded at a dizzying speed and the machine pitched precariously from side to side as it flew, trailing a magnificent cloud of smoke. It seemed to romp rather than glide through the sky.

'By the bells, have you ever seen such a sight?' crowed Galliano, wrestling with the steering rods. 'We're going to sweep your pilgrim sweetheart off her feet!'

'If she comes at all,' Tymon shouted merrily through the headwind. 'She doesn't need us, remember?'

'Well, we need us. We non-men should stick together,' observed the scientist.

Tymon fell silent in the cacophony of the propellers, blinking at the vista below him in a happy daze. Galliano steered them northwest, flying low over the vine-frames. They came perilously close to taking the roof off a farmer's bird-pen and provoked a panic among the margeese. Seconds later the terraced slope of the branch fell away to nothingness and they hurtled out over the west chasm, leaving the environs of Argos city behind. The air-chariot pitched and swayed. Tymon was assailed with a brief succession of contradictory viewpoints. Before him swung the dizzy green depths of the chasm, then the massed leaf-forests, tinged with the glow of the setting sun. There was a swirl of sky and green, and the machine righted itself. It dipped towards the gulf one last time then rose steadily against the western horizon. They climbed upwards for a long time, a dot on the shining clouds, till Galliano pulled hard on the right-hand steering rod. The machine pitched to the south and drew a smoky arc against the sky, turning sharply back towards Argos city. The course change was so abrupt that Tymon let go of the sides of the cockpit and narrowly missed being tipped out.

'We're going to have to get straps for this thing,' he yelled through the wind to Galliano.

'Maps? Who needs maps?' the scientist bellowed, deafly. 'We can steer by the stars, boy!'

The sight that greeted them as they sped over the canopy was breathtaking. The branches and leaf-forests were laid out beneath them like a colossal heaped-up carpet. The complex design formed by the Tree's huge limbs was clearly visible from above, as it never could be from within: boughs spiralled out in all directions, splitting into smaller loops and whorls. Tymon caught a glimpse of a complex, vertiginous symmetry. From the gigantic scale to the most intimate, the world seemed to be drawn in the same pattern, spiral upon spiral, helix into helix, infinitely growing and diminishing. The vision lasted only a moment. The machine shuddered and dipped its nose sickeningly downwards; the wind rushed past his ears and he gripped at the sides of the cockpit, closing his eyes.

When he opened them again he saw that they had lost a great deal of altitude. Ahead of them, cradled between the supporting branch and the mass of the trunk, Argos city stood out like a pale, luminous flower, glimmering in the dusk with a thousand Festival lights. They had agreed not to fly too close for fear of discovery, and Galliano kept the machine at a respectable distance from the town, veering east. Tymon stared at the faraway buildings and tried to imagine how he could ever have been impressed with the grandeur of the place. The coloured stalls and pavilions on the air-harbour resembled decorated sweetmeats on a plate, and the temple Hall on the buttress was a child's toy. He made out the green College pavilion at the western end of the quays. He was thrown against the side of the cockpit once more as Galliano pulled on the lever and the machine changed course again. This time they were caught in an updraft and the air-chariot rocked dangerously forward. It occurred to Tymon that he did not know whether he would manage to hang on in the event the craft flipped completely. He hooked an arm around one of the support beams, bracing himself.

'Witless creature that I am!' cried Galliano frantically, struggling with the steering rods. 'Hold on to something, Tymon!'

After a few heart-churning dips the machine regained balance and they swerved to safety, speeding away from the city.

'We need straps in this thing, not maps,' sighed the old man, shaking his head.

The town disappeared behind them and they puttered on in a wide arc over the leaf-forests, looping back towards Galliano's workshop. The light was failing and the sky had turned a deep, fathomless blue. The brightest evening star, the Friend, appeared directly overhead. With a shiver, Tymon felt the vastness of the world. The stars looked as if they were somehow further away from a height — not the benign 'fruits of heaven' he had been taught about in Treeology, but brilliant, burning orbs in an unimaginably distant void. He turned his eyes back to the comfort of the fading west. He judged by the light that the eighth hour had come and gone. As exhilarating as the flight had been, he realised he would be glad to feel the solid bark beneath his feet. It was late and they still had much to do to prepare for their departure the next day. His head buzzed with schemes and stratagems for the journey to Lantria. There was the matter of procuring more food and better equipment, now that he had a clearer idea of the length of the voyage; he wondered whether it might be possible to restock their supplies, and wished once again, in vain, for the valuable flask of ether oil.

At last he made out the windmill's ragged silhouette on the top of Galliano's knot. With a slow thrill of shock, he noticed lights twinkling like fireflies on the slope beside it. A line of people bearing torches stood on the path outside the workshop. Some already waited beside the tumbledown wall and more were mounting the knot in an unbroken string. The brief expedition in the air-chariot had drawn an audience, after all.

'Already?' Galliano joked, feebly. 'I didn't think we'd get away with nobody noticing, but I must say I wasn't expecting our admirers to be here so soon.'

He dampened the engine and inflated the ether balloon under the craft, allowing the machine to drift the last hundred yards or so down to the knot. They floated in eerie silence towards the flickering torches. A formless suspicion gripped Tymon.

'Turn around, Apu,' he begged. 'Let's leave now, while we still can.'

The old man shook his head forlornly. 'No more fuel, boy,' he whispered. 'I left the extra barrels at the workshop.'

Tymon grasped with steadily mounting dismay that the figures by the workshop were priests. All the members of the Council were present on the knot, along with a throng of ordinary townsfolk. He recognised the Dean among the waiting crowd, a gaunt, unsmiling figure, and his spirits plummeted to his toes. The game was up, he thought. His absence from the seminary had been found out and his tutors were there to retrieve him. The priests' faces were severe. He reflected gloomily on the punishments likely to be meted out to him and tried to imagine how long his trip with Galliano would have to be postponed. There was now no question of helping the pilgrim girl.

'Payback,' murmured Galliano as they touched down on the knot.

The perfect descent barely registered. Tymon climbed out of the craft and made his way slowly up the slope beside his mentor, resigned to being chastised in front of half the town. Father Mossing detached himself from the group of priests and stepped forwards to meet them. He held up a leaf-scroll to the torchlight.

'Let it be duly noted by witnesses,' he proclaimed, 'that on the twenty-first day of the seventh month, this Year of the Root, the Council declares Jonas Galliano guilty of grievous heresy and a danger to his fellow citizens.'

Tymon stopped short in confusion. These were not the words he had been expecting to hear. He realised with a rush of shame that he had thought only of his own punishment, not of the scientist's. His pulse quickened as two members of the Council Guard left the line of onlookers and positioned themselves officiously on each side of Galliano, brandishing their hardwood pikes.

'What are you doing?' he protested to one of the soldiers. 'He's just an old man. He's no threat to anyone.'

The man ignored him, lifting his chin and adjusting his uniform self-consciously.

'Moreover, since the accused has been found to be a corrupting influence on young minds,' continued Mossing, 'he must face immediate trial. Take him away.'

The guards began to propel Galliano down the path with their pikes. The scientist appeared ridiculously small beside his hulking custodians. He looked back at Tymon one last time.

'Goodbye, my friend,' he called. 'Don't ever trade your wings in for a lie like I did!'

'Wait!' cried the boy. 'It isn't heresy, just science!'

His confusion gave way to panic. The townsfolk must have somehow heard of Galliano's plan to enter the Storm, he thought. They should be told the truth, made to understand that the old man had given up on his suicidal notion. He ran after the soldiers.

'He wasn't going to do it!' he exclaimed. 'He was going to Lantria instead!'

Someone caught his arm and pulled him back. He fell in fury on this adversary, kicking and flailing. More hands took hold of him. At last he was forced to remain motionless, cursing the people around him to the roots of Hell.

'Green grace, you really have been exposed to bad influences,' observed a mild voice behind Tymon. 'If going to Lantria seems preferable to what you were planning originally then it's about time this nonsense was stopped.'

The grip of his captors relaxed and he was allowed to turn around. There stood Father Fallow, calm as a coiled snake. At his elbow hovered a glowering and defiant Wick. At the sight of his friend, understanding hit Tymon with the full force of a blow. He thought, with a wrench, of the number of guild-meetings the other boy had been called to, far more than any leaf-binding apprenticeship would warrant. He berated himself for being a trusting fool. Every one of his confidences must have found their way through Wick to the Dean, from the scrawled note in the study hall to his dreamy plans of escape. He had simply been allowed to leave the seminary that night, allowed to accompany Galliano, the better to ensnare the old scientist. He turned on his classmate in furious disappointment.

'You were reporting on me all along!' he burst out. 'Some friend.'

'You lied to me,' retorted Wick. 'You were barred from the Rites for talking to a pilgrim. You didn't see fit to tell me that, did you? What were you going to do? Give the dirty foreigner a ride in that Hell-machine?'

Tymon felt his heart constrict. For a terrible moment he feared that the worst had happened, that his plan had been exposed and the pilgrim girl's identity discovered. But as Wick looked away with an angry shrug, he realised that the accusation had only been a gibe. The other boy had spoken the truth inadvertently, in a fit of spite.

'Now, now,' admonished Fallow. 'There is no betrayal here, only wisdom. You were about to make the worst choice of your life, Tymon, and associate yourself with a man who has proven himself to be a dangerous deviant. Your friend did you a favour.'

Tymon scowled at his toes and made no answer. The hours since his dawn awakening seemed long; like the dream that morning, his youthful assumptions had dissolved and drained away, leaving a sense of disillusionment. He wondered what rewards had been offered to Wick in exchange for his duplicity. In the world of adulthood, it seemed, trust and loyalty had no place. Only power mattered.

The Dean addressed the curious bystanders that had gathered near the machine.

'The heretic Jonas Galliano has made a mechanical abomination,' he announced. 'He has constructed a craft that goes without wind and flies without ether. He has flouted natural law and sought to win over young and impressionable minds to his degenerate pursuits. This will not be tolerated.'

Wick had turned away, his mouth twisted in a bitter smile, and seemed about to slope off, to lose himself in the anonymity of the crowd. But Father Fallow did not let him go so easily. He laid a light, irresistible hand on his shoulder.

'You must appreciate,' he sighed as his melancholy gaze settled on Tymon again, 'that your comrade here had to think of his own future. He could not be a party to such grave transgressions and remain silent. If he reported your activities, it was to give you both a second chance.'

He loosed his hold on Wick. The other boy cast a brief, haunted look behind him then plunged into the crowd. Tymon swallowed a dangerous tightness in his throat.

'But Father Galliano's done me no harm,' he pleaded. 'He was only trying out a new kind of dirigible. He was going to take me to Lantria. He would have sponsored me.'

'And we all know,' interrupted the Dean, 'where that would have led. You've had a lucky escape, boy. This dirigible and its creator were demonically inspired. Burn the abomination with the cleansing fire.'

Father Fallow's last instruction was directed to the crowd by the air-chariot. To Tymon's horror, the spectators began to stick their torches into the clinker body of the craft. The bark shifted beneath his feet.

'That's mine.' His voice grew hoarse. 'That was supposed to be mine.' He tried to run towards the

171

machine, but was restrained again by the people around him.

'It seems you've been misled,' remarked the Dean, briskly. 'While you're indentured to the College, you do not have personal belongings. Be thankful: to own such a contraption would invite the attendant penalties.'

Flames leapt up from the air-chariot, bright against the shadow of the leaf-forests. Tymon gazed at the Dean in disbelief, all his pain and disappointment focusing on one man. A surge of hatred for Father Fallow swept through him and the bile rose to his lips. He spat at the priest. The spittle landed on the Dean's green habit, clinging to the ceremonial silk like a small grey mushroom. No one saw it but Fallow himself. At that moment the machine's gall-tank caught fire and a sheet of blue flame ripped through the night, distracting the crowd. Sharp, unpleasant-smelling smoke filled the air.

'Blast-poison!' cried several voices. 'Demon's work!'

Father Fallow reached down and flicked the spittle from his robe, never taking his eyes off the boy. There was a terrible pause. Tymon's heart thudded uncomfortably in his chest; his head began to swim. The burning hulk of the machine collapsed, drawing shouts of consternation from the onlookers. The Dean's glance snapped towards it and he straightened up, frowning at the noise. He strode down the slope.

'Get everyone out,' he called. 'This place is bewitched.'

He herded the crowd away from the air-chariot, intoning the fire-watch prayer. People hurried off, casting fearful glances at the machine. It sputtered blue sparks after them. Father Mossing shuffled up to Tymon.

'Come walk with me, my boy,' he offered, holding out his bandaged hand. 'Nobody blames you. It's understandable you're feeling angry right now. It'll all work out for the best, you'll see.'

Tymon made no move, his fists clenched at his sides. The fire in the carcass of the machine was falling low once more. No punishment, no beating or humiliation could have made a deeper mark on him than the ruin of his dreams. Mossing retracted the hand with a strained smile.

'If you ever feel the need,' he said, 'remember, you can talk to me.'

The inhabitants of Argos city considered themselves a tolerant people. For years they had endured Galliano, and even treated him well after a fashion, like an embarrassing family member whom no one expects to reform. But now, he had tested their patience to the limit. Most of the townsfolk were ready to see the old man pay for his crimes. If there were a few people, like the kindly Masha, who were not happy about the situation, they bit their tongues and remained silent for fear of the priests. The Council's verdict was announced three days later: the heretic had made a full confession, admitting to counts of witchcraft and demonic possession. He was sentenced to banishment for the rest of his natural life. He had been spared execution due to his advanced age; no one expected him to survive for long.

Tymon came down with a mild case of fly-fever after the trial and spent a week isolated in the College hospital. In many ways the sickness was a blessing. He did not have to watch the public denunciation of his mentor or endure the sight of him hobbling onto a prison ship, bound for an unknown destination. Long before the boy was well enough to leave his bed, all external memories of Galliano had been destroyed by the city militia. His work-leaves, tools and sketches were burnt. The workshop and mill were razed to the ground and the place marked with demon-binding runes. His name was struck from the citizens' register in the College library and by the beginning of summer, all that remained of the old man's indiscretions were a few odd-looking hardwood beams lying twisted and charred on the side of the knot.

It was of little comfort to Tymon to learn that on the same night his mentor had been apprehended, a group of five tithe-pilgrims had escaped from the city jail. The breakout was said to be so embarrassing to the local militia that all details of the episode had been suppressed. The runaways were soon tracked down in the leaf-forests outside the city and returned to the custody of the seminary — all except for one. One of the foreigners, a thin youth with red hair, was still at large. A reward was posted for his capture. The Council had no doubt that he would be found in time.

PART TWO

BRANCHES

We are the same branch, the same leaf,
the same blood:
one life in many, and all lives in one.
— Nurian saying

9

Shafts of afternoon sunlight filtered through the open windows of the Dean's office. Ornate wall-tapestries hung alongside shelves filled with musty tomes; the room was thick with learning, dusty with importance. No sound from the quadrangle outside disturbed the peace. Over a month had passed since Galliano's trial. It was bean-harvest season and most of the students had left the seminary to stay with their families for the summer. The College was tranquil and bathed in dappled light, the silence broken only by the low, chuckling call of the messenger birds in their roosts under the eaves.

Father Fallow sighed as he surveyed the pile of letters, petitions and leaf-bound edicts on his desk. The weeks passed by and yet certain annoyances continued to plague him. The Dean was not given to a contemplative life, taking a great deal of relish in his administrative role. But lately he was feeling the pressure of his duties. His position as chairman of the Colonial Board had proven particularly tiresome. Session after session that year had dragged on over the same issues: the water problem in the colonies, whether the water problem was any worse than it had always been, and what to do about it. Fallow wished to see what the winter rains were like before implementing any change in policy. But the majority of the Board was in favour of more drastic action. This time political leverage had failed to play in the Dean's favour. To make matters worse, petitions were arriving daily from the Eastern Canopy claiming that the rain-wells were running dry, that water stocks had reached an all-time low. Rebellion stirred among natives and colonists alike. It was the mutiny among these so-called 'white-necks' that irritated Fallow the most. The Governor of one of the colonial outposts had even threatened to declare his flyblown garrison independent. His posturing was ridiculous, of course — the outpost could no more survive without Argosian trade than a greatship could float without ether. All the same, the situation riled Fallow. It was an embarrassment.

As if drought and conspiracy were not enough, a further vexation awaited him that afternoon. The Dean glanced up at the youth seated opposite him with distaste. The professors at the seminary might have been forgiven for not remembering the names of all the pupils who trooped through the halls of the seminary. Few students remained to pursue their careers at the College. But this particular boy's identity was etched permanently into the Dean's memory, despite the fact that he had failed, rather than succeeded in his studies. The image of spittle dangling on his Festival robes flashed before Fallow's eyes. His fingers twitched convulsively.

The boy named Tymon was a study in silent resentment. He sat hunched on a bench opposite the Dean, glaring at the edge of the desk. It was his last day in the seminary before leaving on his mission service and every inch of his scrawny young body proclaimed aversion to the fact. He had been taken sick after the old scientist's trial, Fallow remembered; the illness had left him hollow-eyed, scowling at the world through a shock of overlong hair. He would have been better looking if he smiled and taller if he did not slouch, thought the priest. He could have made something of himself, turned himself around, if he had only stopped sulking and concentrated on his studies. But where he went after his indenture, and what would become of him when no one would foot the bill for his upkeep, were matters that did not seem to interest Tymon in the slightest. He simply did what he was told, no more and no less, with an air of injured virtue. It was almost as if he was the one who had been tried and found guilty, not the old heretic.

Few pupils left the seminary under bad auspices. *No fruit shall wither on the branch*, the professors liked to say, quoting Saint Loa. All young people could be encouraged to have an upright character, they pontificated. It was only a question of training the sapling to grow straight. The Priests' Council had been lenient with Tymon, for although heresy was the ultimate crime in Argos, the criminal needed certain qualifications. He had to be mature and fully in charge of his faculties. Young people and most women were not considered mentally developed enough for heresy. Their conduct was seen more as a sickness than a sin, one that could be cured by teaching them better habits. *Doubt is a canker of the mind*, proclaimed the header in the novices' psalm book. *Cauterise it with proper thought.* But if the young person refused to take his medicine — if he remained stubbornly unrepentant — then, like a canker, he should be cut out, thought the Dean. He gazed back steadily at the mass of mute fury on the other side of the table. It took some concentration to keep his face neutral and his words kind.

'In the beauty, master Tymon.'

'In the beauty, Father.' The boy did not look up.

'Well. This is the end of your life as a student and the start of your two-year mission service.'

Silence. Fallow's expression became harder.

'Since you haven't shown any aptitude for the various options here,' he said, 'we have decided to send you to complete your indenture on one of the colonial outposts, where manpower is needed.'

'I'm glad to be of use.' Tymon spoke in a monotone, his voice devoid of emotion. Fallow wondered briefly if he was making fun of him.

'Had you shown the slightest willingness to cooperate, to pursue your studies, we would have kept you with us,' he snapped. 'We might even have given you another chance to pass your Rites. But you haven't made yourself easy to live with, Tymon. Your tutors tell me you give them the strict minimum and no more. Your classmates avoid you, and I can't blame them. You have a marked tendency to rebellion and flirt dangerously with heresy. After endeavouring this past month, with the best of intentions, to give you the benefit of the doubt, I now find myself coming to the unavoidable conclusion that you have no interest in staying on at the seminary.'

The youth was still fixing the edge of the desk with that idiot scowl, playing him for a fool. The Dean's voice became harsh.

'You are withdrawn, resentful — yes, resentful, despite the mercy the Council has shown towards you — and show no sign of remorse for the actions you have taken. We are forbearing but you push the limits of our patience.'

There was an uncomfortable pause. Tymon stared wordlessly at the desk.

'Considering your attitude, I suppose we needn't waste any more time,' resumed the Dean. 'You're being sent to the colonial mission in the hope that hard work will remedy your character. I see nothing else that can.'

With a flick of his wrist, he pushed a folded leaf-scrap across the table. The boy picked it up slowly. It was a travel pass for a voyage by greatship. Scrawled at the bottom, beside the official College stamp, were three summary words: *Service only. Marak.* Where the captain had countersigned the pass, Tymon saw the name *Stargazer.*

'You will catch tomorrow's season departure to Marak, under Captain Safah,' said Fallow. 'A working ticket, of course. I'm not sure what use he'll find for you on a greatship, but the Captain is an imaginative man. I expect you to perform to best of your capacities.'

He paused and gazed at Tymon quizzically, as if trying to decide whether any such capacities existed at all.

'Once in Marak you'll make your way to the mission,' he continued, after obtaining no further reaction from his charge. 'You'll present yourself to Father Verlain. I already sent him an introductory letter. It went by bird and will arrive before you do. I trust you will fulfil your obligations at the mission promptly and cheerfully. Your service period is two years. After that, you will receive an official clearance and are free to do as you wish, returning to Argos city if you desire.'

He nodded in curt dismissal, indicating the doorway. But as Tymon stood up, he added casually: 'I hope you aren't thinking of deserting the service, young man. You know that to leave before the period of indenture is over invites severe punishment. You'll be thrown into prison. And if you escape, you'll be outlawed and never welcome in Argos again.'

'It's no different to a banishment then, is it?' murmured the boy.

'Don't be absurd. If you behave yourself — and I sincerely hope you do — you'll get a commendation from Father Verlain and find gainful employment in Argos after your service is up. *The hardest heart may find eternal springtime,*' finished Fallow, floridly quoting scripture, '*though in its depths the frost may now hold sway.*' He waved his audience away like a troublesome fly. 'Go in beauty, my child. Go in beauty.'

Tymon set his mouth and walked heavily out of

the room. As soon as he was gone, the tapestry on the wall by Fallow's desk stirred and a man dressed in a tightly buttoned black coat emerged from a hidden alcove. The Envoy still had his white kerchief wrapped around his throat, though the weather was close and hot. He strode to the open doorway and scrutinised the empty corridor outside. Then he shut the door, sliding the hardwood bolt noiselessly home.

'Well, I thought you were remarkably patient with him,' he said, turning to the Dean.

'Are you sure he's the one?' asked Fallow, with a worried frown. 'He battles me every inch of the way.'

'Precisely the trait that makes him so useful to us,' replied the Envoy, stalking back to the windows. He closed the shutters, plunging the office into waxy darkness. 'Rebels are always the easiest to control,' he noted, a disembodied voice in the gloom. 'You know that, Holiness.'

'His spirit is chaotic and unfocused.'

A spark of light pierced the darkness as the Envoy held a burning fire-stick up to the candleholder on the Dean's desk. The flame guttered feebly.

'Again, qualities that make him an ideal candidate for our purposes,' he remarked. 'We do not want a thinking ally, we want a pawn.'

'I don't know,' the Head of the College rubbed his temples wearily. 'Something about him ... resists. I find it exhausting, to tell you the truth.'

The Envoy looked up sharply. 'I am not at all sure the boy is the one doing the resisting, Holiness,' he said.

'Meaning?' The Dean gazed at him with a pained expression.

'Meaning, he is susceptible to other influences. We'd best make use of him quickly.'

'I was afraid you might say that,' sighed Fallow.

'It is time, Holiness,' observed his companion. 'The Veil thins.' His tone was polite but brooked no argument. He came to stand behind Fallow's chair.

The Dean straightened hurriedly in his seat, nodding in agreement, and rifled through a nearby drawer, from which he retrieved a bundle of black silk. This he opened on the table to reveal an ornate hardwood disc made up of several moving parts mounted by a rotating rule marked with degrees in the manner of an astrolabe. But instead of the position of the sun and stars, the carved interior of the disc depicted a Tree motif. Both the underlying design and the adjustable pointers which formed its 'branches' were fashioned from a bright material like highly polished Treesap. The rotating rule was made of the same gleaming substance. Fallow's fingers caressed the object. He glanced up at the Envoy.

'What divergence do you recommend today?' he enquired respectfully.

The Envoy's smile was predatory. He bent over the intricate instrument, but did not touch it.

'Pass forty degrees into the sign of the Hunter,' he said. 'Direct the *orah* through the Letter of Dominion. Keep it there and do not let it stray to Loss.'

'No Loss,' murmured Fallow, adjusting the settings on the disc. 'Forty degrees. It hates it when we try this combination.'

'Hates?' echoed Lace in surprise. 'We're dealing with a mindless force, Holiness. It neither hates nor loves. It only serves.'

The Dean was covered in confusion. 'I only meant that avoiding Loss is difficult,' he explained hastily. 'The Sap seems naturally to tend towards dissipation, rather than accumulation. From what I've seen.'

The Envoy contemplated him for a moment. His eyes were fathomless.

'Well, that's precisely our challenge,' he remarked. 'We are the fashioners of the universe. We control the Sap and focus it on a higher goal. Our task is made the more difficult because our enemies counter us at every turn. Now, Holiness, I am going to ask you to put aside this discussion and concentrate on the matter at hand. We do not have much time; the source of my power grows distant.'

The Dean nodded once more, abashed, and cleared his throat. The flame on the candle grew bright and sharp as he began to chant over the disc, a soft invocation.

'*Weakness be strength,*' he intoned.

'*Emptiness, power,*' droned his companion.

'*Worlds that were severed,*' continued Fallow.

'*We bind to our pleasure,*' finished the Envoy solemnly.

As they pronounced the words, the parts of the disc made of the translucent material glowed like hot embers. The pointers leapt into position on the Tree, quivering, and the rule began to rotate, moved by an unseen force. Fallow attempted to nudge it towards a specific setting. It jerked away from his fingers.

'Green grace, it's impossible,' he burst out at last.

Without speaking, the Envoy placed his large, slab-like hand on the Dean's shoulder and waited, his broad features impassive in the candlelight. The rule no longer jerked away from Fallow's grasp and its brightness dimmed. The Dean breathed a sigh of relief as the instrument slid obediently into position.

Tymon stumbled out of the Dean's office building and onto the College quadrangle, stopping a moment by the library steps to catch his breath. His front of glowering indifference had barely lasted through the interview with Fallow. The afternoon shadows edged across the quiet buildings and the air was full of the high chirping of fruit bats nesting in the slope of the branch above the seminary. He stared vacantly upwards for a few minutes then realised he was trembling with shock.

Ever since the night on the knot, he had been unable bear the Dean's presence. Humiliation, anger and a sense of aching loss choked him every time he was in Fallow's company, and his only defence was surly silence. The priest's sarcasm hurt him more than he cared to admit. His mind seemed to go to pieces under his withering scorn. The smell of burning Tree-gall filled his nostrils once again and the memory of his futile act of defiance returned to haunt him. Though he had never been punished for the minor heresy of spitting on the Head of the College, Tymon read his sentence clearly in the service pass. He held it up to the light with unsteady fingers. The Dean's writing crawled like a spider across the bottom: *Marak*. The name reverberated with unpleasant associations. It was a place of convicts and undesirables, a destination when all other options had been exhausted. No fortune or glory ever came out of Marak.

The irony of being sent to his fate on the very greatship he had so often dreamed about was not lost on Tymon. The voyage was the zest in his cup of bitterness. Though he had always fantasised about travelling, his idea had been to visit romantic and exciting places — the magnificent shipyards of Lantria, or the rich and barbaric northern fifes, where it was said no man had less than seven wives. Marak was a drought-infested military outpost on the fringes of the Eastern Canopy. It did not even have the allure of history, being a new settlement built to protect the trade route between Argos and its colonies. The voyage aboard the greatship was a reminder of just how much he would miss by being indentured to the College for two more years. His service stretched out before him like a prison sentence.

He walked across the empty courtyard, a lone figure in the sunlight. His classmates had all left the seminary earlier that week. Bolas had begun his apprenticeship at an architect's trade in the city and Piri had gone back to work on his family's keep for the summer. As for Wick, he had disappeared for two weeks after the heresy trial, sent home, it was said, for health reasons. When he had returned to the seminary there was no further pretence of a leaf-binding apprenticeship: he was wearing the dark green robes of the priesthood. His full initiation to the rank of acolyte had taken place soon afterwards. After that, he no longer slept or ate with the other novices, spending most of his time cloistered at the monastery or studying in the College library. He had hardly exchanged a word with his classmates since his return. Tymon had not been given the opportunity to confront or forgive his former ally.

He approached the kitchen compound and ducked through the narrow entrance. The garden beyond was deserted. Margeese whistled nervously in their pen as he passed.

'Amu!' he called across the compound.

The answer came from within the kitchen building. 'Here, my sprout.'

Masha appeared in the doorway, wiping her hands on her apron. Today her round, kindly face bore the marks of anxiety. She emerged with a brisk attempt at humour.

'So, what did that old killjoy have to say? Did he set you to work in the screaming shillee-pens, or award you an apprenticeship peeling frogapples?'

She eased herself down with an explosive sigh onto the steps leading up to the kitchen door. Tymon sat down beside her, his gaze fixed miserably on the dusty floor of the compound.

'What have they said to you?' she exclaimed. 'Out with it!'

'They have no use for me here,' he said. 'The Dean gave me a service pass for Marak. Leaving tomorrow at dawn on the *Stargazer*.'

Masha's mouth contracted. 'Green grace,' she said, turning her face from him.

She sounded so dismal that Tymon took her work-worn hands in his own to comfort her. She squeezed his fingers silently. As a child the old cook had seemed to him huge and indestructible, a force to be reckoned with. Now she was somehow shrunken and fragile. He contemplated her frumpy, familiar form, her serviceable sleeves rolled up to her elbows and the grey hairs escaping her headscarf in handfuls. He saw with surprise that her cheeks were wet with tears.

'Are you all right, Amu?' he asked gently.

'Don't you worry about me,' she said, wiping the offending liquid angrily with a corner of her apron. 'I'm a foolish old woman. Listen, you promise me you'll take good care of yourself in that fly-hole, you hear? Promise.' She hugged him fiercely, mumbling a torrent of advice into his neck. 'Only eat boiled greens. And make sure you get bird-meat: I hear they cook monkey and snake in Marak. Don't touch their dirty animals. And don't drink their *kush*, it makes Argosians ill.'

'I will,' he answered. 'I mean I won't.' He suddenly felt like laughing. A light, defiant mood took him. 'I'll be fine, Amu. Don't be upset.' He patted her back awkwardly. 'I'll make my fortune in Tree-spice and buy you your own house on Temple road.'

She laughed then too, through her tears, and pinched his cheeks and called him her little captain, as she had when he was a boy. Tymon realised with a pang that he would miss her. Although she could only counsel him to resignation, her kindness had been a balm in the hard days following the loss of Galliano, when he had been laid up with fever in the College ward. During his illness she had cared for him and visited him daily; his battle had been successful thanks in great part to her efforts.

Lying alone that night in his hammock, the only occupant of the forsaken dormitory, he tried to summon up his first childhood memory. He expected it to be a kitchen scene, the warm enveloping perfume of Masha's skirts or the sound of lentils on a tray. But although there were many such recollections, they were not the earliest. Something else lingered behind them — remembered a kind voice crooning over him, a shadowy figure gathering him up in the folds of a cloak. He could not recall if the voice and figure belonged to a woman or a man.

10

Tymon arrived at the city gates in the dark hour before sunrise, hugging his small bundle of belongings — a change of clothes wrapped in a worsted blanket Masha had given him, all he had in the way of worldly possessions. A sleepy guard slouched to the far end of the gate-tunnel to open the postern for him. He stepped onto the quays, shivering in the pre-dawn chill. The door thudded to on his heels. The *Stargazer* could be seen towering over the other dirigibles in the air-harbour, a giant looming shape above the central docks. Ether sacks lined her hull like storm clouds. He craned his neck to stare up at the sheer bulk of her sides. Already she was a hive of activity, with boxes and bales being loaded up a gangplank and into her hold. Sailors whistled and called to each other in her rigging. He was about to move towards the hurrying figures when he heard his name shouted out across the docks.

'Tymon. Wait up.'

The well-known figure of Bolas strode towards him on the boardwalk. His old schoolfellow had a bundle of hardwood planks slung over one shoulder. He laid down his burden and stood awkwardly before Tymon, twisting his brown apprentice's apron around his hands.

'Masha told me you were off this morning,' he said with a shy smile. 'I wanted to say goodbye — to wish you the best of luck in the service, and all.'

'Thank you, Bolas.'

Tymon was assailed by a sense of regret and could barely smile at his friend in return. Of all his former companions at the seminary, Bolas was the only one who had never lied to him, or turned his back on him after the trial. It was doubly mortifying to think that he had shrugged off that one real friendship in favour of Wick's.

'Same to you,' he rushed on. 'I'm really happy things have worked out for you. You're a full citizen now, and an architect! Your old man must be proud.'

A shadow passed over Bolas' round face at the mention of citizenship. 'You didn't miss anything, you know,' he mumbled. 'The Rites, I mean. Pointless. Not worth all the fuss.'

Tymon nodded mutely. He did not trust himself to speak. Bolas picked up the bundle of planks. Before moving away, however, he half-turned towards Tymon again and spoke in a low voice.

'I wanted to tell you while I had the chance,' he muttered. 'I never believed the old scientist meant any harm. It was wrong to do what they did to him. There's more than one of us in the city who thinks that, you know. You take care of yourself, Ty, and come home safe.'

Then he turned and stomped off along the west quays. Tymon was almost inclined to call him back. But he did not know what he would say if he did, and could only watch his friend's solid, reliable form diminish in the distance. After a while he made his way, slowly and with a heavy heart, towards the sailors loading up the *Stargazer*.

The season voyage that departed that morning for Marak was one of only four trips to the Eastern Domains all year. If the winds were favourable, the greatship would plot a course through the wild leaf-forests between Argos and its colony in a month-long journey, navigating the hot and cold air-currents that flowed like rivers between the branches of the Tree. The trip was difficult once the winter rains began, and impossible at the height of summer, when the trade winds failed. Season voyages were therefore something of a gamble for the ship's captain. The time of departure was crucial. Tymon waited for an opportunity to speak to someone on the cargo bay, but there was such an atmosphere of grim concentration among the crew that none of them took any notice of him. At last he approached a cross-eyed, burly sailor shouting orders to the other men. The fellow clutched a wad of torn leaves on which he scribbled figures with a worn reed pen, his lazy eye rolling sideways over the page. Another pen was wedged behind his ear; several more poked out of a pocket in his breeches.

'Please, sir,' Tymon began. He was interrupted by a long piercing whistle from the burly man, directed up to the activity in the hold.

'Not there, you bleary fools ... Up, over the water kegs ... Yes, on top ... No, on top, you pasty-faced morons ...'

'Please, sir,' Tymon tried again, 'could you help me? I have a working pass —'

The sailor ignored him completely, starting forwards with a bark of annoyance towards the door of the hold. Tymon had no alternative but to trot after him.

'On top,' the other reiterated, jabbing the air with his pen. 'I don't care if you don't think it fits Aran, make it fit.'

Tymon took a breath and tried again, tentatively holding out his travel pass from the Dean. 'Sir. I have working passage on the *Stargazer*. Where should I go?'

There was a sudden silence. The sailor fixed Tymon for the first time with his good eye, his face suffused with an expression of mock surprise. Someone somewhere stifled a laugh.

'Well, look what we have here, by the beauty! A working passage, eh? Then how come you aren't doing any work? What do I look like, a charity institution?'

Tymon started at the vehemence of this speech. A youth standing nearby heaved up a bale of barley vine and threw it straight at him with a wide grin. It caught him awkwardly in the ribs, knocking the air from his lungs. He struggled to hold onto it at the same time as keeping a grip on his own bundle. Laughter rippled through the group of workers.

'Move it!' roared the man with the pens, and everyone sprang into action again.

Tymon staggered off with the bale up the gangplank, handing his load to the lanky, toothless crewman waiting in the hold. He was greeted with a broad wink and a gummy smile.

'You'll soon get used to the captain,' the toothless sailor whispered. 'He screams worse than he bites.' Louder he added, 'I'm Aran, first mate here on the *Stargazer*. That devil who threw you the bale is Misho — pay no heed to him, he's more than half a Jay.'

'Did I say, "stop and chat"?' stormed the captain from below, pens bristling. 'Move, move, move!'

An hour later the last of the boxes were stowed in the hold and the *Stargazer* was ready to drop her moorings. The crewmembers climbed high in the rigging, whistling signals to each other and pushing the dirigible loose from the dock with long wooden poles. Tymon stood on deck as the greatship was coaxed out of the air-harbour. The experience was completely different from riding in Galliano's wheezing, convulsing engine. The only sound accompanying the *Stargazer*'s passage was the occasional hiss of ether: the greatship was heavy and graceful, both beautiful and powerful. The dawn breeze picked up and the sails billowed out taut. Slowly, the *Stargazer* swung round over the West Chasm. The captain boomed an order and a second set of sackcloth balloons inflated around the hull. The ship rose in stately splendour, its prow facing due east.

At that moment the first rays of morning sun pierced the leaf-forests immediately above the city, and a long bright beam of light came to rest with uncanny precision on the roof of the Temple, standing out on its buttress. As if in answer, the sound that had greeted Tymon every morning since he could remember pealed out from the seminary. The bells sent up the call to prayer, clanging over the city in dull repetition. As the dirigible picked up speed and the town receded below them, the harsh notes seemed to reach after the boy like grasping fingers. They rang on and on, echoing off the trunk-wall; he felt that the noise would never stop, never let him go. The din became unbearable to him and he crouched down on a corner of the deck, covering his ears. The first mate found him sitting there long after the bells had ceased tolling, his ears still resolutely plugged. He was given a stiff warning against laziness and sent to receive his orders from the captain.

On first sight, Captain Safah exemplified the typical hard-nosed Lantrian businessman, notorious for parsimony. He set Tymon to work as a swab, keeping careful note of the hours he spent at each task, the food he ate and the supplies he used. The boy had the distinct impression that if any of his requirements exceeded a certain, very frugal sum, Safah would hold him personally responsible for the difference. His days passed in a grinding tedium of labour. He cleaned the entire deck of the ship, the cabins, the hold and the galley, scrimping and saving each shred of soap. He peeled and sliced more frogapples than he thought possible in a lifetime. The novelty of flying in a huge dirigible soon wore off and the changeless galley diet began to pall on him. He came to abhor the smell of lentil soup.

The *Stargazer* was built more like a floating fortress than a dirigible. From the tip of her prow to the high towers on her stern, she was bolstered against the world's winds by a tough, resilient shell of bark. Her masts were of the strongest hardwood harvested from Lantrian Tree-mines, her sails great sections of heavy leaf-canvas. Three large reinforced balloons assured her buoyancy. Directional ether jets could be released from barrels at her stern and a squadron of smaller sacks inflated and emptied for vertical movement. A complete set of spares hung at her sides, ready to replace a torn or missing sack at a moment's notice. The whole effect was one of a huge, stately dowager in gathered skirts, moving through the sky with surprising speed. Tymon had never seen such a quantity of polished hardwood and billowing sackcloth, and it seemed as if he was going to have to clean every inch of it.

There were certain advantages to his duties above deck, however. He was able, during his long hours of stair-scrubbing, and wall- and mast- and sail-scrubbing, to keep a surreptitious eye on the vista unfolding beneath the ship. For the first few days the *Stargazer* passed over a familiar panorama of leaf-forests, carefully terraced branches and vine plantations. Safah took a bowed course about the circumference of the Central Canopy, following a strong southeasterly air-current that swept them towards their goal. They flew at a steady altitude just above the leaf-tips during the day and spent the nights moored in the safety of the lower twigs. About six days into the voyage they put down in the market town of Ethis, where they traded hardwood for water and fresh food. The settlement was built in a steep trench between two vertical branches, the houses carved directly into the walls of bark. Doors and windows gaped like myriad blind eyes from the sides of the trench. Tymon could not help thinking, with a shudder, of the Divine Mouth far away in Argos city. The market town seemed plunged in a green gloom to his unaccustomed vision, and its residents struck him as equally dim and gloomy, in keeping with their surroundings. He was glad when the barter was done and the ship returned to the sunlit world above the leaves.

For he began, in spite of himself, to relish his new existence. The departure from the world of the priests turned out to be a true liberation. No one on the dirigible cared beyond a joke or two where his family came from, or whether he had any lack of it. The rigour of the days tired out his body and his nights were spent in untroubled slumber. The knife-edge of his experiences at the seminary grew dull. There was certainly more to life aboard the *Stargazer* than backbreaking routine: in the mild summer evenings, when the dirigible descended into the creaking, swaying leaves for the night, the sailors would gather for an hour of relaxation on the stern deck, playing cards or dice for money. Tymon had no riches to squander on gambling but watched his fellows from the edge of the group, and soon learned to trade insults and banter with the best of them. He found the men on the ship gruff but essentially kind.

Although the *Stargazer* was an Argosian vessel, its crew hailed from the Four Canopies, for few of Tymon's countrymen wished to make a living far from home. Only the first mate, Aran, had been born anywhere near Argos city. The boy heard several Lantrian accents on board as well as the dialect of the Jay folk, a nomadic tribe of actors and musicians barely tolerated in his home town. The ship's cook, his taciturn companion in the galley, was a sallow-skinned barbarian from the North Fringes. The stocky northerner's greasy cooking spoke of cold winters and spice rationing. But once a seemingly inexhaustible pile of frogapples had been boiled for syrup, and the next day's lentil soup prepared, even Cook — Tymon never found out his real name — emerged on the stern deck of an evening to join the others. There he would conduct a game of dice in comfortable silence, almost always going away the winner.

The mild evenings continued, week after week. The weather was hotter than usual for the time of year and the dry spell intensified as they rounded the southernmost marches of the Central Canopy, within sight of the Lantrian leaf-table. The appearance of the hazy depression on the horizon cost Tymon a twinge of bereavement. He thought of his own naïve optimism in planning a trip to the South Fringes with nothing but a bag of Festival cakes. That former self, the optimistically scheming student, seemed insuperably far from him now. The world around him was changing, too. As they turned northwards again and abandoned the glimpse of Lantria, the Treescape below them grew wilder. The terraced barley vine and frogapple farms disappeared and the leaf-forests became dense and dishevelled. By the third week of the voyage they had left all traces of human habitation behind. On the morning of the twenty-second day, Misho whistled an urgent signal from his lookout in the rigging. The sailors crowded together at the prow to scan the eastern horizon. A blue line had appeared there, cutting the leaf-forests short.

'That's it,' murmured Aran, standing beside Tymon. 'That's the Gap, and the end of everything we know, young man.'

The boy glanced in surprise at the usually dauntless first mate. He was making a sailor's sign against bad luck, touching his hand to his forehead.

'Why?' he asked. 'You've been to the Domains before, haven't you, Aran?'

His companion grinned toothlessly. 'Oh, I've been to Marak many times,' he said. 'I've been all over the colonies, at least where there's any point in going. But it doesn't change the basic fact. We don't belong there. You'll be expecting to stand out like a sore thumb, choirboy.'

Tymon only grunted in answer, mesmerised by the blue line on the horizon. The infamous Gap, the gulf of air between the Central and Eastern Canopies, was both a natural barrier and a great cultural divide. The atlases he remembered from the seminary showed the vast tangled canopy beyond it split into a multitude of vassal states, coloured green on the map to indicate that they were Argosian colonies. But the empire that had stretched across the length and breadth of the Eastern Canopy in days gone by was millennia old before the first priest set foot in Argos city. The Kingdom of Nur, light of the ancient world! Half the parables in the novices' readers had been associated with it. Until today, Tymon had not directly associated these narratives with everyday people and places in the Tree. The humdrum eastern colonies with their tithes and pilgrims had borne no relation in his mind to the Nur of the old stories. Now the tales hovered against a backdrop of sudden reality. The East was just beyond the horizon. The blue line grew into a long jagged smudge under his dreaming gaze; he stood in silence by the prow until the Captain emerged onto the forecastle, roaring in fury at the crew's idleness.

The men slunk back to their allotted work. Tymon was relegated to the galley pantry but could not bring himself to concentrate on peeling frogapples. His imagination wandered the streets of the fabled capital of Nur, built — or so accounts claimed — entirely of the rare and mysterious *orah*. The secrets to obtaining this petrified hardwood were lost, predating even the Nurian Empire. The gleaming substance had been the hallmark of the Old Ones, of whom nothing more was remembered than that they were the first to settle and build in the Tree. Legend told that the walls of Nur city had shone like sunlight on water. Tymon would have dearly loved to see the ruins for himself, but that was hardly probable. They lay in the East Fringes of the canopy, beyond the limits of the Domains, in an area overrun by bandits and other, more shadowy horrors. No Argosian greatship would venture near it.

'More slice, less dream,' snapped Cook, startling him from his reverie. The stocky northerner loomed over Tymon in the narrow pantry, brandishing a soup ladle. He jabbed at the boy's chopping board. 'Never I see work so bad. You eat half you chop!'

'What?' Tymon recoiled in surprise. 'I may be slow but I'm not eating the food, if that's what you mean.'

'So say you.' Cook scooped up the pitiful quantity of slices he had managed to deposit in the pail at his feet, and gave a snort of disgust. 'You chop, you slice, not enough to feed rats.'

He trudged out of the pantry, cursing in his own guttural language. Tymon stifled a furious retort and resumed his chopping. After a short interval he re-entered the main galley, swinging the pail of sliced frogapples in his hand, full of righteous indignation. The accomplishment was lost on his nemesis, however. Cook was nowhere to be seen, and Tymon remembered that at that time of day he would be above deck in the ship's tiny greenhouse, tending to his beloved vines. He moved with a sigh of resignation towards the stove. But as he was about to add the contents of his bucket to the vat of perpetually boiling fruit, he noticed that the pot was half-empty.

He frowned. Three desultory pink slivers swam about the ladle at the bottom of the vessel. The quantity Cook had taken to the galley had been small, but there should have been more in the pot, all the same. The mention of rats suddenly took on more literal implications. Tymon's skin crawled. No greatship was free of the hardy grey rodents that lived in the hold, comfortably insulated from all efforts to dislodge them. Although the *Stargazer* was a tightly run ship, it still had its share of these unwelcome guests. In spite of his disgust Tymon felt a reluctant admiration for the rats. Were the dirty beasts so brazen that they ventured into the galley during daylight hours, and stole food from under his very nose? He resolved to catch the thief in the act. He filled the pot with fresh fruit and returned to the pantry, moving his bucket and chopping board nearer to the entrance, where he might spy on the stove.

He did not have long to wait. Soon his straining ears picked up a slight sound at the far end of the galley, a soft creaking noise from an open hatch in the floor leading to a storeroom under the kitchen. Tymon kept his eyes fixed the trapdoor, determined not to miss a whisker of the interloper. But instead of the twitching nose and pink paws of a rat, a familiar face framed with red hair peeped over the hatch before his astonished gaze. The pilgrim girl climbed cautiously up the ladder into the galley.

'You!' Tymon exclaimed, scrambling to his feet in the doorway.

She saw him almost as soon as he saw her. If she was startled, she did not show it. She stood up and smoothed the creases from her grey tunic. She was even thinner than before and as pale as a sheet of bark-paper. But her eyes flashed with the old, fierce spirit. She had discarded the pilgrim's cap. Her fiery hair hung loose about her face.

'Well,' she whispered, 'we meet again, novice.'

11

Tymon hastened to her side in the galley.

'I don't believe it,' he hissed, his resentment mixed with a thrill of unexpected pleasure at finding her again, alive and whole. 'If you had trusted me I could have helped get you food. As it is, Cook's already noticed things going missing.'

'I didn't know you were on board.' She raised her hands, placatory. 'I only came out of the hold when I really needed to. There's just so long a body can survive on biscuits and water.'

Tymon glanced up the stairs leading out of the galley. A group of sailors stamped by on the deck above, their backs to the open hatchway. He nudged the pilgrim girl out of their line of sight and lowered his voice.

'And you've been here since the night of the escape?'

'Hidden in an empty crate for a month and a half, yes. I must say, it's good to see a friendly face.'

She smiled at him then, for the first time in their brief acquaintance. Tymon could not help noticing how the smile lit up her features and how she looked almost pretty, despite the grime and the sun-starved, sickly pallor of her skin. She was less haughty towards him than she had been on the two previous occasions they had spoken. Perhaps six weeks in a ship's hold with no one but rats to talk to had softened her towards Argosians, he thought wryly.

'Well, don't stay here and wait for unfriendly ones.' He strode to the stove, scooped up a ladleful of tepid fruit from the pot and emptied it into her hands. Then he steered her by the elbow towards the trapdoor. 'Let's talk below. Less chance of being overheard.'

She allowed herself to be led meekly down the ladder to the dim, windowless storeroom. They made a brief search of the shelves for provisions she could use, squinting at labels and sniffing the contents of boxes in the half-light. Most of the ship's fresh food was stocked in the pantry, but Tymon found some packets of smoked shillee meat wrapped in leaf-strips and opened one for her; he could explain that away to Cook as a ploy for catching the thieving rats. The rest of the provisions in the storeroom, the supplies of barleyflour, vine-sugar, lentils and dried beans, were useless without a means for cooking. The dry, unpalatable 'bark-biscuits', a sailor's staple fare, she had enough of in the hold. Water she had there too, in luxurious abundance, carefully transported in barrels sealed with Tree-pitch. It was the main currency for trade in the Eastern Domains, each drop of life-giving liquid more valuable than any carved tenders of money.

'We can work out a system for the food,' he told her as they sat crouched behind some flour sacks in the spice-scented stores, and the girl devoured her handful of fruit. 'I'll always hide a bit of fresh stuff, whatever I'm helping Cook with in the mornings, just inside that doorway.' He indicated the entrance to the ship's main hold nearby. 'That's where you came through, right?'

She nodded. 'My box is one of the spare ones at the back of the hold,' she explained between mouthfuls. 'They always keep a few big empty crates on board, for ballast.'

The fruit was already gone. She licked her fingers quickly and daintily, the habit of someone used to eating without a fork, and moved briskly on to the dried meat.

'Perfect. I'll put a trap by the door as well,' continued Tymon, taken up with his strategising. He finally had an outlet for all his frustrated plans of escape. 'If someone finds the victuals they'll think I'm after rats in the hold.'

'Very appropriate,' she grinned, and gave her attention to the food.

As he watched her bowed hungrily over her meal, single-mindedly demolishing the contents of the leaf-packet, he realised that the mystery surrounding her was still complete. He did not know where she came from or why she had travelled to Argos, apart from a vague reference she had made to finding out what really happened to the pilgrims. He did not even know if the name he had called out during the Festival on a desperate whim was hers, or how she had finally escaped from her prison. She had erupted into his life like a whirlwind — shaking it apart, practically causing his expulsion from the Rites — and he still had no idea who she was.

'Samiha?' he trialled softly.

'Yes.' She finished off the last crumbs of her stolen meal, carefully folding the leaf-packet and stowing it away in a pocket of her tunic. 'Yes, I am Samiha. And now, novice of Argos —' she settled back against a sack with a sigh of contentment '— you must satisfy my curiosity. I wish to know your name and how you guessed mine.'

'I'm Tymon.' He felt a rush of embarrassment at the remembrance of his dream. It was impossible to describe such a bizarre coincidence without coming across as either a liar or a fool. 'To be honest, I had no idea it was your name,' he hedged. 'I wanted to get your attention that day on the quays. The word was on my mind — I must have heard it, somewhere. It just popped out.'

She frowned, her mouth twisted with disbelief. 'So let me understand this: you called out a name you did not know, on impulse, without any guarantee that it would mean something to me, just in order to get my attention?'

'I was angry,' he mumbled. Even now, when he had her at a disadvantage, she made him squirm like a first-year student under interrogation. 'I wanted you to listen. I wanted to help.'

'In the middle of your Green Rites?' she pursued, with stubborn insistence. 'You called out a completely random name — no, a rare name, a Nurian name, goodness knows where you heard it — and you can't even tell me why?'

He shook his head, awkward and silent.

208

'Very well, Tymon,' she said after a pause, scrutinising him intently through the shadows of the storeroom. 'Have it your own way. In any case, I am now listening. You may notice I need all the help I can get on this ship.'

'And you'll have it, once I know a few more things about you,' he responded, stubborn in his turn. 'I'd like some questions answered.'

'Fair enough,' she said.

He peered up at the lighted square of the trapdoor. All was quiet in the galley.

'How did you break out of prison?' he whispered to the girl. 'No one would talk about it, as if it were a national embarrassment or something. And you still haven't told me what you were doing in Argos. Why take the risk of dressing up as a man? I think you'll agree, the experiment was doomed to failure sooner or later.'

She laughed softly. 'One question at a time, novice! It was surprisingly easy to escape from the prison. I stole the guards' keys from the bathhouse. The captain was drunk. No wonder they were embarrassed.' Her mirth died away, and she sighed in the gloom. 'Did any of the others make it?'

He understood that she meant the runaways. 'No, they were all caught.'

'Naturally,' she groaned under her breath. 'I should never have involved them. They knew nothing.'

She faltered and sat in silence a while, lost in private rumination. 'Knew nothing about what?' he prompted.

'Nothing about why I came to Argos,' she replied, rousing herself from her thoughts. 'They knew less about me than you do, really. They were just pilgrims, just trying to survive. They sold their freedom for a bit of water to help their families.' Her voice became a low, indignant growl. 'I have friends in Marak who would dearly love to put a stop to the Council's game. I came on their behalf, to gather information. I wish I could have done more. We have stood by long enough while our people are led to slaughter.'

Sudden realisation dawned on Tymon. 'You're a spy for the Nurian rebellion,' he blurted.

Now that the idea had occurred to him, it was the only explanation of her behaviour that made any sense. Who else but a rebel would risk all to come to Argos? Who else but a spy would have friends in Marak who opposed the seminary? Insurgents in the Eastern Domains were accused by the Council of everything from political agitation to grand heresy; in Tymon's current frame of mind, this only enhanced the pilgrim girl's appeal. It was highly gratifying to be aiding and abetting a sworn enemy of the priests.

Her gaze searched out his. She seemed to be sizing him up, measuring him against some internal gauge. 'You might say I was a spy, of sorts,' she conceded. 'Though not for rebels. Not in the sense you mean, anyway.'

He gave a shrug. 'Rebels to some, freedom fighters to others,' he noted. 'But there's one thing I don't understand. Why didn't your friends just send a man?'

His question seemed to throw her. She answered with a flash of her old scorn. 'Why, don't you think a mere slip of a girl is up for such a dangerous job?'

'That's not what I meant,' he clarified hastily. 'You said the other pilgrims didn't know who you were. Surely the disguise made things more difficult? Or did you have help?'

'Juno knew who I was. He was a —' She stopped abruptly, as if she had been about to say something else and thought better of it. 'We came together,' she continued. 'He was going to help me against the priests, until — until we arrived in the city, and he became ill ...'

'What happened to your friend was a tragedy,' put in Tymon as her voice trailed off. 'I must have come across as a fool during the Rites. I didn't want to think about what was happening right there, in front of me. I'm sorry.'

She gave a quick, sad half-smile. 'That's alright. I wasn't much use either that day. I almost missed it.'

'Missed what?'

'Missed why I really came to Argos.'

He sat up eagerly. 'You mean you found out how the seminary does it? How they trick the pilgrims into volunteering for the Sacrifice?'

'Yes and no,' she replied, evasive. 'My suspicions about that were confirmed, yes. But I was referring to something else.'

'Which was?' he pressed. He was not about to let her wriggle out of a response.

'I will tell you that,' she said with deliberate emphasis, 'when you remember where you heard my name.'

They stared at each other a moment, neither willing to make the first move. Cook's heavy tread shook the galley above, dispelling the tension. Tymon jumped up.

'I have to go. I'll see you in the hold tomorrow morning,' he whispered. 'And I promise I'll try and explain about the name, though it sounds crazy —'

The northerner's brusque tones reverberated through the trapdoor, interrupting him. 'Boy! You down there?'

Tymon signalled a hasty farewell to Samiha. 'I'm here,' he shouted as he skipped up the ladder to the galley. 'The rats are back. Saw one stealing from the pot, bold as bark. Where are the traps?'

He disappeared, slamming the hatch behind him with a dull thump. The girl remained in her place after he had gone, a slim, straight shadow in the darkened room. After a while she rose and slipped through the door to the main hold, closing it noiselessly behind her.

By noon the dirigible had approached the last towers of swaying leaves on the fringes of the Central Canopy. The Gap stretched beyond, an abyss of blue-grey cloud. Tymon went about his tasks on deck in a state of suppressed excitement. His conversation with Samiha had left him elated. He had the dim sense of exhilarating possibilities, a grand adventure just over the horizon. He was no longer simply an indentured student on his way to complete his service. He was friend to a wanted fugitive, an ally to a rebel. It was the perfect way to thumb his nose at the seminary. He had taken centre stage in his own dreams once again.

Not everyone aboard the greatship shared his enthusiasm for adventure, however. As the *Stargazer* drifted out over the Void, the members of her crew grew irritable and morose, stiffly avoiding the sides of the ship. Gravity menaced from the airy depths. The Gap was too wide for the other side to be seen: to set sail across it was an act of faith. Superstitious to the last, the men turned their backs on the offensive emptiness as long as they could. Tymon alone gazed eagerly ahead as the sky expanded into a cold grey dome and whistling space surrounded the dirigible. It drew him irresistibly; he stopped even pretending to drag his brush over the deck boards, distracted by curiosity. He sidled closer to the side of the ship and, when no one was watching, shirked his scrubbing duties to peep over the deck-rails.

The Storm stared back at him. A brazen expanse of cloud lay beneath the dirigible, vast and fathomless, and an updraft whipped his face. He gawked at the abyss, fascinated. Within the Central Canopy the view downwards was obscured by the lower branchways and leaf-forests, where it was not entirely blocked by the supporting column of the trunk. Argosians never saw more of the Storm than a smear of purple at the bottom of the West Chasm. But in the wide-open Gap no such protective barrier existed. The mass of churning clouds spread unbroken to the horizon. Tymon forced himself to look steadily into the Void though every fibre of his being, every ounce of his training and upbringing screamed at him to turn away, to flee the dangerous emptiness. The proximity of the Storm shocked him. The highest clouds lay only two hundred feet beneath the dirigible, if he could trust his eyes. He had never imagined the final boundary of the world would be right there, so close to his everyday life. He felt the sudden, irrational urge to jump over the railing, to give himself up to the grey gulf and fall, fall, fall forever.

A hand clapped onto his shoulder, breaking the spell. Misho pulled him back from the railing and rapped his forehead smartly with his knuckles.

'Don't stare at the wind,' growled the Jay. 'You'll call up the Storm, choirboy!'

Tymon returned to his deck-swabbing in subdued silence. The glimpse of the Storm had put him in mind of Galliano and of all the opportunities that were irretrievably lost to him. As the afternoon wore on and the buoyant air-currents that had spurred them through the canopy dissipated in the Gap, the ship began to drift at the mercy of the winds. The anxiety of the crew deepened. Even the captain restricted his orders to clipped monosyllables, and for hours the only sound was the creak of ropes and the breath of the men. Several times Tymon noticed his crewmates gazing askance at the slack sails and mouthing charms, or touching their forelocks in the sign to ward off evil. It occurred to him that he was very far from the world of his childhood. Neither the serene faith of the priests nor the plainspoken piety of the common folk of Argos had any place on the greatship. Here, only the unforgiving weather spirits held sway.

By the end of the afternoon, the sailors' whispered entreaties appeared to have had their desired effect. A brisk breeze filled the mainsail and the dirigible sped through the final furlongs of the Gap, her weatherboards creaking. At the fifth hour a cheer went up from the lookout on the main mast: the Eastern Canopy had been sighted. The mood on board the *Stargazer* lifted, though the work redoubled as the crew battled to keep control of the ship in the rising wind. By sunset the arms of the canopy stretched out to meet them, a bank of shadow in the failing light. Tymon squinted apprehensively at the sky. The ship was heading directly for bad weather. The Eastern Canopy lay between a rack of high thunderclouds and the seething blanket of the Storm. Funnels of vapour had formed between the two levels, glinting hypnotically in the evening sun. From a distance they looked almost beautiful. The boy gazed at them curiously. He turned to Aran as the first mate emerged from a nearby cargo hatch.

'What are those cloud-things, sir?' he asked. He pointed to the funnels.

Aran did not answer him but muttered an oath, hurrying to the deck-rail. He scowled at the murky eastern horizon.

'Wake up, Misho!' he hollered up to the watchtower. The Jay's surprised face peeped over the edge of the crow's nest as the first mate gestured in exasperation towards the columns of cloud. 'Were you going to let us fly into the Maelstrom, Jay fool?'

Misho's warning whistle echoed over the ship. Aran hurried back towards the captain's quarters, pushing past the bewildered Tymon.

'Those pretty things are funnel-winds,' he barked over his shoulder. 'They'll tear up this ship like a piece of bread if we don't out-run 'em!'

The door to Safah's cabin burst open before the first mate could reach it.

'Storm-posts,' boomed the Captain, striding onto the deck. 'We've got a runner, boys!'

The ship's crew sprang into action. The wind, longed-for at first, had now intensified to an unwelcome gale. They fought to trim the sails and tie down any loose equipment. The dirigible hurtled towards the canopy and the sky dimmed rapidly above them. The first drops of rain were already splattering Tymon's face and hands as he helped Misho pull canvas coverings over the dirigible's life-craft. The four ether balloons were mounted on what appeared to be ridiculously small passenger baskets. He wondered how all the men could possibly fit inside them. It was the first time he had encountered anything but clement weather on their journey; although the *Stargazer* was solidly made and as safe as a dirigible could be, the experience was unnerving. He could not help glancing up from his work every few minutes at the tossing gloom of the Eastern Canopy. The funnels of cloud were much larger than he had thought. One rose almost directly in the path of the dirigible, a spinning trunk of vapour at least a hundred feet across, inky black against the fading sky. He could make out what appeared to be shards of bark caught in the vortex.

'I told you not to stare at the Storm,' grumbled Misho, struggling to pin down his corner of the flapping canvas over the life-craft. 'Now look what you've done.'

Tymon could not tear his eyes away from the column of cloud bearing down on the ship. With growing alarm, he realised that he had misjudged the scale of the whirlwind once more. It was not shards of bark but entire twigs of the Tree that spun in the vortex. To reach the canopy they would have to pass between two of the writhing funnels, through a rapidly shrinking space. He stared in horror as the dirigible rode towards the columns on the screeching wind, bound for certain destruction. A wall of impassable black cloud rose before them. The rain abruptly intensified and became a downpour, plunging the dirigible into obscurity. The ship shook like a leaf in the wind. The Captain's bellows grew distant in the watery uproar and Misho yelled something that Tymon could not make out. The boy shook his head uncomprehendingly.

'Get below!' the other screamed in his face. 'Now!'

He lurched away from Tymon towards the last open hatchway. The rest of the crew were already retreating down the stairs to the hold, ducking beneath a piece of canvas that had been stretched in front of the doorway. Tymon had hardly taken three paces after them before a swift shadow loomed above the deck, accompanied by a blast of air so strong that it pulled him off his feet and threw him against the portside railing. A gigantic shape swept over his head, missing it by inches. Something smashed into the main mast with a crack like a colossal whiplash. The whole dirigible shuddered and groaned. The deck tilted sideways at an extreme angle, jerking him treacherously close to oblivion. He recovered from his shock just in time to hang grimly on to the rails, and began to pull himself back up the pitching deck, hand over hand. He dared not imagine what had hit the mast. It sounded as if an entire crossbeam had been ripped off the greatship.

'All ... below.' The Captain's words were ripped away by the squall. '... sacks ... gone. Drop ... ballast. Fill ... sacks ...'

Tymon grasped that the ether sacks on the port side of the dirigible were damaged. The ship was listing dangerously. He could not tell if they were losing altitude, for the space beyond the dirigible was a roaring darkness. He crawled on all fours towards the open hatchway, blinking in the rain. A feeble luminosity escaped from its doors. He fixed his eyes on the guttering beacon until he was able to roll himself under the wildly flapping canvas, scrabbling with aching fingers over the threshold. A hand came out of the hole to grab the collar of his tunic and drag him to safety. In another moment he was propped, dripping and breathless, against the wall of the stairwell. Safah's mad eye gleamed at him in the light of a drunken basket-lantern.

'*So shall the unbeliever be chastised by the tempests of divine wrath,*' he intoned.

Tymon had learned that there was a hidden side to the bluff Lantrian's character. Safah was a closet mystic, a quoter of scripture and saga, known to emerge on the stern deck armed with a book of poetry, which he proceeded to read aloud to his captive audience. The storm seemed to reawaken this dramatic urge; his gaze was wild as he grinned at the boy. It was a moment before he remembered to release Tymon's collar.

'Now, get below and make yourself useful, or make yourself scarce,' he said, collecting himself. 'We're going to lose some ballast.'

'What was that noise, sir?' Tymon asked. 'Did one of the masts break?'

Safah gave a harsh guffaw. 'Good Lantrian hardwood?' he scoffed. 'Never. We clipped the edges of the twister. That sound you heard was a twig caught in the wind. Could have taken your head off. Out of the way now, boy — there's no room here for layabouts!'

The last part of the Captain's speech coincided with the appearance of two sailors in the stairwell, staggering out of the hold with a large crate balanced on their shoulders. Tymon was pushed roughly aside as they hoisted their burden up the stairs and out of the hatch. He stared after them, his heart pounding. He had suddenly remembered that the pilgrim girl would be hiding in just such an empty crate, marked for ballast. The thrashing rain caught the light of Safah's lamp, spraying bright droplets off the sailors' backs and heads as they inched down the tilted deck. He watched, aghast, as the crate tumbled over the railing into the dark abyss. It was an agonising minute before he was sure. The box had been open, and empty.

'... ones at the back, by the galley stores,' he heard Aran crying from below. 'Should be good to go.'

Tymon waited no longer but leapt down the steps towards the hold. Everything was skewed with the slant of the ship and he tripped in the uneven stairwell, staggering desperately on. He knew he had to find the pilgrim girl before the crew did. The sanctions for stowaways on board an Argosian dirigible were harsh, and Samiha's crime was compounded by her origins and her sex. Even if she did not go down with her crate, it was likely the Captain would have her thrown overboard as punishment. The boy stumbled over the last few steps and came up short against the entrance to the hold.

He could hardly make sense of what he saw through the doors. Monstrous, jittering shadows danced up from the sailors' lamps along the walls of the cargo bay, creating more confusion than light. The crates were all heaped on the port side, dislodged when the ship had been hit. The timbers of the hull rasped and groaned. The men were checking the contents of the boxes under Aran's direction, forming a chain to the stairs. Tymon moved hurriedly aside before he could be pressed into service. He threaded a path between the jumbled crates towards the back of the hold, examining each of the boxes he passed as thoroughly as he dared. But the pilgrim girl was nowhere to be seen. He began to hope that she had abandoned her hiding place before the sailors arrived, perhaps making for the storeroom or the galley. He was about to test out his theory when he heard Misho complaining loudly nearby.

'I swear it's full, Aran.'

The sailor stood on the far side of a large crate; he examined it with an air of puzzlement.

'All the ones marked "Marak depot" are empty, numbskull.' The first mate answered him from across the hold, his voice hoarse with shouting over the din of the tempest. 'The spice was unloaded in Argos city.'

'This one weren't.'

'Green grace, I don't have time for this —' The flickering shadows from Aran's basket lantern approached. 'Did you check inside?'

'No,' Misho answered in sullen tones. 'Lid's stuck. Wedged shut.'

He was wrong. Tymon saw with a jolt of dismay that the lid was moving. The crate was almost the height of a man and rested on its end, opening on the side facing away from Misho. The boy watched in horror as thin white fingers emerged and gripped the edges of the lid, sliding it open.

'Let's have a look then— ' The lantern light jumped around the box ahead of the men.

Tymon threw himself at the crate. Before the sailors could reach the opening he had smashed the lid shut with his body's momentum. He must have pinched Samiha's fingers in the process, but he heard no cry of pain from inside the box. She would have bitten her lips through rather than make a sound, he thought with admiration.

'It's empty,' he gabbled, as Aran and Misho stared curiously at him around the corner of the box. He opened the lid a crack, taking care to do so on the edge furthest from the two men, and made a show of looking within to make sure. 'Yes. Totally empty. I'll help you carry it, Misho.'

He had caught a glimpse of Samiha's pale face at the back of the crate, her eyes wide in the darkness. He did not meet his crewmates' gaze. The white, staring visage was burned into the air in front of him and hung everywhere he looked, giving the lie to his words.

'Well,' Aran responded slowly, 'That's what it should be. Empty.' He grimaced and pushed Misho back the way they had come. 'Just like your head is, you Jay fool.'

The other sailor scowled in suspicion at Tymon, and only suffered himself to be dragged reluctantly after Aran, protesting: 'It was stuck. I swear it.'

'It's stuck, it's stuck,' jeered the first mate. 'Your mother said that when your fat head came through. No, I don't want to hear another word. We have work to do.'

The two men disappeared, still arguing. Tymon seized the opportunity to open the lid a crack. A ray of light illuminated a staring eye inches away from his. Samiha was right there, a breath away from him.

'Quick, let me out,' she murmured.

'Where to?' objected the boy. There was no shelter nearby, nowhere she could go without being seen by one of the crewmen. He shook his head. 'There's no safe place.'

'You know where this box is going, don't you?' she retorted. 'We must try!'

The sailors' discussion had come to a close. Aran's light bobbed away and Tymon could hear Misho approaching the other side of the crate, cursing.

'Too late,' he whispered. 'I'll find something else. Trust me.'

'Wait —'

He did not allow her to finish, but pushed the lid shut again just as Misho poked his head around the box.

'Well, choirboy,' the Jay ground out sulkily, 'you'd better be some use to me now. Get ready to heave.'

Heave they did, lugging their burden through the chaos and clamour of the hold, past the men redistributing the empty cargo boxes. The ship was already righting itself, Tymon noticed distractedly. The emergency sacks had been inflated. He felt as if he were moving through a dream. The waking world had become a nightmare, turning his best intentions awry. He had told Samiha to trust him but he did not know how to help her. They moved in plain sight of the sailors — there was no opportunity to let her out of the box. His anxiety intensified as they climbed the stairs, past Safah holding up the flapping canvas in the hatchway. He felt numb, unable to make a decision.

On the deck, raindrops whipped his face and hair, slapping him awake. It was difficult to see more than a few feet ahead in the downpour. He could just make out the lumping forms of the port life-craft beneath their coverings. As his eye settled on the vague outline of the deck-rail, he knew at last what he must do. He forced himself to wait for the right moment, to stumble after Misho all the way to the rail and hoist the box upwards until it was poised over the howling emptiness. Then, gritting his teeth in a silent prayer, he allowed the corners of rough wood to slip between his fingers.

For a heartbeat he thought that he had miscalculated the distance. The crate was too far over the edge. It would fall into the gulf. The box teetered and balanced a precarious instant before crashing down onto the deck, knocking him backwards. He skidded, slipped and fell flat on his back on the sodden planks. Misho gave a yelp of surprise and let go of his end of the box. Gasping, Tymon reached out one flailing arm to push the lid off the crate. It rolled away and clattered against the railing. He was dimly aware of a dark silhouette leaping over him in the pouring rain. The box provided a momentary screen between it and Misho, leaving the path clear to the life-craft. He could only hope that the girl had seen her opportunity and made for one of the covered baskets. There was an instant of breathless expectation as he stared into the swirling drops of rain. Then Misho was bending over him through the deluge.

'You all right?' he cried. He gave no indication that he had seen the shadow jumping from the crate. His concern quickly turned to annoyance as Tymon dragged himself to a seated position and regained his breath. 'Anything broken, mulch-brain?' snapped the Jay.

'No.' Tymon rose shakily to his feet. A quick glance confirmed that the deck was clear. The pilgrim girl was nowhere to be seen. 'I slipped,' he said. 'The boards are wet —'

'Damn right they're wet. You're a sharp one,' Misho spat sideways onto the waterlogged boards in disgust. 'Any more words of wisdom for us tonight, choirboy?'

Tymon gave a weak smile. Relief coursed over him like rain, and a glow of pride warmed him through the squall. He had succeeded. Samiha was safe. He fell back a step as the captain materialised in front him, shielding his basket-lantern with an oilcloth.

'You! Into the hatch. And this time stay out of trouble,' Safah growled.

He thrust the lantern and the cloth at Tymon, who nodded, took the guttering light and limped back to the shelter of the hatchway. Behind him, the two men tipped the empty crate over the railing. It fell soundlessly into the night.

By dawn the next morning the fury of the gale was spent. The boy arrived on deck to find the ship washed clean for him and an eggshell-blue sky glistening overhead. The *Stargazer* drifted above the canopy at a slight angle, one sail torn and fluttering in the breeze. They had outrun the storm, though the winds had taken their toll on the dirigible. Where the two starboard life-craft should have been, there was now only a flapping hole in the rigging. The sailors gathered together on that side of the ship, whispering among themselves and pointing at the severed ropes in dismay. Tymon hurried to the place where he had dropped the crate the night before. To his relief, the portside balloons were still safe, their covers intact. Samiha might be in either one of them.

He peered furtively under the cover of one of the vessels, an eye cocked on the men on the opposite side of the deck. The basket was empty. The sailors' voices erupted in a babble of protest, bemoaning the loss of the life-craft. He felt a sudden misgiving.

'Calm down.' Aran's voice rose through the clamour, reassuring the crew. 'We'll be in Marak in a few hours. They might not have ether in the colonies, but they won't have forgotten how to weave a basket or sew a seam.'

Tymon sidled over to the last balloon. He knew before he lifted the canvas that the pilgrim girl would be gone. The vacant interior of the basket gaped at him as he twitched aside the covering, and he wondered why she had not simply used the balloon she had first hidden in; why she had taken the trouble of cutting one loose from the other side of the ship. Then he noticed something lying in a far corner of the basket. He reached under the canvas, straining towards the object. With a dull click of hardwood he drew out a set of keys on a ring, of a kind commonly used in Argos city. They were immediately identifiable. Inside the ring, painted in dirty white letters, ran the inscription: *If found, please return to*. The subsequent words, *Argos municipal prison*, had been painstakingly blacked out with what looked like dry Tree-gum. These were Samiha's prison keys, the ones that she had stolen from the guards. She had left them for him.

If it was a message, it was not one that he could understand. The key ring lay in the palm of his hand, a big enigmatic 'o', meaning everything and nothing. He slipped it into his tunic pocket and walked over to the starboard rail, scrutinising the calm blue horizon. The life-craft was nowhere to be seen. Where was she now? Had she managed to safely navigate the tempest, or was she scuttled on some remote leaf-island? He gazed out over the expanse of the Eastern Canopy for the first time in the light of day, trying to revel in the knowledge that he had helped her escape. He felt only a sense of abandonment.

He shielded his eyes against the glare of the rising sun. There was something unsettling about the view from the deck-rail, an insistent and niggling detail that upset his sense of proportion. He had been too preoccupied to notice it before. He blinked in disbelief at the Treescape. He had heard of the fact but forgotten it in the turmoil of his arrival: the branches of the Eastern Canopy were bare. No leaves clad the naked limbs beneath the dirigible. Skeletal twigs gaped openly at the sky; bare boughs wound, arid and shorn, into the distance. It was as if the Storm itself had risen up and whipped the greenery away, leaving only the sad grey bones of the world behind.

12

Everyone on the greatship had their own theory about the Eastern Canopy and expressed it loudly as the ship sped over the acres of leafless twigs. God had withdrawn Her blessings from the East, the sailors affirmed. No Sap flowed through Her veins to give life to its inhabitants. Even the rains were scarce by divine decree. The consensus aboard the *Stargazer* was that Easterners were lazy and immoral and that the colonies were fighting a losing battle against chaos. The Nurian natives were thieves at worst, beggars at best, clamouring for Argosian handouts.

'Marak is a hole of iniquity in a rotten blanket,' the Captain announced, mixing his metaphors without compunction as he trudged past Tymon on the deck that morning. He added a dash of scripture for good measure. '*For thou shalt flee the domain of the unbeliever and fear his mercy even as thou dost fear his wrath.*'

Normal duties were suspended in favour of sewing in the wake of the storm, and the boy sat cross-legged on the rain-washed boards with the rest of the crew, patching up the torn and punctured ether sacks. He eyed the Captain warily. Safah liked to impart reams of doctrinal wisdom to his crew but might count the time spent listening to it against their food allowance. The thrifty Lantrian appeared to have other plans in mind for the day, however.

'*Seek ye not friendship with him, for he hath drunk of his own Mother's blood, even to Her death,*' he pontificated, before stamping into his cabin. Tymon stared after him in puzzlement: he was not entirely familiar with the colourful episodes of Lantrian holy writ.

'Who wants to be friends,' muttered Misho from nearby. 'Easterners stink, they don't know how to wash themselves. And their women have no honour.'

'The old Nurians drilled too deep,' Aran explained for Tymon's benefit as he tore off a section of sackcloth into an expert square. 'They mined for Treesap till they sucked the canopy dry. They used special contraptions — you can see what's left of one, over there.' He jerked his chin at the view beyond the deck rails. 'Wind-wells, they were called. Sucked up the Sap faster than it could flow.'

Tymon followed his gaze, scrutinising the alien world that stretched out naked and unapologetic beneath the dirigible. The flight through the night had shortened their journey; Aran had assured him that they would arrive at the colonial capital no later than noon that day. Until now there had been nothing to indicate it, no hint of life in the desolate branches. The bare twig-thickets extended in all directions, grey and dismal, swelling gently towards the canopy's summit. The only marks of human civilisation Tymon had yet seen were the miles of barkwood canal that wound alongside their course: rain-catchers, the sailors called them, though most seemed to be dry and in various states of disrepair. Now, as he lifted his eyes to the grey desolation, he caught sight of other structures, abandoned pulleys and great wheels covered in torn webbing mounted on platforms among the twigs. They stood out against the sky like monstrous distortions of Galliano's workshop.

'After a while God lost patience with them,' Aran continued cheerily. 'She gave them no more Sap and no Tree-water. They farmed using the rain-catchers for a while, but lately the rain isn't enough. They trade us their precious *attar*, their Tree-spice, for a barrel of our rainwater.'

'Why don't they just leave?' Tymon mumbled, more forlornly than he had intended. He wrestled his needle through the stubborn sackcloth.

He could not help feeling nonplussed at Samiha's sudden departure, as well as anxious about her safety. He was alone again, with no prospect but his mission service looming over him. It seemed harsh to lose his damsel in distress just when he was warming to his heroic role. He could no longer help her; she had slipped away from him once more. All that remained of her were the keys. The hardwood ring lay hidden in his pocket, reassuringly solid, proof that he had not dreamt up his adventures with the red-headed spy. Perhaps she meant for the two of them to meet again in

Marak, he thought. He mentally compared the speeds of the balloon and the dirigible and calculated when she might arrive in the city, only half-listening to the sailors' discussion.

His reaction bewildered the first mate.

'Leave? What do you mean, leave?' demanded the toothless sailor. 'Where else would they go? Even if they tried to leave, there's no ether left to float the dirigibles. Argosian ships are the only ones flying to Marak. Besides, they hung the hammock, let 'em lie in it, I say. Why should we save them?'

'Don't they want to save themselves?' Tymon replied without thinking. 'Don't they want freedom from Argos?'

Misho gave a low whistle of astonishment and applied himself with renewed diligence to his work. Aran glanced at Tymon curiously.

'Where d'you hear that?' he asked.

The boy shrugged in embarrassment, aware that he had said too much. 'Oh, I don't know. Isn't there a rebellion in Marak, or something?'

'A few crazy zealots don't qualify as a rebellion,' noted the sailor. He cleared his throat and leaned towards Tymon, speaking softly. 'You'd do well not to talk too much about rebels while you're in Marak. First of all, the Governor isn't friendly towards us home-borns right now, and comments like that can get you into trouble. Second, these so-called rebels are nothing but troublemakers. They don't want freedom. They just want to create as much grief and chaos as possible. Mark my words.'

Tymon nodded, feeling like a fool for his indiscretion. He would have to be more careful in the future, he realised. He was an Argosian on his mission service and a direct representative of the seminary. If he was to have any chance of carrying on his friendship with Samiha, he would have to be a model of caution in the colonies.

By noon the bare knots and exposed branches of the canopy were showing signs of habitation at last. Sections of sackcloth had been stretched from twig to twig for dew farming, and dirty white sheets wound between the bare thickets like the webbing of some gigantic, erratic spider. In these were grown the only crops that could easily bear drought: *melata* beans, the eastern staple crop, and shortwheat, a bitter, grassy grain used for flour and fermented to make the local beer. Tymon scanned the huts and platforms huddled under the shade of the dew-fields. Thin figures stopped their work to watch the greatship pass by and tiny, pot-bellied children waved and shouted in faraway voices. There was a sense of unreality to the naked canopy and its inhabitants. He searched the dreary vista through the deck-rails for a glimpse of the city. But it was sound, not sight, that welcomed him to the fabled kingdom of Nur.

The sun had just passed its zenith when he heard it. The call to prayer floated towards him on the breeze — not a clamour of bells, but a single voice chanting. The hairs on Tymon's neck prickled and he scrambled to his feet on the deck, as if summoned to attention. The disembodied voice reached out to him from the hazy space ahead, from the future. The sound was both strange and intimately familiar. Though the words of the chant were in Nurian and incomprehensible, the melody was well known to him. It was the First Liturgy, the psalm sung at the start of every temple ritual in Argos.

I saw the shape of God
Like to a mighty Tree ...

The dirigible flew above a crest in the twig-forests and over a wide basin, a dip in the general level of the canopy. The lookout gave his cry. Before them, in the grey heart of the hollow, lay the colonial outpost of Marak.

It was far from beautiful. The three shabby tiers of the town clung like pale lichen to a minor limb in a cheap parody of Argos city. The bough supporting the outpost was relatively small, a subsidiary branch only five hundred feet wide. Beyond the highest tier of buildings it split off into ever-narrowing conduits topped by clumps of ungainly bare twigs. Rank upon rank of the leafless twig-thickets extended about the city, closing off the horizon. The houses were crowded together too, the narrow buildings competing for space behind a rough palisade. A sprawling edifice, marked by its gaudy pomp as the Governor's palace, dominated the highest level of the town, and rows of bright yellow military barracks proliferated along the air-harbour like mould. Behind them, to the south, a tent city spread in a fetid jumble, petering out where the supporting branch turned vertical and plunged steeply downwards. A disagreeable smell wafted towards Tymon on the deck and he saw that compost-cloths bulged beneath the air-harbour quays. The call to prayer faded on the breeze, dissolved in the face of dull reality. Marak was unclean and unenchanting.

Safah's barked orders sent the crew scurrying to their posts as the ship descended towards the city. A short while later the *Stargazer's* magnificent bulk towered over the dilapidated docks, and Tymon was consigned to the hold, passing boxes and barrels out of the main cargo hatch. He realised that hiding Samiha in these circumstances would have been almost impossible. It was just as well that she had made her getaway. He heard the commotion of many voices echoing dimly through the walls of the hull as he worked, and wondered what was happening outside on the quays. But it was only after the last box was whisked to the safety of the custom house that the pace on the dirigible slackened, and he was able to return above deck once more to satisfy his curiosity.

A chorus of voices sang out as he peered over the port railing.

'Missa! Missa! Job need doing? Hey, *Argosi!*'

Pale faces gazed up from the docks, a mass of dirty white flecks. The air-harbour was teeming with humanity. Tymon stared at the people jostling each other by the side of the greatship: he had never witnessed such a crowd welcoming an ordinary merchant dirigible in Argos city, nor had he ever seen so many foreigners together in one place. The Nurians in Marak seemed no better off, or cleaner, than those who left to go on pilgrimage.

'Missa! Need stay? Need girl?' the voices cried.

'Quiet, you scum.'

The order cut through the chorus like a lash. Colonial soldiers patrolled the docks. Some of them pushed individual members of the crowd away from the greatship with their short, heavy clubs.

'Move along, Nurry,' they jeered, flattening their vowels, an echo of Father Rede. 'That's it, nice and easy.'

Tymon was astounded. These soldiers were utterly different from the sentries in Argos city. They were cruel and efficient and there were a great many of them. They had cordoned off the main way up to the town, as well as the area between the *Stargazer* and the custom house a little further along the quays. He thought better of calling out a merry answer to the massed faces below, and retreated from the rail.

'Hey, choirboy, quit wasting space,' yelled Misho, emerging from the door to the hold. 'Message from the first mate: you're done and docked. Go see the captain. And don't talk to the natives if you want to live, frog-wit.'

Tymon only shrugged in answer and sauntered off to the captain's quarters. He found Safah seated at his desk, deep in one of his metaphysical moods. The Lantrian's notebooks lay idle on the table before him and he chewed meditatively on one of his pens, his dreamy eye rolling to starboard.

'The path to heaven is tortuous,' he sighed as the boy entered his office. 'Well, it's a sad sight,

235

this place. I wish I wasn't leaving you here, aye —
I'd offer you work myself if I could. But adversity
shall call the true believer! *Yea,*' he intoned in his
best scripture voice, signing Tymon's work pass
and handing it back to him with a flourish, '*the
seeker of truth shall walk through the very Maelstrom
of Hell.* Take this to Father Verlain and go in
beauty, young one. We'll see you again in two
years, eh?'

'In the beauty, Captain,' answered Tymon.

The words stuck in his throat. He suddenly felt
very fondly towards the belligerent Lantrian,
though he was in no hurry now to sign his future
away to the greatship. Samiha had given him a
glimpse of something larger. The pilgrim girl and
her mysterious friends in Marak inhabited a sphere
more exotic than anything he had yet experienced;
even the remote chance of meeting her again was
intoxicating.

'Well, go on then,' snorted Safah, his squint eye
searching a corner of the cabin. 'Ask Aran or
someone to tell you the way to the mission. But
don't look for salvation in these parts.'

Tymon was given a lively farewell by his
crewmates, who threw frogapple peels and light-
hearted insults after him as he walked down the
gangplank. Creaking on its moorings, the dirigible
seemed familiar and safe, a lost haven. The fact
that Marak was host to the seminary mission as
well as being Samiha's home, and that he was
about to officially begin his indenture service,
weighed with sudden heaviness on his spirits. As

he stepped onto the quays a sense of difference, of being completely alien, descended on him like a shroud. The crowd of onlookers surged behind the soldiers' cordon. An officer detached himself from the line, striding towards him. The militiaman had a cold slab of a face. He blocked Tymon's path with both his girth and frigid lack of cordiality.

'Pass, please,' he snapped.

Tymon gave him his signed travel document. The man threw a cursory glance over it.

'How long will you be staying in Marak city.' He spoke as if the question were a statement, with no inflection in his voice.

'Two years, sir.' The boy fidgeted in embarrassment.

'For what purpose are you sojourning in Marak city.'

'It says on the pass, sir —'

'For what purpose are you sojourning in Marak city.'

'My mission service, sir.'

The soldier's lip curled into a faint sneer. 'You'll be going straight to the Argosian mission, then. It's near the second tier temple. Proceed.'

He handed the pass back and waved Tymon on perfunctorily. A faint hiss escaped from the crowd, a collective sigh.

The boy made his way through the area cleared by the soldiers up to the city palisade. The day was turning fine and his tunic clung to him in sticky, smothering folds. Sunlight glanced, blinding, on the dusty boards of the dock and beat down on the bodies pressed together behind the line of militiamen. The soldiers stuck out their chests and swung their short clubs purposefully. Hungry eyes followed Tymon along the quays. Sometimes a voice sang out from the crowd, promising him delights, but it was soon silenced by a gruff word or the crack of a club. The throng shifted, swallowing the perpetrator into oblivion. He tried to keep his gaze evasive and his expression non-committal, but he could not help glancing back curiously at the people behind the military cordon. They were mostly children.

The docks were packed with boys and young men, none of whom were much older than Tymon himself. He was to learn later that they came from the tent-town on the outskirts of the city, refugees who had fled the drought in the outlying reaches of the canopy. The urchins were a ragged, fluid lot, their faces pinched with starvation under a veneer of grime. They were full of the smiling, terrible exuberance of those who have nothing to lose. A few of the younger ones broke away from the back of the crowd and shadowed him to the palisade gates, crying for alms. When he did not respond, they danced about him, yelling, *'Putar! Putar!'*, which he guessed was a local insult. They gave up their chant only at the start of the main thoroughfare into the city, where they dispersed in a hail of shrieks. He was left standing in a crowded street market, gazing up at the tiers of Marak city.

The town was even filthier up close than it had appeared from the ship. The houses were made of tawdry lightwood, jammed together and overflowing with refuse. The stink of the gutters in the lowest tier was overpowering, for they opened directly onto the compost cloths below. He had been told to follow the main ramp through the first and second tiers until it reached the entrance to the Governor's palace; he walked slowly on, gazing about him. The market, where he had expected to see Argosian colonials, was overrun by Nurians: traders, artisans, servants and errand-boys. The only 'white-necks' in the vicinity were the omnipresent soldiers. Tymon wondered that his countrymen did not seem to go out in the streets at all. Everything in the town was unfamiliar, pungent, chaotic. He saw no vehicles, for there was no space for anything bigger than a handcart to pass. Several times he caught sight of swaying, curtained boxes held aloft on the shoulders of four men and accompanied by a retinue of guards. He realised after a while that these were covered litters for the transport of paying passengers, probably his fellow Argosians. There were animals forever underfoot, herds of yellow-eyed, lop-eared shillees and diseased-looking dock birds squabbling at the refuse-holes. His head reeled with new sounds and smells, and he was glad when the market came to an end and the ramp was a little freer.

Through the compost odour receded in the second level of the city, the narrow streets were eclipsed by the looming presence of the Governor's palace. The higher tiers were given over to the official buildings and colonial residences. Crowds and shops disappeared and the curtained litters multiplied. The few pedestrians stared at Tymon coldly. He peered up in trepidation at the Governor's oversized mansion. The temple and the mission would be next to it, at the entrance to the third tier. Every step made him feel as if a noose were tightening about his neck. He drifted past the headquarters of the Spice Guild, a dour hardwood fortress surrounded by what seemed to be an overabundance of walls, before arriving at last at the imposing gates to the palace. There he stopped, searching in vain for the temple.

It was several moments before he grasped that he was looking straight at it. To his right, set back from the ramp, stood an eight-sided building. It was locked and appeared singularly deserted, even disused. The decorative shingles on the dome were chipped and the whitewash on the walls had faded to oblivion. He sat down on the front steps and waited, hoping someone would turn up. No one did. Eventually he rose to his feet and crossed to the far side of the building, where a movement in the narrow quadrangle behind the temple caught his attention. An old woman in a shapeless black headscarf was sweeping the back courtyard. Temple cleaners were a familiar sight to Tymon; the black crone was a shrivelled icon so universal that her presence put him at his ease. He hurried forward, calling, 'In the beauty, Amu! Where is Father Verlain?'

She turned and gazed at him wordlessly. The boy saw with a thrill of surprise that her eyes were almost colourless, as clear as Tree-water. He came to an uncertain halt; she was a Nurian. He had been warned not to speak to the natives. Besides, she might not even understand him. But just as he was about to leave, the answer came in a cracked and weedy whisper.

'In beauty, *nami*. Father in mission compound, there.' She pointed a knobbed and wrinkled finger at the gated archway on the other side of the courtyard. 'He sleep, you wake. Good?' She smiled, exposing a line of astonishingly perfect teeth, the tip of her nose almost touching her chin.

'Oh, I don't want to bother him if he's resting,' protested Tymon. 'I'll just wait.'

'Nah, nah, you go now,' insisted the crone, suddenly imperious, brandishing her straw broom. '*Vaz*, go, go.'

She rapped him on the back with the handle, pushing him along. He submitted in bewilderment and headed towards the open gate. She mumbled a stream of Nurian after him, nodding vigorously until he lost sight of her.

Beyond the arch he entered another, smaller compound, paved with barkwood tiles and blissfully shaded by a wide sackcloth awning. Under the awning stood a tattered-looking couch, and on the couch lay a fat man in priest's robes, sound asleep. A grass-weave fan rested on his rotund stomach, trembling slightly with each breath. One bare foot was propped up on the threadbare pillows while the other trailed on the floor, graced by a stained green slipper. The second slipper was nowhere to be seen. Beside the man, within easy reach, stood a large and complicated jar-pipe, quietly bubbling. He was lying turned towards Tymon. The boy saw a flaccid, corpulent face, as blotched and bloated as a drowned spider. He tiptoed closer, fascinated by the priest's ugliness. He noticed that a pool of spittle had collected in a corner of the sleeper's mouth and was slowly trickling onto the couch.

Tymon might have continued watching the fat man in a state of hypnotised horror had it not been for a very large, very loud fly that appeared from behind the awning and settled unceremoniously on the priest's nose. For such a bloated bag of a face, the nose was disproportionately small. It quickly wrinkled under the weight of the fly and with a snort and a splutter, the fat man was awake. He waved his hands about his head, chasing the buzzing offender off with an oath. Then he saw Tymon standing above him and squealed.

The sound was ludicrous. The boy disguised his laughter with some difficulty as a cough, and stepped back. Flustered, the priest gathered himself into a semi-sitting position, his bare toes searching the floor in vain for the missing slipper.

'Who ... who the devil are you, creeping up on me like that? Didn't anyone tell you it was rude to play jokes on a priest, you damned Nurry?' He stared blearily at Tymon and paused. 'You're no Nurry.'

'In the beauty, Father. My name is Tymon, and I'm here on my mission service. Sorry to have woken you.' Tymon looked down, furiously fighting the urge to smile.

'Ah, the indentured student,' yawned the priest grumpily. 'You certainly do know how to make an entrance! I'm Verlain. No need for "beauties", or "fathers", or any such like. We're at the rotten rear end of the world, and there's no point in standing on ceremony. But you'll soon learn that ...' He heaved himself up with a resigned grunt and salvaged the remaining green slipper from under the couch.

'Would you like to see my papers, sir?' Tymon could not bring himself to do without an honorific altogether. He held out his travel pass to the priest, who waved it away impatiently.

'None of that, no need. Why bother? They sent you to this hole, that's good enough for me.'

He lumbered off towards a room opening onto the courtyard and motioned the boy to follow him. Inside, the stale smell of jar-weed hung in the air, as well as another cloying odour Tymon could not identify. The room was sparsely furnished with a crude table, two chairs and a rickety cabinet. The fat priest rummaged in this last item, retrieving a stoppered cask and two small bowls, which he brought to the table. Then he squeezed himself into one of the chairs, wheezing heavily, and indicated that Tymon should join him. He opened the cask and poured a clear, pungent liquid into the bowls.

'To Argos city!' he announced, raising his bowl in a toast. 'And the mean-spirited bastards who live there!'

Tymon stared at his companion in shock. The other shrugged his ample shoulders, gulped down the contents of the bowl in one go and poured himself another.

'To Argos city,' he said again. 'May they rot in their own damn rainfall.'

Down went the priest's second bowl. A third was poured. Tymon sipped his portion of the acrid liquid in an attempt at courtesy. He was barely able to swallow a mouthful.

'To Argosh city,' said the priest, a little more blurrily, 'love of my life.'

Like a sudden shower of rain, the prayer-call drifted through the open window once more. The sound sent a shiver down Tymon's spine. The chant was mesmerising. Why couldn't the temple in Argos have a human voice? he thought. Why was it always bells, bells, bells, fit to tear his eardrums apart? But the music did not come from the direction of the Marak temple, or from anywhere near the deserted, dusty mission buildings. It echoed out far below, beyond the first tier of the city.

'You see, my boy, we're useless here,' Verlain giggled, leaning towards him conspiratorially. His breath was foul. 'The Nurries don't even go to our temple. They prefer the old shrine in the tent-town. Ha, ha! We're the joke of the day, the laughing-stock of the natives! To Argos!'

He raised his bowl again, drank, and slumped onto the table, snoring.

13

So began Tymon's colonial service. He soon realised that the fat priest was right: the Marak mission was a resounding failure. The temple remained locked and disused even on seventh nights, and the painted dome and fluted columns of the edifice were sadly dilapidated. No one bothered to visit the mission or enquire after Father Verlain. The city's Argosian elite, so disparagingly called 'white-necks' by the novices at the seminary — a term almost unheard-of in the colony — attended the Governor's chapel in the third tier, while the natives preferred their own heretical shrine in the refugee quarter. This state of affairs was tacitly condoned by the authorities, more out of a desire to snub the seminary than any spirit of tolerance. For a split had developed between the colonists and their superiors in Argos. The Colonial Board would not waive taxes during the drought, or provide aid in the form of extra water to the outpost. The Governor of Marak had retaliated by threatening to declare his town independent. Argosian trade dirigibles were still permitted into the air-harbour, as were the seminary's recruitment vessels, ferrying tithe-pilgrims back to Argos. But the mission itself had fallen out of favour.

The circumstances of Tymon's indenture were unlike anything he could have imagined or predicted. Far from the suffocating restrictiveness of the seminary, he was propelled into a life of unexpected licence. None of the usual clerical laws were in force at the mission. He could smoke jar-weed and eat on fast days, if he wished. There was no longer any question of rising at dawn, no morning ritual to hurry to, no sermons to endure. In fact, there were no sacred activities at the mission at all. When he asked how he should observe daily prayer, Verlain laughed in his face.

'Pray all you like, my dear boy,' the priest tittered. 'But as to ablutions, remember that water is rationed in Marak. You may find that we have a different attitude to such things. One shouldn't judge a leaf by its colour, eh?'

True to his word, Father Verlain did not use one drop of the mission's water allowance to bathe and passed his days tippling on the courtyard couch in a cloud of sweat and weed-smoke. He began drinking from his acrid bowl as soon as he emerged from his sleeping quarters around noon, and continued steadily through lunch and the hours that followed until by dinner he was either incoherent or inert. His only contact with the outside world was Amu Bibi, the temple crone. The old woman swept the courtyard in a daily rite of futility and cooked quantities of spiced *melata* for the mission meals, muttering to herself in a hotchpotch of Nurian and Argosian. Tymon suspected that she was half-witted in any language. She seemed to think she knew a devastating joke at the priest's expense, for she would wink at Tymon behind his back when he spoke, tapping her long nose with a bony finger. It was some time before the boy's stomach became accustomed to her indigestible cooking.

Initially, he relished the lack of discipline under Verlain's tutelage. He had few obligations at the mission. So long as he completed the daily supply run and carried out some secretarial duties for his employer, his time was his own. He would rise gloriously late each morning, grab a mobile breakfast from the mission kitchen and quit the compound, unwashed and tousle-headed, for the madness of the first-tier bazaar. There he would purchase the everlasting beans and bread that made up Amu Bibi's meals, as well as casks of the harsh *kush* which Verlain consumed in vast quantities. He did not hurry on these errands, dawdling in the streets for hours before returning to the mission for lunch. He calculated that Samiha must by now have reached the city, barring accident or mishap; he waited in the market and on the air-harbour quays, anxious and full of hope, to catch a glimpse of the familiar red head. He had told himself that his service was only temporary. When he found her again, he would run away from the priests for good. He would join the rebels and fight for Nurian freedom. Everything would change. It was only a matter of time.

Time went by, however, with no news of the red-haired spy. As the first week of his indenture gave way grudgingly to a second, and then a third, his confidence began to flag in the sultry heat of the eastern summer, and the reality of the colony settled on his spirit like dust. Despite his encounter with Samiha, he had not been prepared for the grinding poverty and misery that confronted him in Marak. There was little in the way of a livelihood to be had in the parched outer reaches of the canopy. But there were no jobs waiting for the Nurians in the city, either, no way out of their predicament except to sell their freedom to the tithe-ships. The refugees seethed with anger beneath their mask of servility and their masters reacted as if they were under siege. Well-to-do colonials restricted themselves to fortified compounds and never left without an armed escort. Nurian revolutionary slogans were a common sight scrawled on the walls and doorways of the town, erased by colonial soldiers to the tune of a patriotic song. No love was lost between the two strata of Marak society.

Putar! The epithet — insulting, untranslatable — dogged Tymon's heels whenever he ventured near the market or docks, or into the tent-town. He would hear the word hissed out on a daily basis in the cramped and stinking alleyways. The Nurian traders dealt abruptly with him, as if they wished to have as little to do with him as possible and only took his money out of necessity. There seemed no hope of approaching the locals in friendship. It was a stark lesson for the boy. His simplistic vision of joining the rebels began to fray at the edges, and he wondered whether even

Samiha's support would be enough to buy him credibility with her friends.

To make matters worse, he learned to his chagrin that the lack of strictures at the mission was double-edged. Verlain's peculiarities were to prove as disagreeable in their own way as the rigid routine at the seminary. Every day when his errands in the market were done, he was expected to take dictation for his employer, copying out petitions to the Governor and to the seminary bemoaning the state of the mission and asking for funds. The priest would insist that he sit beside him on the tattered courtyard divan to accomplish this task, not on the floor at his feet as was customary for a student — a dubious privilege made particularly gruesome by Verlain's lack of personal hygiene. The dictation became less intelligible and more unpleasant with each passing hour, as the fat man's letter writing gave way to his drinking, and his drinking to wallowing despair.

For Father Verlain was a tortured soul. He claimed to have been a victim of political intrigue, cheated out of his rightful position at the seminary and sent off to the colonies as punishment. He hated both his colleagues in Argos for sending him to Marak and the 'white-necks' for failing to appreciate him once he was there. He had an almost morbid fear of the Nurian natives, considering them no better than animals and ready to slit his throat at the slightest provocation. His post, he would moan to Tymon, was an emotional exile, a spiritual death. Much to his dismay, the boy found himself becoming his employer's confidant, a party to tearful reminiscences and sodden confessions. Verlain had cried on his shoulder by the end of his first week at the mission. By the third they were, in the fat man's florid terms, 'bosom companions'. One airless afternoon, about a month after his arrival, Tymon was obliged to contend with more than Verlain's unpleasant smell.

'My dear, you speak with the sweet voice of an angel, in the accent of my beloved home. *Argos city, tall and bright, you hold my captive heart tonight.*'

Tymon started up from his copy. The day's dictation, a report to the seminary, had given way as usual to self-pitying reminiscences on the part of his employer. Fountains of drunken nostalgia accompanied Verlain's letters, and this time the priest had broken into tuneless doggerel, mid-phrase. He had also laid his sweaty palm on the boy's knee and was leaning far too close for comfort. Perspiration stained his armpits and the stench rose like a miasma from his robes. Tymon gritted his teeth.

'Maybe one day you'll return home, sir,' he answered with an effort.

'Not with those old buzzards sitting on the Council,' oozed Verlain. 'You know that! Anyone who's a little different gets sent off to rot in the service ...'

'Shall I leave this for tomorrow?' Tymon tried to deflect the priest's attention to his copy-leaf.

Verlain ignored the question. 'I suppose they sent you away for a reason too, my angel, hmm?' he murmured. 'Remember you can tell me anything, I'll understand.' His fat fingers squeezed Tymon's leg and he bent closer, breathing heavily.

Tymon wavered between hilarity and disgust. The foul-smelling priest was the last person he wished to confide in, or compare himself with. He shifted further away from Verlain on the couch.

'I'm afraid I don't understand you very well, sir.'

The fat man sighed petulantly. 'Well, I suppose we all have our thorny vine to bear,' he wheezed, releasing the boy's knee. 'The colonies can be confusing for a fresh young bud like yourself. I am your friend. If you have any needs ... any needs at all ... do not hesitate to ask me for help.'

They were thankfully interrupted by the call to prayer rising from the tent-town. Verlain took up his jar-pipe and bubbled loudly all the way through the song. Tymon paused to listen to the voice. He found it achingly beautiful.

Morning, noon and night, the disembodied chant floated over the stink and poverty of Marak like a balm. The seminary taught that the Eastern Doctrine was a heathen heresy, and he was surprised to find that the Nurians had a First Liturgy at all, let alone one he recognised. He had never visited the tent-town shrine, never ventured into that heart of darkness. Verlain had warned him that the Nurian temple was the province of criminal gangs, to be avoided by Argosians at all costs. The threat of violence lurked beneath the haunting music as it did all else in the city.

'That horrific noise,' moaned the priest as the song faded away, 'frays my poor nerves to shreds. I shall need more medicine tomorrow, if you don't mind.'

Tymon's heart sank. Verlain had of late taken advantage of their supposed complicity to send him on personal errands, questionable commissions that required him to extend the scope of his supply run to the black market in the tent-town. In the squalid alleyways behind the custom house, traders hawked everything from the luxury of fresh vegetables to a staple of prostitutes. In return, the Nurians insisted on being paid in water, or at least in Argosian money for their wares. The local strawpaper currency bearing the large-nosed likeness of the Governor was almost valueless, and only a whole *talek*, the hardwood disc making a guilty lump in Tymon's pocket as he hastened through the streets, was enough to buy Verlain his daily fill of *som*.

The priest could not seem to do without this powerful sedative. He would put a generous portion of the stuff into his pipe every evening, exhaling a noxious sweet smoke that clung to the compound rooms like oil. The sticky vapour seeped over the low partition wall from his quarters into Tymon's cubicle, and the boy's nights became unpleasantly heavy, troubled by dreams of fire and flight. He loathed purchasing the packets of dull grey powder from the taciturn dealers in the tent-town, paying the equivalent of a month's room and board for one paltry dose. It was doubly galling to him that Verlain did not appear to think it at all inconsistent, in this instance, to send him straight into the arms of the Nurion gangs he so deplored.

That day, trapped on the couch in the ghostly wake of the prayer call, he felt a rising sense of panic. Maybe this was it, he thought. Maybe this was all he could hope for from life in Marak. Samiha's balloon had gone down in the pathless thickets and he would spend the next two years running errands for a disreputable drunk. The idea that the elusive red-haired spy might actually have arrived in the city, but chosen not to contact him for reasons of her own, was more unbearable than any thought of accident or injury. For she had left him to fend for himself in a world without hope.

The Harvest month came to a dry and unproductive end; the official start of the rainy season brought with it only a stifling rise in temperature. Not one drop of water fell on the parched city. The mission compound sagged in the heat and huge, mottled flies flew lazily around the incense-burners in the courtyard, expiring with a pop when they were caught in the flames. Although Verlain never again offered his assistance to Tymon in any capacity, his afternoon transcriptions became a torture of sweat and immobility. Day after interminable day, the boy counted the annihilated insects between the fat man's phrases, gagging on his smell until the dinner hour brought his misery to an end. There was never the slightest response to the volumes he copied out for his employer. The storm of correspondence simply vanished into thin air. He did not see the letters being given to messengers or dispatched by bird. The more time he passed in Verlain's company, the more irksome the priest and his habits became. He began to hate every waking minute at the mission.

'Father, why do the Nurians sing the First Liturgy?'

The voice from the tent-town filled the space after Tymon's question with longing. Verlain paused in his dictation and gave a spasmodic cough, peering sharply at him over his pipe-draw. For an instant, he appeared entirely sober.

By the fourth day of the Water month and his fifth week in the city, Tymon's patience had run out. He had spent over a month at the mission with nothing to do but sit by Verlain's side, listen to the priest's droning voice and plug his nostrils against his smell. He was now convinced that Samiha had run into difficulties in the life-vessel, and the thought tormented him. His employer had kept him trapped on the courtyard couch yet again that day, writing to the Governor to complain of 'the shadow of heresy that sullies the fair face of our city'; the heat was suffocating, and Verlain's prose resolutely purple. There was nothing, never anything but cheap strawpaper to write on at the mission. Tymon's pen snagged on the rough surface of his copy. He had botched and rewritten the word 'heresy' every time the priest had used it and the yellow paper was full of unsightly brown blots. He was considering rewriting the whole thing from start to end when the voice from the shrine rang out for evening prayer. It seemed to mock him. His question to the priest was a last resort, an act of desperation.

The call faded, but the heretical query hung in

the air, dangling unanswered between the priest and the boy. Verlain dissolved into a renewed bout of coughing and wiped his streaming eyes.

'Considering your innocence, your curiosity is understandable,' he gasped at last. 'But I pray lest any taint of the dangerous beliefs rampant in this city mar the purity of your soul.'

'Sir?'

'The shrine in the tent-town. I hope you don't attend it.'

'No, of course not —'

'Good. There is a reason I ask you not to, as your concerned friend and mentor.' The priest took another noisy draw from his pipe, exhaling wetly. 'These damned Nurries say it's a Tree temple, just like ours. They're lying, of course. If it was, the parishioners would want to go on pilgrimage, wouldn't they? Instead here we are, writing letters.'

With slow-dawning hope, Tymon realised what the fat man was saying.

'You mean, people in Marak don't sign up for the tithe?' he murmured. He had difficulty keeping the exultation out of his voice.

'Not the ones who go to the shrine, no.' The priest's chins wobbled as he leaned closer to the boy, his voice dropping to an unctuous whisper. 'The Nurries here think they're better than all that. They believe in the Sap heresy, which basically means they have no end of fine philosophical reasons for not doing an honest day's work. No man shall own another, *for ye are leaves of the same branch*, or some such nonsense.

It's a good thing there're always recruits among the refugees or we'd be reduced to choosing pilgrims by lot.'

Tymon digested this new piece of information. It was hardly surprising that the members of the Council were so keen to stamp out heresy: it threatened their livelihood. 'The Sap heresy?' he prompted cautiously, hoping Verlain's revelatory mood would hold out. Anything was better than dictation.

'Their so-called religion. The Nurries, of course, claim it's no different to proper Tree worship, but there are far too many fundamental —' Verlain coughed, spluttered, and fanned himself '— fundamental variances in dogma for it to qualify as anything but a degenerate sect. They don't even acknowledge the Tree as creator. But the temple rites are by far the worst. The call to prayer is a blasphemy in itself. Take the *shanti*, the local shaman whom we are obliged to hear chanting that awful song.'

'The First Liturgy ...'

'My boy, the First Liturgy is immaterial. The ritual is a deliberate perversion, a heresy. The Nurries have female *shanti*. It's disgraceful. Disgusting. Their very presence in the temple is an outrage.'

To Tymon's sheltered sensibilities the ladies of Marak were loud, pushy and provocative, a fact that went some way to explaining Samiha's extraordinary behaviour. They owned stalls in the market, wore breeches under their long cloaks and looked him straight in the eye when they spoke, in defiance of all Argosian norms of propriety. But this was the first time he had heard they could hold priestly rank. His face must have betrayed his surprise, for Verlain gave a prim little nod of commiseration.

'Oh yes, though it pains me to speak of such things. These so-called priestesses use their charms to lead young men astray. Of course, everyone knows the Sap heresy is just a cover for Nurry rebels. I have it on authority that the local *shanti* recruits in a most unsavoury manner for their cause.'

Where females were concerned, Verlain's permissiveness disappeared completely. The fat man waxed lyrical in condemnation of Nurian customs until late that evening, holding forth on women and heretics all through supper while the flies expired in the flames and Amu Bibi leered at him over her platter of beans. Tymon resigned himself to another wasted day and concentrated on slapping the insects away from his face and neck. He wished morosely that he had some luck with women, any women, even heretical ones. But the Nurian girls in the market did not play the game of seduction by the rules he had been taught. They were not coy, or suggestive, or even attractive, with their garish pale skin and light hair. He thought despairingly of Samiha, wondering what had become of her, and whether she was even alive.

That night he dreamt of fire again. It seemed to him that he heard the bells pealing out from the bell-tower, sounding the dreaded warning. But this time he was lost in a strange city. The smoke was already coiling thick and noisome about him.

'*Foy*,' cried a far-off voice in Nurian. '*Foy!*' He ran down ramps, climbed never-ending ladders in a desperate hunt for the way out. The walls of the buildings were too thin, flimsy, already consumed in the roaring flames. Fear weighted his limbs and his breath came in short gasps. He could no longer see in front of him for the smoke. A terrible pressure mounted in his chest. He opened his mouth to scream.

He woke up with a start, coughing. The stale odour of *som* drifted over the wall from Verlain's quarters, catching in his throat. Over time, his body had grown accustomed to the effects of the drug, and the saccharine vapour no longer made him so drowsy. He slipped out of his hammock and groped his way to the door, sweat slicking the tunic to his back. The courtyard outside was awash with moonlight. He lingered on the threshold, feeling the welcome breeze on his neck, and thought with distaste of the fat priest breathing stupefying fumes in the cubicle next door.

Then he froze. Verlain was not in his room but standing at the entrance to the mission, his unmistakably bulbous form outlined in silver light. He had his back to Tymon and appeared to be waiting for someone. Instinctively, the boy retreated into his cubicle doorway. Soon a second shadow, tall and lithe, flitted across the temple courtyard to join Verlain. The two spoke in whispers, drifting in and out of earshot.

'... not safe any longer.' The priest's tone was wheedling. 'It's really best we communicate through an intermediary.'

'I work alone. No intermediaries.' His companion's yellow hair and beard caught the moonlight. Tymon saw with a shock that the stranger was a Nurian. What had become of Verlain's qualms? 'Do not seek to deceive me, priest. Your life will be worthless.'

'No need ... no need to be suspicious. The Council finds your movement sympathetic to our needs.'

'Expedient, you mean.' The Nurian's pale features broke into a derogatory smile. 'You think you can make use of my revolution!'

'Quietly, Caro,' muttered Verlain. He glanced warily in the direction of the third tier, and the Governor's palace. 'Give me the address of a safe house.'

The man named Caro hesitated before answering. 'Ladder six, Kion Street,' he said. 'The house with the green door.'

'Perfect. I have a little surprise for your enemies. In two days' time your revolution will get a kick-start, my friend ...'

The conversation dropped out of Tymon's hearing and he leaned forward, straining to hear the whispered exchange. At last the priest's nasal murmur became audible once more.

'... meet you there with the goods, if you insist.'

'Very well. Though I will not be present to receive them. Come on the ninth of the month, at sunset — the house will be empty then. The door is never locked. You can leave the delivery in the back alcove, behind the stove.'

'You can rely on me.'

The yellow-haired man bowed his head in farewell, turned on his heel and disappeared from sight. Verlain shambled back into the compound.

Tymon pushed shut the cubicle door, his heart pounding, and dived for his hammock. The shuffling gait of the priest paused an instant outside his room then carried on. The door to his quarters clicked shut and a moment later candlelight bounced soft shadows over the open top of the wall. Tymon heard the fat man manoeuvre himself laboriously onto his sleeping couch. There was the scrape of a fire-stick, and a fresh cloud of *som* drifted over the gap to sting his eyes.

He lay awake in the darkness, his mind buzzing with questions. Why was the seminary brokering a secret deal with Nurian rebels? Who were the members of the 'movement' the Council found sympathetic? Were they Samiha's friends? He racked his brains to imagine why the Council was aiding a revolution in its own colony, and realised that there was only one sure way to solve the mystery. He would have to lie in wait for Verlain's associate on the evening of the ninth. He would have to find out what goods were being delivered to the Nurian safe house, and to whom.

Even after reaching this decision he was unable to rest. Somehow, finding out that Verlain was linked to the rebels did nothing to reassure him or improve his opinion of the fat priest. He bewailed the fact that Samiha was lost to him, and that he was unable to discuss the matter with her. He could not imagine her having anything to do with the Council. He tossed and turned in his hammock through the dark hours till dawn. It was a long time before the smoke from Verlain's pipe lulled him back to sleep.

14

From that moment on, Tymon took nothing for granted at the mission. His unease about Verlain grew. He made an effort to stay awake during the night and noted that although the priest lit up several pipefuls of *som*, he spent very little time in his quarters, pacing outside in the courtyard to the early hours. The pipe was left to smoke on its own, sending sticky clouds into Tymon's cubicle. A cold insight crept over the boy. The sedative was destined for him. He was being kept out of Verlain's way, segregated from whatever business the priest was conducting under cover of darkness. His hatred of the seminary flared up once more. To be drugged and lied to was as vexing as any injustice he had experienced in Argos. He wrapped a damp cloth across his mouth and nose to cut the effects of the smoke, and observed the fat man's every move. But he did not witness any further clandestine activity in the days leading up to the meeting in Kion Street.

That week, the atmosphere of unrest in Marak worsened considerably. The official water-toll soared to ten *taleks* a measure, the equivalent of a barrelful of the useless strawpaper *pon*, and the town rumbled with dissent. Both the heat and the tension reached fever pitch. To add to Tymon's dismay, the mission cistern was running low and he was faced with the prospect of a trip to the official water dispensary at the custom house. He had come to dread the periodic expedition to fill the cistern; the task summed up everything he hated most about life in the colony. The youthful mob of Nurian refugees targeted him every time he arrived on the quays with his heavy shoulder-yoke and two covered buckets, as if his errand were a direct insult to them. He would have to fight through the crowd to the dispensary, wait in line to have his allotment of water doled out by soldiers then lug his precious load back to the mission, pursued all the way by a band of ragged beggar children. He was not allowed to spare them so much as a ladleful, and could only hurry through the streets, feeling guilty and wretched, with their shrill accusations ringing in his ears: *Putar. You kill mother, you eat baby.* He put off each trip for as long as he possibly could and waited until the cistern had attained a murky low before confronting his ordeal again.

By the eighth day of the Water month, he was obliged to face the inevitable. Verlain had luckily dispensed with his copying services, and he delayed his departure for the quays until late that afternoon, hoping that the temperature would abate. It did not. At last he had no choice but to hoist up his heavy yoke in the wilting heat. He was about to exit the compound gates, the cumbersome buckets banging and thumping against his legs, when a door slammed behind him and Verlain's nasal voice echoed out across the courtyard.

'Wait, my boy. I have a job for you, if you're going down to the air-harbour.'

The fat priest waddled up to him with unusual alacrity, his bulk heaving under his stained robe. He had a sheaf of strawpaper in one hand.

'The promotional bills for this year's tithe have arrived,' he announced, flourishing the papers. 'Cost me a fair fortune in bribes to the Governor's office, too. You're to put them up in the main market and on the quays.'

Tymon's shrinking gaze took in the block-printed letters, the ink bleeding through the cheap grain. BE A PILGRIM! SIGN UP FOR THE MARAK TITHE! proclaimed the handbills in cheery capitals. ADVANCE WAGES IN WATER! Then in smaller letters at the bottom: *Candidates present themselves directly to the tithe-ship authorities. Conditions apply.*

'I thought you didn't agree with the seminary's policies, sir,' he muttered, taken aback. The next tithe-ship was not due for months. Why was Verlain suddenly so keen on recruiting pilgrims?

'Agree, disagree, it all comes to the same thing in the end,' gulped the priest, nervously. His eyes searched the corners of the compound, as if he were expecting someone to jump out at him from the shadows. He was not even particularly drunk. 'Truth is relative, so stick to the lies you know, I say,' he babbled.

He thrust the wad of paper at Tymon, who struggled to catch the bills while balancing his yoke. As if on second thoughts, Verlain rummaged in the grimy purse at his belt and withdrew a whole *talek* piece, which he slipped on top of the paper bundle. For a moment the boy thought he was going to ask for yet more *som*. But Verlain only winked connivingly at him.

'Buy the gum for the bills with this and spend whatever's left on yourself,' he breathed, with crude familiarity. 'I know what it's like to be a fine young blade. Go and buy some pretty native thing to amuse you in the tent-town, whatever suits your tastes, eh? I won't expect you back early at the mission tonight.'

The strawpaper bills might have been red-hot embers; they certainly burned a hole in Tymon's hands as he hurried down the main ramp towards the first tier market. He felt hot with disgust, too, revolted by Verlain's insinuations. The bribe of a *talek* piece, more money than he had ever had to call his own, burdened his pocket and his conscience. He was faced with a quandary. He could neither leave the handbills lying in the street, nor throw them away for fear of reprisal. He had absolutely no intention of putting them up on the walls of the town. He might not be anything more than an errand-boy for a drunkard, but he would not stoop to helping the seminary fill its tithe-ships. He clutched the irksome papers in one hand and his yoke in the other, cursing through his teeth all the way to the entrance of the first tier. There, he paused to catch his breath on a relatively deserted section of the ramp.

The start of the bazaar was still some distance away, around a corner and out of sight; its dim, confused murmur reached his ears. He lowered his buckets, wiped the sweat from his face and gazed vacantly at a nearby house-front. It was a moment before he noticed the writing on the wall.

The King shall come,
The King shall come.
The Year returns, all to burn.
Dead wood done, worlds made one.

Tymon stared at the inscription daubed in red paint. The poem, if it could be called one, stirred his heart. The words chimed in his mind as if he had heard them, or something like them, before. An enigmatic signature was scrawled below the verse, a circle attached to what appeared to be a crooked trident. He guessed that it was the handiwork of Nurian rebels, though it conveyed little in the way of a political message. The message was more of an invocation than a slogan.

'Move along now, young fellow, move along.'

A self-important little man in military costume had walked up to him as he stood dreaming over the verse. The soldier bore a scrubbing brush and a straw pail of dirty water, and carried a covered basket on his back.

'Step aside, you're obstructing access,' he sniffed.

The boy stuffed the handbills under his arm and rolled his buckets out of the way. The soldier deposited his basket on the ramp. Then he sauntered up to the wall and began scrubbing off the writing with the aid of his brush.

'Who wrote that?' Tymon asked him curiously. 'What King will come?'

'Damn Nurry rebels, may they rot in hell,' offered the diminutive soldier. He stabbed a finger at the trident sign. 'They mean their own dung-heap saviour, of course. You see before you the sign of the long-lost Nurian royal louse — oh, pardon me, I meant royal house.' He snorted with derision. 'Apparently that dried-up joke of a bloodline is going to produce the High King, the Green Lord who will restore the glory of old Nur and make the canopy bloom again. Remember your temple classes? The End Times.'

And as he said it, Tymon did remember — remembered the nasal voice of Father Rede reciting a passage of Grafting scripture, all fire and judgment and overwrought imagery. *And lo, the Year shall come to pass, and five trumpets blow, and five leaves fall. And all things shall burn, for dead wood is destined to burn. Ye shall see the Tree die, and a third of the things upon Her die, and a third of the things above Her die, and a third of the things below Her die. Then shall the Kingdom be free. Then shall the King return unto his own* ... It appeared that ancient prophecies were still popular reading for Nurians, mused the boy. Perhaps the present held little interest for them.

The little soldier continued to scour the wall, puffing with disdain.

'A King of Nur!' he fumed. 'Imagine! A bunch of dirty lice who can't even wash themselves properly, let alone rule the canopy. They can produce as many royal louses as they like, as far as I'm concerned. None of them will stand up to us!'

Tymon peered over the man's shoulder at the rapidly disappearing words. '*Worlds made one.* What does that mean?'

The militiaman shrugged, exasperated. 'How should I know what this nonsense means? One thing I can tell you: some day, we're going to teach these hoodlums a lesson. No more handouts, you lazy sons of whores. No more civilisation, you stinking barbarians. Yes, things are going to change around here. Just wait and see.'

He gave an unpleasant smirk and began whistling the tune to 'The Merry Bells', an Argosian favourite.

'But ...' The blasphemy came bubbling out of Tymon's mouth. 'Surely there's a way to reach some sort of an agreement with the Nurians? I mean, we're all in this together, aren't we?'

The soldier's eyes grew round in disbelief.

'"In this together"?' he echoed jeeringly. 'You're a bleeding-heart choirboy, aren't you? What do you know about it? All you home-borns can kiss my hardworking colonist's rump. What has Argos ever done for us? Crippling taxes, no water relief and a stinking degenerate for a mission priest. No thank you. We know what you fine religious folks get up to at home. Perverts and drunks. That's not the way we do things here! In Marak, we have pride! We have purity! We won't be overtaken by a horde of dirty whiteys, and we won't let 'em turn our women into whores!'

Tymon retreated under the soldier's tirade, trying his best not to smile and almost tripping over his buckets in the process. The indignant colonist reminded him very much of Father Rede. The physiognomy of the man, his accent, even the attitude of deep disdain were identical to those of his former tutor. Tymon wondered if he had happened upon some long-lost relative, or if the 'white-necks' all came from a certain, limited mould. He recovered his yoke and his composure with some difficulty, and staggered away down the ramp.

As he passed the little man's covered basket, however, he hesitated. The soldier no longer graced him with his notice, applying himself with much diligence and offended dignity to his scrubbing. Tymon glanced about the ramp. None of the passers-by were close enough to mark what he was doing. With a quick movement, he opened the lid of the basket and slipped Verlain's promotional handbills deep beneath a pile of rags and refuse. He could always tell the priest that his bills had been taken down by the soldiers. By the time the colonist's haughty gaze found him once more, he was weaving merrily down the road, his buckets swinging behind him.

He was still grinning to himself over this private triumph when his eye lit on the second inscription. Further along the street another set of words had been daubed on a different doorway, followed by the same trident signature.

There is no haven, no place to shelter in, far from you.

Nowhere to turn, nowhere to run, for every city burns, far from you.

The smile faded from Tymon's face and he shivered. The second verse was darker than the first; it gave him no comfort, made no promises of salvation. He wondered what madman was writing these lines and how he could possibly imagine that they would inspire popular feeling. Flames and death there were in the Nurian revolution, but no hope. No wonder the spectre of fire haunted his nights, he reflected sourly as he hurried on. Marak had rubbed off on him. He took a deep breath before plunging into the clamour and chaos of the bazaar.

His movement in the packed market was reduced to a crawl. A thick, miasmic odour of refuse hung in the air and the crowd oozed past the shops and vending booths with infuriating slowness. By the time the boy had negotiated his way to the foot of the first tier, the sun was westering. He became impatient, worried that the custom house would be closed before he arrived on the air-harbour. But barely fifty feet from the entrance to the city his progress stalled completely. A bleating herd of shillees remained between him and his goal. They blocked his path with their foolish, spotted backs and fixed him with slack-jawed stares, refusing to budge. He could neither move forwards nor backwards.

As he stood there, thwarted and fuming, voices rose in protest from further up the ramp. He turned around to see a gaudy, curtained litter swaying over the heads of the crowd, accompanied by a troupe of bodyguards. The minders whipped everyone out of their way, laying mercilessly into the Nurian bystanders with their hardwood clubs. Again and again they brought their weapons down on the unfortunate people trapped in the path of the litter, shouting at them to be gone, to move aside. But there was no empty space for the Nurians to move to. Figures collapsed under the rain of blows and did not get up. The litter bearers trampled over them.

The water yoke fell from Tymon's shoulders with a clatter. The shillees erupted into a paroxysm of bleating as he backed into the shelter of a nearby doorway. He had never seen such brutality before. The guards appeared to be overtaken by a frenzy of senseless cruelty. They struck at anything within arm's length — man or woman, animal or child. The litter swung by Tymon and the curtains covering its sides parted for an instant. Within, he glimpsed a young Argosian woman wearing a tasselled headdress. Her face was beautiful, smiling and entirely self-satisfied. The litter barged through the city gates, scattering panicked animals on every side.

As soon as the box and its train had disappeared the crowd erupted. Cries of 'putar' and 'Argosi' filled the air. The throng parted and Tymon saw that there were bloodied bodies on the ramp. These were hoisted onto people's shoulders, the piteous, battered limbs dangling over the backs of the bearers. The crowd surged as one towards the gates; the boy was swept along by it, his buckets abandoned. He kept his face lowered, praying that nobody would identify him as a foreigner. For now the mob seemed oblivious to anything but its own headlong momentum. It burst out of the first tier, through the air-harbour and into the tent-town, flowing through the refugee quarter like a torrent of rain. Tymon tried to keep his bearings in the cluttered, canvas-lined streets but was soon hopelessly lost. The din of voices took up a common, rhythmic chant.

'Shanti. Shanti. Shanti.'

The stampede came to an abrupt halt in a narrow alleyway, in front of a makeshift building half-obscured by a jumble of tents and awnings. Tymon was jostled along with everyone else into an unfurnished hall decorated only with patterned weave-mats. The bodies of the victims were set down on the floor and he realised for the first time that they were all dead. The cry of 'shanti, shanti ...' faded away. After a moment, another sound pierced the silence: a single voice chanting, clear and poignant. It reverberated in the domed ceiling of the hall. A shiver passed through the boy. He had heard that lilting voice each day, delivering the First Liturgy in Nurian. The melody it sang now was different, if equally familiar. As the Song of the Dead rang out in the hall with the solemn intonation of a dirge, Tymon understood that he had found the Nurian shrine at last.

This time the ghostly voice did not sing alone. The people in the hall took up the chant, responding to the singer in a repeated refrain. As the lament went on, individuals stepped out of the crowd, approaching the bodies in the central space. Some knelt down hesitantly to touch a bloodied face or hand. Others simply stood there with their heads bowed. One small child squatted by a man and shook his shoulder, as if trying to wake him. The death-rite worked its spell on Tymon. The wrenching melody brought a lump to his throat and the memory of the pointless butchery in the market filled him with anger. He hardly noticed that the people about him had moved away to give the mourners room. The chant came to an end and he was left alone, exposed at the edge of the circle.

'*Putar.*'

The accusation hissed through the gathering, jolting him awake. He became aware of his vulnerable position — too late. He had been seen. The Nurians surrounded him with horrifying speed, and before he could do more than think of retreat, he was enclosed by a wall of hostile faces. Fear dragged at the pit of his stomach.

'*Putar.* You are not welcome here.'

The general buzz of rage resolved itself into one voice. The speaker stepped out of the throng. He was a tall man with a yellow hair and waxy features, his pale blue eyes blank with hatred.

'You are not welcome, Argos,' he sneered, advancing on Tymon.

The mob surged forward. Tymon was pushed violently from behind and lost his balance, stumbling towards the yellow-haired man. The seconds slowed to a crawl as his grinning adversary raised a fist to meet him. He heard the dull crack as the blow connected with his ribs. He stared up at his opponent in surprise, for he had belatedly identified the man as Caro, Verlain's accomplice.

Then a searing agony pulsed through him and he fell to his knees. With a roar of triumph the members of the crowd closed in, kicking him.

'*Bas.*'

The ringing command brought the tumult in the shrine to an abrupt halt. Tymon's attackers pulled away, abandoning him on the floor. He glanced up painfully towards the source of the voice. A figure descended a ladder from a trapdoor in the ceiling; he grasped that the call to prayer was sung on the roof and that this must be the singer. The crowd opened ranks as the boy picked himself up to face his advocate. It was a woman.

'Do not harm the stranger,' said the newcomer, gravely.

It was an instant before he recognised her. Samiha! No longer the half-starved, runaway pilgrim, the red-haired girl was dressed in long green robes and walked tall and straight, with obvious authority. She returned his gaze coolly, as if she had never seen him before in her life.

'Why not, *shanti?*' cried the yellow-haired man. 'He is a *putar*. Our enemy.'

'Not this one, Caro,' she answered. 'The Focals spoke of him.'

Her explanation seemed to be sufficient for the crowd. Nobody challenged her, and although the man named Caro frowned angrily, he did not speak. Tymon was given no chance to respond. The clamour of voices mounted about him and he was seized by many hands and thrust out of the shrine into the relative cool of the evening. The doors slammed shut behind him. He blundered a short distance down the street, his head reeling, before he understood where he was. The Nurian shrine stood not a hundred feet from the air-harbour quays. He had passed the little street almost every day on his errands for Verlain without noticing it. The entrance of the shrine was hidden from where he stood, but he could make out the domed roof of the building, silhouetted against the brilliant evening sky. High above it, the Friend star shone clear and bright.

He made his way slowly back through the first tier, doubled up with pain. The yellow-haired Nurian had cracked his ribs. The memory of the mangled bodies on the floor of the shrine and the unexpected reunion with Samiha all throbbed together in his mind, and he felt sickened and shaken. He wandered into the deserted market and tried to retrieve his water buckets from the side of the ramp. But the yoke was too heavy to lift in his bruised state. He gave up and continued laboriously on to the mission. He met a squadron of soldiers coming towards him who informed him that there had been a riot in the bazaar, and that he should return to the mission immediately. Tymon acquiesced silently. He could not look the guards in their faces. He arrived at the compound exhausted and awash with conflicting emotions. He had no wish to associate himself with the brutality of the colonists. But his crushed ribs confirmed that he had no hope, indeed had never had any hope of finding refuge with Samiha.

The pilgrim girl had been right there in the city all this time, but had obviously thought it unnecessary to contact him. She was a *shanti*, one of the infamous Nurian priestesses. Her responsibility lay with her people, not with him. He did not know whether to hate or respect her for it. The reality of his tenuous position, of being caught between two worlds, came home to him with full force. He understood clearly that if revolt broke out in the city no one would shelter him, not even the one person he had come to consider a friend. And yet she had saved him from being beaten to pulp, or worse. She evidently had no wish to see him hurt. Like the rhyme on the wall, her words haunted him, teasing recollection. Who were the Focals? Why did the mere mention of them suffice the Nurians in the shrine? And why above all was someone like Samiha associated with Caro, an ally of the Council?

His questions had no answers and he was too tired to pursue them. The mission was quiet as he dragged himself through the gates. Verlain was nowhere to be seen. The boy lurched gratefully into his smoke-free cubicle and eased his aching body into his hammock. Whatever the risk to himself, he decided, he had no intention of leaving the matter as it stood. He would find Samiha the next day and attempt to speak with her privately. He would insist that she acknowledge him. He could not simply sit by while the maddening girl with flame-coloured hair slipped through his fingers once again.

15

The next morning, however, he could barely stand up. His ribs were sore and inflamed and he extracted himself from the hammock with great difficulty. Verlain was evidently back in his sleeping quarters, for oily tendrils of *som* crept over the wall, accompanied by the priest's resonant snores. Tymon hobbled out into the courtyard to find Amu Bibi hard at work with her indefatigable broom. She clucked in disapproval at the sight of him, and threatened him with the broom-handle until he stripped off his tunic and showed her his injuries. A large purple weal stretched over his left side.

'Ai,' she expostulated, raising her hands in dismay. 'You fall on angry fist!'

She made him lie on the couch under the awning and disappeared into the kitchen, re-emerging a few moments later with an assortment of salves, ointments and bandages. These she applied to Tymon's bruises, scolding him briskly in her polyglot style. The boy had discovered that her quaint speech was more than a personal eccentricity. Many Nurians in the city spoke a 'twig-tongue', a form of Argosian liberally spiced with words in their own language. Over the past few weeks he had reviewed his first, hasty judgment of the old woman's mental ability: she was as sharp as a hardwood pin.

The searing fire in his side abated. When Amu Bibi was satisfied with her handiwork she sat down beside him, pursed her lips and fixed him with a beady eye.

'*Argosi* not welcome in *Nuri* shrine,' she pronounced. 'You be careful, not hasten next life.'

Tymon glanced at the crone in surprise. 'How do you know about the shrine, Amu?'

'I know all.' She tapped the side of her nose. 'I speak to Sap.'

He stared at her. She erupted into a dry cackle, rocking with mirth. 'I have nephews in tent-town, yes?' she grinned. 'But you not careful! Stupid! Enemies everywhere!'

'Amu,' he pleaded earnestly, 'please tell me. How can I find the *shanti*?'

She watched him a while in silence, her colourless eyes appraising him from top to toe.

'*Shanti* find you,' she answered finally. 'She have powerful friends. See Sap. Find you, if you wish.'

'You really believe in the Grafting, don't you?' He could not keep a note of derision from his voice. 'Does the *shanti* go in for all that prophecy and soothsaying nonsense as well?'

The smile died on the crone's cracked lips and she turned away from him towards the compound entrance. After a moment, the sound of running feet echoed through the gates and a perspiring soldier trotted into the courtyard. He cleared his throat, fixed his gaze somewhere above the heads of his listeners and unrolled an official leaf-scroll with aplomb.

'By order of the Grand High Governor,' he cried, 'Marak city is placed under martial law, on this the ninth day of the Water month. Curfew will begin an hour after sunset and terminate an hour before dawn. No citizen shall go forth into the city after curfew. Furthermore, citizens of Argosian descent, and members of the erstwhile temple mission —' here the soldier licked his lips with evident enjoyment '—are discouraged from leaving their homes unless absolutely necessary, as they are targets for rebel agitators. This state of emergency shall continue until the twelfth of the month. Thereafter a new proclamation will be made.'

At the close of his speech the man rolled up his leaf, turned smartly about and strode away from the compound without another word.

'No time left,' exclaimed Amu Bibi, jumping up from the couch with surprising vigour. 'Must leave now.'

'Wait!' cried Tymon after her. 'Tell me more! I'm sorry I laughed, Amu!'

But the old woman was already gone, her tattered shawl fluttering after her through the gates. The door to Verlain's room creaked open and the priest's heavy tread approached.

'What was all that commotion about?' The fat man's voice was querulous.

Tymon tried to escape the couch before he arrived, but succeeded only in raising himself to a sitting position. Verlain's lard-like mass quivered in front of him.

'By the bells, you're hurt!' he exclaimed.

'It's nothing, sir,' mumbled the boy, mortified.

'Far from it. This is terrible! I feel responsible — I sent you into the tent-town yesterday, may God forgive me.' To his dismay, Verlain squeezed onto the divan beside him, wrapping a flabby arm about his shoulders. 'You were caught in the riot, were you not?'

'I was just in the wrong place at the wrong time, Father,' Tymon protested, ducking his head in vain to be free of the arm. 'Amu Bibi's already seen to it. It's not so bad.'

'Terrible, terrible,' the priest murmured unctuously. 'These Nurries are animals, aggressive by nature. And the local *shanti* incites them to violence, you know ...'

He shook his flaccid chins, his breath reeking in Tymon's face. With a burst of energy born of desperation, the boy pulled himself free and sprang up from the couch. It was his employer's sympathy he dreaded, rather than his displeasure. He had no desire to answer questions from the priest about his experience the previous day, and wished at all costs to avoid the subject of the handbills.

'I'm fine,' he gasped. 'Don't worry about me, Father. I really should be doing the water-run. The cistern's almost dry. I left the buckets down in the market yesterday.'

He limped out of the compound, deaf to Verlain's protestations.

The energy that had propelled him from the mission dissipated by the time he reached the first tier. The bazaar was unusually empty that morning and only a small number of stall-keepers served the people hurrying by. Soldiers stood in knots along the ramp, surveying the street with impenetrable calm. Copies of the Governor's edict had been posted at regular intervals on the walls. Tymon found his buckets near the palisade where he had left them, but did not shoulder the yoke at once. He lingered a moment by the side of the ramp, torn with indecision. He had no real wish to fetch water, to brave the throng on the quays, and certainly no desire to return to the mission. The marketplace seemed steeped in the memory of violence and his ribs ached at the thought of revisiting the shrine in an attempt to locate Samiha. He sat down with a grunt of pain on one of the upturned buckets.

It was then that he saw the signature. Daubed on the doorway above his buckets was the ubiquitous crooked trident, this time without an accompanying verse. He was certain it had not been there during the riot. He frowned at the enigmatic symbol, struck by its form. Almost mechanically, he reached into his tunic pocket and retrieved the key ring that Samiha had given him. The resemblance was obvious. The signature repeated the design of the prison keys, a circular haft above a three-pronged shank. The symbol was a stylised key, not a trident.

Was it a coincidence? Tymon's pulse quickened as he gazed at the key ring. He had not taken it out of his pocket since the day of the tempest aboard the *Stargazer*, initially for fear that someone would discover him in possession of stolen property. Later in Marak, other matters had distracted him and he had not studied the key ring closely. Now, as he held it up and scrutinised it in a shaft of morning sun, he could have sworn there were scratches on the inside surface, on the blackened part of the ring. He turned the bunched keys first this way, then that. At last he hit on the right angle of light. The resin on the ring was indeed scored with faint marks. New words had been added to the existing text.

'*If found, please return to 6 Key Street*,' he whispered, reading the amended inscription.

Samiha had acknowledged him after all! She had wanted him to contact her, left him a message. The horror of the events of the previous day vanished completely and he hurried as quickly as he could to one of the few manned stalls in the market, forsaking his buckets once again.

'I need to find Key Street,' he burst out to the man in the stall, without preamble.

The merchant, a dour-faced Nurian with a long nose like the speckled fruit on his stand, indicated the collection of wizened frogapples before him.

'One *talek* for the lot,' he declared. 'It's a bargain, *Argosi*.'

Tymon hesitated, staggered at the astronomical price and the demand for Argosian currency. 'I just want directions —' he began.

'One *talek*,' snapped the man. 'Do you want them or not?'

His gaze flicked meaningfully towards group of militia soldiers ambling down the ramp. Tymon realised that his conversation was being monitored. Slowly, he withdrew Verlain's money from his tunic pocket.

'Give me the lot,' he sighed, pushing the hardwood counter towards the man.

'With pleasure,' smirked the merchant. The money was whisked away and the pile of dismal fruit dumped into a box in its place.

'You'll find my cousin's stall three streets up, on your right,' remarked the vendor, as he dusted off the table. 'He'll have the beans and greens you want. Brought fresh today in spite of the curfew.'

'Three streets up, on the right,' repeated Tymon. 'You're sure?'

The other pushed the box towards him. 'That's what I said,' he yawned.

The soldiers moved on towards the gates and the boy exhaled with relief.

'Thank you,' he murmured to the stall owner, and hurried away up the ramp, the box of shrivelled fruit under his arm.

'No problem. Come again!' sang out the merchant from behind him.

Tymon had already passed the first narrow road intersecting the main ramp and reached the second before it occurred to him to doubt the trader's word. His pace slowed as he reached the third turn-off to his right. It was more of an alley than a street. There was no sign at the entrance to the dusty by-way, no indication that this was the Key Street he had been told to find. He paused a moment at the mouth of the alley, examining its dingy recesses. Then he continued on, his footsteps echoing in the narrow space between the buildings. He had to take the chance. He had to see if the message on the ring would lead him anywhere. The passage was steep and winding, and spiralled down successive flights of steps. He squinted up at the faded numbers over the doorways; many were missing or illegible, but he established finally that they went in decreasing order. At length he arrived at the address written on the ring, an upper-storey apartment near the city palisade, accessible only by ladder. He stood in the courtyard below, eyeing the non-descript building and shabby balcony overhead.

'I must be mad,' he sighed. He stepped onto the ladder and began to climb, wincing as the movement chafed his ribs.

'Then it is a good madness,' replied a well-known voice from above. 'Welcome to my home, *Argosi*.'

The balcony, empty a moment before, was now occupied. Tymon glanced up with a thrill of joy to see Samiha at the railing. The *shanti* was no longer dressed in her ceremonial green robes but wore a simple white shift and breeches, her hair knotted in a long rope over one shoulder. She smiled at him as he climbed laboriously up the remaining rungs of the ladder.

'I'm truly sorry about what happened in the temple last night,' she said, helping him to install himself somewhat shakily beside her. 'I'm sorry I couldn't let on that I knew you. The trouble in the market — the deaths of those poor people — it

284

wasn't the right time. I hope you'll forgive me.' She glanced at the box he still carried under his arm, pressed to his good side. 'Ah. You brought ... frogapples. How nice.'

He thrust the box to one side of the balcony. 'They're not very fresh,' he muttered. He could not put words to the sweet rush of excitement that took hold of him when he was in her company. 'Don't worry about the temple,' he added hurriedly, opting for her designation of the shrine. 'Did you know anyone caught in the riot?'

'Not personally,' she sighed. 'I fear there will be consequences for what took place yesterday, Tymon. People are very angry.'

'I'll vouch for that,' he replied with feeling. 'I thought I'd never be able to talk to you again without having my bones broken. I didn't see the message on the ring until this morning.'

'So that's what kept you so long.' She laughed. 'Granted, I was writing in the light of the storm-lanterns, with a splinter of wood, but still! A whole month ... Well, they did say you needed to find us on your own, and that you'd do it today.'

'They?'

'The Focals.' She beckoned to him. 'Come inside and meet them. They should be ready soon. Meanwhile, we'll see about some refreshment.'

He followed her, wondering, through a little door leading off the balcony.

'I had no other way of reaching you that night on the ship,' she continued over her shoulder. 'I wanted to tell you I was grateful for your help, among other things.'

They entered a modest apartment under the eaves of the building. The front room was no more than twenty paces wide and unfurnished, like the shrine in the tent-town. Two doorways hung with bright curtains opened out of the far wall; the floors were piled with weave-mats. The cloth on the left-hand doorway was drawn aside, revealing a small and equally austere sleeping alcove. Tymon glimpsed five people, two women and three men, seated in the alcove, forming a circle. They appeared to be in some form of reverie or trance, for their eyes were shut. They sat silent and straight-backed.

'Do not disturb the Focals,' cautioned Samiha, in an undertone. 'Wait here. I'll be back shortly.'

She slipped through the right-hand curtain. The boy settled himself down on the floor of the main room and scrutinised the five individuals in the alcove. They were dressed much like the *shanti*, in loose-fitting white robes. A white-haired old man and a tiny woman, frail and wrinkled, sat on one side of the circle. The young couple across from them might have been only a few years older than Tymon, though it was hard to be sure: Nurians quickly lost their youth to sun and hardship. The final member of the group, a man in his middle age, had his back to the curtained doorway. His weather-beaten face was obscured by a shock of dark hair.

Tymon craned his neck to catch a glimpse of the fifth Focal's features. He could have sworn he had seen the man before — somewhere in the first tier market, perhaps, or half-noticed in the tent quarter the previous evening. The word 'Focal' was also known to him, though he could not place it at once. It had to do with Grafting, he remembered suddenly. The people in the alcove were practising a Grafting trance. He had stumbled onto a group of Nurian heretics, probably the very same 'Sap cult' he had been warned about. He recalled Verlain's stories of an apostate priestess leading young men astray in the city. Nothing, much to his personal regret, seemed further from the truth where Samiha was concerned.

As he thought of her she reappeared and placed a small tray table with folding legs in front of him. It bore two drinking bowls and a hardwood pot.

'I hope you like *yosha*,' she said.

Without waiting for an answer, she knelt down and poured steaming green liquid from the pot into one of the bowls, handing it to him. Tymon lifted the fragrant container to his lips. He had not yet tried the traditional Nurian drink — Verlain would have nothing at the mission that was not at least slightly intoxicating. The sweet infusion was delicious, rich and light. He gulped it down gratefully. He found the apartment hot and airless and the *yosha* refreshed him.

'What's a Focal?' he asked Samiha, although he could guess her reply.

She filled her own bowl with great care, as if the *yosha* were precious. Her face was concentrated over the steaming pot. 'They are Grafters, Tymon. The five chief practitioners in the canopy, to be precise. Few mortals have their power.'

'And they knew in advance that I'd be coming.' He tried to keep his tone non-committal, to suspend judgment until he had heard more. It was difficult. He was used to rejecting claims of magic and sorcery outright.

'Yes. They Saw it during their last trance,' she said, stressing the word.

Tymon smiled. 'Do they have the Sight, then? Does the Tree speak to them, like the Saints in the old days?'

'The Tree you're thinking of, the World Tree, is just that — a giant plant, no more sentient than the frogapples you brought this morning.' She peered at him over the lip of her bowl. 'The Focals speak to the Sap. You know what that is, right?'

'I've been trying to forget what I learned in Treeology class, but yes.'

'If that's all you learned, then we're in trouble,' she chuckled. 'For Nurians, the Sap isn't some mystic force outside you. It's here,' she tapped a finger on her jugular, 'closer than your life's vein. It runs through everything. We're alive because of it.'

She paused to gauge the effect of her words. He stifled his impatience. It appeared that Samiha did indeed believe in soothsaying nonsense of the sort spouted by Amu Bibi. He wished, in vain, that the conversation would take another turn.

'Events and people are connected. They're one thing, like the branches of the Tree,' she resumed, watching him closely. 'That's why the Grafters can See the future — you are the future. You're becoming it. Your priests in Argos have forgotten their own basic teachings. Or perhaps they simply

288

lied to you. I don't suppose they told you that you are part of the Tree of Being, the sacred body of the universe, and that the Sap moves through you —'

'They aren't *my* priests, Samiha,' he interrupted with a sigh. 'And you talk as if there's some mighty conspiracy against Nurian wisdom. How are we Argosians to know what you believe, way out here in the Eastern Canopy?'

She blinked at him in surprise. 'Where do you suppose your own culture comes from? Don't you remember that your people came from Nur, hundreds of years ago?' Her voice had risen a little, and she glanced remorsefully in the direction of the Focals before continuing in a curt whisper. 'What we believe is what you believed, to start with, anyway.'

'Leave me out of it. I don't believe in anything,' he said. 'I'm not interested in being part of some mystic Tree. The ordinary one is enough for me. I think all this is a waste of time.'

'Poor *Argosi*.' She spoke gently, even condescendingly, as if he, not her, were the oppressed member of a slave race. 'The priests have robbed you of your birthright. There's an awesome power at work in the world, a power in you, in the movement of leaves and the flight of birds. *The Tree grows, the Sap flows.* But you don't See it. They've made you blind.'

'Actually, it's more like the reverse,' he growled. 'I've had this sort of craziness repeated to me my whole life. I've had the Saints and prophets and their precious Grafting drummed into my skull until I want to throw the pack of 'em into the

Storm. I don't believe in it because it's ridiculous, that's why.'

'Not even when the Council's Grafters were working under your very nose? Oh yes,' she retorted to his questioning stare, 'Argosian soothsaying didn't come to an end with Saint Loa or Saint Usala. But the Council doesn't like us ordinary folks knowing of such things. They oversee all Grafting activity in Argos — or what they would like to call Grafting. Sorcery, more like. How else would they twist a man's mind until he jumps into a Tree-rift? Think about it.'

He did think about it, and drank his *yosha* in silence, at a loss as to how someone as intelligent as she was could fall for such foolishness. Now that he was in her company again, he recalled her exasperating habit of taking the higher moral tone. So righteous, always so righteous. His eyes strayed irritably to the group in the alcove as he tried to decide whether they, at least, would oblige him by being charlatans.

The Focals sat unmoving, rooted to the floor of the apartment. Their faces were tranquil. The boy was struck by the fact that they were able to sit still in a hot room for so long. They had not moved a muscle since he came in the door. If they were charlatans then they were highly trained and highly talented, like the Jay magicians he had heard could perform miracles, piercing their flesh with hardwood pins or slowing their pulse to appear dead. The figures on the weave-mat might have been made of wood.

'And you really believe they can see the future?'

he asked Samiha, gesturing towards the Focals. 'You believe in the Saints, the Grafting prophecies, all that stuff?'

'Particularly in all that stuff, as you call it,' she observed. 'That's why I travelled to Argos in the first place.' A spasm of regret passed over her face. 'Actually, it was Juno's idea to go. He was studying with the Focals.'

Tymon's heart beat a little faster. He thought he understood now. The five people on the mat were rebels, whatever their bizarre beliefs. They were the friends Samiha had mentioned, the enemies of the Council.

'So the Focals sent you to Argos,' he breathed.

'No one sent me,' she answered quickly, almost defensively. 'I went on behalf of the Focals, yes. But they didn't send me.'

This nicety was beyond Tymon. 'Well then, you went on their behalf,' he said. 'And you say you found the priests using Grafting on the pilgrims.' She nodded. 'But why didn't the Focals do something about that themselves? Or couldn't they stand up to the priests?'

'They can, and they do. Though again not in the way you mean. The Rites were only one concern of ours. Juno and I were looking for a Sign of the Sap in Argos city, the fulfilment of a prophecy. One that predicts the end of Argosian power — the end of all power based on hate and tyranny.' Her smile became eager as she leaned forward. 'There are times when the Sap flows more strongly, Tymon. We're privileged to be alive at such a time. The Year of Fire is upon us.'

He frowned in amazement. She sounded like the poetry on the walls of the city.

'Help me to understand,' he said. 'You came all the way to Argos city, risked your life — your friend lost his life — simply because of some prophecy of the End Times?' It seemed too ridiculous to contemplate.

'It's not just any prophecy. The King returns, remember. Not a King in hiding like we have now, but the Green Lord, the High King of the Four Canopies, crowned in glory. Nur will be free. We'll all be free.'

Her eyes shone as she spoke. Tymon was shocked. He had assumed that, whatever her personal philosophy, the *shanti* was purely pragmatic when it came to fighting for Nurian freedom. Had he not known her better and witnessed her bravery first-hand, he might have dismissed her convictions as those of a crank.

'Why wait around for some mystic King to come and save you?' he scoffed. 'Why not save yourselves?'

'Do I look like I'm waiting around?' she asked dryly. 'The best way to save ourselves is to do the work of the Grafting. We can help the prophecies along.'

'I don't see why you'd want those particular prophecies to come true,' he objected. 'The world dying, and all ... A third of this, a third of that ... What if you're in the wrong third?'

'We Nurians are in the wrong third already, from what I can see,' she said sadly. 'The world is dying, Tymon. The Eastern Canopy has been dead for generations. There's no Tree-water, and precious little rain. We might as well go all the way.'

Tymon was reminded of Galliano's enthusiasm for other, more scientific apocalypses. The thought of his old friend was bittersweet.

'So, did you find it? Your omen?' he asked, deflated.

'Oh yes,' she replied with a mysterious smile. 'I believe we did.'

'What was it?'

As he spoke the group in the alcove stirred. All five people moved simultaneously. Their eyes were still closed, but they took hold of each other's hands.

'It is done,' Samiha murmured. 'Now we'll have some answers.'

He saw that her face was transfigured with hope. She genuinely believed in the prophecies her friends provided; if they were charlatans, then the *shanti* was as much duped as anyone. He considered the possibility warily as, one by one, the Focals opened their eyes and stood up. They exited the tiny alcove and came to join Tymon and Samiha on the floor of the front room. The two elders nodded to the boy but did not address him directly. Samiha rose and fetched more *yosha* to serve them. Once she had completed the round of the room, handing out bowls of the fragrant drink and exchanging a few quiet words in Nurian with her guests, she took her place again beside Tymon.

'Friends,' she announced as the group gazed expectantly at her, 'today is a good day. We have a visitor. This is Tymon of Argos. It is the first time in many years that a foreigner has witnessed a true Grafting. I call on you to tell us what you have Seen, though the tongue is strange.'

'*Beni, shanti*,' replied the old man. 'Forgive my *Argosi* speech, it is not good. Signs are counted. Year has begun.' He acknowledged Tymon with a kindly smile. 'We are glad you found path here, young one. Do not hate weakness —'

'— for weakness is strength,' interjected the old woman.

Tymon stared at her in surprise. The wizened little lady sitting next to the old man had finished his phrase as if it were her own. 'Soon you will choose your loyalties, *Argosi*,' she continued without missing a beat, her grasp of the foreign words easier. 'Choose well, and remember that strength lies in the Sap, not the stick.'

The old man did not appear in the least upset by her interference. He made a bobbing bow to Samiha.

'You have done well, *shanti*,' he said. 'Your journey bears fruit.'

The old woman also bowed to Samiha, murmuring '*shanti*' in turn; '*shanti, shanti, shanti*,' echoed the three other members of the circle, bobbing in succession like rooks in a roost.

'The time of testing has begun,' proclaimed the old woman. 'Events are now in motion that have been spoken of —'

'— for centuries,' put in the Nurian youth on her left. Again, the disruption appeared entirely natural, even expected. The young man went on as if his voice and the old woman's were one. 'Nothing can stand in our way. We have the victory. But that does not mean it will be —'

'— easy,' added the thin, pale girl beside him. She stumbled over the unfamiliar grammar, still holding tightly to the young man's hand though the others had separated. 'Fire Times show quality. Dead wood burns.'

Tymon felt a stab of disappointment. Apart from their unusual style of speech, the Focals' predictions were standard prophetic fare. This, then, was all he could hope for from the Grafting: a series of riddles, vague statements that could apply to anything or anyone. His irritation intensified, his mood exacerbated by the suffocating atmosphere in the room. The apartment was unbearably hot. He told himself that he should not have expected more from a group of wild-eyed zealots, and shifted restlessly in his seat.

'The next few days will be difficult, *shanti*,' resumed the old woman. 'The judgment is passed. The path is chosen. We have failed —'

'— the test,' completed the young man, frowning to himself in recollection. 'The vision was clear. All is not as it should be. We speak the language of hate, the language of fire, and that flame will consume us. Every action has a —'

'— consequence,' stammered the thin girl, her expression troubled. She seemed half-lost in her trance even now. She eyed the empty space at the centre of the room as if she saw something there that terrified her. 'We reap fire. It takes us, hearts and cities, all will —'

'— burn,' finished the fifth man, speaking for the first time.

Tymon shuddered. He was inclined to ask Samiha if he might open the balcony door, for an unpleasant, dizzy sensation had taken hold of him. Waves of dry heat travelled up his body and it occurred to him that the *yosha* might have disagreed with him. He barely listened to the litany of predictions.

'All will burn,' repeated the fifth Focal. 'All will suffer. High and low, rich and poor, guilty and innocent alike. There is no sanctuary. The choice is made, the path taken, all will —'

'— burn,' affirmed the man with white hair.

'Burn!' declared the old woman.

'Burn, burn, burn!' chanted the others in quick succession, their voices rising to a collective shout. All the Grafters now gazed at the space in the centre of the room.

'Burn!' cried Tymon belatedly, as he jumped to his feet, knocking over the tray of *yosha*.

For he had seen it. Rivers of flame had sprung into being before his eyes, consuming the air between the Focals: a vision, brief but unmistakable, of a city at the summit of a branch, burning like a torch. Then the momentary hallucination was gone and he was left standing, open-mouthed, among the spilled bowls. The Focals barely glanced at him. As usual, they showed no surprise at all at the interruption.

'Tymon, are you alright?' Samiha asked anxiously. She alone of the people in the room appeared startled by his outburst. 'Do you feel unwell?'

He passed a hand over his eyes. 'No!' he answered. 'I'm fine. I'm sorry. I don't know what came over me.' He sat down. 'Go on, I'm perfectly well,' he mumbled to the others, wilting in embarrassment.

And he did feel better. The heat and dizziness had drained out of him. The temperature in the room now seemed perfectly normal. He must have been dreaming, he thought. The events of the day before had exhausted him and he had been half asleep, hypnotised by the repetitive predictions. He berated himself for being so susceptible. The burning city had not even resembled Marak. It was a dream, he told himself, breathing deeply to calm his ragged pulse.

Whatever it had been, the episode in the apartment was now clearly over. A point of tension had passed. The Focals bowed their heads as if preparing to pray and took hold of each others' hands again. To his discomfort, Tymon found his own hands grasped by Samiha to his right, and, more awkwardly, by the fifth Focal to his left. He squirmed, unused to the touch of a stranger. The verse the Nurians chanted was part of no liturgy he knew.

'*In weakness, find strength,*' began the white-haired man.

'*In emptiness, power,*' continued the old woman quietly.

'*Worlds that were severed, we now bind together,*' finished the young couple, as one. The fifth Focal said nothing, but remained still, his head bowed.

The words sent a pulse of joy through Tymon, as if his body recognised them even if his mind did not. He quelled the reaction hastily, unwilling to be enthralled by the Grafters yet again. But the Focals seemed uninterested in further dramatics. Much to Tymon's relief, they let go of each other's hands and looked up. The atmosphere in the room lightened. Even the young girl appeared to be fully restored to the ordinary world; she gave Tymon a timid smile. The old man murmured something in the old woman's ear and the old woman made a wry remark in Nurian to her companions. Everyone laughed — except Samiha.

'Is there no more to be done, friends?' she broke in. 'Are we condemned to simply watch and wait for disaster?'

She sat hunched, her hands clenched in her lap. With some surprise, Tymon understood that the Grafters' prophecies had not been to her liking. All was not *as it should be*. He pricked up his ears.

'Advise me,' she pleaded. 'Surely we can do something to stop the worst from happening?'

It was the fifth Focal who answered, his green eyes as merry and kind as if he had just predicted good rainfall and a fine harvest instead of fire, failure and ruin.

'There is nothing you can do for now, *shanti*,' he said gently. 'Sometimes we must let a fever run its course. When the time for intervention comes, you'll know. You'll act swiftly to cut off the rotten member. Right now, any direct action would bring worse results.' He winked at Tymon. 'But here we have something more encouraging. A friend from the West! Samiha has told us of your exploits on the greatship. I'm glad to see you here at last, Tymon of Argos.'

The boy revived a little at the compliment, though he was too shy to do more than mumble his inarticulate thanks. He could not shake off the persistent impression that he had seen the fifth Focal before. Even on his own merits, the man was a complete puzzle. He spoke Argosian like a native, his accent flawless. His face was as dark as that of an Argosian too, and lined with suffering like a map. Only the eyes were too light and too foreign, a youthful flash under his grey locks. They seemed to pierce Tymon's very soul.

Could it be real? the boy wondered suddenly. Had he been wrong to dismiss what was going on in the apartment as foolishness or chicanery? Could these people actually see the future? He recalled that the Grafters of old were able to produce illusions, to conjure images out of thin air. Their creations could have great effect if people believed in them. Was that what he had seen, shimmering for an instant in the middle of the room? Had he witnessed a Seeming?

'Samiha,' he hissed, edging towards the *shanti* on the weave-mat. 'Tell me: did you notice anything strange during the Grafting?'

'Strange?' she repeated. She was preoccupied, staring absently at the pattern on the mat. 'No. What do you mean?'

He shrugged uncomfortably. 'Nothing. I just thought for a moment ... It's nothing. Forget it.'

She raised an eyebrow, but Tymon's embarrassment had won over his curiosity and he refused to be drawn out. He helped the younger Nurians collect and refill the *yosha* bowls, taking advantage of the lull to surreptitiously observe the fifth Focal. The green-eyed man did not say much to the others, but drank from his bowl with quiet contentment. The boy had just regained his seat, determined to ask his neighbour his name, when Samiha addressed the gathering again.

'Thank you for all your help, my friends. *Maz, namis*,' she said graciously, though Tymon could hear an edge of regret in her voice. She turned to him. 'It's time for you to leave now, *Argosi*. There's someone waiting for you at the mission.'

The directive took him by surprise. 'But ... but —' he protested, forgetting both his manners and his embarrassment in his excitement, 'I have so much to ask you! I want to know all about Grafting!'

This drew a general laugh from his listeners. 'All about Grafting?' observed the old woman. 'It would take more than a lifetime to learn that, *Argosi*!'

'Hush, Tuvala, he is thirsty for knowledge,' said the white-haired man. 'As it should be! If Sap wills, you learn more.'

'We'll see each other tomorrow,' Samiha assured him. 'We can talk then.'

She stood up and moved towards the door without further discussion or explanation, as if their next meeting had already been arranged. Tymon scrambled after her. He did not know what else to do, so he bowed to the group in farewell.

'In the beauty,' he said.

'Be blessed,' answered the old man, politely.

'*Sav beni*,' added the woman named Tuvala. The younger couple echoed her words.

'In the beauty,' said the fifth Focal, raising his hand in farewell.

Tymon followed Samiha onto the balcony. 'I'm sorry about the *yosha*,' he told her. 'I don't know what happened back there. I felt very hot. I must have come across like a complete lunatic.'

She gave him a hard look, but her reply was unruffled. 'Don't mention it.'

He did not want to leave, and cast about for an excuse to prolong the conversation.

'Back on the ship I promised to tell you how I knew your name,' he blurted. 'I was worried you wouldn't believe me, but I think you will, now. I dreamt it.'

'Is that so?' She surveyed him calmly from the doorway.

'I thought you'd be surprised,' he said. 'I mean, what are the odds that I dream up the right name? It's almost like Grafting.'

'The odds are quite high, if one is listening, that one will hear. If one looks, one might even See.'

'You sound like the Focals,' he grumbled. 'Don't Nurians ever talk plainly?'

His comment provoked her to wry laughter. 'I'm sorry, Tymon. I've been so used to hiding my true thoughts and intentions ... I want to talk to you plainly. Come again tomorrow and we'll have a good long conversation about the Grafting, and your dreams. Be here by the fifth hour. Right now we have to prepare for the funeral service of those who died yesterday. I hope you will forgive me if I do not invite you.' She smiled apologetically. 'Be blessed, Tymon! *Sav beni.*'

'I'll be back tomorrow! Thank you!' he called, as she shut the door of the apartment.

He grinned a moment at the peeling green paint of the doorway, his thoughts far away. The morning's experiences had filled him with a wild hope. Perhaps there really were Grafters in the world. Perhaps they would share their secrets with him. Even if the fiery vision in Samiha's apartment had been nothing but an aberration, a daydream, it had a salutary effect. He felt lighter than he had when he arrived, as if he had been freed of a layer of binding dust. He took the ladder down from the balcony two rungs at a time, hardly aware of the pain in his ribs. Whether it was sheer chance that had brought him to Samiha's house or the power of the Sap, he had found the red-haired girl again, and found her to be the friend he yearned for. He did not mind for the moment that she seemed always to be teasing him or looking down on him. He wondered briefly what she had meant when she said that someone was waiting for him at the mission. He dropped into the street, whistling to himself. He felt ready to meet anything and anyone.

He decided to brave the quays and collect the mission's water allowance after all, for he felt surprisingly restored after his encounter with Samiha and the Focals. He wound his way back along the alley, towards the main ramp and the city gates. He had almost reached the first-tier market when he chanced on the street sign that had eluded him on his way down. A dirty white board hung on the wall at the corner of the road, indicating its name. Like many places in the colonial city, Samiha's street had both a Nurian and an Argosian designation: the two words were written next to each other on the sign. Tymon peered up at the double marker.

'Kion Street, Key Street,' he whispered, his euphoria evaporating. Half-remembered details pieced themselves together in his mind, and Caro's arrangement with Verlain came rushing back. 'Number six, the house with the green door.'

16

Tymon dragged his buckets down to the custom house, his mind thrown into turmoil. Did Samiha know about Caro's deal with the seminary? If not, why had her address been given as a safe house for Verlain's delivery? Why would someone like her accept the help of her enemies? Gnawing doubts followed him all the way to the air-harbour and he longed for simplicity. Nothing in Marak was as it first appeared to be.

He found the quays teeming with activity. A dirigible had docked in the city that morning, and the usual collection of migrants swarmed at its foot, flanked by soldiers. Tymon edged along the fringes of the crowd as unobtrusively as his clumsy shoulder-yoke allowed, contemplating the craft over the heads of the people. It was smaller and sleeker than the *Stargazer*, a single-masted vessel flying the green and purple standard of Argos city. Only high-level officials, Guild Masters and members of the Priests' Council rode in dirigibles of such quality. As he passed it on the quays he caught the end of a public announcement addressed to the crowd of refugees.

'... barrels of water to all those who sign, payable immediately.'

A man in dark green livery stood on the dirigible's gangplank, reading from a leaf-scroll; he was a recruiting agent for the seminary, Tymon realised with revulsion.

'I repeat: the offer has been increased to seven barrels,' called out the agent. 'Each pilgrim will receive no less than seven full barrels of water for their services. Sign on for a ten-year contract and take home your down payment today. God smiles on your endeavour. Sign up for pilgrimage now!'

A buzz of astonishment passed through the crowd. Seven barrels was an undreamt-of sum. That much water might keep a family for half a year, or be sold on at inflated prices on the black market. People pressed eagerly around the man on the gangplank. Tymon turned away from the spectacle in disgust, angry both with the seminary for making the offer and with the Nurians for listening. He hurried on towards the custom house. There, he found his way barred. The doors to the water dispensary were shut, the entrance closed off by two guards. He joined the group of porters gathered about the soldiers, pleading with them. Their requests for water were stolidly denied.

'New security measures,' one of the guards declared. 'Nothing will be sold to the public until the Argosian dirigible has left Marak air-harbour.'

Tymon found that he was no exception. 'It's the mission's weekly allowance, sir,' he told the soldier. 'We're absolutely dry. I have the money.' He counted out ten *taleks*, but the sum made no impression on the man.

'Not my problem,' he snapped. 'No water's being sold. That's all.'

The throng of carriers reiterated his words in dismay.

'No water?'

'How can we go without for two days?'

'*Mo dia*, my poor babies!'

'*Nosra morti*. We cannot live.'

'They're keeping it all for themselves.'

Caro's gratingly familiar tones caught Tymon's attention. He spied the yellow-haired Nurian loitering at the fringes of the group, his voice rising stridently over the hubbub of the docks.

'There's more than enough water for everyone,' he cried. 'But they won't sell it to us! They would rather we sign our souls away to that travesty.'

He pointed a finger, trembling with rage, at the Argosian vessel. The agent had finished his proclamation and disappeared from the gangplank, and the people on the docks were now drifting towards the dispensary, captivated by another speech.

'They would rather keep the water for themselves and let our children go thirsty!' shouted Caro. 'They would rather we were forced to be slaves!'

Cries of 'Aye!' and 'Well said!' rippled through the throng. The two soldiers straightened their backs and raised their hardwood pikes. Tymon eyed the rabble-rouser with reluctant fascination. He could not help sympathising with him on this occasion. He did not think Caro would confront him in a public setting, but backed away from the custom house doors just in case, slipping into the anonymity of the crowd.

The militant hammered on. 'They tax us till we bleed. They cheat us on the price of *attar*, and stockpile their water till we can no longer afford even the little we need to keep us alive. How long must we bear this injustice? How can we save our families and ourselves?'

A horn blared from the direction of the dirigible and the cordon of soldiers on the docks closed ranks, bearing down on Caro.

'Hoi, you, Nurry, that's enough!' bellowed the captain of the guard. 'You're under arrest for inciting the populace.'

The sheer number of people between the soldiers and their quarry slowed them down, though they beat bystanders out of their path mercilessly. Tymon lost sight of Caro's yellow head. The Nurian's voice drifted over the confusion.

'We will take back what is ours! *Morto putar!* They cannot escape the Year of Fire!'

The crowd dispersed under the militiamen's blows. Tymon retreated back along the quays to the city gates, his empty buckets clattering on their hardwood chains; he had no desire to see further carnage. He hastened through the noise and colour of the first-tier market with the agitator's last words echoing ominously in his ears. The Year of Fire seemed to be as much a part of Caro's vocabulary as it was of the Grafters'. He wondered again, dejectedly, whether there was any difference between them.

His ribs protested every step back to the mission. When he arrived, he found the doors to the compound shut and locked. At last his calls brought Verlain's shuffling steps to the gate. Bolts groaned and one of the doors creaked open.

'Ah, it's you! You took your sweet time! Quickly, quickly, inside!' cried the priest.

Tymon had never seen him so flustered. The fat man peered about him anxiously, brandishing a large hardwood key like a charm. He was barely over the threshold before Verlain had pushed the doors to, sending the heavy bolts home with a grinding thump of finality. The key scraped in the lock. The priest shambled back to the couch, his face the hue of congealed bean curd. He ogled Tymon morosely.

'I told you, my dear boy, not to go out in the city today. I fear for your safety. There's trouble brewing in the tent-town. I heard the soldiers' horn.' He collapsed into his seat, fanning himself. A cloud of dust floated up from the tattered upholstery.

'I'm sorry, sir.' Tymon eased off the shoulder-yoke, grimacing. 'But we won't get water till tomorrow. There's a new trade dirigible being unloaded and the guards aren't allowing anyone in the custom house. That's what the trouble was about.'

'Saints save us!' quivered Verlain. 'These barbarians grow more brazen by the day! All the more reason, all the more reason.' He put down his fan and motioned Tymon closer, his eyes popping with agitation. 'There will be no more unauthorised gadding about the city for now. We've been given direct orders.'

Tymon sat himself gingerly on the edge of the couch, as far from the priest as possible. 'I thought the curfew was only binding at night-time,' he said.

'Our orders,' wheezed Verlain, withdrawing a roll of parchment from his robes, 'come from the Council in Argos, not from the Governor of Marak, whatever you may think of both institutions. We have been told to restrict our movements to the mission for the next few days. Things are going to hot up in the city. I've sent Amu Bibi home for the week.'

Tymon retrieved the delicate bark-skin scroll from Verlain's damp fingers and examined it. It bore the seal of the Council and was without doubt authentic. The Dean's sweeping scrawl covered half the page, followed by the seal and signature of all five Council members.

'To the Marak mission,' he read. 'News has reached us that the security of the colony is threatened by disaffected Nurian elements and that a military curfew is now in place in the city. We advise extreme caution in this situation and a strict policy of containment. All contact or association with the native population is forbidden until further notice. This measure is for the protection of the mission, and shall be considered binding … Yours in the Tree, etc.'

'I don't understand,' he objected as he put the scroll down. 'How can the Council know about the curfew so quickly? It was only announced this morning. Even by bird, the news would have taken a week to get to them.'

'He's no fool,' remarked a soft voice behind them.

Tymon almost jumped out of his seat. Someone had approached the couch noiselessly from the rear and now stood behind him, gazing down at him with a proprietary smile. With a shiver, he recognised the man in the black coat, the Lord Envoy whose presence had so perturbed Rede. He seemed to exert the same destabilising influence on Verlain. The fat priest emitted a nervous, hiccupping noise and sought the refuge of his pipe.

'These are troubled times,' murmured the Envoy, deftly circumnavigating the couch. 'It's a great boon to know friend from foe.'

'Tymon.' The anxiety in Verlain's voice was unmistakable. 'Greet our guest politely. He has come all the way here from Argos seminary.'

'In the beau—'

Tymon's attempt at greeting was interrupted by the Envoy's smooth laughter.

'But I believe we have already met, albeit under less than ideal circumstances! Tymon — a charming name. From the Nurian root *timon*, meaning navigator. Fated to travel, so they say.' The man in black bared his teeth in more of a rictus than a smile. 'Come now, Verlain, tell the boy who I am.'

Verlain took another hurried draw from his pipe, and coughed and choked his way through the introductions. 'This is Father Lace, a Special Envoy of the Council. He is here to take charge of the mission during the state of emergency.'

'I really do wish you would give up that filthy habit, Gerud,' the Envoy sighed.

'Apologies, Reverence.' Verlain promptly dropped the pipe-draw.

Lace took up a stance of studied gravity in front of Tymon, his hands clasped behind his back.

'The moment of truth has come,' he observed. 'The Dean knows full well what is going on in the city and at this mission. Little of import happens in Marak that does not find its way straight back to the Council. And no error on the part of its employees, however minor, escapes its notice.'

Tymon tried to guess what the Envoy was building up to. Had he been sent to replace Verlain and salvage the mission's reputation? No wonder the priest had been so keen on posting recruitment handbills! He must have known Lace was coming, received an advance message by bird. For an instant, the boy allowed himself to imagine that the fat man's nocturnal activities were entirely on his own initiative and that Lace would now set everything to rights. But the Envoy's next words shattered his hopes.

'The current situation with the Nurian rebels was long foreseen. It is inevitable. Though the members of the Council are aware of future events, it is only due to sound judgment and analysis. They see the future, as it were, because they understand the forces that control it.'

'Events and people are connected.' The heresy popped out of Tymon's mouth before he could restrain himself. Too late, he regretted his gaffe.

'What a bright fellow!' exclaimed Lace, his cadaverous smile broader than ever. 'Such insights! The seminary has need of sharp minds like yours!' He nodded meaningfully to Tymon. 'Now the events you speak of are reaching a critical point of development. There is no longer room for divided loyalties. You have a choice. Will you work for your own, or for others?'

'I don't understand, sir.' Tymon hung his head. He felt absurdly guilty, as if the Envoy could see into his mind and isolate every treacherous thought, every dubious action. Had he been observed entering the *shanti*'s house that day?

'Don't give me that.' Lace's smile disappeared as he leaned over Tymon, blocking the light. 'Have you been visiting the Nurry shrine, boy?'

Verlain stirred fitfully, flapping his fan. 'Oh, you should tell him the truth,' he muttered. 'He knows everything we do, everything.' The fat priest seemed to have lost his wits; sweat poured down his flabby cheeks and he trembled visibly.

'Well? I'm waiting.' The Envoy's voice took on a frosty note.

'Only once, sir, by accident,' Tymon mumbled.

'Then let that be the last time,' came the cool reply. Lace turned and paced about the couch again. 'There are factions at work in this city that you would do well to avoid. The shrine is a hub of political agitation.'

'And their despicable woman *shanti* is at the centre of it all,' burst in Verlain, almost falling off the divan in his excitement. 'A shameless hussy, an abomination of nature, worse than all the other brazen females in this city put together ... Why, she even doctors the drink she gives to her guests, in order to win them to her cause ...'

'Doctors it?' Misgiving stabbed through Tymon.

Verlain nodded vigorously. 'With an infusion of bellweed to cause beatific visions. When her victims are good and silly, she gets them to take part in a so-called Grafting trance. Claims the herb dreams are messages from the Sap, and what-not.'

With a rush of dismay, Tymon recalled the vision of fire in Samiha's apartment. He had drunk her *yosha*, after all. He frowned at the dusty flags of the courtyard, unsure what to make of Verlain's insinuations. Had he been taken in by rebel agents? Were Samiha and her friends now laughing behind his back, mocking the naïve Argosian boy who was so easy to dupe?

As if he sensed his advantage, the priest pressed on. 'Why, those people who attacked you yesterday — you were caught in the riot, no? Those people were her minions, her fanatical supporters,' he exclaimed breathlessly. 'She is married to every single one of them. I have it on excellent authority that every Grafting session ends in an abominable orgy —'

'Calm yourself, Gerud,' Lace barked.

The Envoy had allowed Verlain to patter on unsupervised for several seconds. It was a fatal mistake. The priest had gone a step too far: his accusations had become lurid, stretching the point beyond belief. Lace seemed to know it, for he clapped a restraining hand on the fat man's shoulder.

'I'm sure we don't need to hear your opinion of what the *shanti* does or does not do,' he snapped. Verlain deflated like an empty ether balloon. 'Tymon would never get himself into a situation like that to begin with — would you, Tymon?'

The boy shook his head silently. Relief washed over him. The priest's accusations had the opposite effect of that intended. It was clear from Verlain's slander and the Envoy's irritation that Samiha had no place in their schemes.

'Now, I return to my former question, the only real issue of import here.' Lace exhaled with impatience. 'It is time for you to choose your allegiances, young man. Will you prove your loyalty to the Council? Will you become a man and leave boyish things aside?'

'What do you want from me?' Tymon shrank under Lace's scrutiny. The Envoy's oratory style reminded him alarmingly of the Dean.

'Nothing difficult or dangerous. I am offering you a promotion, actually. A position has opened up on my recruiting ship. We need help drafting candidates for the next tribute. The seminary is stepping up its presence in the colonies, and there will soon be two tithe-ships a year sent to Argos to cover expenses. The post would fulfil the obligations of your indenture as well as opening up several interesting avenues for your future. What do you say?'

'It's a great honour,' squawked Verlain from the sidelines. 'You're very, very lucky to get this sort of chance at your age!'

Tymon recalled Samiha's prodding comments. He would not fall short of the mark again.

'Thank you, sir. But I'm afraid I'd be no good at recruiting,' he said carefully. 'I'd rather stay here, if I may.'

Lace had paced all the way round the couch and now stood in front of him again, his lean arms clasped behind his back. When he heard the boy's response, he grunted dismissively.

'I don't think you quite understand what's on offer. I am giving you a chance to do something special, to belong to a select group.' He turned his predatory gaze on Tymon. 'Isn't that what you've always wanted? To belong? To be part of the inner circle? There are secrets to power, novice: secrets the seminary does not reveal to the uninitiated. Don't you wish to know what they are?'

The words fell like small slivers of ice on Tymon's soul. He looked into the abyss reflected in the Envoy's eyes. There were all his hopes and fears, all his needs and desires, hung out like produce in a market stall. He had always been the one on the outside, the one no one took seriously. He did want to have people listen to him and respect him, and Lace knew it. He wavered a moment, drawn to the simplicity of the offer. Then his old resentment against the seminary returned. He would not forget Galliano so easily.

'I'd be no good at recruiting,' he repeated, stubborn.

As soon as he said it, he knew he had made another enemy. Lace's expression was impassive. Only the lines around his mouth hardened slightly.

'Well, to each his own, I'm sure,' he said. The produce in the virtual market was cleared away with lightning speed, and the Envoy's eyes wandered off to a corner of the courtyard. 'Gerud' — Verlain was making a high-pitched whine — 'Stop that. We have asked, and the boy has given his answer.'

Verlain bobbed and shuffled to his feet. His face was drenched in sweat.

'I will rest now. The journey was long and we have much to accomplish in the days ahead. I am in need of refreshment.' Lace was brisk, business-like.

'Yes, of course, of course. I shall be honoured to leave you the use of my quarters.' The priest wobbled obsequiously off towards his room. 'Tymon, be sure to fetch some lunch for his Reverence.'

The Envoy glanced briefly down at him. 'Go in beauty, Tymon. Remember you're restricted to the mission until further notice. Don't behave rashly.'

'In the beauty, Father. I'll remember.'

Lace had his back turned before Tymon finished the sentence, striding after Verlain. The boy sighed with relief and leaned back on the couch. The confirmation of Samiha's honesty made his heart sing, for he was desperate to find a crumb of truth in the lies surrounding him. Even the Focals appeared in a more attractive light after the Envoy's smooth-talk. He doubted now that they had anything to do with Caro, or even knew of his arrangement with Verlain. It had been worth returning to the mission and meeting with Lace, simply to be assured of that.

The interview had left him drained, however; his thoughts unravelled themselves like twine, refusing to cooperate. His stomach grumbled. He remembered Verlain's last injunction and extracted himself from the couch, wandering across the courtyard to the mission's tiny kitchen in quest of food. Most of the cupboards were bare but he found the eternal pot of leftover *melata* beans sitting on Amu Bibi's stove, along with a few pieces of dry flatbread. How the priest thought he would survive for a whole week without the old woman to care for him was a mystery. Tymon snorted scornfully to himself, serving a grey dollop of beans into a bowl. Then he grabbed an unopened cask of *kush* and returned to Verlain's quarters. Repeated knocking on the door brought no answer, and he was obliged to leave the provisions on the doorstep.

He returned to the couch with his own portion, considering his next move as he crammed the gluey repast down his throat. With the knowledge of Samiha's innocence came apprehension for his friend. If rebels were caught delivering goods to the *shanti*'s address, she could be convicted of a crime she had never committed. He remembered belatedly that she was organising the funeral that evening, and would be at the shrine, unaware of goings on in her home. He was the only person who could warn her of Caro's activities. He had to return to see her at once. The mission gate was locked but that would not stop him. He stared blearily at the compound wall, trying to calculate whether it could be scaled.

He stood up. The courtyard was awash with searing light; he swayed, squinting through the white-hot glow. The distance to the gate seemed vast. He took one step beyond the awning, teetered, regained his balance, and took another step. Then he slowly crumpled into a heap on the barkwood flags.

Verlain's many-chinned countenance became gradually visible, a dark stain on the brilliant sky. The sticky, sugary aftertaste of *som* clogged Tymon's mouth. He could neither rouse his sluggish limbs nor lift his head, and realised with dim outrage that his food had been drugged. After all that had happened at the mission, after all the priests had said about Samiha, he had fallen for that simple ruse.

'Nothing to worry about, Reverence,' Verlain murmured. 'He won't be able to move till tomorrow evening at the earliest. He's had enough to soothe a herd of shillies.'

Tymon distinguished the Envoy's dry tones, somewhere above and behind him.

'I hope so for your sake, Gerud. You obviously think something of the boy, one hardly dares wonder why. It would be sad if there were a mishap.'

'There will be no mishap,' the priest breathed. 'I guarantee it.'

Tymon felt himself being picked up and hoisted back onto the couch. He stared at the shivering rolls of fat on Verlain's neck, struggling to speak. He yearned to hurl abuse at his captors but only managed a faint groan. Verlain bent over him and placed a clammy finger on his lips.

'Now, don't exert yourself, my angel,' he rasped. 'You need to rest.'

17

The rain fell in a continual sheet, making a sound like far-off thunder. But it did not wet anything it touched. When the drops met the desiccated bark they evaporated with a hiss of steam. Tymon stood bone dry under the torrent, his mouth open wide in a vain attempt to catch the water on his parched tongue. But instead of water, ash caked his lips, gagging him. The rain thundered on.

It was not rain but liquid fire, exploding into the night like a bright Festival garland, lighting up the city with birds and celebration. The rooftops burst into red and yellow flowers. Tymon stretched his fingers towards the shimmering petals on the palace walls. There must be a party at the Governor's residence, he thought. This must be the night of the Rites, the night everything would change. He could hear the cries and commotion of the Festival-goers. The sharp odour of blast-poison, the demons dancing on the slope outside the workshop: all of it was to be expected. He had seen it before. He laughed at the panic of the people running down the knot and through the streets, away from the burning carcass that was part building, part flower, part mechanical abomination.

'It's only a machine,' he told the shadowy figures. 'Three lengths of lightwood and a propeller. It isn't magic, just science.'

A shadow approached. 'Wake up!' it cried. 'The rain has come at last!'

'You don't understand,' explained Tymon patiently. 'This isn't rain. It's fire.'

Another explosion shook the Governor's residence and flames poured out of the windows. The shadowy figure grew a yellow beard and spat yellow dust from its mouth.

'*Putar*,' it hissed. '*Argosi putar.*'

'You're a filthy, lying demon,' Tymon shouted. 'You have no soul!'

'You're wrong, you know,' said the *shanti*. 'He's part of the Tree of Being just as much as you are.'

The red-haired girl knelt at the centre of the courtyard. She carefully arranged five corpses bound in white cloth on the flags, feet pointing together, heads radiating outwards. Tymon tried to remember her name without success.

'That's possible,' he conceded. 'But I'm thirsty. Will you give me some water?'

She made no answer but rose and walked slowly towards him, her face shadowed and eyeless. As she drew near her form changed, becoming bloated and obscene. Her eyes receded into the fatty folds of her cheeks.

'My boy?'

Verlain's bulbous figure bent over Tymon. 'My boy, can you hear me?'

Tymon shrank back. He could not be sure whether the fat priest was real or not. Verlain hung between his dreams like an unwelcome spider, melting in and out of existence. His face was blurred and indistinct, and his features swam and bled into each other until nothing was left but a blank wall of shivering flesh. It was too much to bear. Tymon let go of the unpleasant image with a sense of liberation. The world became a tunnel of noise and fury and he fell into the Void, leaving light and life behind.

He awoke with the stale taste of *som* gagging in his throat. After a moment of disorientation he realised he was lying in Verlain's quarters. Sweat saturated his rumpled tunic and thirst tortured him, but he felt able to move again. Even the pain in his ribs had improved. He raised himself onto one elbow. The room was dark and shreds of bright hallucination clung to the edges of his vision. A dull red luminescence that was neither daylight nor moonlight seeped under the doorway. He guessed he had slept for many hours, though whether it was still the night after his capture or the evening of the next day was unclear. He shook his head, trying to separate memory from fantasy. Had he imagined a fire in the Governor's palace? Was the red light outside nothing but a delusion, the aftermath of drugged slumber?

He heaved himself up from the bed and staggered to the door. It was locked. He laid his ear against the wood, listening for movement in the courtyard. There was only silence. He had been left alone at the mission. He wrestled fruitlessly with the door-handle, cursing Verlain under his breath. Then he peered into the darkness in an effort to make out the contents of the room. By the bed, on a carved wooden chest, he found the sunken stub of a candle and a box of fire-sticks. He struck a light. The flame sent shadows scuttling into the corners.

Though there were no other exits or windows in the room, the gap between the priest's quarters and his own cubicle caught Tymon's eye. It looked just big enough to squeeze through. With a bit of luck, the cubicle door on the other side might be unlocked. He climbed onto the bed and tried to gain a grip on the high aperture, but it was out of reach. He cast about for something to use as a ladder. The only items of furniture in the room were the chest by the bed and a large hardwood wardrobe, too heavy to move. He descended from the bed and squatted down by the chest, bracing his arms about it. Then he paused. Slowly, he reached out and tried the lock on the box. It flipped open.

He did not know exactly what he was expecting. Perhaps he cherished a wild hope of finding proof of the fat priest's duplicity, some link to the rebels or compromising correspondence with the seminary. There was, of course, nothing of the sort among the documents piled in the unlocked chest. Tymon thumbed through the volumes of strawpaper, the candle weeping over the yellow sheets. A smile of disbelief stretched across his lips. Every letter he had ever copied out for Verlain, every preposterous report and whining petition lay there rotting and unsent. He leaned back against the bed and laughed aloud at his own gullibility. Why had he thought there would be any regular communication at all between the fat priest and the Council? The seminary was not interested in what Gerud Verlain, a disgraced and deported failure, had to say about mission life in the colonies. The priest was there to do a specific job and was given the funds and means necessary to do it. It was enough for the Dean to send him a few missives by bird with his instructions. Lace would take care of the rest.

The candle burned low, singeing Tymon's fingers. With a swift movement he kicked the box over and spilled its contents onto the floor. A mountain of useless paper slid over his feet. It was with difficulty that he restrained himself from dropping the remains of the candle into the heap and reducing the legacy of his indenture to a crisp. He took a deep breath, stuck the candle stub on one of the bedposts and hoisted the empty and much lighter chest onto the bed. The gap by the ceiling was narrow but passable. He wriggled over the wall and dropped down into his cubicle, ignoring the spasm in his side. The candle he had left in Verlain's quarters guttered and went out. He groped in the darkness towards the faint red line of the doorway. To his relief the handle turned in his grasp and the door opened.

The courtyard beyond was deserted and still. There was no sign of either Verlain or Lace, although he waited in the doorway for several minutes before venturing outside. The blush of firelight hung unmistakably over the compound and the caustic whiff of smoke caught in his nostrils. The area in front of the mission gates appeared to be strewn with empty boxes. Propelled by thirst, he hurried at last to the water cistern by the kitchen and scraped up a ladleful of brackish liquid from its depths. The drink was only enough to wet his mouth. He returned to the gates, licking his cracked lips with discomfort, and prepared to scale the compound wall.

But the gates were hanging half-open. The heavy hardwood bolts had been splintered, the doors bludgeoned and wrenched off their axis. What he had taken in his haste for empty boxes was wreckage littering the flags. The mission had been vandalised, though by whom and for what purpose he could not tell. Nothing in the compound had been touched. He picked his way through the ruined gates, scanning the temple courtyard beyond for movement. It was quiet and empty. The temple was bathed in a fitful orange glow, as were the walls of the third tier above. His new vantage point afforded a better view of the Governor's residence than the mission compound. He was able to take in the full extent of the damage inflicted on the palace.

He had heard accounts of the power of blast-poison, a substance said to unleash a ball of fire so intense it could consume the heaviest of buildings in an instant. The secret of its making was a Dark Art — the first taught to men by demons, according to Argosian legend. He half expected the devastation before him to evaporate like one of his hallucinatory dreams. The Governor's palace was gutted. A large section at the top of the city had been gouged out of existence, leaving a gaping wound that belched thick black smoke. Flames leapt at its heart. Only blast-poison could have wreaked such havoc with the foot-thick walls of the palace, and few but the Fathers at the seminary had access to the knowledge necessary to re-create the formula. Tymon shuddered. This must have been the 'little surprise' that would kick-start Caro's revolution. No demons were needed to perpetuate the crime, however; he guessed now what goods the Nurian might have received from Verlain.

He set off warily across the temple courtyard, keeping a sharp eye out for the fat priest. The city might be in the throes of a revolution but it was also theoretically under curfew. He had no desire to be caught and questioned by soldiers, or returned to the custody of his masters. The second tier was quiet but he had the disagreeable impression that he was being watched from behind closed shutters. The murderous glare from the Governor's residence lit up the streets better than any torch as he hastened down the deserted main ramp to the first tier and market.

There the signs of trouble multiplied. Market stalls had been demolished and crates and wheelbarrows overturned by the side of the road. Several of the houses had been ransacked, their doors and shutters forced open and left to swing in the smoky breeze. Broken furniture lay scattered about on the ramp. A dim uproar drifted towards Tymon from beyond the city gates. He saw the telltale glimmer of orange rising above the palisade — the tent-town was on fire. Far away, a militia horn blew four victorious blasts, and through the faint cries from the tent-quarter came the sound of singing. Strains of 'The Merry Bells' pierced the night. It seemed that the soldiers were finally teaching the natives their salutary lesson.

The boy broke into a run, gripped by a new and terrible certainty. The vigilante crowd would look for an easy target. They would blame a well-known figure for the explosion. Samiha was the obvious choice. He skidded down Kion Street and almost tripped over ladder six, all thought of personal danger gone. But as he scrambled onto the balcony, he saw with cold shock that he was too late. The green door gaped wide, its lock smashed.

'Samiha!' he cried, plunging into the dark apartment.

Someone was sitting in the middle of the room. He could make out a bowed shape in the fitful glimmer from the doorway.

'Are you there?' he called.

His foot struck something soft; he hesitated. He reached down and touched a human arm. There were bodies lying on the floor in front of him. He recoiled in confusion as the bowed figure lifted its head.

'I'm here,' said Samiha quietly.

There was a brief scrape and a fire-stick leapt to life, its small flame cupped in the *shanti*'s hands. She was dressed in a hooded travel cloak as if she had just come in from outside. Her red hair fell in long folds about her face.

'What's going on?' Tymon frowned as he caught a glimpse of huddled figures on the floor. 'Are you hurt?' he asked anxiously. 'What happened here?'

'I'm unhurt,' she replied, her tones flat and weary. 'Soldiers came. I wasn't at home. But they were — the Focals.'

The flame went out. She struck another, lighting a small basket-lantern beside her. Tymon shrank from the scene before him in horror. Five corpses lay on the floor of the apartment. The Focals had been slaughtered, their throats cut. The old man and the old woman were curled together in curiously child-like postures; the young couple still clasped each other's hands. They had been attacked during their trance. Beside them lay the man with green eyes, his bright gaze now empty and dull. With a jolt, Tymon recalled where he had met the fifth Focal. The scar on the Nurian's face was clearly visible in the flickering lantern light: he could not think why he had not noticed it before. There was the stranger who had spoken to him at the gates of Argos city, what seemed like a lifetime ago. There lay the beggar from the prison cart — dead.

He barely had time to register the startling fact. Samiha stumbled to him over the bodies of her companions, her light throwing wild shadows on the walls. He could see that she had been crying. He reached out his arms and steadied her, pulled her close. She laid her head against his shoulder.

'They were butchered,' she whispered. 'Elder Tuvala and Elder Brek. Little Payah and her Sem. Wise Ash. Every one of them.'

'I'm sorry,' he mumbled ineffectually. With a twinge of shame he noticed that he was thinking more about the sweet smell of Samiha's hair than the murdered people at his feet. 'It's not your fault,' he assured her. 'You couldn't have stopped it.'

To his regret, she raised her head and pulled away from him.

'You don't understand,' she said. 'They died because of me. My choices have been all wrong, from the start —' she broke off, flustered, before continuing. 'In any case, the soldiers came looking for me. People have been saying I called down the demon fire on the Governor's palace.'

'There's something you should know about that —' began Tymon.

He was interrupted by the sound of a military horn blaring outside the palisade. The tramp of booted feet approached from the direction of the city gates, accompanied by a chorus of 'The Merry Bells'.

'You'd better leave now. They'll be back soon.' Samiha pushed him towards the door.

'What do you mean, I'd better leave?' Tymon protested. 'If they're looking for you, aren't you the one who should be leaving?'

'I'm staying here.' She half thrust him onto the balcony.

'Never!' Tymon arrested his progress, catching himself on the doorframe. 'I'm not going unless you come with me!'

'That isn't your decision to make.'

The clamour of the crowd drew closer. Tymon realised with alarm that she intended to give herself up to the mob, to be caught or killed.

'Why throw your life away?' he cried. 'What good would it do? It won't bring the others back.'

'At least I'll die with my brothers.'

'That's ridiculous and you know it!' he exclaimed impatiently. 'What about all the rest of your brothers who are alive, *shanti*? Are you going to abandon them?'

Samiha hesitated, her face half-hidden by its veil of hair. When she spoke at last her voice was low and hoarse.

'Without the Focals, I'm blind, Tymon. What use am I to my people? I have no gift for Grafting. Without them, I'm lost. I can't see the future.'

She was rocking herself in grief. He took her in his arms again and steered her gently but firmly away from the door.

'Neither can the rest of us,' he admonished. 'And we muddle along. That's no reason to give up!'

There was no longer any mistaking the intentions of the vigilantes. The roar of the crowd rolled down Kion Street, swelling to a crescendo. The flicker of torches played through the shutters on the apartment windows.

'Is there any way out of here?' pleaded Tymon. 'Samiha, I need you.'

She stirred at last, lifting her face from his shoulder. From below the balcony, the cries echoed out: *Kill the sorceress! Burn her! Burn the witch!*

'There's a trapdoor to the roof,' she whispered. 'In the back, over the stove.'

'Let's go, then.'

He pulled her behind him, diving through the curtain at the rear of the main room. It opened into a tiny kitchen area dominated by a hardwood oven. There was a small hatch in the ceiling. He scrambled onto the unlit stove and strained his fingers towards the trapdoor, but it was too high. He could hear people mounting the ladder outside. Time was running out. He jumped down and grasped Samiha firmly by the waist. Ignoring her exclamation of protest, he hoisted her up towards the hole in the ceiling. Her body felt taut and warm in his hands.

'Open the trapdoor and get in,' he urged. 'I need you to help me afterwards!'

She threw him an indecipherable look and pushed the door ajar, manoeuvring herself into the space above. As she turned and stretched her arm down to him, a babble of voices erupted into the main room. Torchlight danced through the curtain. Tymon seized Samiha's arm and swung himself up towards the hatch. It seemed to take forever to haul his body through the opening, an excruciating scrape on sore bone. At last he dragged himself to safety, kicking the trapdoor shut behind him.

There was a space under the roof just wide enough to crawl through. They shuffled as quickly as they dared along the rafters until they reached the periphery of the building, where a second hatch led onto the roof. The door was wedged fast and could only be pried open by the two of them in a concerted effort. It came loose with a screech of warped wood. They waited for an agonised interval, listening for sounds of pursuit as the night breeze whistled through the gap, carrying with it the smell of smoke. No noise came from the direction of the apartment. Tymon sighed with relief and turned towards the hatch. He was arrested by the look of alarm on Samiha's face. An orange flicker leapt in her eyes. He glanced back over his shoulder: where they had just passed, tiny tongues of flame licked through the rafters.

'They've set fire to the apartment,' gasped Samiha. 'We'll be burnt alive.'

'It's not over yet,' Tymon rallied her. 'The roof is still whole.'

'Not for long. The fire will break through before we get halfway to the palisade. The tiles are only made of lightwood.'

'We don't know till we try! Come on, Samiha!'

'It's no use, we need to reach the —'

'Will you stop arguing and go, woman?' he snapped, exasperated. The greedy crackle of flames was now clearly audible.

Samiha glared at him then turned to slip through the half-open door. Tymon squeezed after her with rather more difficulty. He found himself on a narrow ledge running along the front of the building. A hot wind hit him in the face and he heard the roar of flames from the lower storey windows. The sound of chanting drifted up on eddies of hot ash. *Kill the sorceress. Burn the witch.* He did not dare look down at the mob in the street, but clung to the eaves and crept forward, step by step. At the extremity of the ledge Samiha helped him onto the low point of the roof. Fire was now darting through the hatch behind them.

'Careful,' she warned. 'The tiles are unstable.'

They moved diagonally across the rooftop, heading for the ragged crest of the city palisade, a line of rough-hewn posts flanking the building on its far side. Colonial architecture stubbornly followed the Argosian model despite differences in climate, and the roof was steeply inclined. Their progress became painfully slow. The tiles felt warm under Tymon's fingers. To his alarm he saw smoke and bright sparks escaping from several points on their trajectory.

'It won't hold much longer,' called Samiha. 'Watch where you step!' The roar of the flames swallowed her words as a section of tiles on Tymon's left fell inwards with a sickening crunch.

'Why are we going up so far?' he shouted after her. Samiha seemed to be leading him on an unnecessarily precipitous arc up the roof. They could have reached the palisade more quickly in a straight line.

'There's rope at the top,' she answered, indicating the ridgepole. 'We need it to get down the other side.'

They crawled on, crouched almost flat against the hot tiles. Tymon felt the building creak and groan beneath him as another section of the roof collapsed with a crash nearby. A tile came loose under his hand and skittered away. It was several anxious seconds before he was able to find another secure hold. Samiha had reached the top of the roof ahead of him and was busy untying a roll of rope from the ridgepole.

'Straight along to the end now,' she said, when Tymon hoisted himself up beside her, panting with exertion. 'It's the safest part of the roof, anyway.'

'I feel better already,' he muttered. The ridgepole cut uncomfortably through his breeches.

'What?'

'Let's get this over with,' he sighed.

'You were the one who wanted to come.'

'Just ... lead on.'

They inched along the top of the roof, aiming for the line of the palisade. Tymon prayed silently that their precarious perch would hold. The lower tiles were now caving in to the fire, disappearing in showers of bright sparks. Heat rose up in a suffocating wave and whipped their faces raw, and smoke stung their eyes. It seemed an eternity before they reached the end of the ridgepole and dropped down onto the top of the palisade. Samiha secured a loop of rope around one of the posts; they lowered themselves into a quiet corner of the tent-town below. A sullen pall of smoke hung over the refugee camp. Eastwards, the bare thickets above the city were outlined in the faint light of dawn.

They paused at the base of the palisade. Tymon blinked, his eyes dazzled by the memory of flame. Samiha's voice carried softly through the shadows.

'You are brave, *Argosi*. But never call me "woman" in that tone again, or you'll find yourself alone on a hot roof, with no rope.'

18

Tymon felt the blood rush painfully to his cheeks. His face and palms were chapped by the heat of the fire and the raw skin tingled. He was unable to tell in the darkness whether Samiha was actually offended. Her approval meant more to him than he had realised.

'I'm sorry,' he said stiffly. 'Please don't hold my words against me. I spoke in haste.'

There was a softening in her voice that reassured him.

'Don't apologise,' she replied. 'Whatever else I regret about this night, I'll always remember your courage and your persistence in getting me out of that apartment. You're a true friend. You can return to the mission now. The way should be clear.'

'The mission?' he repeated dumbly. He had not thought he would be parted from her so soon.

'The mob will still be in Kion Street. Hurry and you won't be noticed.'

He shook his head. 'I'm not going back to the mission. I'm deserting the service. I've already made up my mind.'

She did not answer immediately. A single tongue of flame ripped up from within the city palisade and subsided.

'Well, I hope you don't think you're coming with me.' She spoke with finality.

'Why not?' demanded Tymon, taken aback.

'It's too dangerous.'

'More dangerous than a collapsing roof?'

'I've a long road ahead of me. I have to leave the city and join my companions. They're outlaws, Tymon.'

'Then let me come with you. I'm an outlaw too, from the seminary's point of view.'

'You can't come. You don't understand.'

'Why not? Do you still think I'm no use to you?' His answer was tinged with pique.

'Please!' she breathed. She glanced uneasily at the walls of canvas flanking the alley. 'Speak quietly!'

He lowered his voice to a growl of annoyance. 'After all we've been through, I thought you might trust me by now.'

'You just don't know what you're asking.' She exhaled in frustration. 'It's too complicated.'

'You think your friends won't accept me, right? Well, let me meet them. I'll prove you wrong.'

'This isn't about proving anything —' she began.

'You're ashamed of me, aren't you?' he interrupted. 'Because I'm an Argosian.' The accusation sounded shrill in his own ears.

There was an awkward pause. The sky grew lighter as one by one, the stars faded above them.

'I'd never be ashamed of a friend,' she remarked after a while. 'The Sap has brought us together and I have no doubt that we will meet again. But it's too risky to let you accompany me out of the city right now. Farewell, *nami*.' She turned abruptly and walked down the shadowy alley between the rows of tents.

He hesitated, battling his pride. He wanted to tell her that he had no place left to go, that he was homeless and alone. But he could not bear to beg for her help. At last he thrust away his scruples and hurried to catch up with her.

'I didn't mean that, Samiha,' he said. 'I was out of line again. I'm sorry.'

She did not slow her pace.

'Let me come with you,' he persisted. 'I have information that might be useful.'

'I'm sure you do.'

'I learnt several things while I was at the mission. Your rebel friends would benefit from hearing about them —'

She spun around on her heel so that he almost collided with her.

'You have nowhere else to go, do you?' she said quietly.

Her expression was now clearly visible in the growing light; she surveyed him with pursed lips. He hung his head in mortification.

'If I agree to this, you'll remember two things,' she continued. 'Firstly: I do not condone rebellion and I do not have rebel friends. Secondly: you will be discreet. No shouting at me in the road. While we're in the city, you do as I say. No discussion. Are we clear?'

'Absolutely clear, *shanti*,' he replied, relief welling up through his embarrassment.

'*Sav vay*, what have I let myself in for?' she sighed. 'Follow me and if you want to live, be quiet.'

She glanced at the paling sky and flipped up the hood at the back of her shift. Then she walked on down the alley, motioning him after her. They emerged into a street near the air-harbour. All was still in the tent-town. Ashes drifted across the wind and a cloud of dingy smoke hung over the area behind the custom house.

'They've set fire to the temple,' noted Samiha, in an undertone. 'The fools. They might have destroyed their own food supplies.'

She led them eastwards, away from the docks, avoiding the main thoroughfares. Dotted along their way were the casualties of the night's violence. The colonial mob had carried out indiscriminate attacks in the tent quarter; every few yards they passed the black and smoking remnants of a shack or tent. Looming over all, a dark column of ash drifted over the city. A red dawn broke above the ruin of the Governor's palace. Tymon peered up at the remains of the third tier, wondering if his absence from the mission had yet been discovered. He dreaded a chance meeting with Lace or Verlain in the street.

A tense calm reigned in the refugee quarter. Only a few hurrying figures crossed their path, heads bowed and hoods drawn up. The normal business of the morning had been abandoned. Tymon's thirst returned to torment him as he plodded after Samiha, winding between the tents and pole-houses. She came to a halt quite suddenly in a nondescript walkway at the south end of the tent-town, bending her head close to one of the canvas walls to whisper a stream of Nurian. A voice answered in muffled tones and a loose flap was raised to let them through. They stepped into an empty tent, lit only by the light seeping through the white fabric of the roof. A freckle-faced youth of about Tymon's age knelt at the foot of the canvas, lacing it shut.

'Tymon, this is Oren.' Samiha introduced the young stranger. 'He will help us leave the city — at least until things calm down a little.'

Oren rose and made a deep bow to the *shanti*. Then he checked himself, visibly shocked at the sight of Samiha's companion. Even in the faint light of the tent, Tymon's skin was conspicuously darker than a Nurian's.

'*Shanti … Argosi* —' began the other youth.

'He is a friend, Oren.' Samiha's tone was unequivocal. 'If it wasn't for him, I wouldn't be here this morning. He saved my life. There are others who have not fared as well as I.'

She laid a hand on the youth's arm as if to comfort him, and continued to speak in Nurian. Tymon caught the mention of the Focals' names and guessed that she was reporting the tragedy of the night before. Oren's rather comical, round face grew grave as he listened. When Samiha was done, the Nurian youth stood silent a moment, as if lost in thought. Then he collected himself and bowed to Tymon, addressing him in the curt idiom current among the townsfolk.

'Welcome, *nami*,' he said. 'You save more than one life last night. You keep all hearts beating.'

As he straightened up, a medallion slipped into view around his neck, a piece of hardwood bearing the key signature Tymon had seen painted on the walls of the city. The carving was inlaid with a bright material that glinted in the light. It occurred to Tymon that he might be face to face with the author of the peculiar wall-poetry. His ribs prevented him from bowing properly in return, and he could only bob his head awkwardly to Oren.

The Nurian gave a sudden, radiant grin. '*Shanti* — it is Sign!' he said. 'Friend in west. *Sav beni!* Year of Fire!'

'Perhaps. But there is no time to lose, Oren. Bring another cloak for Tymon and enough food for three days' journey. We should be out of the town by mid-morning.'

The youth bowed once more and disappeared through a door-flap. Samiha settled herself on the bare floor with her back against one of the interior poles. To Tymon's joy, she produced a small water gourd from the folds of her cloak.

'He may be a while out there,' she said. 'Rest now, and have some water.'

He sat down beside her and accepted the drink gratefully, watching her over the edge of the gourd. She seemed weary: the pale skin of her face was waxy and there were bluish shadows under her eyes. He had taken a deep draught from the gourd before he remembered that in Marak water was a luxury. He handed it hastily back to her, wiping the drops from his mouth with his hand.

'Thank you. *Maz*,' he ventured.

She smiled at his use of the Nurian word. 'You're very welcome.'

He wanted to ask her more about what had happened the previous evening, about how she escaped the fate of the Focals. But he was afraid of upsetting her. He steered clear of the difficult subject and concentrated on the details of their flight.

'Where are we going now, Samiha?' he enquired. 'Where are your companions?'

'At a Freehold. We should be able to meet up with a dirigible that will take us there, but we have at least a day's journey on foot before we reach the pick-up point.'

Tymon nodded. He recalled Verlain mentioning the existence of Nurian Freeholds in the Eastern Canopy, concessions to self-governance the priest had loudly deplored. Despite Samiha's protestations to the contrary, he was sure that he was finally about to meet members of the elusive Nurian rebellion.

'That medallion Oren was wearing,' he continued, after a while. 'I've seen the same sign on the walls of the city. What is it?'

She glanced up at him keenly. 'Oh, you noticed that, did you? It's the mark of the Nurian king. The symbol of the royal house of Nur.'

'Is Oren some kind of royalty, then?'

'No. The medallion just shows where his allegiance lies.'

'Did he write those verses on the walls?'

'Did you like them?'

Her response took Tymon by surprise. 'Well ... I don't know if "like" is the word I'd use,' he stammered. 'Personal taste doesn't apply to that sort of thing ... I mean, they seemed more like prophecies than poetry ...'

'Ah.' She looked away. 'Yes. You're absolutely right. They weren't really poetry. I wrote them.'

There was a pause. He berated himself silently for his blunder and decided to try a different angle of conversation.

'There's another thing I've been meaning to ask you,' he said. 'Who is this *Sav* person everyone keeps mentioning? Is he a prophet of yours?'

She gave a grunt of ironic laughter and settled herself more comfortably against the tent-pole. 'It's not a person. *Sav* means "Sap". When Oren says *Sav beni*, he means "may the Sap bless you".'

'I still don't understand what the Sap is. How can a life-force speak to you?'

'You're full of questions this morning,' she noted, her voice husky. She rubbed a hand across her face and he regretted blurting out his thoughts at a time like this. 'I don't have the energy to talk philosophy just now, Tymon. But I do promise it will all become much clearer to you when you learn the Grafting.'

'When I learn the Grafting?' he echoed doubtfully. 'How is that possible, Samiha? I'm not like the Focals. I can't predict the future.'

'Oh, but you can,' she murmured. Her eyelids drifted shut. 'You have the raw talent to become a Grafter. That's what I came to Argos to find. A Sign of the Sap, a westerner with the Sight. You just need training. Now, I really must rest, forgive me.'

She was asleep almost as soon as she said it, her head propped against the tent pole. Tymon was left with the mad claim jangling in his ears: unanswerable, impossible. He bit his lip with frustration. He had meant to tell her of Caro's dealings with Verlain when the opportunity presented itself. Instead, he had asked utterly useless questions about poetry and semantics, and received more in answer than he had bargained for. He understood now, with a plummeting heart, why Samiha tolerated his presence. He was supposed to fulfil her prophecies, to be the omen that set off her precious Year of Fire. He wished that it were true, that he were a Grafter, if only for her sake. To learn that he was not — that the trip to Argos, even the death of her friend, had been in vain — would be a terrible disappointment for her.

He watched her, lingering over the line of her profile in the diffuse light of the tent. In sleep her face lost its air of fatigue and preoccupation and she looked younger, hardly more than a girl. Tear marks stained her cheeks. Long strands of fiery hair had ensnared themselves in her mouth, rising and falling with each breath. He felt the urge to reach out and free the snarled strands, to caress her lips. His fingers were already stretching towards her face before he came to his senses and drew back his hand. He found himself speculating whether she liked him at all. He wanted to show her that he was a man, not a Sign, alive and ordinary, in the ordinary Tree, and worthy of her interest. He realised then, for the first time, that he cared very much indeed for the red-haired Nurian girl. Slowly, insidiously, his curiosity about her had turned into fascination, and fascination had developed into something more profound. He was falling in love.

Love was not a virtue taught to novices at Argos seminary. To an Argosian male an unmarried woman was a plaything, and a married one little more than a prudent investment. Marriage was about social standing, not romantic affection. Tymon's classmates had boasted of manly conquests, encounters in the back alleys of the city, but the stories seldom reflected reality. Tenderness between a man and a woman was seen more as a weakness than a blessing by the youth of Argos. All a student of the seminary could usually hope for in the way of romance was a kiss — or perhaps a pancake — stolen from a kitchen maid, on the sly.

No voice gave the call to prayer that morning in Marak. Tymon fidgeted restlessly on the tent floor, diverted from his unaccustomed musings by the rumbling in his belly. Now that his thirst was quenched a gnawing hunger had taken its place. He had eaten his last, tainted meal at the mission, what he guessed was almost two days ago. Perhaps it was only another hour before the door-flap lifted

344

and Oren re-entered the tent, bearing a bundle of supplies, but the wait might have been eternal. The smell of fried beans emanated from the bundle like clouds of glory. Samiha roused herself with a yawn and shook the tumbled strands of hair from her face. She smiled at Oren.

'What news, *nami?*'

The freckled youth answered in his abbreviated jargon. 'Things bad. Palace burn, no one ever see demon-fire so big. Soldiers angry, look for rebels, nobody find. Governor Bignose run away to *Argosi* ship.'

'The Governor's on the Envoy's ship?' Tymon interrupted, astounded. 'I thought he hated the seminary!'

Oren nodded solemnly. 'Governor hate everybody. He go with *Argosi* boss-man now, while is trouble. He say: all refugees out of tent-town. All without job have to leave city, otherwise off to *Argosi* plantation. All must pay for rebel attack.'

'But what about Verlain?' insisted Tymon. The smell of food was mouth-watering, but anxiety still gnawed at him. 'Is Father Verlain on the dirigible with them, or up at the mission?'

'I doubt if the *Argosi* priest will trouble us now,' put in Samiha. 'What about the bridge, Oren?'

The youth shook his head. 'I know nothing of this Varl-Ayn. But there is price for your life, *shanti*. Difficult to pass bridge, soldiers make checkpoint.'

Samiha sighed. 'That's going to be a problem.'

'No worry, there is plan!' Oren pronounced. 'My sister, Noni.'

He appeared to consider this truncated explanation sufficient. He rummaged through his bundle, taking out three pockets of hot, stuffed flatbread. He handed two to his guests and squatted down on the floor, applying himself with single-minded attention to his meal. Tymon followed suit. Samiha frowned, dissatisfied, her eyes searching out Oren's.

'Noni?' she prompted.

The Nurian youth swallowed his mouthful and finished his thought. 'She make soldiers busy. You pass.'

'I'm worried it's too dangerous. Your sister's so young —'

'Old enough, *shanti*,' replied Oren, mildly. 'Her idea. She help, you pass, everything fine.'

The Nurian youth seemed able to sit and eat his flatbread with perfect equanimity, despite all the night's reversals and bereavements. Tymon eyed the other boy impatiently, suspecting him of dim-wittedness. Now that his breakfast was secured he wished that Oren would leave the tent. He still had to tell Samiha about Caro and had convinced himself that the best way of doing so was when they were alone. Besides, he wanted to reason with her, to warn her that she was mistaken about him and his so-called talents. The issue was awkward for him to bring up in front of other people.

'*Shanti*, may I have a word with you — in private?' he whispered to her.

'Is it important?' Samiha rummaged through the provisions in the bundle and withdrew a long

346

cloak, which she handed to him. 'Put this on, it'll help you get by the guards unnoticed.'

'Yes, it's important. I found something out at the mission, something you should know.'

'I trust Oren. You can say anything in front of him.'

'It's a delicate subject.'

'In that case, wait until we're outside the city. We'll have a chance to talk privately then.'

It was hard for Tymon to swallow his irritation. He had not thought through his motives in wanting to speak with her, and the information he wished to convey seemed suddenly less significant than being alone with her. Sulking slightly, he tried on the cloak she had given him. It was a grey worsted cape with a deep hood, a style he had often seen on the streets of Marak. His chapped brown hands and raw cheeks were completely hidden under its folds. He strapped the provisions for their journey on his back and refused point blank to let Samiha carry anything. She submitted with a laugh.

'*Maz*,' she said. 'Be careful, *Argosi*, you're acquiring the native courtesies. Soon we won't be able to tell you apart from one of our own.'

They left the shelter of the tent with the hoods of their cloaks pulled over their faces, and slipped through the back alleys of the refugee quarter, making their way steadily southwards. It must have been at least mid-morning, but the sun remained hidden behind a blanket of cloud that filled the city with a harsh, hazy light. Tymon scrutinised the overcast sky with distaste. He was not used to the *mora*, the breathless, stifling season before the onset of the eastern rains. Flakes of hot ash still floated on the breeze. Behind him, the charred silhouette of the Governor's palace sat hunched on the third tier like a bird of ill omen.

As he had noticed from on board the *Stargazer*, the branch supporting the city changed direction at its southern extremity and plunged downwards, losing itself in a tangle of twigs. The tent-town came to a ragged halt at the edge of the chasm. On the other side of the drop another twisting branch rose up, surrounded by ranks of bare twig-thickets. A single bridge of rope and planks spanned the gap, anchored at both ends by hardwood posts driven deep into the Tree. A line of people now filed along the slender road, their possessions tied to their backs or balanced on their heads. Militia guards stood in front of the bridge, questioning each of the travellers before waving them on. Tymon's heartbeat quickened as they mingled with the throng. The mood of the refugees was grim and subdued. Their eyes were on the soldiers' checkpoint. He wondered how Oren expected them to pass unnoticed. He caught the brusque, sarcastic tones of the soldiers: they were requiring everyone in the queue to remove their hoods.

'Where's your sister, Oren?' he whispered worriedly. 'How's this going to work?'

'She have plan. She make busy, you go,' replied the Nurian youth, imperturbed.

He slipped in front of them, leaving Tymon alone beside Samiha in the line. The boy pondered all the possible meanings of 'making busy' but was unable to see how anyone could distract so many guards. There were four soldiers at the checkpoint. Three stood by the bridge, while a sallow-faced official lounged at a makeshift desk on one side, interrogating the passers-by. To Tymon's discomfiture the interrogator was none other than the soldier who had scrubbed the poem off the first-tier wall. It was too late now to leave without attracting the notice of the guards, and there appeared to be no way of avoiding identification. A flutter of panic rose inside him. He would be found out, Samiha would be found out. He doubted whether he would escape the Envoy a second time. He glanced desperately about him.

Only one person remained in front of Oren in the queue. She was a young girl, and the pallid bureaucrat had taken a bullying tone towards her. She appeared to be refusing a request. As the exchange grew heated Oren stirred. He strode up to the desk and pulled the girl aside, spitting at the militiaman's feet.

'She say no. You leave my sister alone, *Argosi putar*,' he cried.

'This is a government checkpoint. You're obliged to comply with militia requests,' snarled the little bureaucrat.

Two of the soldiers left their posts at the bridge and laid hold of the young Nurian's shoulders. The official leaned forward on his desk, his lips twitching as he eyed the girl.

'Do as you're told, Nurry. Take off the damn cloak,' he snarled.

She stared at her feet, unresponsive. She wore a long worsted cape of the type Tymon had on, her face hidden by a deep hood.

'Remove your head covering, rebel slut, or I will be obliged to do it for you.'

The girl made no move. '*Putar!*' shouted Oren, wrestling against the men holding him. 'She my sister! She no rebel!'

The sallow-faced officer got up from his seat and walked slowly and deliberately over to the girl, his mouth curled into a leer. With one finger he reached out and flicked the hood off her head. Her bright hair tumbled onto her shoulders, shining like orange flame in the midday sun. The colour was a shade too light and the cut a trace too short, but Tymon found his eyes darting back towards Samiha, to make sure she was still at his side. She was — tense and silent, her eyes glinting out from the depths of her own hood as she watched her young double intently.

At that point several things happened. The last guard at the checkpoint moved towards the red-haired girl with a yell, abandoning his post. Tymon felt Samiha grab hold of his arm and jerk him behind the people who had gathered to watch the altercation, dodging onto the foot of the bridge. He craned over his shoulder to see what was going on. Oren was flailing against his captors like a madman. Through a gap in the confusion he caught a glimpse of Noni. She was painfully young, barely more than a child, standing straight-backed and proud in the grip of the soldiers.

Then they were running, scurrying helter-skelter along the bridge. They kept out of sight of the guards at the checkpoint, slipping through the line of travellers filing away from the city. As if complicit in the escape, none of the refugees turned towards them or remarked upon them in any way. When they were past the midpoint of the bridge they stopped, gasping for breath.

'What'll happen to them?' Tymon burst out, to Samiha.

The *shanti* did not reply. She leaned on the parapet, staring into the twigs below.

'What will the soldiers do to them?' he cried. 'Samiha, we can't just leave them there! It isn't right!'

He peered under the low brim of her hood, and saw with a shock that her eyes were glistening with tears.

'Oh yes, we can just leave them there, and we will,' she returned fiercely. 'Because if we don't, we'll throw away everything they've done for us. This is what it means to follow me, Tymon. This is what it means to be a Grafter. There is no glorious rebellion. You won't do as you wish. You won't even do what you think is right. You'll only do what you must. It's possible those two children will die to help us escape. Can you understand now why I told you to stay behind?'

She let go of the rope and continued on her way without waiting to see if he would keep up. Tymon stared after her, shaken to his core. The planks trembled intermittently as people passed by. Finally he roused himself from his torpor and pursued her across the bridge.

They walked on until evening, leaving the path to plunge directly into the knotted twig-thickets. It was possible to thread one's way from branch tip to dwindling branch tip in the higher regions of the canopy, following a tortuous route through the massed twigs. Their pace soon slackened, however, for the clumps of spiky growth on the scalp of the Tree were hard to penetrate. The grey, mournful thickets opened reluctantly before them and closed behind them like the bars of a cage. The old leaf-forests were drab and dour without their cloak of green. The surroundings did little to improve Tymon's spirits; he trudged silently after Samiha, her last words echoing in his memory. He could not rid himself of the image of Noni standing straight and slim, clutched in the militiaman's paw, and he burned with shame when he thought of how he had misjudged Oren and mistaken bravery for stupidity. He had never thanked the young Nurian for his help, or even for his breakfast. All he had thought of was being left alone with Samiha — and now that he was alone with her for hours on end, he dared not utter a word.

By the close of day he guessed that they had put at least fifteen miles behind them. His feet ached from scrambling over the knobbed and twisted remains of old growth. Just as he was thinking he could stand the pace no longer, they arrived at a clearing between the twigs spanned by a wooden platform. Over it towered a scaffold surmounted by a decaying, skeletal wheel. Tymon recognised one of the ancient Nurian wind-wells marooned incongruously in the depths of the canopy. A long snake-like irrigation canal left the far end of the platform and disappeared into the thickets on the other side.

'We'll spend the night here,' said Samiha. It was the first time she had opened her mouth since they left the city. She lowered herself onto the boards with a sigh.

He joined her, pensive. 'Samiha.'

'Yes.'

'Oren and his sister ... I feel terrible.'

She shook her head. 'Don't. Don't take my words there on the bridge too much to heart. I was upset. None of this is your fault.'

'If it wasn't for me, would they have found another way of getting you across?'

'Maybe not. It was a risky business in any case. Tymon, I have to confess something to you.' She turned to face him, her expression anguished. 'The reason I've been so hard on you is that I've done something terrible myself. I went to Argos — I found you — without the Focals' blessing.'

He gazed at her, uncomprehending.

'They were against the idea,' she explained, miserably. 'They said it would lead to the wrong sequence of events, that the right things would happen, but too quickly, and we'd pay a price. I was impatient. I said I was ready to pay the price. I thought it would be me — I had no idea it would be Juno, and them — and now maybe Oren and Noni ...'

Her voice trailed off and she hunched over her knees, a ball of dejection. He moved to sit next to her, taking advantage of the moment to place an arm about her shoulders.

'You can't blame yourself for what the soldiers did,' he said. 'They committed murder, not you.' He gave her a gentle shake. 'Listen: you can't go on thinking this way. It'll cut the bark out from under your feet.'

She said nothing, but did not disengage herself.

'When I was a little boy,' he continued, happy simply to be close to her, 'Masha, my adoptive mother, would tell me a story. I haven't thought of it in ages. She'd say, "My sprout, don't be telling the wind which way to blow. The wind will blow the way it does and if you go telling it what to do the whole time, you'll always be thinking it did something else to spite you, or to punish you because you did wrong. But that's not the way the world works. The wind blows and the leaves grow, and you can fuss and fret about it till you're brown and curling at the edges: it makes no difference. Sometimes the wind blows for you, sometimes against you."'

He cleared his throat, surprised that he had gone on talking for so long. She looked up at him in wonderment.

'Tymon, that's a marvellous story!' she exclaimed. She extracted herself from under his arm, much to his disappointment, and squeezed his hand in her own.

'Your Masha must have been a wise woman,' she declared. 'And you are definitely her son in every way that counts. Those are the true words of a Grafter. *Beni!* What's done is done. I just have to be better at sniffing out the wind.'

She laughed. It was the first genuine spark of mirth he had seen in her since the death of the Focals, and he could not bear to ruin her mood by contradicting her on the subject of the Grafting. He resolved to speak to her about it the next day. They sat comfortably together for a few more minutes, contemplating the decrepit remains of the wind-well. Then he remembered Caro.

'There's something I must tell you,' he said. 'Caro's been dealing with Father Verlain. I heard the two of them arranging for a delivery at your address in Kion Street. I think the seminary gave him blast-poison in return for information.'

A flicker of anger moved across Samiha's face. 'I know.'

He glanced at her in surprise. 'How? How could you possibly know that?'

'Wise Ash told me. The Focals Saw it.'

'When?'

She hesitated a long moment before answering.

'I was uneasy yesterday,' she replied, at last. 'You never came back when you said you would. I went out to see if I could gather some news, but all I could discover was that the priest had left the mission with the Special Envoy to return to the seminary's dirigible. I wasn't home when the Focals were attacked. I returned after curfew using the roof access, and found them ... It couldn't have been too long after the soldiers came, because — because Ash was still alive, badly wounded. He told me the full story of Caro's treachery before he died. I had suspected Caro was unhappy, though I had no idea he would go so far or show such lack of judgment.'

Her lips were thin, pressed together in fury. 'He might as well have pulled a knife on the Focals himself,' she murmured. 'What makes me despair is that others will support this madness. He'll be treated like a hero instead of a criminal. He isn't the only one who thinks the Argosians should be chased out of Nur in fire and blood. There are quite a few disaffected Nurians in Marak city and elsewhere. Their foolishness will make us all suffer in the end.'

She volunteered no more on the subject, and Tymon did not press her. That evening they dined frugally on the provisions from the bundle, taking care not to waste their limited water supply. Samiha seemed glad of his company, though they did not talk much. As soon as their meal was over she wrapped herself in her cloak and bid him goodnight, curling up on the hard planks as easily as on a feather mattress.

Tymon tossed and turned sleeplessly beside her. He was distracted by her presence, the sound of her steady breathing in the warm darkness. All the events of the past few days jostled through his mind, giving him no rest. He was particularly baffled by the man with the scar. How had Ash really known about Caro? Had someone else told him about the militant's activities? Caro had said he worked alone. And what had the fifth Focal been doing in a prison cart in Argos city, over two months ago? How had he escaped custody? Why, above all, had he said nothing whatsoever about the incident when he met Tymon in Marak? The entire affair left the boy with a sense of aggravation, as if he were the butt of some private joke from the hereafter. He shrank in embarrassment from mentioning yet another inexplicable coincidence to Samiha. But the mystery remained, niggling at him until he promised himself that he would talk to her about that, too, the following day.

When he finally fell into a fitful doze he dreamt that he was looking desperately for something he had lost. There was a pattern to the world that just escaped him, a meaning to everything that happened. He rummaged through branches, sorted out twigs, leaves, stalks. The Tree had become a tiny replica of itself and every limb and stem was a letter in an unknown alphabet. If he could just see the message in the leaves, he would understand everything. But just as the letters were beginning to coalesce, to form some kind of meaning, he awoke from his dream with a jerk. The platform was bathed in pale moonlight. A stealthy noise emanating from the thickets nearby set his nerves tingling, and he leapt to his feet. Someone was approaching along the irrigation troughs.

'Who goes there?' he shouted.

The figure on the canal path stopped short and gave an answering challenge in Nurian. The words jostled in Tymon's ears incomprehensibly. It occurred to him that bounty hunters from Marak had come to claim the price on Samiha's head. For a wild instant he looked for her where she had been and could not find her. Then he realised that she was standing beside him, her face joyful. She laid a reassuring hand on his arm and called out to the stranger in Nurian. The man replied, an edge of relief in his voice. Other figures emerged from the thickets behind him and crept down the irrigation canal. Samiha turned to Tymon with a flash of her old mischievous smile.

'You almost had your ribs broken again, *Argosi*,' she said, leading him towards the people gathered at the edge of the platform. 'These are my friends. They arrived earlier than expected! *Laska, Sav beni.*' She halted in front of the man who had called out the challenge. 'Laska, this is Tymon. He says he wants to join us. Tell me if you think we should convert him to our cause.'

There was a smattering of general merriment. The man named Laska was a tall, grey-haired Nurian in his middle age, his bony features washed a ghostly white in the moonlight. He did not laugh with the others but bowed low to Tymon, placing his hand on his heart.

'Welcome, friend,' he said. He smiled at the boy. 'Strange to say, you are not the first *Argosi* we have converted.'

'Nonsense!' called another voice from the background. The group parted and Tymon felt his heart skip a beat. He noticed a little figure standing behind the rest. It was small and bent and crowned by an ugly cap with earflaps.

'Nonsense!' repeated the voice. 'I didn't convert. I expressed my sympathies for your cause, which is something completely different.'

'Apu?' muttered the boy, hardly trusting his senses.

'Tymon! Is that you? What luck!' came the answering cackle. Galliano stretched out his hands. 'You'd better come closer. I'm no good at finding other people any more!'

Tymon leapt forward with a whoop of delight and caught the old man up in his arms, pulling him clean off the platform. 'Why — where — how come you're here?' he exclaimed.

'Goodness me, you've grown tall!' squeaked his friend. 'However it was that I came, I did. So here I am. Now put me down.'

Tymon deposited him back on the platform and peered into his face. The scientist seemed even tinier and more bird-like than before. His smile was entirely toothless. Then, with a shock like a slap, he saw the two scars on the old man's eyelids, still red and puffed with healing, and the gouged, empty eye-sockets.

'Apu, your poor eyes!' he cried, aghast. 'Who did this to you?'

'Oh, a parting gift from the seminary,' replied the scientist, his beard bristling in defiance. 'A special souvenir to take with me on my journeys.'

'That's — that's murderous! They should be hanged for doing this to an old man!'

'That's life.' Galliano patted his shoulder comfortingly. 'It really doesn't stop me doing my work, you know.'

'For which we are grateful,' interjected Samiha. 'I did not know of your friendship with *syor* Galliano here, Tymon, or I would have asked you to build us one of the magic dirigibles I hear he has made, to spirit us out of Marak.'

Tymon smiled wistfully. 'I wanted to spirit you away already, back in Argos city,' he said. 'It seems that we never catch the easy ride.'

'Not this time,' noted Galliano mysteriously. 'Guide me down the canal path, boy. I have something to show you. Bend down a little, I think you've doubled in height over the past few months.'

He hobbled forward, leaning on Tymon's arm; he seemed completely sure of his direction, blind though he was. They filed along the barkwood troughs for about half a mile, winding between the moonlit thickets. The boy bombarded his friend with a torrent of questions, most of which the scientist deflected with a wry comment or deprecatory remark. Tymon gathered that he had first been banished to a small garrison city north of Marak, where he had been found and aided by Laska's spies. They had brought him to live with them on the Freehold.

'They are good people, you know, despite everything,' Galliano announced, without worrying that everyone nearby could hear him. 'A bit caught up in their beliefs and superstitions but good people, nonetheless. The very best. Without them, I would not be alive today. And I would not be able to work.'

As he spoke they reached the end of the canal. Before them rose a small, irregular knot in a subsidiary branch. Clinging to its crest was a beetle-like, hulking form, black and monstrous in the moonlight.

'Is that what I think it is?' whispered Tymon in awe, coming to a halt at the foot of the knot. Joy welled up inside him.

'That's right, boy!' crowed Galliano. 'It's my new air-chariot. Two cylinders of fuel and a double set of propellers! This one won't dip and churn like the first — she soars like a bird!'

PART THREE

LEAVES

All things are in motion.
Like a leaf caught in the wind,
Creation never rests.
Do you think you are safe from change?
The sun can dim, and the stars may one day go out.
— Usala the Green
(Excerpts from the trial of Saint Usala)

19

Smoke drifted up from the carcass of the Governor's palace in coils, floating across the dawn sky like loops of hazy calligraphy. From the vantage point of the Envoy's dirigible, hovering over the bare twigs a mile distant from Marak, the heavens seemed to be scrawled with enigmatic warnings. Two figures stood shadowed on the deck of the vessel: the Envoy himself, easily recognisable in his somber black coat and white kerchief, and a portly gentleman dressed in rich robes. Neither man was taking in the glory of the sunrise. They conferred in hushed tones, heads bent close together.

'You may rest easy, my Lord.' The Envoy smiled his ashen smile. 'Everything is going to plan. The insurgent is returning to the Freehold to play the hero and won't think twice about security. We'll follow at our leisure and wait for reports. We need only choose the right moment to intercept the *shanti*.'

His companion's large nose was a perfect replica of the profile on the city's worthless paper currency.

'Your idea of using our enemies against themselves was a good one, Excellency,' replied the Governor comfortably. 'Popular feeling is running high since the attack and I can get people to do whatever I like. But I still don't see why my men couldn't just comb the canopy for that witch. It seems a pity to let her escape.'

'Patience, my Lord. The Council advises me it's better this way. The rebels will let down their guard and lead us straight to the source of all the trouble, their skulking native king. If I know anything, he'll come out of the woodwork to gloat over their great victory. Besides, you need your soldiers in the city.'

The other man snorted. 'Maybe so. But I do wish your masters in Argos had sent reinforcements as well as advice. I could dispense with all the fuss and simply take on that gaggle of beggars in a military strike.'

'With due respect, you tried that twenty years ago,' Lace replied, smoothly. 'Weaken the enemy from within. When the time is right, strike hard, once and for all.'

'Very well.' The end of the Governor's nose twitched in disgust. 'We'll do it your way. But I want the witch, you hear? She's been a thorn in my side for years. And if we catch that snivelling, holed-up rat of a king at the same time, I'll be a happy man. I could do without some cursed Grafting prophecy coming to life.'

'Believe me, the seminary wants the *shanti* and her so-called sovereign as much as you do.' The Envoy's teeth flashed once more, bone-white in the sunlight. 'You'd like them out of your hair. We'd like them put on trial for heresy. Our interests coincide.'

The Governor gazed dolefully up at the ruined carcass of his palace and gave a grunt of assent. 'And all you want in return is a second shipment.'

'The seminary is short on manpower.' Father Lace shrugged, as if the matter were negligible. 'Two tithe-ships per year should cover our losses. We'll be taking the city's undesirables off your hands.'

'And the spice tax?'

'Lifted. You have the Council's guarantee. We pledge to back you in your fight against these fanatics. We must remember that we are one people. Whatever our past differences, we are Argosians, the chosen children of the Tree.' The Envoy's voice was syrupy.

The Governor nodded his bulbous beak with satisfaction. 'We understand each other, Excellency. But the people will want a scapegoat to blame for the attack. A middleman, someone of no importance.' He leered. 'Justice must be served.'

Lace turned on his heel and stalked towards the captain's cabin. 'Give them the drunk priest,' he threw out nonchalantly.

The Governor's eyebrows rose as he hurried after the Envoy. 'And his crime?'

'Trading blast-poison to rebel gangs to feed his own filthy habits.'

The Governor rubbed his hands together with glee. 'That will do very well, Excellency,' he said. 'That will do very well indeed.'

His complacence faded as a third, slighter figure emerged from the cabin to meet them. A youth in acolyte's robes bowed to the pair on the deck.

'If my Lord Governor would care to step inside the cabin, breakfast is served,' announced the boy deferentially.

Wick's face had lost its bland, childish innocence in the months following Galliano's arrest. His expression was hard and proud, despite the show of respect. The Governor gave an involuntary shudder as he passed him in the doorway.

Nine people were gathered that night at the camp on the knot. Four of them, including Galliano and the man named Laska, had arrived from the Nurian Freehold earlier the same evening. Three others were refugees fleeing the Governor's reprisals in Marak. The Nurians were stoical about their predicament. Though they did not speak to Tymon in Argosian, they shared their cold meal of bean patties with him and seemed welcoming enough. He settled himself to sleep again not far from Galliano and the machine, well content with the turn of events. His hopes of freedom and adventure had been given a new lease of life, tempered this time by a sense of responsibility. He did not forget the scene at the bridge. It was as if he had been accorded a second chance, an opportunity to show that he deserved both Samiha's trust and Oren's generosity. He boiled with outrage at what had been done to Galliano; he was determined to accompany the old man in his exile, to be his eyes and to make a new life for them both on the Freehold.

His attitude toward Samiha reflected this fresh surge of optimism. He would prove himself indispensable to her, he decided. He would convince her that she needed him more than she needed her prophecies. He fixed once more on the air-chariot as a means to an end, and imagined himself piloting the machine by Galliano's side, hurtling across the canopy at the *shanti*'s command. He would earn her undying admiration by becoming a champion of the Nurian cause. He would even learn about Grafting, he thought in a fit of extravagance, to prove to her that he was open-minded and willing to make an effort to fit into her scheme of things. And if the heretics' hopes were a fantasy — a delusion born of poverty and suffering, as he suspected — there would be no harm in showing Samiha, gently, where his real talents lay. One thing was certain: he would be a hero. Dramatic visions danced before his eyes under the winking stars. He saw himself roaring to the *shanti*'s aid in the air-chariot. He would save her, save her people, save the world.

He awoke from these pleasant fantasies late the next morning, to the echo of a shout. He sat up, rumpled and befuddled. He was the last to rise at the camp. Samiha was nowhere to be seen. Several of the Nurians had collected at the foot of the knot, debating urgently with each other in their own language: it was this altercation that had awoken him. The discussion escalated to a babble of argument then subsided. Some of the refugees glanced in Tymon's direction, their expressions less than friendly. But no one said anything, or approached him. Presently the men set to work packing up the camp as if nothing had happened. It was mystifying to the boy.

He decided that he must have been mistaken in what he had seen, and applied himself hungrily to the remains of a breakfast of dried vine-fruit that had been left out for him, peering about in search of his friends. He glimpsed Galliano's tiny figure on the crest of the slope by the hulking form of the air-chariot. Laska and Samiha were both conspicuously absent. The older Nurian, though he wore no insignia of rank, was evidently the senior member of the group, a captain or leader of the Freehold. He and Samiha had stayed huddled together over a basket lantern a long while the night before, conversing in whispers. Tymon supposed that the two of them were now continuing their discussion in private. He felt a prick of jealousy. He would have liked to be the one who was granted Samiha's confidences.

When he had finished eating he hurried to join Galliano beneath the air-chariot's blunt nose. The old man stood beaming sightlessly at his creation, his head cocked in a listening attitude. Occasionally he reached out a gnarled hand to touch the machine's pulsating frame. He appeared to know exactly what state the engine was in at any given moment and shouted vilification and encouragement alternately to the men tinkering under the craft. The spark in the furnace grew to a blaze and clouds of smoke and steam billowed over the surrounding thickets. The propellers started up and died down again, sending up a storm of outraged birds from the canopy. Tymon gazed at the beetled form of the machine with a warm emotion akin to family pride. It was gloriously ugly.

'In the beauty, Apu,' he said cheerfully.

'You sleep like the proverbial log, my friend,' observed the scientist. 'I trust you are rested and ready for a journey. What do you think of my new creation? She purrs like a Tree-cat. No wheezing in this engine.'

The second air-chariot was significantly larger than the original model, with the capacity to carry five people comfortably as well as to store provisions and extra fuel. The steering cockpit and seats were enclosed and accessible by a hatch, and a row of round window-holes pierced each side of the craft. As with the first craft, the main propeller was mounted over the roof, but the whole construction was better balanced and less prone to instability. An additional steering propeller sat on the tapered tail. The furnace burned twice as efficiently as before; three barrels of fuel were enough, Galliano affirmed, to take them all the way back to Argos city.

'We could make the journey inside six days,' he exulted. 'Not that we would ever want to, of course. But we could.'

'Where do they get the Tree-sap to make the gall?' asked Tymon. 'There was none to be had in Marak at any price!'

'It's not just liquid gall that can be used for fuel, boy,' chuckled his friend. 'Tree-spice will do as well, and there's enough of that in the Eastern Canopy to feed a legion of air-chariots. Nurians with their own wings and able to travel the canopy again: you can see why the Council doesn't like it! We're setting up a production line. By next year, there will be ten more air-chariots like this one — the year after, maybe fifty. Good riddance to the seminary, eh? Perhaps this way they'll leave us in peace. That's what Captain Laska's hoping for, anyway, and I agrre with him.'

The mention of Laska's name distracted Tymon. He glanced restively about the knot. 'What was all that fuss about, earlier?' he asked the scientist, dropping his voice. 'That discussion between the Nurians, I mean?'

'What discussion?' replied Galliano unconcernedly, patting the machine's vibrating hull. 'I've been here, working. No time for discussions. We have to get back to the Freehold. We have a production schedule to keep.'

Notwithstanding Galliano's schedule, it was past noon when the grey-haired captain and the *shanti* finally reappeared on the dry canal path. The others hurried to the foot of the knot to meet them. The Freeholders seemed uneasy, Tymon noticed, less ready to laugh than they had been the night before, and certainly less welcoming towards him. No one smiled as he joined the gathering. He wondered what had occurred to change their minds. Laska made an announcement to the group in Nurian, holding up his hands as if appealing for calm; his words caused a ripple of surprise. Some of the Marak refugees shook their heads in disbelief. But the captain's tone was uncompromising, and after a moment of shuffling hesitation the men dispersed. Most cast black looks at Tymon. The boy had no time to reflect on this development, however, for Laska now turned to him.

'Well, *Argosi*, it seems we have much to thank you for,' he said calmly. There was nothing in his voice to explain the tension with the men. His Argosian was impeccable, formal. 'The *shanti* has told me of your courage the night of the fire and your part in helping her escape. The death of the Focals was a terrible blow. It would have been a crippling one if she had gone with them.'

Samiha had occupied herself with packing up the camp. She seemed to be deliberately avoiding Tymon and would not catch his eye as he spoke to Laska. He shrugged, a little annoyed at being kept in the dark by her of all people.

'I did nothing special,' he said. Then he remembered the reality of the escape. 'Though I'm afraid it may have cost two of your people's lives to get me out of the city, sir,' he added. 'I regret that.'

'That was their choice and their honour,' replied Laska. 'And we haven't yet heard the last word on Oren and Noni. They may still be alive.'

'What's all this, boy?' piped Galliano from nearby. 'There are details of your stay in Marak you haven't acquainted me with yet, I see.'

'It's a long story,' muttered Tymon.

He found himself shrinking from describing the exact circumstances that had led to his flight from the mission. The memory of Verlain's pawing duplicity was too fresh. Besides, a full account of the experiences in Marak would include a plausible motive for following the *shanti*. He was as yet too self-conscious to voice his feelings on the subject, even to his old friend.

Samiha left her bags to join them, but it was only to hook an arm through Galliano's and steer him away.

'I would be grateful if you would come with me, Apu,' she said. 'I want to consult you on a matter of some importance.'

'I'd be flattered,' grinned the old man. 'Lead me to the edge of the world and I'd probably walk off it for you.'

They moved out of earshot. Laska appraised Tymon from head to toe with a slight, inscrutable smile.

'The *shanti* tells me you wish to throw your lot in with us,' he said. 'Forgive me if I ask: why? Why would you want to give up your privileges as an Argosian and join a group of beleaguered heretics?'

Tymon's embarrassment mounted, confronted by that awkward question sooner than he would have liked.

'This is where my friends are, I guess,' he answered lamely. 'I'd rather throw my lot in with Galliano and Samiha than the priests, any day.'

'Ah, but you did not know the old scientist was with us when you decided to accompany the *shanti*.'

'That's true,' sighed Tymon. 'Well, I suppose that once I got to know Samiha, I was very impressed — I mean, I think she's right about a lot of things. She's right about the need for Nurian independence, and I wanted to help —'

'We aren't a rebel organisation, of course,' interrupted Laska. 'We're a Freehold. We have our independence already, in theory.'

Tymon realised that he had no adequate explanations for the older man. He nodded mutely, hot with discomfort.

'I don't wish to hurt your feelings,' continued Laska. 'But you must realise how strange this all sounds to us. Why would you give up everything to accompany Samiha? You see our problem.'

'Is that why the men were angry, earlier?' said Tymon suddenly. 'Do they believe I'm lying about why I came here, or something? I'm not a spy for the seminary, if that's what they're saying.'

Laska gazed at him, his expression thoughtful. 'You must understand they have no guarantee but the *shanti's* word,' he replied. 'That goes a long way, but in these days of suspicion, we do need more, unfortunately. The Freehold judges will want these sorts of questions answered once you arrive in the village.'

The boy felt a glimmer of hope: he would be given a chance to explain himself properly on the Freehold, then. He had begun to wonder over the course of the conversation whether the captain intended to let him travel with them at all. If Samiha had mentioned her convictions regarding his unusual abilities, or her obsession with the Grafting prophecies, Laska did not say so. He appeared to be treating him just like any other potential recruit.

'There is another thing,' he cautioned. 'All Freeholders are heretics and troublemakers, according to the Argosian authorities. If you come with us, you'll also be considered a heretic and a troublemaker. You could find yourself thrown in prison if you return home. Be certain that you wish to take that chance.'

'I've already taken it,' answered Tymon. 'I deserted my mission service: I'm no longer welcome in Argos. But I don't mind that.' He did not want Laska, too, to think of him as nothing more than a runaway, a homeless beggar. It was bad enough to have given that impression to Samiha. 'I like travelling,' he declared. 'I've always wanted to see the Tree.'

'That in itself is unusual, for an *Argosi*,' noted the Nurian, with dry humour. 'But don't you want to go home eventually? Would the priests not forgive you?'

Tymon remembered the Dean's smooth severity, the Envoy's chilly calm. 'I doubt it,' he replied truthfully. 'Argos city isn't my home any more.'

As he said it he realised, with a pang, that it never really had been.

'Well, then. We should make sure you choose a new one properly. What do you know about us Freeholders, lad?'

'Not much that's reliable,' admitted Tymon, glad to turn the focus away from himself. 'Verl— the priest in charge at the mission seemed to think you were all murderers and thieves. I didn't pay much attention to what he said, obviously.'

'Then hear the facts. We do want freedom for all Nur, but we will not use violence to achieve it. Neither will we use underhand means to accomplish our goal. Unfortunately, the rank and file of Nurians do not always agree with our methods, more's the pity. What happened in Marak recently is a case in point. The Focals were clearly opposed to violence, but that didn't stop someone who said he believed in them from using blast-poison on the Governor's mansion.'

Tymon relaxed. The captain seemed like a straightforward, bluff character. He had obviously respected the Focals, but he was a soldier and a man of action, and did not live his life by dreams and prophecies. The boy admired that trait. He wanted to be entirely honest with Laska.

'I should be up front about the Grafting,' he put in. 'I don't know whether I believe in it myself. I realise the Focals were wise people. Samiha set a lot of store by their advice. But I can't accept they actually saw the future until I have proof. Is that going to be a problem?'

Laska gave a bark of laughter. 'Not for me,' he said. 'The proof has to be personal, you're right.'

He inclined his head politely to Tymon, signifying that their interview was at a close. 'You will be questioned further on these subjects by the judges, so expect to do some explaining,' he warned. 'But for now you may stay with us, *Argosi*. All going well, you'll be sworn in as an honorary member of the Freehold tonight. I've sent word of our arrival by bird.'

He was about to move away when Tymon reached out on impulse to touch his sleeve. 'Please, sir ... I have a question of my own, if you're willing.'

Laska glanced at him enquiringly.

'One of the Focals in Marak. Ash, a man with a scar on his cheek ...' He indicated the right side of his face. 'Did he ever travel to Argos city?'

'Not that I know of,' answered Laska, slowly.

'It's just that I think I might have seen him,' Tymon rushed on, half regretting his indiscretion. 'Or perhaps it was someone like him ...'

Laska's smile faded. 'You saw Ash? In Argos?'

His regard was so intense, his face so hard, that the boy backed down in surprise and panic.

'No, I realise that would be impossible,' he gabbled. 'I must be wrong. Sorry to have bothered you with it, sir.'

'As long as you're certain,' remarked the captain, after a moment of looking searchingly at Tymon. 'I apologise, but I cannot help you more right now. There is much to do to prepare for our journey to the Freehold.'

He bowed abruptly and strode away. Tymon released a pent-up breath, relieved that the exchange was over. His mention of the Focal had evidently displeased Laska: he regretted bringing up the subject. It was ridiculous to think that he had seen Ash in Argos city. He had almost begun to doubt the fact himself. He watched glumly as the captain ordered the other men to unload the air-chariot's stock of food and water and divide it up between them; he did not dare approach the group himself or offer to help, for the Nurians glared at him over the boxes and bundles as if he were diseased. At least he had an ally in Samiha, he thought. Whatever their quarrel with him, the men would listen to her. He decided to count his blessings and trust that time would take care of any misunderstandings.

By early afternoon, the company on the knot was ready to part ways. Tymon was to accompany Galliano, Laska and Samiha in the air-chariot, while the rest of the men awaited a second transport that was to meet them at the wind-well by prior arrangement. There was now no avoiding the fact that Tymon's inclusion in the party posed a problem, especially for the refugees. The men from Marak fixed him with hostile stares, whispering angrily among themselves as he helped Galliano through the hatchway of the machine. Even the two Freehold guards seemed none too happy to send him off alone with their captain. Both Laska and Samiha had spoken on separate occasions to the Nurians before boarding the craft in an attempt to quell the rising unrest. But the affair, whatever it was, was far from closed. Tymon tried to cheer himself up by concentrating on the journey ahead. He was eager to experience Galliano's boisterous new creation.

The scientist appeared oblivious to the tension on the knot. 'We've done it, boy,' he proclaimed, as he manoeuvred himself into the air-chariot's cabin. 'We've finally found a name for her.'

'A name for who, Apu?'

'For my machine, of course. It was the *shanti*'s suggestion, actually. We've called her the *Lyla*, after *Juno and Lyla*. You know, the story of impossible love. It seemed appropriate.'

'Very appropriate. Though I'm not sure what I think of your taste in women, Apu. Can a man marry a machine?'

'I see your wit has not improved since we were last together,' the old man complained.

The *Lyla*'s propellers gyrated noisily on the roof of the machine, building up speed. Galliano felt his way along the curved walls to the front of the cockpit where Laska worked the steering rods. Samiha leaned out of one of the windows, shouting her farewells to the men on the knot. Tymon watched as the bright strands of hair on the nape of her neck tugged to and fro in the breeze. She appeared to be reassuring or encouraging her listeners one last time. He heard the word '*Argosi*' repeated. As she drew her head back through the window, she allowed herself to catch his eye at last.

'Times are difficult,' she observed ruefully. 'You'll have to get used to everyone being suspicious of you for a while, Tymon.'

Here was his opportunity to ask her frankly what was going on. But an obscure sense of pride stopped him. He wanted to appear unconcerned, fearless, on top of the situation. He wanted to impress her.

'They're wondering why I get to ride with the captain and the *shanti* while they have to wait for a mean old dirigible,' he quipped. 'I can't blame them.'

To his joy, she sat down beside him on one of the air-chariot's narrow benches. His jest fell flat, however; she did not seem to hear him, and gazed at the floor of the cockpit. The silence between them was filled with the pounding of the propellers.

'What happens when they swear me in on the Freehold?' he asked, after a pause.

She glanced at him uneasily then, as if that very question had been troubling her.

'There will be a public hearing,' she replied. 'You'll be interviewed by the judges. It's very important that you answer them truthfully, Tymon. I'm sure ... I'm sure whatever doubts they have will be laid to rest, if you do. After that you'll be asked to pledge your allegiance to the Freehold. The King of Nur will be there in person to receive your oath.'

'The King?' Tymon sat up, almost knocking his head on the low ceiling of the cabin. 'He's on the Freehold? The real one, I mean, not the prophecy?'

'Yes, yes, the current king, just your average monarch in hiding.' She smiled. 'The King's identity has to be kept a secret, you understand. When the time comes, you'll know who it is.'

'Do you think,' Tymon leaned eagerly towards Samiha, taken up by the engaging possibility, 'do you think that if I swear allegiance to him, in public — if I promise to defend Nur, and all that — then people here would accept me better?'

'And all that?' The wicked gleam returned to her eyes. 'Yes. It's possible. Though I warn you, Nurians are very independent. They have their own ideas, king or no king. But yes, it might help.'

'I wouldn't do anything to hurt the folks back home,' mused the boy. 'But I do think the Council should get its claws out of Nur. And the Rites — that's got to stop. I'd be happy to fight for those ideas.'

He was happy to fight for her too, but he did not know how to say it.

'No fighting required for now,' Samiha laughed. 'Though I'm having difficulty convincing anyone of that.'

The propellers thudded with increasing ferocity as the *Lyla* climbed slowly into the sky. Tymon articulated his next question through the deafening noise.

'There's something I still don't understand, *shanti*. Don't be angry if I say this, but if the Focals really could see the future, why didn't they predict what happened to them? If I was a Grafter — and mind, I haven't said I am, and I've been meaning to talk to you about that — then I'd certainly want to know how I was going to die!'

She seemed taken aback by the comment. He wondered if he had offended her again.

'They did predict it,' she shouted over the din of the propellers. 'Though I didn't find out until the end, of course. All was as it should be, however difficult it was for me to accept.'

'What, you mean they allowed themselves to be killed?' he cried, astounded. 'They didn't even try to save themselves?'

'A Grafter doesn't run around changing events to suit him, Tymon. All that business about cultivating the future, as if it were a fruit vine — that's a misinterpretation. The Grafters align themselves with the flow of the Sap, not the other way around. Sometimes it leads to great personal hardship. The Focals' deaths were part of a certain branch of prophecy. The right one, the one that gives joy and life and happiness to the greatest number of people. They died so that we could live.'

Tymon gave a skeptical shrug. Samiha's heresy seemed to repeat the same old tired themes of martyrdom and sacrifice he had heard spouted so many times at the seminary. It was hardly a creed for powerful heroes.

'That's the silliest thing I've ever heard,' he grumbled unthinkingly. He was still smarting from the hostility of the Nurians at the camp, and his discomfort expressed itself as sarcasm. 'Why bother seeing the future if you can't change it?'

'It may sound foolish to you, but please try and respect our beliefs, at least while you're with us,' she said. Her smile had become strained. 'I promised that much to those men back there.'

He immediately regretted having made fun of her. 'Don't pay attention to the ignorant foreigner,' he joked, in an effort to lighten her mood. 'I promise to behave better on the Freehold and say all the right things.'

'Say the right things to the Freehold judges. That's what counts.'

'Do you think they'll allow me to stay?' he asked, with somewhat tardy anxiety.

Her answer was almost lost in the surrounding cacophony. 'I think that may be the least of our problems,' she murmured.

Tymon fell silent, vanquished by the uproar of the machine's engine. What he wanted to say could not be bawled out over the sound of hacking propellers. He would have liked Samiha to share her troubles with him as an equal, to talk to him as she could obviously talk to Laska. It occurred to him, with a pang of frustration, that the Nurian captain fulfilled the very role he had wanted for himself: that of Samiha's protector and confidant, hero and helper. He had even usurped Tymon's cherished dream of flying the air-chariot. The boy tried to guess whether there was something other than friendship between Laska and the *shanti*, and studied her expression for a clue to her thoughts. After a few minutes she noticed him staring, and raised an eyebrow. He gave an awkward grin and took refuge by the nearest window, thrusting his head through the gap and into the wind.

They had already climbed high over the topmost twigs of the canopy. Only once before, during the test flight in Argos, had Tymon experienced such dizzying heights. It was exhilarating to hurtle over the twig-tips, to race beyond the normal confines of the world. The thin air carried a sparkling lightness, fresh and sharp. He let the wind whip his cheeks until his chapped skin glowed. Up here, nothing mattered but the speed of the machine and the open horizon. Here there were no people, no prophecies, no complications to worry about. He spent a long time with his nose in the wind. When he looked for Samiha again, he saw that she had left the bench to join Laska at the controls. She was crouched next to the captain, speaking in his ear. Tymon consoled himself by adopting an attitude of indifference and spent much of the remainder of the trip glued to the *Lyla*'s windows.

The hour-long flight passed quickly. The sun was angling towards mid-afternoon when he noticed a change in the canopy. A sharp protuberance broke the thickets to the southeast. There, several branches of the Tree formed a high promontory, the bare twigs draped in a net of dry, desiccated vines that obscured the area beneath. Laska steered the machine towards a lone spur jutting out from the mass and touched down on a flat section of the branch, near the tip. The machine bounced gently on the bark before coming to a halt. The maelstrom of the propellers gave way to blissful calm.

They climbed from the air-chariot in silence, stretching their cramped joints and unwilling to break the peace with conversation. Tymon gazed about him admiringly as he helped Galliano out of the hatchway. The outlook from the spur was magnificent. To the west and north, beginning a hundred feet or so below him, the twig-forests of the lower canopy spread out in a gently undulating slope. Behind and above him rose the western face of the promontory, a tangled net of vegetation. The air was cooler than in Marak, even autumnal, and the sun shone pleasantly warm through the drapery of plants. He saw that these were dead frogapple vines woven together in a grid pattern, although he had never seen specimens so big. The long strands overhead were as sturdy as his forearm. He noticed grey bulges in the vegetation, too big to be fruit, and tried to guess what sort of birds might nest in the ancient plantation. Then, with a prickling thrill of shock, he realised that the lumps were people.

Grey-cloaked men hung among the dead vines, their faces shadowed under deep hoods, eyes alive.

20

The men dropped from their perches and ranged themselves across the inner side of the spur, blocking the path into the promontory. Tymon counted twenty of them. Each was armed with a long grey staff at the ready. Neither Laska nor Samiha spoke a word. They stood patiently, as if waiting for a signal. Finally one of the figures threw back the hood of his cloak. He was a tall youth, as dark-haired and dark-skinned as an Argosian.

'*Beni, shanti.*' The youth bowed in Samiha's direction. He then inclined his head politely towards Laska and Galliano. '*Beni, syors.*'

The others did the same, removing their hoods and bowing to Samiha. They were boys of about Tymon's age, lean and lanky with barely a beard between them. They stepped back and opened a way down the spur.

'*Beni,* Solis,' answered Laska.

He gripped the dark youth's arm in a brief salute, whispering something in his ear. When he withdrew, the guard surveyed Tymon with ill-concealed dislike.

'This way, please, *syors*,' he grated, indicating stiffly that they should proceed. His accent was marked and each syllable of the foreign tongue seemed to be wrung out of him. 'Welcome to Freehold of Sheb.'

The manner in which he pronounced 'Freehold' was almost an accusation; the welcoming bow hardly creased his waist. He allowed Samiha and Laska to walk on unmolested. But when Tymon tried to pass the line of guards, supporting Galliano by the arm, the dark lad's staff whistled down with a crack, barring his way.

'Not you, *Argosi*,' he breathed. There was a spark of satisfaction in his eye.

'But I have to go with Galliano,' protested Tymon. 'You realise he can't walk on his own, right?'

'Scientist goes. Not you.' Solis stood, immovable, in front of him.

'It'll be alright, Tymon,' said Laska. He took Galliano's hand gently in his own. 'I'll take care of our friend. You go with the Freehold guards. I promise no harm will come to you.'

'Go on, go on,' smiled Galliano, waving him away. 'These young fellows have to be sure they aren't letting enemies into the village. Just answer their questions honestly and you'll be fine. I'll see you later, boy.'

Tymon was left standing, tongue-tied with surprise, as the others walked off along the spur. It did not seem to worry his friends one jot that they were abandoning him to the guards. Laska had probably known in advance of Solis' intentions, and Galliano did not seem to appreciate his predicament at all. He felt a stirring of resentment. Samiha, at the very least, might have warned him that he would be singled out for questioning so soon. But she barely glanced back in farewell. It did not occur to him to ask when he would be meeting the judges until it was too late, and he was on his own with Solis and his band.

'*Maz, syors*,' remarked the dark youth as the adults disappeared over a ridge in the path. The sarcasm in his voice was obvious.

The guards sprang into action and Tymon found himself surrounded by a thicket of grey staves. He tried to remain as still and as calm as possible. Laska had given these boys their orders, he thought. Their posturing was mere bluff and bravado. He would show them that he was not afraid.

'Well, *putar*,' smirked Solis, 'it seems we have problem. *Syor* Laska wishes you meet judges tonight. But to meet judges, *putar*, you must be worthy. *Las*, I not believe you are.'

His words drew a round of derogatory laughter from the rest of the youths, who chanted '*las, putar, las*', in mock commiseration. They fixed Tymon with hateful looks and spat on the bark at his feet. The message was clear. Argosians were not only unwelcome on the Freehold, they were reviled. Tymon's confidence wavered. Did Laska really know how much these young Freeholders hated him and his kind?

'*Shanti* too good. She believe too good of everyone,' continued Solis in his guttural, broken Argosian. He jabbed at Tymon with his staff, shoving him backwards. 'So, we have job. We protect village. We see who is worthy.'

The other boys mimicked their leader, feinting and thrusting at Tymon with their weapons then jeering as he shied away. Often the quick and expert blows found their mark and made contact with his bruised ribs. He gritted his teeth to avoid crying out with pain and fury. The guards harried him from side to side amid gales of laughter. At last he could bear it no longer.

'What kind of cowards are you?' he burst out. 'If anyone dared stand up to me alone, I'd take him, by the bells!'

This pleased the youths no end. They whooped with scorn, crying, 'We give you bells! We ring your head, *putar*!' But Solis held up his hands for silence.

'*Beni!*' he grinned. He cast aside his staff and stepped into the ring, beckoning Tymon towards him contemptuously. 'Show me, *Argosi*. Can you fight or just talk?'

Tymon clenched his fists, bracing himself. So much for non-violence, he reflected as he moved about the ring, waiting for an opportunity to attack. Occasionally one of the boys would reach out a hand to shove him between the shoulders as he passed, until Solis growled at them to stop. Then, without warning, the Nurian threw himself forward. He was lighter than Tymon, but caught him by surprise and laid him flat on his back on the bark, to howls of mirth from the youthful audience. Two well-placed cuffs sent a stabbing pain through Tymon's side; he swung out wildly, landing a glancing blow on the side of his opponent's head. But before he could strike again Solis was on his feet, dancing away from him.

'One for Freehold,' called the dark boy, triumphant.

Tymon jumped up, incensed, and lunged out, catching the other in a wrestling grip. It was a manoeuvre taught by the priests at the seminary and he had always been good at it. He threw Solis down in turn, grunting with satisfaction. They rolled over each other on the bark, neither holding the advantage for long, until an irate voice interrupted the spat.

'*Solis! Bas!* You should be ashamed!'

A man appeared, striding up the spur towards the ring of youths. 'What's going on here?' he bellowed in Argosian. 'You are to take the prisoner to the holding area. What's all this nonsense?'

He was a short, powerful Nurian, his grizzled hair and beard fairly bristling with indignation. He gestured peremptorily to Solis. The dark youth scrambled up shame-faced and hastily saluted the stranger.

'At ease, citizen. I won't report you,' observed his superior with an impatient sigh. But his gaze as he surveyed Tymon was cold. 'You. *Argosi.* Your chances at the trial would be better if you behaved with more dignity, like an adult, not a brawling child.'

Tymon rose, dusting off his tunic in embarrassment and surprise. From what Samiha had told him, he had assumed his upcoming hearing would be a formality, a chance to tell the story of their escape and answer any questions the leaders of the Freehold might put to him. Now it seemed that he was a prisoner to be put on trial. He could not think of anything he might have done to offend these people, apart from simply being who he was. Again, he wondered why Samiha and Laska had said nothing to prepare him. He made no answer as the stocky man turned his back on him and gave orders to the youths in Nurian. The guards formed an orderly enclave about Tymon. Solis motioned him on with a curt nod, and they marched away down the spur, the picture of efficiency. But when they had put some distance between them and the grizzled man, the young captain leaned close to Tymon's ear and whispered: 'You wait, *Argosi*. What we not finish, judges finish. Enjoy last minutes of peace, *putar*.'

He said no more, content to corral Tymon ahead of him in silence. The boy was left to ponder his words and do his best to gain his bearings as he jogged along. Their path soon diverged from the main road, winding along the steep, sloping side of the spur rather than its crest. To the left of the little-used track yawned a dizzy drop. Their precarious position did not appear to deter the Freehold guards. On the contrary, they redoubled their pace along the ledge, driving Tymon relentlessly before them towards the heart of the promontory.

From what he could tell in the course of his breathless, skidding progress, the outcrop in the canopy was a Tree in miniature, complete with a trunk, axial limbs and a spreading crown of twigs. The largest horizontal limbs, including the western spur, all radiated out from a single vertical axis at its core. The village itself nestled in the highest and least accessible of the branches. The boy glimpsed houses made of canvas and straw among the twig-forests at the summit of the central column; there did not seem to be any heavier structures. The buildings, the delicate rope-bridges, the camouflage netting — all were built for defence, discreet and mobile. He realised with a sinking heart that the Freeholders lived in a permanent state of war. The fact that he had ever thought he would find a welcome among these people was laughable. It occurred to him that he could not rely on Samiha's good word, or even Laska's orders, to protect him now. Who would complain if there were a regrettable accident on the way to the holding area, and the *Argosi* prisoner fell to his death in the abyss?

He hugged the slope of the spur as he ran, determined not to give his captors the satisfaction. His breath came in gasps and the sweat dripped down his forehead, but he dared not stop to wipe it away. The little track made directly for the vertical limb at the hub of the promontory. There it became a tunnel, a black wormhole bored straight into the face of the column. He had no choice but to plunge into the narrow opening ahead of the guards, passing from sunny afternoon into swift, moist night. The darkness in the passageway was almost tangible. The footsteps of the other boys echoed strangely behind him; he could no longer be sure if he was being followed. With a stab of misgiving, he slowed his pace in the gloom, reached out to touch the wall beside him — and fell.

The hole was not deep, but it was as black as Tree-pitch. Tymon tumbled onto something soft and springy. From the dusty odour that rose about him he guessed that his fall had been broken by a heap of dried moss. He rolled off the sweet-smelling pile and scrambled to his feet. His outstretched arms touched a wall behind the heap of moss. He was in an empty chamber, a cavity within the limb. He tried reaching up the wall, but the lip of the passageway above was too high and the wall itself hopelessly smooth, offering no handhold.

'Come back, you cowards!' he cried in outrage. 'Tell me why I'm on trial!'

There was no answer. A draught hit his ear; the cavity had some other exit. He followed the wall to his left, tracing the smooth, curved surface with his fingers, his breathing loud in the darkness. His heart jumped as he found the edges of a door. But it was locked, without even a handle on his side as far as he could determine. A steady flow of air seeped through the hairline crack beneath. On he walked, feeling his way along the wall until he stumbled onto the pile of moss once more. The chamber was round, and he had come full circle. There was nothing else in his prison.

'You can't just leave me here!' he shouted, helpless with fury.

But they did leave him. Time slowed to a standstill in the impenetrable darkness of the chamber. It was a torture for Tymon. He told himself that help would come soon, that Galliano would miss him and Samiha would enquire after him. Laska would ask if his orders had been carried out. They were surely not a party to this treatment. Or were they? Had his friends all betrayed him, consented to his imprisonment for reasons of their own? Was this some elaborate initiation, some test, as Solis had suggested, of his worth? He continued to wait, waited interminably, waited until he was almost beside himself with frustration. He rose and kicked the smooth walls of his prison. He yelled until he was hoarse. At last he sat back down on the pile of moss and attempted to gather his thoughts.

If there was a way out of his predicament, it was by cunning, not force, he reasoned. The Freeholders had all mentioned he was to be interviewed by judges, so they would not leave him there forever. The stocky man was right: it was time to grow up. He would be ready to prove his worth, to take up any challenge the leaders of the Freehold offered, even if it meant returning to Marak at the risk of life and limb to spy on the priests. If he really was going to meet the Nurian King that evening, as Samiha had said — it seemed out of character for her to lie outright, even if she had been less than forthcoming about what awaited him on the Freehold — then he would use the opportunity to throw himself on the mercy of the sovereign. He would beg for a chance to prove his loyalty. If only they would give him a chance to speak! He would be eloquent. He would be brave. No one would be able to refuse him. He rehearsed grand gestures and heartfelt pledges, murmuring to himself in the darkness.

He did not know whether he had been sitting there for an hour, or two, or three, crouched over his knees and furiously dreaming, when suddenly the deep, rolling voice of a bass drum vibrated through the chamber. The beat reverberated from above, penetrating the woody heart of the limb. Even the floor trembled. From somewhere beyond the chamber roof came the muffled roar of many voices, as if a crowd had gathered right overhead. Before he could do more than scramble to his feet, his nerves stretched taut in the darkness, there was a scrape of a key in a lock and a luminous crack appeared on the opposite side of the chamber. It widened to an archway. A figure stood in the doorway, black against a glare of reddish light. Voices chanted in Nurian beyond. They sounded as if they were resonating inside a well.

'You go meet judges now.' Solis' dry tones rang out. The red glow of the evening sun, dazzling to Tymon after his hours of incarceration, spilled down the spiral staircase behind him. '*Vaz*. Go. They wait for you.'

The youth jerked his staff impatiently upwards. Tymon was hardly at the bottom of the stairwell before the Nurian had locked the door behind him and followed on his heels. *Doom, doom*, thrilled the drums, quickening along with Tymon's pulse. He mounted the stairs with a beating heart, at a loss as to what to expect next.

He could not have been prepared for the sight that greeted him as he stepped through the arch at the top of the stairwell. He blinked, blinded by the light-filled space ahead. His first impression was of a large and unnaturally flat surface. Then he caught his breath in astonishment. He was indeed standing in something similar to a giant well. At the summit of the hub-like limb, where the many branches of the promontory met and merged, an arena had been built a gigantic amphitheatre carved straight into the living Tree. Terraced seating stretched up on three sides above Tymon. At his feet lay a wide circular platform surrounded by eight giant torches, each the height of a man. He had emerged in an alcove under the west terraces. The fourth quarter of the round, the eastern side, was empty. A gap in the twig-forests opposite showed clear through to the evening sky. His steps faltered and he came to a halt, checked by the expanse of the arena. The drums thundered on. He could see the great hide-bound tubs poking out from alcoves under the terraces to the north and south. Another guard glared balefully at him from the edge of the stage.

Tymon had never been inside a theatre, but he had heard tales of the Nurian 'pleasure pits' from his tutors at the seminary. He gawked at the central platform. It seemed like an outrageous waste of horizontal space. He felt dwarfed by the steep sides of the well, oppressed by the twelve levels of seating above him. The people on the terraces were a blur of colour; the drums rolled and the torches smoked impressively into a red and purple sky. He was reminded uncomfortably of the Rites procession in Argos. Only the first three tiers of the arena were actually occupied, but that was quite enough. He felt his lips go dry. In front of him, forming a semicircle at the centre of the stage, stood nine figures robed in grey.

'Go!' breathed Solis at his elbow. 'You go to judges! No wait!'

He pushed Tymon past the second guard, who scowled in disapproval, as if he objected to an *Argosi* setting foot on the stage at all. As the boy stumbled gracelessly onto the platform, the drums rumbled to a halt. A hush descended on the terraces. Solis herded him into the middle of the stage then stepped back, leaving him on his own. The nine robed figures turned slowly towards him: he noticed that they all wore bone-white masks.

'Tymon of Argos,' pronounced a short, stocky figure at the centre of the arc. His voice reminded Tymon of the man who had interrupted the fight on the spur. 'You have been brought before the Freehold to receive judgment. The charges are murder and conspiracy to murder. How do you plead?'

Even after listening to Solis' jibes, Tymon would never have expected a charge as grave as murder. He felt the injustice of the allegations keenly and forgot all his rehearsed eloquence.

'Not guilty!' he blurted out. 'Of course not guilty! Why are you doing this to me?'

His outburst provoked a buzz of anger from the terraces.

'This court does what it sees fit,' growled the stocky judge. 'We ask the questions. You answer. Let the prosecution make its case, *syors*.'

A second judge, a tall, thin man, paced forward, his finger pointed in accusation at Tymon.

'Here we have a liar and an impostor,' he declared, stalking about the boy like a Tree-cat about its prey. 'You are a spy for the seminary, novice, and have been since you met the *shanti* in Argos city. Once a priest, always a priest.'

Tymon opened his mouth to protest, only to hear another masked figure cry out: 'As soon as you discovered Samiha's identity, you reported to your superiors. You were assigned to follow her, to find out what was going on in the Nurian community. To that end you cultivated her friendship and her trust. To that end you helped her escape.'

'You insinuated yourself into her company again in Marak,' put in yet another, reproachfully, before he had a chance to answer. 'You went so far as to attend a Grafting. Then, when the moment was right, you betrayed the Focals to the Governor's men.'

The judges paced to and fro on the stage, delivering their indictment of him as if it were undisputed fact. They formed a restlessly moving circle about Tymon. Despite what the stocky man had said, they asked no real questions, and gave him no chance to respond. There was no occasion to try out his prepared speeches. Viewed in a cynical light, his whole association with the *shanti* was suspect. The wheel of masked figures revolved as the charges against him mounted inexorably.

'You had other plans for Samiha, of course. After the death of the Focals, you were conveniently to hand in her hour of need —'

'You won her trust, only to lure her into a trap, *Argosi*.'

'If Laska had not arrived early and foiled your plans —'

'She'd be in an Argosian brig by now, on her way to stand trial for treason!'

'That's not how it was!' pleaded Tymon, flustered at the unrelenting litany of accusations. 'There was no trap! You're wrong! I had nothing to do with the deaths of the Focals and I'd never do anything to hurt the *shanti* —'

'Did you, or did you not, meet a man known as the Lord Envoy before you left Marak city?' interrupted the short man again, ignoring his appeal.

Tymon's heart froze. The judges' procession came to an abrupt stop. They made a tight circle about him, a wall of eyeless faces far more intimidating than the guards' boisterous ring on the spur.

'I did,' he admitted reluctantly. 'But only because I had to. He was waiting for me at the mission. I had no choice.'

'Did you tell him about the Focals, novice?' snarled the thin man. 'Did you give him the time and place of their next Grafting, so he could send the Governor's soldiers to slit their throats?'

The audience rumbled with righteous indignation. This was the main charge, the question that the crowd had been waiting for.

'Of course not!' Tymon answered. 'He asked me if I wanted a promotion. I didn't even agree to that —'

'Did he ask you to betray the *shanti*?' enquired another figure, soft-voiced. With a shock, Tymon recognised the tones of an older woman, rich and mellow. He had assumed that all the judges were men. 'Did he threaten you, perhaps?' suggested the feminine voice. 'Force you to give away her position?'

'Give away her position?' echoed Tymon, perplexed. 'I don't know what you mean. We escaped from her house together —'

'The better to ensnare her in the wilds of the canopy,' spat out the thin judge. His hands were twitching with annoyance, as if he ached to throttle the upstart foreigner.

'I'd never do such a thing!' exclaimed Tymon hotly. 'Why don't you ask Samiha? Why don't you ask Laska?' He tried to peer between the bodies of the judges, towards the terraces, searching in vain for his friends. 'Why don't you ask your captain?' he cried. 'He's the one who invited me to the Freehold in the first place. He wouldn't approve of all this.'

'I should be up front about that,' observed one of the judges who had not yet spoken. 'I'm afraid that invitation has been suspended.'

The figure took off its mask. There stood Laska, baiting him with his own words. Laughter bubbled briefly through the crowd. Despite the banter, however, no trace of the captain's old, courteous manner remained. With a swift movement he grabbed hold of Tymon's arm and twisted it behind his back, forcing him to his knees. The boy was too surprised to resist. He found himself thrust down on the dusty floor of the stage.

'The Envoy's ship was sighted over the canopy this morning, before we left the campsite,' he barked in Tymon's ear. 'Lucky for you it was headed south and did not approach the knot. Did you signal the priests, novice? Did you send them a message about the *shanti*'s whereabouts?'

'No!' gasped the boy, in pain and resentment. 'I hate them as much as you do!'

'I do not hate them,' replied Laska, grimly. 'Hate clouds the judgment. But I will defend my people, and my sovereign, to my last breath. The *shanti* may believe you're a friend but I'm harder to convince. If you've been signalling the enemy I'll break both your arms myself.'

The fact that Samiha apparently still thought well of him was a ray of hope for Tymon. 'I swear I had no idea that ship was on our tail,' he insisted. 'You have to believe me!'

'Why should we believe you?' cried another, all too recognisable voice, taut with emotion. One more robed figure lifted its mask. Samiha gazed at him, her face full of sorrow. 'You never told us the whole truth, did you, Tymon?'

Laska released him and he rose unsteadily. Even she had turned against him, then. The glimpse of the Envoy's ship had been enough to erase everything else. She must have suspected him ever since that morning on the knot, mistrusted every word of their conversation on the air-chariot.

'What do you mean?' he asked her, despairing. If she did not believe in him, no one could.

But it was the thin man who answered. 'Don't you remember?' he jeered. 'You told her you saw her coming in a dream. You pulled her name out of a hat like a conjurer. You played on her hopes until she was convinced you were one of the five Leaves of the Divine Springtime, a Sign of the Sap. You are a false prophet, *Argosi*.'

His statement drew a furious uproar from the terraces. Howls of contempt rang through the arena.

'I never claimed to be any sort of prophet!' shouted Tymon in vain, through the clamour. He turned imploringly to Samiha. 'You know I didn't! I don't even believe in the Grafting!'

This confession only seemed to make his situation worse. There were calls of 'Shame, shame!' from the crowd and Samiha bowed her head, as if she could do no more for him.

Laska's reply was cutting. 'Oh, but you needn't lay a claim to it. Just plant a few seeds and the idea will grow all on its own.' He gazed at the boy, his face bleak. 'The truth now, novice,' he said. 'How did you know the *shanti*'s name?'

'The name, the name,' muttered the judges. 'Who told you the name?'

'You know the truth,' Tymon cried hoarsely. He could not retreat from the captain: there was nowhere left to go. 'I dreamt it. It was a complete coincidence.'

Some of the judges laughed scornfully at this. Others shrugged as if they had expected no better from him, and turned away, talking among themselves. Insults echoed from the terraces. Laska conferred briefly with Samiha; the *shanti* seemed downcast. Only one out of the nine judges made no move. One robed figure, silent and unimposing, took no part in the discussions and stood to one side, scrutinising Tymon through the black holes of the mask. He squirmed uncomfortably under that empty gaze. At last the stocky man spoke for the court.

'We will give you one more chance, novice,' he said. There were hoots and whistles from the terraces. 'Describe your dream. Furnish details. Try to convince us. I assure you, your life depends upon it.'

The hubbub in the arena died down. The torches about the stage flared bright with a faint whiff of Tree-spice, and Tymon found that he was sweating in the heat of the flames. The robed judges loomed taller in the uncertain light, menacing.

'I dreamt of the Focal with the scar on his face!' he replied with sudden vehemence, hating them all for putting him on the spot. 'I dreamt of Ash. He told me the key was in the bathhouse —'

'The Key?' The older woman cut him off, her voice perilously quiet. 'What do you know about a Key, novice?'

'The key to the prison in Argos,' answered Tymon recklessly. 'It turned out to be true. But that doesn't mean anything to you, I suppose.' He rummaged in his pocket and threw down the key ring Samiha had given him. It landed with a clatter on the hardwood flags at Laska's feet.

The captain bent down to pick up the ring. 'Is that all?' he asked coldly.

Tymon could not imagine why, but his story appeared to aggravate his listeners even further. Laska's expression was severe. Samiha covered her face with her hands. Tymon felt that should she lose faith in him, all would be lost. He panicked.

'There's more!' he babbled. 'The Focal said to tell you — to tell Samiha to come home. He said she'd found what she was looking for, but I couldn't have known what she was looking for, then, and besides, when I met him for real, the first time, he didn't mention any name or the keys. He only asked me who I was ...'

He broke off in alarm as he realised what he was saying. He had no wish to invite disaster by mentioning his waking meeting with Ash. A dream was bad enough: claiming any further association with the Grafter might be suicide.

'I thought you denied encountering *penta* Ash in Argos city,' observed Laska dryly. 'Is this not another of your extraordinary dreams?'

Dusk had fallen. The audience could be heard shifting restlessly in the darkness beyond the ring of torchlight. Tymon hesitated, torn between two unpleasant options. He could lie and risk being found out, or he could confess to a dangerous truth. He had forgotten about his encounter with the fifth Focal in the excitement of his arrival, and remembered it now almost in spite of himself. The memory was hard to hold on to, slippery, as if the event itself did not wish to be recalled. A thousand qualms on the subject, long overdue, raced through his mind. Were the judges already aware that Ash had been in Argos? Had the Grafter been on a secret journey that no one was supposed to know about, certainly not an *Argosi putar* on trial for his murder? Was that why the mention of the Focal was so displeasing to Laska? Would admitting his knowledge condemn him further? He writhed with indecision, melting in the glare of the torches. Why did the arena have to be so hot on top of it all?

'This is pointless,' snapped the thin judge. 'He's been coached on what to say, obviously. I don't see why we're even discussing it. Someone signalled the ship. Who else could it be but him?'

'Patience, citizen,' the older woman admonished from the sidelines. 'Let the *Argosi* continue. We'll soon know if he's lying.'

'Tymon,' Laska prompted him patiently. 'Answer the court. Did you meet the Focal named Ash in Argos city?'

The boy took a deep breath and made his choice.

'Yes,' he said, glancing apologetically at Laska. He had to raise his voice through the mounting hum of disapproval in the arena. 'Yes, I met him there. I'm sorry I said it didn't happen, sir. I panicked a bit when you questioned me. It was about two months ago. He spoke to me from a prison cart. He didn't really look foreign, so I never thought ... I took him for a beggar. I only remembered the whole thing when I saw him at the *shanti*'s apartment the other night — when I saw him dead.'

'Are you absolutely certain of this?' asked the older woman again. 'Couldn't it have been someone else?'

Tymon shook his head. 'No, *syora*. I met that man.'

Samiha was watching him intently, as if she would have liked to read his thoughts. He wished there was some way he could convince her that he had never lied, that he had omitted some parts of the truth simply because they seemed unimportant at the time, or because other issues had preoccupied him. If only he had made a clean breast of everything while he had the chance, on their journey together from Marak city!

'Think about what you're claiming for a moment, *Argosi*,' remarked the stocky man. Most of the judges had moved away and were conversing with each other in low voices, but he ambled towards Tymon, speaking half to the boy and half to the audience above, in the skilful manner of an orator. 'Imagine: the only Nurians to go to Argos are pilgrims, and to my knowledge only one pilgrim has ever returned. Why would *penta* Ash travel to Argos city? What ship would have him for the journey? Who would take a 'Nurry' all the way to the Central Canopy, and bring him back again?'

Tymon had not considered the matter from a practical point of view. The judge's objections were entirely correct.

'I don't know,' he answered feebly. 'I hadn't thought of that.'

'He hadn't thought of that,' snorted the short judge, gesturing to the audience, to his colleagues, to the whole world in exasperation. The crowd was his: laughter rippled through the arena. 'If you're going to advance a claim of the Sight, boy, at least do so openly and honestly. What kind of fool would you have us believe you are?'

'The Sight?' gulped Tymon. 'This wasn't a dream —'

'And we're telling you: the Focal was not in Argos,' shrugged the other. 'If you persist in your story, you're saying that you experienced a Sending, a waking vision. Anyone can have a dream, novice. Only someone with the Sight can perceive a Sending. Is that the claim you wish to make in this court? I thought you did not believe in Grafting?'

The terraces erupted with whistles and catcalls. Tymon stared helplessly at the stocky judge. He had been caught and betrayed by his own truth.

'It was him,' he murmured wretchedly. He felt unable to lie, or even to avoid a straight answer on the subject any longer. 'I can't explain it. It just was.'

At that the crowd burst into a storm of debate. Some of the spectators climbed to their feet on the terraces and shook their fists at the boy. Others argued heatedly in Nurian. The judges huddled together in a concentrated deliberation of their own. Even Laska and Samiha joined the fray. It was all too much for Tymon. He was sure now that he would be condemned by the court as a liar, for no one could believe such a ridiculous tale. He wiped his sweating palms on his tunic miserably. All his optimism, all his hopes for a new start had fallen apart at the seams. What would he tell Galliano? He could not see the old man anywhere on the terraces. Was the scientist now a prisoner too, damned by association?

He felt the prick of eyes and glanced up to find the silent judge still watching him steadily. Again, that one masked figure took no part in the debate;

again, it was singularly disengaged from the whole process of the trial. As Tymon met that compelling, empty gaze, he knew with a jolt of certainty that the ninth judge had said nothing whatsoever throughout the entire hearing. Not one word of accusation or argument had passed those hidden lips. The figure's silence was deafening, its mute presence a clanging gong. Tymon felt the overwhelming urge to lift up the mask and see the face beneath.

As if it sensed his interest, the grey form stirred. To Tymon's amazement it raised a finger and pointed directly at its debating colleagues. All other sounds faded away as the judges' words reverberated in the arena, clear and strong.

'... say it's too convenient.' The thin man's complaint rang out. 'It's a ploy to distract our energies. Why does he turn up now, when we finally have some real hope, some military advantages? As Laska said this afternoon —'

'I'm not so sure now of my former assessment, if you recall,' broke in the captain. 'We already discussed this, Davil.'

'Don't you see? This is our real hope!' Samiha's eager tones cut through the others. Tymon wondered vaguely why all the judges were speaking in Argosian. His head spun. 'Now I understand what the Fifth told me, his last words —'

'Which we all agreed should not be dragged through a public court of law, out of respect for the dead,' interposed the stocky man. 'Remember our arrangement, Highness. You have your pet project, we have ours ...'

The figure dropped its hand, and the voices of the judges were snuffed out abruptly in the general din. Warmth travelled up Tymon's chest in waves and a sensation of dizziness engulfed him. He remembered the Grafting session in Marak, remembered the fiery vision in Samiha's apartment. Something other than natural was taking place in the arena. He took a shaky step towards the ninth judge.

'Who are you?' he whispered, awe-struck.

The figure held up its hand in a brief gesture of warning. Footsteps echoed behind Tymon and someone gave a gruff shout. Solis grabbed his arm.

'No move!' hissed the young guard. His companion from the alcove arrived at his side, brandishing his staff, but Solis waved him away.

'Think we not watch you, *putar*?' he sneered. 'You stay. Judges make vote. Silence in face of betters, *Argosi*.'

Tymon squinted through the haze of light that seemed to have enveloped the stage. He grasped that the judges had finished their discussion. Those who had been debating stepped back to their original places, reforming the arc. The ninth figure did not move from its post on the far right. No one spoke to it — no one appeared to have seen it. The clamour in the arena subsided as the stocky man addressed the audience again.

'*Syors, syoras*,' he called up to the terraces. 'The time has come for the judges to make their decision known. Justice will be done.' There was a brief, thunderous cheer as he continued. 'This court has debated on two counts. Firstly: whether the *Argosi*, Tymon, is guilty of the charges already mentioned. Secondly: whether his claim of meeting *penta* Ash in his own city is to be taken seriously. The last, of course, has a direct bearing on the first.'

Shouts, boos. To his own surprise, Tymon realised that he did not care any longer whether the court found him guilty or innocent. Another matter altogether occupied his attention. One by one, as the stocky man delivered his speech, the judges lifted up their masks. One by one, the faceless figures became human again. At last seven men and two women stood unveiled in the circle of flickering light.

'... will be dropped, due to lack of direct evidence.' The short man's voice dipped in and out of Tymon's hearing. '... security of the Freehold at risk. For that reason, the court defers judgment on the second count until a proper investigation can be made ...'

The boy passed a trembling hand over his eyes. The judges guttered like wind-blown candles, knots of weaving shadow and flame. Only one figure remained sharp, in focus, completely distinct.

'... headed by a committee of enquiry, to look into the claim ...'

The ninth figure was unmasked, its identity now unmistakable. There before Tymon, his scarred face brighter than any torch, stood the fifth Focal. A dead man watched him from the flickering shadows of the stage.

And smiled.

21

It might have been a hundred years that he stood there, facing the Focal: it might only have been an instant. Tymon blinked, and the dead man was gone. The thunder of drums filled a suddenly dim and ordinary arena. The proceedings were over. The judges had broken ranks, filing off the platform towards the northern terraces. Another ring of torches had been lit on the upper rim of the arena and most of the Freeholders were now climbing up the north stairs out of the hollow. Through the broken crown of the twig-forests, the night sky was bright with stars, an inverse well.

Tymon would have liked to sit down, but there was nowhere to sit on the empty stage. He would have liked to cry out in alarm, or perhaps laugh aloud, but some lingering notion of where he was and what was going on stopped him. Someone plucked at his elbow. He turned, distracted, to find Laska waiting beside him.

'Wake up, lad,' remarked the captain. He was back to his old self, polite and genial, as if nothing untoward had occurred between them. 'It's all over for now. You passed the test and came out with flying colours, I must say.'

'Please ...' Tymon stammered, pointing at the spot where the apparition had been. He could see Solis and his companion guard skulking in the shadows at the edge of the stage, following his every move. 'Please tell me — there — did you see him — him ...'

His throat tightened with panic and wonderment. He could not pronounce Ash's name.

Laska peered into his face quizzically. 'See who? The guards? Are you well, Tymon?'

The boy opened his mouth and then shut it again without saying a word. He did not know if he was 'well'. The conviction that something truly extraordinary had just happened pulsed through him like the beat of the arena drum. He knew, down to the marrow of his bones, that this was no dream, no simple hallucination born of sickness or *som*. He was not 'unwell': he was bewildered, thrilled, terrorised. He did not trust himself to do more than nod dumbly at the captain.

'In that case, we should leave,' said Laska. 'Don't worry, you're under the protection of the court now. No more Freehold guards, I promise.'

He offered his arm, smiling. Tymon allowed himself to be steered away in the wake of the judges. The knot of mingled fear and wonder remained lodged in his throat. The normal rules of existence had been turned inside out. The dead walked among the living — and he could see it. He could See it. The fact repeated itself again and again in his mind. He did have the Sight. Samiha had been right, after all. The Grafting was real. He

413

felt a dim sense of outrage. How could he have lived his whole life among people who said they believed in such things, and remained unaware? He had indeed been robbed of his birthright, he reflected as he stumbled across the stage. He had been entirely despoiled of the truth.

The captain's voice broke through his thoughts.

'I hope you'll forgive me for hauling you over the coals earlier,' he observed through the din of the drums. 'You've made quite a claim, lad. We had to be sure.'

'Then you do believe me?' asked Tymon quickly.

They had reached the north stairs on the heels of the crowd. He saw Samiha among the people ahead, deep in conversation with the stocky judge. He itched to run up to her, to tell her what he had just experienced. She would believe him. She would understand. But she did not look down. The arena drums reached a deafening climax and crashed to a longed-for halt.

'I believed you as soon as you told your story properly,' answered Laska, when conversation was again possible. 'Once you stopped beating about like a panicked shillee and told us what really happened. You've no great talent for lying, young one.'

'I had no idea I came across so badly,' mumbled Tymon, abashed. 'I just ... forgot about things, mostly. Or maybe I didn't want to admit they existed.'

They strolled up the steps at the tail end of the throng, too slowly for his liking, too slowly to catch up with Samiha. She disappeared over the rim of the arena.

'I see that you did not believe in yourself before tonight,' the captain noted astutely. 'That would account for much. Have you since revised your opinion?'

'Yes. And I feel like a fool, sir. I didn't think it all through beforehand. I had no idea I'd be claiming the Sight.'

'So it seems.' Laska lowered his voice in the renewed silence. 'Though if I were you, I would not protest your innocence too strongly. Many of my colleagues are now convinced you are as subtle as the summer breeze, and have conjured up the only defence that would let you off the hook in a Nurian court of law. I suppose you weren't aware that anyone making a good case for possessing the Sight is entitled to protection from the Freehold?'

'No, I didn't know that,' muttered the boy.

It was hard after the intensity of his experience in the arena to return to the mundane reality of politics and compromise. He was conscious that his vision, however overwhelming it may have been for him, carried no weight in a court of law. His proof, as Laska had said, had been intimately personal. The apparition had meant to warn him about the judges — of that he was sure. He recalled what he had overheard of their debate. There was something they had not brought up during the trial, some detail regarding the Focals the stocky man had not wanted repeated in public. Samiha had agreed to remain silent about it in exchange for support on another issue. *You all have your pet projects*, he reflected. *And I am one of them.*

'Is that what the others think?' he asked Laska as they trudged up the steps. 'That I planned it? That I made up the business with ... with the Grafter on purpose, just to get myself treated leniently?'

He choked again on Ash's name. The memory of the dead man was at odds with such concerns.

'Yes and no,' sighed the captain. 'To be honest, most of the judges would rather not deal with your claim at all. But they cannot be perceived as acting foolishly or hastily. A concession was necessary. A committee is now in charge of examining your case.' He gave another dry laugh. 'I imagine the verdict on your abilities will be deferred.'

The stalemate was disappointing to Tymon. Were the Nurians as hypocritical as the priests in Argos, then? Was the Sight just a convenient tool to them, a vehicle to advance one faction against another?

'What will you do with me now?' he asked, with some degree of weary cynicism. 'Am I going back to prison?'

Laska's eyebrows shot up. 'No, lad. You're under our protection, as I said. You're to be sworn in as an honorary member of the Freehold. We're all invited to the feast-hall to celebrate the King's arrival. You'll be making your pledge there.'

Tymon subsided, mortified. He had entirely forgotten Samiha's promise that he would meet the Nurian King. All his planned gestures and speeches seemed foolish and out of place, and the last thing he wanted was to be thrust into the public eye again. He trailed reluctantly after the older man as they reached the top of the stairs and exited the arena.

'Don't worry,' said Laska kindly, noting his discomfort. 'The ceremony is short and you'll be among friends. Don't be misled by the trial tactics, they're meant to shock. That's how we Nurians get to the root of things. I don't mind telling you that Samiha supported you throughout, no matter how hard you made it for her.'

Tymon picked out the *shanti*'s bright head among the people climbing the slope of the promontory's main northern limb. But Laska did not pursue the other villagers immediately. He pulled Tymon to one side of the branch-path, just beyond the ring of light cast by the arena torches.

'There's something I must be sure you understand, before we go on,' he said in an undertone. 'The King's identity is not generally given out to foreigners. I'm sure you realise by now that many people here would object strongly to your knowing it.'

He broke off as Solis and the second guard emerged from the arena. The trial did not appear to have softened them towards Tymon in the slightest. The youths' eyes glinted with resentment as they walked by.

'The fact that you are being told at all is a sign of great trust,' resumed the captain, when they were alone. 'It is your reward for being honest with us. The Kion wanted you to know that trust is repaid by trust, and truth by truth. Is that clear?'

'Kion? I'm to be sworn in by a key?' Tymon asked in puzzlement.

'The Key,' emphasised Laska. 'The official title of the Nurian King.' He frowned worriedly. 'I might as well tell you right now, I'm against the idea. I think it's unwise for you to know the true identity of the Kion, trust or no trust. You're no threat to us but you've been in close contact with people who are. One day, they might find you. The information they would force out of you would be a blow to us, certainly, but the experience would be most devastating for you, I fear.'

'Why?' Tymon argued. He was beginning to recover from his encounter in the arena, to feel more like himself. 'Why would it be worse for me, I mean? If everyone knows who the King is, wouldn't any one of the Freeholders be just as much at risk?'

Laska contemplated him in the shifting light of the torches.

'Now that you know what you are, you ought to consider that there are others like you in the world,' he said softly. 'They may have greater ability and training, and they may be in the employ of the Council. Not only that: there are Beings in existence unbound by our human laws and limitations, whose power exceeds that of the mightiest Grafter. Not all are righteous. Not all are good. Someone with your untrained talent is particularly vulnerable to their attentions.'

Tymon shivered. The night seemed to deepen about him as Laska spoke. Part of him was curious to know about such extraordinary Beings; he remembered that the scripture lessons he had been so eager to dismiss at the seminary contained references to sorcerers, as well as to the demonic powers they served. He wondered if the captain was referring to them. But Laska seemed unwilling to dwell on the subject. He suddenly smiled, and clapped the boy on the back.

'In any case, the Kion's wishes are clear,' he declared. 'All may yet be well. We'll deal with any problems as they arise, and trust in the Sap — *Sav vay, Argosi*. Now, we'd best be getting on, or they'll finish the feast without us!'

He turned and strode up the path the villagers had taken. Tymon trudged after him in silence. He found that he was grateful not to talk any more, glad of a respite. It was simply too much to have his eyes opened to a whole new world and have to consider its denizens as well, both high and low. The intense emotions of the past few hours ebbed away; he felt suddenly very hungry, and very tired. He had eaten nothing since his midday meal.

The night air was warm and dry about them. Many of the village dwellings favoured the north side of the promontory, and the twig-thickets above the path were filled with twinkling lights. Tymon could hear children talking excitedly, clattering along the high ramps and bridges between the houses. The Freehold seemed an altogether more pleasant place under cover of darkness, more attractive than it had been on his precipitous arrival. His spirits rose. Perhaps the people of Sheb were not such bad sorts. Perhaps they would welcome him, after all. Haunting strains of music carried towards him on the night breeze; over a hump in the path their source, and the destination of the crowd, became apparent. A large building was perched in the thickets directly overhead, its windows aflame with lamplight.

At that moment he caught sight of a small, bent figure on the ramp leading up to the hall and forgot all other concerns. 'Apu!' he cried, hastening to Galliano's side.

The old man turned his ruined, beaming face on him. 'Ah! Welcome back, boy!' he said. 'Not too shaken up, I hope? Sorry you had to go through all that trial business.'

One of the Freeholders, a powerful man wearing a sooty workshop apron, was helping Galliano up the ramp. The scientist grinned blindly at the people making their way past him. Several greeted him politely in return.

'After what happened to me, I was afraid they had arrested you, too!' confided Tymon, falling into step with him.

'Arrested me, eh? Why would they do that?' scoffed his friend. 'No, they just asked me to stay away from the trial. Unacceptable bias and all. I think they wanted to spare my fragile nerves. I told them I'd go on strike if they found you guilty, anyway. Come and tell me how it went. I presume well, otherwise you would not be here.'

That evening, Tymon had the distinction of sharing the only table in the feast-hall with the leaders of Sheb. As was usual among the Nurians, there was little furniture in evidence in the high-beamed, airy dining hall. Most of the villagers served themselves from communal pots along one side of the room and gathered in informal groups on the floor, holding their plates on their laps. There were no chairs for the judges, either: they were installed cross-legged around the low table. Tymon sat crouched between Galliano and Laska at one corner, some distance away from Samiha. If the King was present, he was accorded no special honour or distinctive place in the company, as far as the boy could tell. He could not have decided which of the simply dressed villagers, or for that matter which of the judges was the Nurian sovereign in hiding. The leaders of the Freehold, once they removed their masks and gowns, were indistinguishable from the rest of the population.

He spent most of the meal listening to Galliano's often comical descriptions of the characters and ambitions of each of the judges. He learned that the stocky man, *syor* Kosta, was the judges' Speaker, something analogous to the Dean in Argos. Kosta was the main backer for Galliano's air-chariot production line, a responsibility he shared, surprisingly enough, with the thin, vociferous man, the *syor* Davil who had taken such exception to Tymon.

'Davil's a demagogue,' shrugged the scientist dismissively when he heard Tymon's account of the trial and the thin man's accusations. 'It pays in votes to take the hard line against Argosians — when they don't offer you military advantages, that is. He's an opportunist. He'll bend any way the wind blows.'

Tymon's description of the older woman, *syora* Gardan, elicited an admiring chuckle from his friend, however.

'Now there's a character,' confided the old man. 'I wish I had my eyes. You won't find a sharper mind or a sharper beak in the roost. She's the one you have to look out for, along with Kosta. Protect your brain-pans, gentlemen.'

Gardan sat not far from them, on the other side of the table. As Galliano spoke, she glanced up and with uncanny accuracy caught Tymon's gaze. Her eyes were bright and blue under a short crop of snow-white hair, and her smile did have something sharp about it, as if she were about to make a brisk reply. But she only leaned over the table and offered the boy a bowl of froggapples. He shook his head, squirming with embarrassment. He had already eaten and indeed drunk to his heart's content, for despite the drought and general want in the Eastern Canopy — Galliano assured him that this was the first time they had tasted meat in a fortnight — the villagers had laid out a splendid feast in honour of their invisible king. No less than three roast shillees were served up on woven platters filled with gravy, and the side dishes brimmed with vegetables Tymon had not seen since he left Argos city. They were grown in special Tree cavities protected by ingenious methods from too much heat and sunlight, the scientist informed him proudly. Despite his caustic observations, the old man seemed to think a great deal of the Freeholders. He was more than willing to forgive them their exacerbated suspicion of outsiders and their flair for courtroom dramatics.

'They gave me a bit of a scrubbing when I first came, too,' he laughed. 'Though any masks were wasted on me, I'm afraid! I must say I can't top an accusation of murder. But they're solid to the core, Tymon. As long as they feel you're being entirely honest, they'll come round and accept you, you'll see. Frankly, I'd rather the accusations were out in the open like that. No sessions behind closed doors, like the Priests' Council, don't you know.'

Tymon thought of the judges' covert dealings and was not sure that he did know. But in the aftermath of the meal he felt inclined to let the matter go. He was now bursting with the desire to share his discovery of the Sight with someone; nothing else was really of any consequence. He had searched for an opportunity during the feast to mention his vision to Galliano, but the moment never seemed right. Finally, when everyone had finished eating and the conversation in the hall dropped to a satisfied hum, he could contain himself no longer.

'Apu,' he whispered in the old man's ear. 'Something else happened to me during the trial. I have to tell you about it —'

'Eh? What? I'll be deaf as well as blind at this rate, boy. Speak up!'

'I said, I saw something during the trial —'

'Sorry to interrupt,' put in Laska, from Tymon's other side. 'But you should be ready to stand up when you're called, lad. The Kion is about to make an address.'

'Now, this is important,' whispered Galliano excitedly, as Tymon groaned in irritation at the delay. 'I'm sure what you saw was very interesting, but you can tell me later. I must admit I've been hoping you'd be allowed to know about the Kion. It's a great honour — you're only the second Argosian who does!'

Tymon felt the stirrings of curiosity through his frustration. He had never met royalty before. The Priests' Council had abolished the monarchy in Argos as a relic of a decadent empire; he had only the dimmest notion of what a king was, let alone how to talk to one. It was a surprise to him, therefore, when Samiha rose from the table. She held herself as straight and tall as a leaf-stem, gazing out over the suddenly quiet room.

'*Sav beni, namis,*' she announced.

The atmosphere in the hall had shifted subtly, as if everyone knew what was coming. The people on either side of Tymon hung on the *shanti*'s every word. He guessed that she would be introducing the Kion, doubtless under another name.

'Today we welcome a new recruit to Sheb,' she continued, in Argosian.

A faint sigh of protest ran through the gathering. The villagers had accepted a foreign tongue at the court proceedings out of fairness to the defendant, but enough was enough. Samiha waited for the noise to subside. Slowly, deliberately, she persisted in the alien language.

'He is worthy. He has been tested and found loyal. We are all children of the Tree, whether *Nuri* or *Argosi*. You've heard by now of the events in Marak: heard that our brethren died because of the unwise and short-sighted actions of a few.'

Silence hung palpably over the hall. Tymon fidgeted, eyeing the rapt faces of the audience and only half listening to Samiha's words. Who would she introduce?

'It's time to put our differences aside and work together,' she said. 'Without the Focals we can only see our past mistakes. What lies ahead is veiled to us. Nothing can be accomplished through hatred. *Beni.* In the spirit of reconciliation, let us welcome the new member of our fellowship and a possible heir to the five Focals of Marak. Come forward, Tymon of Argos.'

She turned to Tymon and held out her arms, beckoning to him. It was the call to the pledge. She had extended the invitation herself. He was perplexed an instant; what of the Kion?

And then, at long last, understanding dawned. He recalled in a rush the unquestioning self-sacrifice of Oren and his sister; Laska's fierce loyalty; the deference shown to the *shanti* even by the most belligerent of her people. No ordinary priestess would command such wide respect. No temple singer would keep an audience on tenterhooks in this fashion. 'Highness,' Kosta had said during the trial, he remembered belatedly. He had been sharing his bread and berth with a queen. He felt Laska nudge him urgently and staggered to his feet in astonishment, knocking the edge of the table and causing cups and bowls to teeter. He retained his wits sufficiently to hurry to where she stood, and take her hands in his own. Her fingers were cool and light in his hot palms. Kion, he thought. She was the Kion. Of course she was.

'Do you wish to join the Freehold?' she asked gravely.

'You!' he breathed, with sudden comprehension. 'He was talking about you!'

He could have smote his forehead at his own stupidity. The words of the fifth Focal came back to him with new meaning. *The Key is in the bathhouse.* Key, Kion. He had known her identity all along. Even her street address had proclaimed it to the world.

She smiled at him briefly, and he realised that the public question still hung between them.

'Yes,' he managed. He hoped his voice would carry. The day's successive revelations had robbed him of the power of speech.

'Do you swear allegiance to Nur?'

'I do,' he answered again, stronger.

'Do you accept that all life is sacred, that all are part of the Tree of Being and that the Sap flows through us?'

'I do,' he repeated. It sounded like Treeology class all over again, he thought.

And then he wondered, with a stab of anxiety, whether it was. If it was possible to See the dead, what of the Grafters' other powers? What of Samiha's troublesome beliefs about the End Times? Were all Grafting prophecies equally valid? Tymon's experience of the Sight had done nothing to lessen his dislike of lurid predictions and pious apocalypses. Did he now have to believe in all that, too? But this was no moment to consider such matters. The villagers had their eyes fixed on him, waiting for him to flub his chance, to commit some error of protocol. Samiha scanned the crowded hall carefully before resuming her speech.

'Bearing in mind the verdict of the judges, does anyone here have good reason —' she paused, allowing the word 'good' to sink in '— to oppose this union?'

Tymon almost dropped her hands. He had not expected a direct question of this sort and winced, waiting for the blow. There was a crackle here, a rustle there, but the throng remained mute. No one dared openly contradict the Kion. She allowed an interminable instant to pass before turning her gaze back to Tymon.

'Then you have joined our fellowship. Our pain, our joy, is yours to share.'

He assumed that the pledge was over and waited for her to withdraw. But instead, with simple solemnity, she pulled him close and kissed him on the mouth. Another ripple of surprise, pleasant this time, curled his toes.

'*Sav beni*. Be blessed, Tymon,' she said.

She let go of his hands and returned to her seat. Tymon wandered back to his own end of the table in a daze. Nurian customs did not cease to amaze him. He reminded himself that it had been a ceremonial gesture, and that she had probably delivered similar greetings to others. But the kiss lingered, oddly personal, a burr on his lips.

'*Beni*, Tymon,' whispered Laska as he sat down again. Both he and Galliano grinned gleefully at the boy.

'You all enjoyed that,' muttered Tymon. 'You enjoyed holding out on me about who she was.' He glanced down the length of the table at Samiha. Her eyes slid away from his, but her colour was high. 'She enjoyed it even more!' he added indignantly.

'Now, boy, this is no joke. You don't talk about it to anybody,' admonished the scientist in a whisper, as the buzz of conversation mounted again in the room. 'If you must speak of it, do so only to Laska or myself.'

'Is there anything else I should know?' asked Tymon. 'She hasn't stopped changing identity since we met ... pilgrim, priestess, judge, queen ... is there any more?'

Galliano chuckled. 'Without a doubt,' he said. 'There's always more where the ladies are concerned.'

Tymon finally found the time to tell his friend about his vision later that evening, after he had taken the old man back to his living quarters. He had immediately accepted Galliano's invitation to stay in his hut among the twig-thickets; the thought of ghosts peering over his shoulder during the night was disturbing, and he had no wish to be alone. The scientist's response to his dilemma was typically sanguine.

'If you say you saw the Focal then I believe you,' he said. 'What that actually means, however, is a different story. You'll have to figure that out for yourself.'

Tymon settled himself on his sleeping pallet. The night was clear and the two of them had brought their bedding out onto the terrace, under the stars.

'I don't know what to think, Apu,' he sighed. 'It's spooky. And there are some things — well, many things, really — that I don't like about the Grafting prophecies. Do I have to believe in them, too?'

Galliano laughed softly. 'It's a shame I can't help you more. I never much went in for metaphysics at the seminary. Applied Treeology was my line. But I don't think you need to decide what to believe just now. Learn as much as you can and keep an open mind. Perhaps Grafting is just a kind of science we haven't understood much about yet.'

There was a moment of silence. Then the old man spoke again, meditatively.

'If such things as the Sap exist, mind you, I'd be inclined to think they had bounds and limitations. Everything has limitations, Tymon. That's the way the world works. Know the rules — learn the language — and you'll see how it fits together. Gravity, polarity, the behaviour of the stars ... every mysterious thing, even the Grafting. Everything has its own grammar and logic. Sometimes I wonder whether there isn't one mother-tongue that describes it all ...'

This time, the silence was longer. Tymon had just decided that Galliano had gone to sleep in mid-sentence when the old man's querulous voice piped up once more.

'Oh, and do me a favour, would you? Talk to Samiha about this, for once. Tell her what you saw in the arena. And tell her how you feel about her, too, for the sake of all things green. Your torch is burning rather too visibly.'

Tymon dissolved with embarrassment in the darkness and could produce nothing better in answer than a grunt. He had not imagined that he had been so obvious. Did Samiha see through his fumbling attempts at friendship, too? It was all very well being told to declare himself, but how was he to start? With the language of the stars? She might as well have existed on a far-distant orb herself. Her rank confused him, set her apart. She seemed further out of his reach than she had been before they arrived in Sheb. How could a runaway servant court a head of state, albeit one in hiding? How could an upstart novice, even one with the Sight, be of interest to a queen?

22

He had missed something. He rifled through Samiha's apartment, peering under weave-mats, behind curtains. Something eluded him and although he could not remember what it was, he was sure that he had left it here, in the rooms above Kion street, number six, the house with the green door. The apartment kept changing shape in the most disagreeable manner. Sometimes there were two chambers, sometimes four or five, even a panelled hallway reminiscent of the College library in Argos. If he could just find the fifth Focal again, he told himself, pacing through room after empty room, he would be able to ask him what he had mislaid. Ash would know. But the Grafters were gone, invisible. Infuriatingly, he had just missed them, too. He caught teasing glimpses — the brim of a hat through a doorway, the sound of far-off laughter. He hurried through the bewilderingly expanded apartment. They would not escape him.

Then he hesitated, struck by a thought. It was no surprise that he could not find the Focals: they were dead. How could he have forgotten? They were dead and he was back where he had started, in the room where he had sat and drunk *yosha* with Samiha. He had the sense that whatever it was he was looking for, it was right here, tantalisingly close. And there was the fifth Focal, after all, he realised. A dark figure wearing a hat and cloak stood in the open door, its back to him. Tymon approached it gladly. He was about to tug at the edge of the long cloak with his fingers like a little child, when the figure turned around. But instead of Ash it was Father Lace who loomed above him, blocking the light from the doorway.

'Greetings, novice,' remarked the Envoy. The lifeless smile spread slowly across his face.

Tymon recoiled. He glanced about him in alarm; from too many rooms, the apartment had shrunk to having only one. There was only one door, and that was obstructed by Lace.

The Envoy took a menacing step towards him. 'I have given your post away to someone else,' he whispered. 'You're a fool, boy. You missed your chance and now you have nothing left.'

'That's not true.' Tymon's voice was small and choked. 'I have friends.'

Lace erupted into laughter, but his face stayed rigid, a mask. The boy stared in horror as the hollow sound emerged from behind frozen, grinning lips. Where the Envoy's eyes should have been there were two empty holes.

'Your friends,' he gloated, 'are all dead, or soon will be. Your hopes are an illusion. You think you're a Grafter but you can't even understand what you have Seen. You think that you've found a new home in that rat-hole of a village, but no one will accept you. You're weak and deluded and pathetic.'

He reached out. Long, searching fingers grasped at Tymon's throat. The boy was paralysed with fear. He tried to speak but could not; tried to scream, but no sound emerged from his mouth. He seemed to hear a voice in the distance, chanting joyously in a language he did not understand. There was a blinding flash of light. He woke up from his nightmare to find that he had rolled off his mattress and was lying at the edge of Galliano's terrace with the morning sun full in his eyes. Someone was chanting the First Liturgy in the central arena. It was not Samiha's voice.

Of fire were Her branches made
Fearful Her symmetry …

Tymon jumped to his feet. He tripped on Galliano's bedding in the process, waking the old man up.

'By the bells!' grumbled his friend. 'If sharing a house with you means being kicked out of bed every morning, then you can go back to Marak!'

'I've made a mistake, Apu!' cried Tymon. 'I've missed something!'

The sense of having lost or misunderstood a vital truth was so strong that he had to lean on the terrace balustrade, breathing deeply of the fresh morning air until he was calm. He could not explain his anxiety. He tried recounting his nightmare to Galliano, but the details slipped away from him, tame and washed-out in the sunlight. Until the day before, he would have shrugged off the dream as a product of recent events, as meaningless as indigestion. Now he did not dare. Was there some significance to it? Was this a sliver of prophecy? How was he to know? How did the Grafters ever know?

The feeling of unease clung to him all morning. When he accompanied the scientist to the dining hall for breakfast, neither Laska nor Samiha, nor indeed any of the other judges were in evidence. Despite what Laska had said, he did not feel himself to be in the presence of friends. The villagers, especially the youth, were resolutely unsympathetic towards him. It was as if the trial and the pledge had never happened. No one challenged him, but no one spoke to him either, or made him feel at home. People turned their backs as he approached. He felt patently unwelcome as he sat on the floor of the hall beside Galliano — they avoided the low table this time — shovelling dry bean-flour patties into his mouth in miserable silence. He was deeply relieved when the old man suggested that they move on to his workshop and he was able to leave the taciturn Freeholders behind.

A hollowed-out knot in one of the southern branches of the promontory served as Galliano's new workshop and hangar. It was here that the *Lyla* had recently been assembled. The structure for a third machine was now under way, its skeletal beginnings laid out in the hangar like the bones of a giant bird. It would emerge from the open top of the knot on its maiden flight. Galliano supervised the proceedings from a ramshackle basket-chair in one corner; although he could not see the progress of construction himself, he kept tabs on everything by haranguing his co-workers in broken Nurian. The assembly team consisted of nine Freeholders who tolerated the scientist's exacerbated perfectionism with surprising good humour. Jamil, the large man Tymon had seen escorting Galliano to the feast the night before, was workshop supervisor. The huge, light-haired Nurian and the tiny Argosian scientist made a humorous pair, the giant bending patiently over the old man to receive instructions he had probably carried out himself a long time ago. He seemed to genuinely like and respect Galliano.

The spectacle of his friend's success, his ability to overcome huge odds to settle in a new place and carry on his work, was both heart-warming and slightly exasperating to Tymon. It underscored for him how far he was from achieving the same goal. After some initial awkwardness, Jamil was able to persuade his companions to let the boy join their team, and Tymon spent the rest of the morning in the cheerful chaos of the hangar, splitting planks for the new air-chariot's hull. The Nurians seemed happy enough to have an extra pair of hands on the job. When he ventured back to the dining hall, however, he came face to face with crushing indifference. Lunch was a torture; everyone but Galliano ignored him. Dinner was worse. The old scientist did not accompany him, pleading fatigue, and Samiha and Laska were still absent. Even his workshop mates shunned him, neglecting to invite him into their laughing groups. His own attempts at communication were met with blank stares from the villagers or an apologetic shrug, as if none of the Freeholders understood him. He was eager to tell Samiha about his experience of the Sight. But she seemed to have slipped away from him again, abandoning him just as they reached some form of understanding.

Matters did not improve over the next two days, and by his third morning in Sheb, Tymon's enthusiasm for life on the Freehold had plummeted. He was tired of being treated as if he did not exist and desperately needed someone to talk to besides Galliano. Samiha's continued absence vexed him. Did she consider herself too good for him now, he wondered? Did the Kion not associate with mere foreigners when she was among her own? Despite the fact that he had everything, or almost everything, that he had originally wanted — a chance to help Galliano, an opportunity to learn about the air-chariot and a new home, however imperfect — he was deeply dissatisfied. He could not shake off the low spirits that had clung to him since his dream of the Envoy. That morning, he did not go straight back to work on the planks, but squatted glumly on a twig-stump beside Galliano's chair, answering the scientist's good-natured banter with monosyllables.

'Take an old-timer's word,' his friend observed at last. 'Life is short. It's a pity to waste it on being miserable!'

Tymon's reply was muffled, out of earshot of the workmen. 'Why don't the Freeholders like me, Apu?' he mumbled forlornly.

Galliano smiled. 'Because you're an Argosian, and Argosians are faithless oppressors, as far as they are concerned.'

'But Sheb isn't even a colony. They govern themselves, don't they?'

'So it would seem,' answered the scientist.

'I can't help where I was born, can I? It's not fair.'

'Like many things.'

'All I want,' muttered the boy, 'is a new start. I want to learn how to live with these people. I'm willing to work hard. But I'm wondering if it's worth it.'

Galliano did not respond immediately. He lifted his scarred face to the sky and rocked back in his chair, making the basketwork creak dangerously. Then he said, 'For centuries this Freehold was the site of one of the great Grafting temples. It was a centre of learning. They kept an astronomical calendar here, among other things, and calculated the paths of the stars. There used to be a spur to the east of the promontory — you must have seen the gap in the branches on that side of the arena, during the trial, no? Well, the temple stood there. Quite an extraordinary construction. It had ninety-five columns and ninety-five doors, and was built fifteen hundred years before Saint Loa set foot in Argos city.'

He paused and cleared his throat. 'The seminary ordered it destroyed twenty years ago. I remember the occasion. The Freehold had a treaty with the Council. It was never supposed to provide tribute. But recruiters came anyway, demanding a quota of pilgrims. The judges refused. The Council didn't take the matter up themselves: they used the Governor of Marak to do their dirty work. The Governor accused the judges of conspiring with rebels and sent what he called a "warning strike". I'm sorry to say, the colonial troops didn't do our people any credit on that raid. Apart from demolishing the temple and hacking down a whole section of the promontory, they tore down every house in the village and left the inhabitants starving and homeless. There were Grafters-in-training at the temple; they were all killed. All their finest minds, Tymon, imagine. Everyone who had any education. It would be like burning down the seminary and killing all the priests.

'Anyway, to cut a long story short, the soldiers only left when they had forced a group of Freeholders to go with them. Women, mostly. The Tree knows where they took them. Certainly, none of them became pilgrims or arrived in Argos. It was just plain revenge. After that, as you can imagine, Argosians were welcomed here with less than open arms. The Council never acknowledged their part in the affair. It was a shameful episode and one of the reasons why I left the seminary. Ironic that I should end up here myself, don't you think?'

Tymon eyed Galliano with surprise and renewed respect. The scientist had not mentioned this story when they had last spoken on the subject of the pilgrims. He had assumed that Galliano had lost his post at the seminary because of his experiments. Now he grasped that the old man had actually given up his career over the Nurians. He had made a stand.

'I didn't know —' he began, then stopped, struck by an unpleasant realisation. The hatred of the Freeholders suddenly acquired new meaning. 'Solis, the one who looks like an Argosian ...'

'His mother was one of the lucky ones,' said Galliano quietly. 'The soldiers abandoned her in the wild canopy south of here when she became pregnant. She found her way back — eventually.'

Tymon battled a rush of conflicting emotions. He remembered the pronouncement of the wall-scrubbing militiaman in Marak: *we won't let 'em make our women whores.* He imagined Samiha with her independent spirit in the hands of such people. He, too, would have been eager to take revenge on anyone who hurt her. He was simultaneously overcome with the need to see her again, to catch the sweet fragrance of her hair. He thrust the thought away angrily.

'They have to know I'm not like that,' he exclaimed.

'They don't know. But they have faith in the Kion, and she vouches for you. So does Laska.'

'Teach me to fly the air-chariot, Apu!' demanded the boy, hotly. 'I'll go on their most dangerous missions, the ones no one else wants to do. I'll win their respect. I'll prove I'm not like those brutes in Marak.'

'We'll see about that, young daredevil,' said Galliano. He leaned forward in the chair, and an eager note crept into his voice. 'Be patient. In a few months' time, I guarantee you'll be flying a new machine on one of the most exciting missions possible.'

'What do you mean?'

'When we've built a squadron of air-chariots, one will be allowed to depart on a journey to the World Below. I made the request already: you are to pilot it.'

Tymon drew a swift breath. 'The World Below?'

'Yes, my friend! The Freeholders accept my theories. Apparently there are Grafting prophecies about a second world and a second heaven under the Storm. Anyway, the judges have decided it's time to investigate.'

Tymon could not suppress a smile. After all this time, his friend's zeal was still infectious. It lifted his gloom.

'I'm glad your dreams are alive and well, Apu. And that other people are just as crazy as you are,' he said gently.

'This is no dream! Some of the Nurians have seen it.'

'Seen what?'

'The World Below, numbskull. There's a place in the Southern Fringes where you can catch glimpses of it — they call it the Well of Worlds. I imagine they mean a hole in the Storm. I wish I could witness it for myself. Maybe one day you will go there for me.'

Tymon gaped at the old scientist. He had always thought the Storm clouds went on forever, endless, pointless, part of the infinite Void about the Tree. His impatience with Galliano's ideas had stemmed from the fact that he believed nothing at all lay under the Storm, whether mystical or material. Now, for the first time, doubt assailed him on that score. It seemed that everything he had been eager to write off as myth and delusion had at least some basis in reality.

'What do they see down there?' he asked humbly.

'They say there's another canopy. Or maybe several, it's hard to tell. The accounts are confused. Whatever it is, it's huge.'

'No demons?'

'No demons,' replied the old man. 'And no brooms.'

Tymon contemplated the ribs of the mechanical creature before him, tugging at the scanty crop of hairs on his chin. Volunteering for a trip to the World Below was certainly a worthy way of proving his capabilities to Samiha, and compensating for the behaviour of his fellow Argosians at the same time. He returned to his work with renewed energy, and spent the rest of the morning splitting bark for the air-chariot's hull. At noon he went so far as to offer to fetch lunch for his workmates. He returned to the dreaded dining hall with his chin held high, the lightness back in his step. A tangible goal made the villagers' hostility far easier to bear.

On his way back to the workshop, a packet of warm bean patties in his hands, he noticed people congregating on the path ahead of him. He had been skirting the rim of the arena, threading a circle about the promontory's central hub from north to south; the Freeholders were turning off the central axis and hurrying along the crest of the western spur towards the spot where Tymon had first disembarked from the air-chariot. The villagers called out to each other excitedly as they ran. No one paid any attention to him. He could not resist his curiosity, and followed cautiously behind, craning his neck to discover what was causing the stir. He was within sight of the *Lyla*, insect-like on the exposed tip of the branch, when he heard a shout resonate from the net of vines above him. He recalled with a stab of anxiety that he had entered the domain of Solis and his band. Figures dropped from the vines. But they had their backs to him, their gaze fixed on the foggy western horizon. The day was hot and overcast in a return of the *mora* weather that had so weighed on Tymon's spirits in Marak. He squinted at the hazy sky, shading his eyes. At last he spotted a black speck over the lower canopy. A dirigible was approaching.

For a terrible instant he thought it was the Envoy's ship. He saw the sleek line of the hull, the green banners of the Council flowing at the mast. Fear gripped him, an icy, reasonless panic. Had his old masters come all the way here to claim him? Then, belatedly, he understood that the fog had played a trick on his eyes. The craft was far too small and dilapidated to be an Argosian vessel, or for that matter any other attack force. The banners were simply dark ropes that swung on the crossbeams. The cries of the people on the spur as they caught sight of the arriving ship were joyful, and he remembered that the refugees they had left behind at the wind-well were to return to the Freehold on another vessel. This was the transport from Marak. As the old merchant ship tacked round and descended towards the waiting crowd, Tymon suddenly became conscious of his vulnerable position, alone and without friends on the spur. He had no wish to be caught between the youth of Sheb and the Marak refugees. He beat a hasty retreat to the workshop with his rapidly cooling lunch.

The false glimpse of the Envoy's ship proved hard to dislodge, however, and hung like a shadow on his mind all afternoon. He was still mulling over his mistake that evening, sweeping chips off the floor of the hangar, when he heard a commotion outside the hollow knot. Strident voices echoed on the branch-path leading to the workshop. One by one, the men ceased their hammering and drew together in tight, whispering groups. No amount of scolding from Jamil or Galliano could persuade them to carry on with their tasks. At last the angry voices resonated directly outside the hollow. Footsteps thudded along the narrow tunnel connecting the surface of the branch with the hangar, and the doors were thrown wide. Caro burst in, followed by a gaggle of villagers. He pointed straight to Tymon.

'You! *Argosi* traitor!' he cried. 'You will pay for your crimes! I will not sit by while my people are taken in by a spy and a scoundrel!'

Tymon laid down his hardwood axe in order to respond, then regretted doing so. Caro strode towards him as if he intended to pulverise him on the spot. Only the intervention of Jamil prevented a scuffle. The workshop supervisor stepped in front of the boy and spoke quietly to Caro in his own language. Even the militant was no match for the huge man. He drew back, glaring at Tymon. The other villagers talked among themselves excitedly. Tymon recognised Solis and several of the Freehold guards.

'What in green grace is going on?' Galliano protested, unheeded, through the babble of voices. 'Be careful where you step, there's delicate work going on here!'

'I cannot bear it!' Caro broke out. 'He must be made to pay! He's guilty — how could they not see it —'

'Guilty of what?' shouted Tymon defiantly. It felt unbearably unjust to be faced with yet more accusations, even after the trial. 'All I'm guilty of is being who I am, Caro.'

'Don't speak to me, *putar*!' Caro screamed. 'Don't dirty my ears with your lies —' He tried to move around Jamil but the giant placed two gentle, immovable hands on his shoulders, stopping him in his tracks. Several of the villagers reasoned with the militant in undertones. One was the judge named Davil, Tymon noticed with alarm.

'So be it,' pronounced Caro, after listening to the whispered counsel. He shook himself free of Jamil and smiled disdainfully. 'So be it, *Argosi*,' he said to Tymon. 'I will treat you with the respect you do not deserve. Come to the *askar* — to the old temple — tomorrow morning. Be prepared to defend yourself. You will be given no quarter.'

444

Tymon stared in dismay as the yellow-haired Nurian marched out of the workshop, followed by his hangers-on. He had no doubt that he had been handed a personal challenge. Caro meant to confront him, perhaps even to fight a duel with him in front of the entire village. He guessed, after what Galliano had told him, that the 'old temple' was the central arena and wondered what he had done to provoke the militant's hatred to new heights. He seemed to hear the voice from his dream once more. *You think you have found a home*, it jeered. *But no one will accept you.*

'I can't believe that man is still angry at me,' he sighed.

'Caro is angry with everyone,' observed Jamil, at his side. 'He lives on anger, *Argosi*. It consumes him.'

'Well,' commented Galliano in disgust, creaking up from his basket-chair, 'I for one have had quite enough anger for today. Everyone go home and calm down.'

He shuffled out of the workshop on Tymon's arm. They avoided the dining hall and made directly for their quarters, unwilling to face Caro or his supporters again. As they climbed the ramp towards Galliano's hut, they saw Laska and Samiha hurrying down the north branch below them. The *shanti* waved eagerly to Tymon, calling his name. His heart pitched in his chest. He turned and waited for the others to join them.

'*Syor* Galliano, my sincerest apologies for what just occurred,' cried Samiha as they drew level with each other on the ramp. 'We could not stop

Caro or reason with him. This is a very unfortunate affair.' She turned to Tymon. 'We need to have a little talk, *Argosi*.'

She murmured a few words to Laska in Nurian. The captain took hold of Galliano's arm.

'Come, friend,' he offered. 'I will help you to your quarters.'

'Very well,' grumbled the old man. 'But I won't have any more raving lunatics interrupting my work and holding up my schedule. I've several things to say to that Caro of yours tomorrow morning.'

They walked off, leaving the two young people alone. The evening twilight had faded and the lights of the village shimmered like glowworms through the twig-thickets. Tymon waited in uncomfortable silence. The episode with Caro had shaken him and now that he was alone with Samiha, his embarrassment about protocol returned in full force. He did not know how to have a 'little talk' with the Queen of Nur. He could no longer think of her simply as his friend, the *shanti* from the Marak temple. He eyed her as she leaned on the balustrade at the side of the ramp, gazing over the twig-thickets.

'I regret that I've had no time to be with you during the past few days,' she remarked. 'I wanted to visit you at the workshop, to see how you were settling in, but there have been a hundred things to attend to. And it seems that whenever I do see you, I must be telling you things you probably don't want to hear. Though I do have some good news for you tonight, as well as bad. Which do you want first?'

He came to stand at the balustrade beside her. 'The bad, I suppose,' he answered. 'Give me something to look forward to. Besides talking to you, I mean.'

It had not been meant as a joke, but the piece of flattery elicited a dry chuckle from her. He revived a little.

'*Beni*,' she said. 'The bad news, as you have no doubt gathered, is that Caro arrived this afternoon on the refugee ship. He is determined to re-open your trial. He was, shall we say, unimpressed by the judges' ruling. He's anxious to prove you responsible for the deaths of the Focals.'

'Then it's the same old story.' Tymon snorted in disbelief. 'It's rich, coming from him. I don't understand why the judges let him come back to the Freehold.'

'It's not a question of "letting",' replied Samiha. 'The judges might disapprove of Caro's actions in Marak — actually, some of them don't — but he still has a right of asylum here. And the average Freeholder thinks he's a hero.'

'But the Focals! He sold them out for blast-poison!'

'That's not his version of events, as you'll see. I agree with you whole-heartedly: I think it's unconscionable to allow Caro to get away with what he did. Unfortunately, mine is not the only opinion in play. Don't worry, the judges' decision will not be overturned by one man's hatred. But there is something else, unfortunately.' She almost growled in exasperation. 'An old Nurian law. When a private citizen is unhappy with the judges' ruling, he can challenge the other party to a "trial by branch". It's like a duel. No one ordinarily uses the law. It's ancient. But Caro has done it: he's asking the judges for a trial by branch on your account, tomorrow.'

'Excellent!' Tymon declared. 'I'll prove I'm innocent any way he likes! So much the better if it's a duel —'

'You mistake me!' she interrupted in alarm. 'You're not bound by the law as a foreigner. You aren't obliged to take up the challenge. You just have to make a public refusal tomorrow morning in the arena. Everyone will understand.'

'They'll understand I'm a coward,' objected Tymon. 'That's the last thing I need right now!'

'The last thing you need, or I need, is for you to be killed in some idiotic duel,' she snapped, with a burst of impatience. 'Don't you see? You have a destiny. I didn't go through what I did — I didn't lose Juno and the Focals — just to see you throw it all away on a personal feud — before there's a chance, a chance —'

She broke off, and took a deep breath before continuing. 'You know you're a Grafter now, don't you, Tymon?' she said carefully. 'You told Laska you did, anyway.'

Her eyes glinted in the far-off light of the house lanterns.

'I know I am,' he ground out.

'Well, that means you have responsibilities. You're important to us. Too important to waste on a duel. You're one of the five Signs of the Sap that set off the Year of Fire, whatever you may think about that. These events go beyond us. They're bigger than us. The part we each have to play may be small, but it's crucial.'

'What are the other Signs?' he asked, resigned to her certainties.

She shrugged. 'You went to Treeology class. *The Tree shall die*. That's no riddle. *And a third of the things upon her shall die*. Since the withering of the leaf-forests, and especially since the Tree-water dried up in the Eastern Canopy, we've lost most of our wildlife. I don't know whether that makes a third of what lives *above*, but it's close enough. I can't speak for what lives *below*.'

'That's only three Signs, and you're stretching it. What are the other two?'

'They're apocryphal,' she said. 'Grafting prophecies from after the times of Saint Loa, so it's fair enough that you wouldn't have heard of them. *A friend from the west*: a Grafter from Argos who joins our fellowship and uses his powers for good. That's you. There's a lot more about what you'll do for the people of Nur, but I won't burden you with it.' She grinned.

'And the last?'

'*A king in chains.*'

'There are far too many kings in these prophecies,' Tymon noted laconically. He was beginning to relax, to forget the difficulties posed by her rank. 'Which one is this? Not the Green Lord again, I suppose, otherwise there wouldn't be any chains.'

Her answer was muffled as she hunched over the balustrade.

'What?' he asked, taking advantage of the opportunity to move closer to her.

'It's me, I said. The prophecy refers to the twelfth Kion. I'm the twelfth direct descendant of the first king of Nur. The chains aren't literal. They just mean that under my reign, Nur is enslaved. A whole people in chains, as it were. The yoke of tyranny.'

'Well.' He whistled. 'So I'm not the only Divine Leaf and Sacred Trumpet around here. Nice to know.'

'Tymon, be serious.' Her eyes flashed dangerously in the darkness. 'The Year of Fire is no laughing matter.'

'Alright, alright,' he protested feebly. 'I'm just not used to thinking of any of this as real.'

'Then get used to it, and quickly. We don't know exactly what we have in store for us, but it will be momentous. We have to be ready. If we aren't ... If we don't step up to the mark ... Others will take our place. It'll be harder. We'll be swept aside and the Sap will find some other channel.'

'I understand,' he assured her, though he did not. This sort of apocalyptic fervour was beyond him. The more he heard of Samiha's beliefs, the more he dreaded that they might turn out to be true.

'The stakes are high,' she mused, still gazing over the balustrade at the twinkling lights of the village. 'The Council in Argos knows that well enough. They stand to lose the most during the Year of Fire. They are the old world, the dead wood. They will be burnt away.'

'I'm guessing this is not a literal burning or Caro would be a happy man.'

She barely smiled, lost in her own thoughts. 'The priests in Argos, particularly the Council and inner sanctum, are well aware that their fate is bound up with the Grafting prophecies,' she murmured. 'With the Nurian Grafters in particular. There are very few people left in the world with the Sight. The Council flushes them out, one by one: those they cannot persuade to join them, they kill. We've lost far too many that way.'

He made no reply, as she did not seem to require one. The Friend star had appeared above them, shining through the twig-thickets. He stifled a sigh. It was a moment before he realised that she was looking at him again, gazing earnestly into his face.

'I can't lose you too,' she whispered. 'Please, Tymon.'

She was the one who moved close to him now. He caught a hint of the light perfume that clung to her. Then, without knowing quite how it happened, his arms were about her and she was pressed against him in the warm darkness. He tried to hold her, his hands fumbling through her hair, touching her face; he felt like a thirsty wanderer who had found a pure Tree-well after days of drought. He wanted to kiss her again, properly this time. But she was rigid and unyielding. He just managed to bump his mouth awkwardly against hers before she pushed him away and stepped back.

'Ah,' she murmured. 'That, on the other hand, is not a good idea. For many, many reasons.'

He bowed, hot with humiliation and regret. 'I'll be on my way then,' he said, turning aside. 'Don't worry, *shanti*, I'll make sure you have your Grafter intact tomorrow. I won't fight the duel.' He could not look her in the eye.

'Wait,' she called after him, as he stalked up the ramp. 'Wait, *Argosi*.'

She ran to him and took his hand, hesitating and shy as a little girl. 'Please don't be upset with me,' she said. 'I want us to be friends. I do care about you. I just can't give you anything else right now, do you understand?'

She looked at him so pleadingly that he nodded, relenting.

'Besides, I haven't told you the good news yet,' she reminded him. 'A letter also arrived today, from Marak. Though if Caro had known to whom it was partly addressed, I doubt he would have brought it.' She withdrew a strip of delicate paper from her pocket, the sort that would be attached to the leg of a messenger bird, and handed it to him. 'It's from Noni, Oren's sister. She says the authorities released her after only a day of questioning. Oren's still in prison but he was well enough to write to you.'

The translucent paper was covered in densely packed lines of Nurian script, almost invisible in the dim light. The writing crawled sideways, diagonally and upside down, filling every available inch of the page. Tymon squinted at it as if it were a nest of snakes, wondering how she expected him to read it.

'What does he say?' he asked.

She pointed a finger to a corner of the paper. He saw that one line at the base of the text was written in Oren's condensed brand of Argosian.

'*Timon, friend*,' he read aloud, '*You have Seen. Congratulation.*' He glanced up at Samiha in surprise. 'How did he know?' he stammered. 'I mean, I have ... I've been meaning to tell you ... I Saw the Focal, in the arena ...'

Briefly, he recounted his vision during the trial, the encounter with the dead man. Samiha listened attentively. When he reported the fragment of conversation he had overheard among the judges, a sharp hiss of breath escaped her lips and she rapped the railing with one hand, triumphant.

'If only Kosta could hear that ... Well, no matter. He'd still listen with stumps in his ears,' she said. 'What he didn't want repeated at the trial was the fact that Ash knew perfectly well what you were capable of, Tymon. He told me all about his meeting with the novice of Argos when I came back to Marak. He had high hopes for you. He said that you'd admit to knowing him in your own way, in your own time, when you were ready. That's the odd thing: a Grafter can't be a Grafter until he's ready.' She gazed at him with shining eyes. 'You've come into your power, *Argosi*. I'm very glad to see it, because we need all the help we can get.'

He felt a flush of pride, his disappointment at her rebuff somewhat mollified.

'But how did Oren know?' he enquired. 'Is he a Grafter, too?'

'Sadly, only a Grafter-in-training, though a very talented one. The Focals were among the last full-fledged Grafters in the canopy. Oren was only halfway through his studies with them. The other young people in his class were even less advanced. We lost much when the Focals were taken from us.'

She shook her head ruefully and turned her attention to the purse at her belt, taking out a small object on a string and holding it up to the light. He saw that it was the pendant Oren had worn the day of their escape from Marak, an oblong of hardwood carved with the sign of the key. The symbol caught the glimmer of the lanterns and shone as if it were on fire.

'Noni also sent this,' she continued softly. 'This sort of pendant is very old and very rare. The key-rune is inlaid with *orah*, some of the last of that material known to exist. *Orah* focuses a Grafter's power. It also protects him.'

Tymon stared in wonder at the bright inlay. It really did look like trapped sunlight, he thought. 'Why does it help Grafters?' he asked.

'No one knows exactly. I've heard people say that all the *orah* was blessed by a powerful sage when it was first mined from the Tree. There are only five such pendants left in existence, anyway. They are worn by trusted warriors who have sworn to defend the Kion. Oren is passing this one on to you, since he's no longer able to serve in that capacity. You already noticed it in Marak — that's a good sign. Do you accept it?'

The pendant sparkled merrily in her hand as she offered it to him. He suddenly smiled. All the stories he had listened to as a child and learned to scoff at later had come to life; there really were Grafters and sorcerers, lost kingdoms and hidden worlds beneath the Storm. The only thing that had been missing was a radiant glimpse of *orah*. He took the pendant and slipped it over his neck. Then he went down on one knee before Samiha.

'I'd be honoured, Highness,' he said quietly.

23

At dawn the next day he arrived at his appointment in the arena, a dull knot of apprehension in his belly. He had promised Samiha he would not take up Caro's challenge, much as it irked him, and dreaded the public announcement he would have to make to the villagers. He knew the refusal could only come off as a lack of nerve and therefore lack of integrity on his part. The Nurians whose path he crossed on his stared at him with open dislike. The clouds hung low over the promontory and silence wrapped the twig-thickets like a shroud. Even the birds appeared to have forgotten to sing at sunrise, misled by the *mora*. As Tymon trudged down the stairs to the well, supporting Galliano, he found himself longing for rain, for the touch of real water on his skin. His eyes were drawn to the foggy hole on the east side of the arena. There was now no mistaking the remains of the broken branch peeping out from under the stage. He shivered as he stepped for the second time onto the wide central platform.

The space ahead of him was full of people. On this occasion the spectators had not remained on the terraces, but stood about on the stage in murmuring groups. Tymon saw that the only individuals seated in the arena were the judges themselves. They occupied the lowest tier on the western terraces, their unmasked faces stern. He identified Laska, Kosta, Gardan and the man named Davil, and made out Samiha's lithe form at the end of the row. His spirits sagged as he identified the figure with the yellow hair and beard standing beside her. Caro stared at him insolently as he approached.

'You won't get away with this treachery, *Argosi*,' pronounced the militant. 'I'm here to see that justice is done.'

Tymon scowled at his adversary and helped Galliano onto the terrace next to Samiha.

'Ha!' grunted the old man in an undertone as he eased himself down on the ledge. 'Justice is as justice does.'

'The Freehold judges have already seen to justice, citizen Caro,' noted Laska crisply. 'If you were wise, you would accept their ruling and go in peace.'

Galliano had taken the last available spot on the judges' terrace and no one offered Tymon another seat. He was left loitering uneasily by Caro on the stage. Somehow, although he appreciated Laska and Samiha rallying to his defence, he would have rather defeated the yellow-haired Nurian on his own merits. The prospect of backing down in the face of the challenge weighed heavily on him.

'You may proceed, citizen,' said Kosta to Caro. 'State your aims in calling us here this morning but be brief. The court does not have time for idle chatter.'

The militant bowed and addressed the row of judges in strident tones.

'*Syors*: forgive me. I disturb the court only because I must. I came to you yesterday with news of our losses in Marak, only to find that you have allowed another *Argosi* to join our sacred fellowship. That's bad enough. But as to him possessing the Sight — I cannot comprehend how you even begin to speak of it! He is a *putar*! He is the enemy!'

'That isn't your decision to make, Caro,' put in Samiha. 'We must allow the committee time to deliberate on this matter.'

Caro scarcely glanced at her. He paced on the stage in mounting excitement, his voice reverberating through the arena.

'These are no times for pious sentiments, overtures of peace and brotherly love,' he announced to the people about him. 'Nor do we have time for committees and long deliberations. We are facing annihilation: we are defending our very right to exist! Would the Council in Argos extend such courtesies as we have to the *Argosi*, if one of us were in their city? *Neni, o Sav!* A Nurian in Argos would be clapped in hardwood fetters in the deepest dungeon of the seminary, if he was not thrown into their Sacred Mouth as fodder for their Rites!'

The sneering statement had the desired effect, and his audience rippled with outrage. Tymon stood miserably silent. How was he to answer such a deft mixture of fact and fiction? With a simple denial? No one on the Freehold would believe him if he were not willing to put his life on the line. Caro turned to the judges once more, his pale face flushed in triumph.

'If you are handicapped by your own concern for law and precedent, then let me help you!' he urged. 'I have no doubt the *putar* is a liar. I'll prove it in a trial by branch! The Tree will decide between us. Let him answer that challenge, if he dares!'

'I'll answer it!' piped a querulous voice at Tymon's side. Galliano tried to struggle up from the terrace before giving up and continuing from a seated position. 'I don't understand why we're listening to this troublemaker,' he objected. 'He's taking up our time and energy, and has held back my work schedule something terrible. I've known Tymon all his life and I know he's a good boy. The judges examined the evidence against him already and threw it out. Why are we even discussing this?'

'Be still, old man,' barked Caro. 'You're here on sufferance, and only because of your knowledge —'

'Which we appreciate tremendously,' interjected Kosta. He gave Caro a meaningful stare. 'Do not misunderstand us, *syor* Galliano,' he said in an aside to the scientist. 'I believe the issue is only one of Freehold security. We must be sure Tymon is not an unwitting tool of our enemies.'

Galliano subsided, mumbling in protest, as Samiha joined the debate.

'Trial by branch is an ancient custom and a barbaric way of making your point, citizen,' she pleaded with Caro. 'I beg you to reconsider. The ruling of this court is law.'

Once again, the militant did not deign to look at her, but focused his attention on the villagers.

'Well, if we turn to barbarism, it might be because we're left with no other choice,' he replied, slow and droll, engaging the crowd. 'Perhaps dreams and prophecies are not enough, *shanti*. Perhaps the current laws no longer fit our needs and we need new laws, a new kind of leadership. This is no longer the Kingdom of Light, after all. The old ways are dead. The old Kings are dead. Why do we hold on to them? Give power to the people, I say, power to those people who know how to defend us.'

The open declaration of revolt seemed to strike his audience dumb. The villagers gaped at him in shock. Laska, Samiha and most of the other judges sat by, grey-faced and speechless. Only Davil and Kosta huddled together in whispered debate, their heads bent close together. Tymon suddenly understood that this was what the yellow-haired Nurian had been aiming at from the outset. The duel was not about him at all: it was about politics and jockeying for power. Punishing the *putar* was secondary to seizing control of the Freehold, aided perhaps by judges such as Davil and Kosta, quick to see an opportunity to extend their influence.

'If you wish to dispute leadership of this Freehold with the judges and the Kion, then say so clearly, citizen,' answered Samiha. 'Don't play games and don't hide behind other issues.'

Her voice shook a little as she stood up from

the terrace to face Caro. She seemed tiny beside the powerful Marak man.

Caro's eyes flicked towards her at last, and he allowed himself a moment to look her up and down, scornful. Then he laughed. The harsh sound echoed in the arena.

'For now, I only ask that the *Argosi* respond to my challenge,' he said with exaggerated politeness. 'Or is the *putar* too much of a coward to speak for himself?'

Tymon's frustration finally boiled over. He could not bear to see Samiha treated with disrespect. He could have borne any insult but this.

'I accept your challenge,' he cried, stepping around Samiha. 'I'll fight for the honour of this court and for the Kion.'

The whispering between the judges suddenly ceased. Davil and Kosta's startled faces turned towards him. Gardan, who sat nearby, gave a short, dry laugh.

'Tymon, no!' gasped Samiha. 'You promised!'

'The monkey has broken his leash,' said Caro, flashing his unpleasant grin.

'You don't have to accept the challenge, Tymon,' interjected Laska. 'Your opponent is older and heavier than you are, and you do not know our ways. It's an antiquated custom. Normally,' he glanced grimly at Caro, 'no one would think of using such a rule.'

The militant made no response, his smile smug.

'I'll do it,' Tymon declared. He avoided Samiha's furious gaze.

'I ask you all to bear witness!' Caro raised his voice to the crowd. 'The *Argosi* accepts my challenge! It is lawful —'

Laska interrupted again, stern. 'Not so fast. You have not told us which rules you wish to fight under, citizen. Did you think we would sit by and allow you to take advantage of the ignorance of a stranger?'

'I said I'll do it,' broke in Tymon. 'I'm not afraid to fight under any —'

'Peace, young man,' observed Gardan. Her face was grave but her eyes twinkled, as if she were proud of him. 'Listen a moment, and learn.'

'This duel is a test of strength,' resumed Laska. 'Breaking your enemy's club or knocking him unconscious confers victory. In case you had forgotten, Caro, I will remind you that a fight to the death is prohibited, as one of the claimants is a foreigner. You may choose a duel in three blows or in one.'

The yellow-haired Nurian glared at him sullenly. 'Then I choose a duel in three blows, *syor*,' he spat. 'It's the only honourable option you leave me.'

Laska sighed as he turned to Tymon. 'Do you accept a duel in three blows, *Argosi*?' he asked.

'I accept it.'

Tymon was conscious of the people on the stage drinking in his words, savouring the syllables. The villagers pressed in a tight, eager semi-circle about him. He saw Solis and his band in the front row, their faces shining. After a brief deliberation with his colleagues, Kosta spoke again.

'This court acknowledges your request for a trial by branch, citizen. It is your right. You may proceed if both parties are willing, but without our blessing.'

'*Maz, syors,*' said the militant, making another florid bow. He did not bother to hide his satisfaction. 'May justice be served.'

Without further preamble, he pushed through the crowd of spectators towards the eastern side of the stage.

'You don't know the meaning of the word,' murmured Samiha, beside Tymon. She noticed him watching her and added in a low, terse voice, 'You — this is unworthy of you. A Grafter does not engage in personal duels.'

'I don't see as I have much choice, *shanti,*' he replied.

'There's always a choice,' she retorted, moving away from him. 'Violence breeds violence.'

'What are you doing, boy?' Galliano called from the terrace. 'I thought you were going to refuse the challenge?'

'It's all right, Apu,' he answered, gazing after Samiha with dim resentment. Why did she always have to disapprove of him? He walked back to Galliano's side and placed a hand on the old man's shoulder. 'I'll be fine,' he reassured him, summoning up the confidence he did not feel. 'I have to do this.'

Caro climbed off the platform onto the broken branch beneath. Only his upper body was visible above the level of the stage.

'Are you coming, *Argosi?*' he jeered over his shoulder. 'Take your weapon from the temple

463

branch, but choose wisely! The branch isn't what it used to be, since it was desecrated by your brethren.'

'Remember this is a lawful event, Caro,' cautioned Samiha, from the edge of the stage. 'Not an excuse for revenge.'

The audience had already lined up along the eastern rim of the platform. Only the seven remaining judges lingered on the terrace, debating heatedly with one another in Nurian. They ignored Tymon as if he was of no further consequence. He swallowed a sense of injured decency, and left Galliano frowning after him to follow in Caro's footsteps. The reference to desecration was calculated to incite the crowd; angry catcalls echoed out as he swung his legs over the side of the platform and dropped onto the branch. He landed on a loose piece of bark, almost twisting his ankle. The militant gave a guffaw.

'Bad luck,' he sneered. 'Perhaps it's an indication of things to come.'

He strode off towards the mutilated edge of the branch. The broken limb was as massive as its counterpart on the west side of the promontory, at least seventy feet in diameter, though the flanks sloped steeply. Lengthwise it came to an abrupt halt twenty feet from the stage. The charred extremity cut a stark silhouette against the sky. Caro knelt on the blackened rim, reaching over the edge. He strained a moment, grimacing with effort. With a sound uncannily like a child's shriek, a shard of wood broke away in his hand. He lifted up a jagged beam as tall as he was with a jubilant yell.

'The branch favours me!' he cried. Answering cheers rose from the spectators on the lip of the stage.

'Now it's your turn!' crowed Caro. 'Choose well, *Argosi!*'

Tymon approached the edge of the branch peering over the brink. He was alive to Caro's reasons for selecting this particular place to fight his duel. The wounded face of the great limb was a mute accusation against any and all Argosians. The boy surveyed the scorched collection of shattered spikes with disgust. He tried to gauge the size of each, seeking one similar to Caro's. His eye lit on a likely candidate and he leaned forward, closing his fist around the shard. It crumbled to dust in his hand.

'Choose well!' repeated the yellow-haired Nurian. 'A strong club is proof of sincerity.'

He smiled easily, leaning on his great, pointed stake, but there was a tension in his muscles that belied his calm. Tymon's first flush of anger was cooling. He kept a wary watch on the other man as he manoevered himself closer to the brink of the broken limb. His rival was taller, broader and at least ten years older than he was, a warrior in his physical prime, sure of his power.

'Having second thoughts?' Caro whispered, mocking. 'Yield now if your conscience fails you.'

Tymon did not waste time on an answer. He laid himself on his stomach on the branch and peered over the dizzy drop. Tentacles of fog drifted up to meet him. He stretched his arm down as far as it would go. An updraft stirred his hair, and his

465

fingers brushed against something solid. He grasped the fragment and pulled. The shard was difficult to break loose. When it finally came free the recoil nearly sent him rolling into the gulf. He picked himself up and dusted off his tunic. The piece of wood in his hand was black and gnarled and about the length of his leg. It looked sturdy, but was nowhere near as massive as Caro's club.

'Say your *Argosi* prayers, *putar*,' taunted the militant. 'You'll need them.'

Excitement rippled through the spectators on the stage. Rows of faces leered down at them. Samiha held out both arms at the front of the crowd, palms outward. She did not look at Tymon, but her whole body radiated her displeasure. The whispering of the throng died away.

'I remind you both this duel is not a free-for-all,' she said flatly. 'You will not exceed three blows. Be ready on my mark.'

Caro retreated a few steps and raised his weapon. Tymon mirrored the move cautiously. Fear clutched at his throat, an animal force, instinctive and irresistible. He wondered if he was making a terrible mistake. But it was too late to withdraw. He registered the downwards sweep of Samiha's arms. The duel had begun.

Caro's first lunge was so quick that he was caught off his guard. He lifted his club only just in time to ward off the militant's strike. The shock of the blow jarred through him and splinters flew into his eyes. When he blinked them clean again he saw Caro step back with an unconcerned smile. Both clubs were still whole. A sigh went up from the audience. Tymon's arms ached as he lowered his weapon.

'*Bas*,' called Samiha.

'You were lucky,' Caro remarked. 'Luck won't see you through three rounds, however.'

The boy panted, too breathless to make a reply. The heavy atmosphere of the *mora* seemed to steal the very air out of his lungs. He glanced at the people pressed together at the edge of the stage. The Freehold guards were right there in the front row, their expressions exultant. This was what the youths of Sheb had been hoping for since his arrival, he reflected — an official extension of the fight on the spur. And there beside them, with her own, entirely different set of expectations, stood Samiha. It was impossible to satisfy both parties. The *shanti* stared over his head, white-faced. He had lost her for good now, he thought dully. Even if by some fluke he won this contest, she would still be angry with him.

'On my mark,' she announced, lifting her arms.

Caro paced forward. 'We finish what we started in Marak,' he snarled, raising the bludgeoning shard.

Tymon readied his weapon. He had come to the sobering realisation that he did not have the brute force to withstand Caro. A numb terror took hold of him. Samiha's hands came down and Caro's club whistled through the air a heartbeat later. The two shards screeched together, releasing a sharp scent of burnt sap. The force of the blow sent Tymon staggering to one side. He flailed wildly, teetered on the broken rim of the branch and regained his balance only in the nick of time. A great shout went up from the stage.

'*Bas*.' Samiha's voice rang out like a bell.

'Ah, you fail, *Argosi*, you fail!' chuckled Caro. He barely seemed affected by his exertions at all.

Tymon's head reeled. Rivulets of sweat stained his tunic. He could not focus properly on his opponent, as if some of the splinters had lodged in his eye. He had not caught Samiha's last signal but knew that the third round must have begun. Caro was circling him again, his weapon raised and his mouth curled into a greedy smile. The boy's shoulders throbbed. His arms had lost all their strength. He heaved up his burdensome shard of wood and braced himself for the final blow.

It never came. Far-off, urgent, a cry pierced the breathless silence in the arena. A voice rose beyond the confines of the well.

'*Foy!*'

There was a pause, a frozen moment. The villagers glanced away from the duel, towards the source of the sound.

'*Bas*,' said Samiha, almost as an afterthought. She frowned at the western stairs.

'No.' Caro struck the end of his club against the bark, incensed. 'We haven't finished here yet.'

But no one was watching him any more. Footsteps thudded on the rim of the arena, and a man appeared at the top of the stairs, waving his arms to the people below.

'*Foy!*' he called, as he hastened down the steps. '*Foy!*'

'No,' Caro whispered furiously.

In a sudden lurch he swung his weapon at Tymon. The boy had no opportunity to lift his own shard of wood or ward off the blow. The instant of danger stretched out to an eternity, as it had in the Marak shrine; all he could do was watch, helpless, as Caro's club plummeted towards his head. He had time to appreciate with calm certainty that it would split open his skull. No one else noticed the illicit strike. The Freeholders were crowding about the messenger at the foot of the stairs. *Foy, foy* — the word swept through the arena like a swift wind.

'Fire.' Tymon muttered the translation to himself, a distracted echo.

What happened next took place all at once, in a blur, so that he could not remember later which event came first. As he said the word, Oren's pendant, hidden in the collar of his tunic, glowed with a vivid pulse of heat. Almost simultaneously, Caro's club burst into flames. The militant skidded to a halt and dropped the burning wood with a stifled oath. He gazed at Tymon in rage and astonishment. A now familiar sense of dizziness washed through the boy, the slight disorientation that seemed to be accessory to the Grafter's power. On the stage the messenger talked and gesticulated excitedly. The judges had risen from their terrace to join the people gathering about him. Only a few heads turned to note the pair on the broken limb, the smoking remains of the shard on the floor of the stage.

In his bemused state Tymon did not immediately understand what had happened. He could only stare dumbly at Caro. Behind the militant's anger lurked a terrible fear, the look of a man confronted with something he had thought impossible. For a brief moment, Tymon wondered whether his opponent was going to rush at him and push him over the edge of the branch with his bare hands. He certainly could not have prevented him from doing so, had he tried. But Caro merely collected himself with a visible effort, turned on his heel and vaulted up onto the stage. Relief washed over Tymon. He bowed his head.

'Come with me, you fool,' whispered a voice in his ear.

Samiha took hold of his elbow and led him back towards the platform.

'What's going on?' he asked her thickly. His tongue felt swollen and clumsy in his mouth. 'Is the village on fire?'

'No, Tymon. The western watch-fires have been lit.'

'What does that mean?'

She helped him up onto the stage and propelled him towards Galliano, still perched alone at the end of the judges' terrace.

'It means we're under attack, or soon will be,' she replied quietly. 'A fleet has been sighted bearing down on the Freehold.'

'An attack?' He peered at her in consternation. 'By the Governor of Marak?'

'The watch signalled Argosian ships, not colonial dirigibles. Argos has launched a direct assault against us.'

'But that's impossible!' he cried, halting in his tracks.

She waited for him, patient and sad. 'Why impossible?' she asked.

'Because I didn't See it,' he whispered dismally. 'I didn't See it coming.'

24

There would be a period of about half an hour's
grace between the lighting of the watch fires some
ten miles distant from Sheb, and the arrival of the
enemy on the Freehold horizon. Although the
villagers had long expected another attack, indeed
scrupulously planned and drilled for one, everyone
was painfully aware of how little time remained.
Tymon and Samiha had barely climbed onto the
stage before the great drums beneath the terraces
began rolling out their urgent warning. All
Freeholders who were not already in the arena
hurried there in response to the signal. Mothers
came trailing infants and bundles of hastily
gathered belongings; elders shuffled down the steps
on the arms of their grandchildren. Tymon was
astounded at the rapidity with which the villagers
organised themselves, and by their self-discipline.
Their mood was tense but purposeful. All personal
quarrels, all questions of pride and politics were
forgotten. No one mentioned the outcome of the
duel. The whole affair faded to insignificance in
the face of an outside threat. Even Caro appeared
to have set his criticisms of the judges aside,
accepting Laska's orders without question.

The yellow-haired Nurian was given the task of organising the evacuation. Those unable to fight were to leave immediately for Tree-caves beneath the promontory, and most of the hasty conference in the arena was spent making sure all of Caro's charges were present and accounted for. To Tymon's surprise, the militant assumed this less than glamorous role without a murmur of protest. A successful evacuation was the Freehold's only guarantee of survival and Caro seemed to understand the importance of the job. The Freehold's one decrepit trading dirigible, too slow to be used in combat, would be sent south to a secret meeting point to pick up the refugees. Those staying behind on the front lines — a pitifully small group, though it included women as well as men, Tymon noted — would join the fugitives if things turned out badly for the village.

The boy was left feeling only embarrassment at his part in the morning's fiasco. The duel had not even ended in a decisive victory. He had no idea whether he had the right to use the Grafter's power in such a situation, consciously or not. No one clarified the point for him and in the current circumstances he dared not ask. Despite the fact that he was weary and dispirited, therefore, and that his arms ached from Caro's blows, he insisted on accepting an assignment on one of the catapults on the western defences. He had convinced himself that there was no other way to make amends for his conspicuous failure to predict the Argosian attack. He was only good at fighting, he thought gloomily. He may as well fight some more.

To his relief, no one objected to the posting, not even Samiha. There were too few able soldiers on the Freehold to quibble about an *Argosi* on the front lines, and since the fight with Caro, Samiha appeared to be resigned to leaving him to his own devices. He could not shake the sense that she was disappointed in him — and rightly so, he told himself. The facts haunted him as he trooped after the other members of his squadron towards the western stairs. What use was his ability if it foretold the details, but left out the main event? Why was he able to set fire to shards of wood but not predict the arrival of an entire war-fleet? He could have torn off Oren's pendant and thrown it away in a fit of self-reproach.

'Tymon.'

Samiha's voice recalled him from his maudlin thoughts, sent a quick thrill through him as it always did. She caught up with him at the edge of the stage and took his hand in her own. When she spoke, however, it was not to bolster up his confidence or to tell him that she did not blame him for his lack of foresight.

'Promise me. We get through this without any more heroics,' she begged.

'I promise.' He peered solemnly into her face. 'I mean it this time, Samiha.'

She made a small noise that could have been either agreement or scepticism and let go of his hand. '*Sav vay*, Tymon. Come back from that catapult in one piece.'

His wilting spirits revived a little and he permitted himself a witticism as he turned back towards the stairs.

'I'll see you all when the hard work's done,' he grinned.

'Oh, you'll be seeing me before that,' she remarked. 'I'll be out on the defences just like you, my friend.'

'What?' He almost tripped on the bottom step, shocked. 'Aren't you going to the Tree-caves?'

'No, *Argosi*, I am not.'

'But what about your beliefs? I thought you didn't hold with violence?'

'I don't hold with needless violence, no. I do believe in defending my people.'

'But, but ...' he stammered, at a loss for words. Even if some of the Freehold women were warriors, he had assumed her position as the Kion would oblige her to accompany the evacuees.

'I'm not the only member of the Nurian royal house,' she said softly, as if he had spoken his worries aloud. 'There are people left to carry on the bloodline if I die.'

'Why take the chance?' he protested. 'We're all fighting for you, Samiha. I'd rather you didn't put yourself in unnecessary danger, I really would.'

She smiled. 'Now,' she noted, with a distinct purr of satisfaction, 'you know exactly how I feel regarding you, *Argosi*.'

And then Laska was calling out her name, beckoning to her from the far side of the arena. She gave Tymon's hand another quick squeeze and hurried off. He gazed after her, at once exasperated, anxious and admiring.

Catapult seven, dubbed the *Flea* by the youths assigned to her, was the smallest of three engines defending the west flank of the village. It was positioned on a platform in the twigs above the western spur, conveniently camouflaged by the net of dry vines Tymon had seen on the day of his arrival. The site commanded a wide panorama of the lower canopy and a view of the main docking port. The *Lyla* had been whisked away by Jamil and Galliano and the end of the spur was empty and still beneath the catapult platform. Far off on the grey horizon sprang the watch fires' baleful glow. The *Flea*'s bite was modest, but it was more manoeuverable than its heavier counterparts to the north and south: the neat, compact arm was mounted on a swivelling base and could be pointed in any direction, even back towards the heart of the village. It fired 'gum-balls', flammable shot made of dried bird guano that burned — Tymon's companions informed him, straight-faced — with a distinctive smell of flatulence. A well aimed gum-ball, they hastened to add, could do more serious damage to a dirigible's flotation sacks than the bark-shot deployed by the larger engines.

His fellow fighters were all members of Solis' band, of course. The western spur was their realm and they guarded it jealously. The dark youth himself led the squadron operating the catapult. Tymon had expected to be treated with suspicion and blame by the young Nurians who shared his assignment. In his current mood of self-recrimination, he almost welcomed the prospect as a form of penance. It was a surprise to him when he learned that the boy guards had specifically asked for him to join their team. What he had assumed to be Laska's decision in the arena turned out to be a request made by Solis himself, with the support of his fellows.

'I bring you here for purpose, *Argosi*,' the young captain explained as he directed Tymon to his post at the catapult's loading station. 'You stay with us — live or die with us. Show quality.'

Tymon was happy enough with this arrangement. He was willing to die on the Freehold defences, he told himself, if it would help Samiha. It was a refreshing change to be accepted by the Nurians, if only on probation. With the brief exception of Oren in Marak city, he had not had the opportunity to associate with lads his own age since he left the seminary. The boys on the catapult platform talked and joked with him in broken Argosian as they uncovered the *Flea* and prepped it for use. They were inordinately proud of their position on the vanguard of defence, the trust placed in them by the Freehold judges. Just let the *putar* come, they gloated. Just let them come and taste the fury of the *Flea*.

As the minutes slipped by with no hint of the Argosian ships, however, their jokes petered out and their gaze turned more often and more anxiously towards the west. The bright point of the watch fires shone changeless on the horizon. Surely a half hour had passed already? Where was the Argosian armada? Had the lookout been mistaken? The youths hunched their shoulders against the breeze and squinted at the dark clouds forming over the lower canopy; even the promise of an end to the drought provoked little commentary among them. For there was now no doubt that the day would see rain. The western horizon had darkened to a deep purple and the wind was hard, driving the clouds before it. Tymon shivered where he stood at the edge of the platform, shading his eyes. Pale flecks had materialised against the backdrop of rolling grey. He wondered whether they were wind-funnels like the ones he had seen from on board the greatship. A moment later, he knew that they were not.

Delicate, deceptively small, a bloom of green and white sails appeared on the horizon, the colours of the Argosian fleet. And still the young people about him said nothing, staring at the approaching ships. Each one knew what the others were thinking. There was no need to comment, no need to put words to their dismay. There were so many — no one had expected so many. The line of flecks expanded, spread out and solidified to reveal no less than thirty vessels on course for the promontory. Every one of them was a greatship, the finest and fastest in the Council's line. It was a disproportionate force, more suited to a wholesale invasion than a raid. No longer in any way delicate, the greatships swept past the watch fires ahead of the storm, snuffing them out. By the time the dirigibles were ranged in impressive formation about a mile from the promontory, they seemed to take up the entire sky. It was clear that the Council meant to crush the Freehold once and for all.

The fleet did not immediately attack the village. Secure in their display of strength, the Argosian dirigibles simply hung there out of range of the Freehold defences, dropping tethers to the lower canopy. Another age seemed to pass and the cold wind picked up, penetrating Tymon's bones. At last one vessel, smaller than the rest, moved towards the promontory. It flew the green flag of parley. With a shudder, the boy recognised the Envoy's sleek ship. A delegation of Freeholders headed by Kosta and Laska walked out to meet it on the spur, accompanied by a group of seasoned warriors, all older and sterner than Solis' crowd. They passed directly below the *Flea* on their way to the docking port. The Envoy's dirigible descended to just above the tip of the spur, suspended over the heads of the Nurians. It hovered perhaps a hundred feet away from the youths on their platform. Argosian soldiers armed with crossbows lined the deck.

Tymon could not hear the parley through the noise of slowly venting ether, but someone must have issued a challenge. Kosta and Laska moved up to the side of the ship. He felt, rather than saw, the familiar black-coated figure step up to the side of the deck in answer. The Envoy leaned easily against the rail, talking down to the men on the spur. Tymon shrank behind the squat form of the *Flea*. It was impossible for Lace to see him, veiled by the net of vines and the bulk of the catapult, but he had a sense of being exposed on his little outcrop of twigs, as if a hungry beast were sniffing him out.

'They offer terms,' Solis observed scathingly from his post nearby. 'They offer, just like before. Accept tithe, and all well! Sell children, you go free.'

Tymon shuddered again. Even at a distance the sight of the Envoy provoked a deep unease in him, a visceral reaction. He cowered behind the catapult, annoyed at himself for losing his nerve. What was wrong with him?

'I not understand why we even listen,' grumbled Solis, more to himself than to his companions. He spat meditatively off the edge of the platform.

Tymon forced himself to look through the vines, to concentrate on what was happening below instead of his own discomfort. As far as he could tell, no negotiation was taking place at all. Once the preliminary words were over, the Envoy did not appear interested in the parley. He lolled on the rail as if he were out on a relaxed excursion from the seminary. The boy squinted in disbelief at the scene. Something was wrong. The tone of the judges' voices had changed. The Freeholders were arguing with each other instead of the enemy. Although he could not make out the exact words, he saw that Kosta was behaving oddly, shouting at Laska. The captain's responses were quiet, cajoling. He seemed to be trying to calm his colleague. Kosta almost screamed in response. With an effort, Tymon shook off the leeching fear that had taken hold of him.

'Something's not right,' he blurted. Oren's

pendant pulsed briefly about his neck as if the *orah* agreed with him. 'That shouldn't be happening. It's not —'

He faltered. He had been about to say, *not as it should be.*

The note of concern in his voice roused Solis. The dark youth peered through the net of vines, his brow furrowed. 'Why judges talk like enemies?' he muttered.

A giddy certainty gripped Tymon. He scrambled to his feet.

'Because Lace is a sorcerer!' he exclaimed. He hastened to Solis' side, his fear forgotten. 'That man's one of the Council's Grafters, I'd bet my life on it. He's done something to the judges — I felt it all the way up here. Look at them arguing with each other! I'd swear — I'd swear it was a Seeming!'

Solis tensed. He looked searchingly at Tymon's face, and down again at Kosta. Then he turned abruptly to his companions and barked out an order in his own tongue. The guards leapt into action. In a trice the *Flea* was locked and loaded, a dull grey gum-ball in its maw. Solis' lips moved in silent prayer. He struck a fire-stick and lit the shot.

'What are you doing?' asked Tymon, belatedly aware of what was happening behind him.

He was too late. The safety had been released and the catapult arm whistled through the air, launching the flaming shot in a high arc.

'Save Freehold,' declared Solis. He watched with grim satisfaction as the gum-ball made contact with the sacks on the Envoy's ship, burying itself in the soft folds almost without a sound.

There was an instant of shocked silence. Then a sheet of flame burst over the vessel and chaos erupted on the spur. The soldiers next to Lace fired their crossbows in a mosquito whine at the judges, and the Freeholders fell back, forming a protective shield about their leaders. Several succumbed to the Argosian crossbows. One of the fallen might have been Kosta, but Tymon could not be sure what was happening before the group had passed below the *Flea* in a welter of voices and hurried on towards the heart of the promontory. A tall figure separated itself out from the villagers and climbed swiftly up the long ladder towards the *Flea*. Laska pulled himself over the edge of platform seven; his gaze took in the guilty faces of the boy guards, the smoking catapult, the released safety.

'What's going on here?' he roared. 'You broke parley!'

'My fault, *syor*,' announced Solis, without hesitation. 'My mistake. Punish only me.' He bent his head like a prisoner awaiting execution.

Laska frowned at him. 'You are responsible for our dishonour —' he began.

'Begging your pardon, sir,' put in Tymon. He stepped forward to join the dark youth, his chin stuck out stubbornly as he faced Laska. 'I told him the Envoy was a Grafter. He was using his power. Solis just did what he had to do to save the Freehold. If you're going to punish anyone, it should be me.'

'Not listen to him!' cried Solis, jumping up. 'It was me! He have nothing to do!'

Laska stared in surprise at the two unlikely allies. He gave a rueful smile.

'*Bas*, Solis,' he said. 'And no, Tymon. The Council's Envoy is no Grafter. A Grafter tries to help the world. That man was concerned only with controlling or destroying it.'

'But he did a Seeming!' objected Tymon. 'He made Kosta angry with you —'

'I do not deny what he did.' Laska's voice was sharp, cautionary. 'As to *syor* Kosta, he was a better man than you or I. Who knows how we would have fared under similar pressure.'

He paused, as if weary. 'Would that the Focals were here,' he muttered. 'I have no strength for such contests.'

He fell silent, his eyes on the Envoy's dirigible. Lace was gone from the deck, Tymon saw with relief. The flames to the aft of the vessel had been extinguished and the ship was already leaving, rising in a graceful arc from the spur, its green flag at half-mast. Nothing remained of the attack but a pall of blue smoke over the branch. Far away, the fleet's signal drums thundered out, irrevocable.

'*Syor* Kosta is dead,' sighed the captain. 'I am now Speaker for the Freehold. There is much to do. Do not think you will not be punished for your conduct, you two. If we get through this you'll both face a disciplinary hearing. But since you precipitated hostilities, as it were, we now have a battle to fight. A battle that was inevitable from the start, unfortunately. Back to your posts, all of you.'

He motioned Solis away with a gesture and sent the guards scurrying to their positions with a single glance.

'Please, sir.' Tymon hesitated behind the others, curious. He was itching to know what had taken place on the spur. 'Did the enemy negotiate? What were their demands?'

Laska strode back to the ladder and swung himself over the edge of the platform.

'They wanted Samiha,' he answered, simply. 'You have your orders,' he called to the youths. 'We are few but this is our home. Defend it well. *Sav vay.*'

Then he was gone. Tymon hurried to his own post by the *Flea*. The Envoy's vessel had reached the other dirigibles now and the Argosian ships were breaking ranks, spreading into attack formation. The fleet bore down on the promontory under a darkened sky. Everything seemed to be happening very quickly after the long wait, and the boy realised that he was afraid of the coming battle, afraid of dying. It was a very different fear from the one he had experienced under the Envoy's influence — a sharp, mindful fear, as bracing as the breeze. It was a tonic to his spirit. If people like the Envoy were sorcerers in the employ of the Council, then his duty was clear. This practical Grafting, rather than grandiose prophecies, was what he could believe in. He was happy his ability allowed him to frustrate his enemies.

'Well,' he said to Solis, 'let's do this properly. I don't care to meet that Father Lace again.'

The Nurian youth gave him a rakish grin. 'Most certain, *Argosi*,' he replied. 'You not meet *putar* sorcerer again. You die right here with us, no problem. *Beni!*'

The sound was the worst. It was like the night of the attack on the Governor's palace, only louder, a hundred times louder, and continuous. The planks beneath Tymon's feet shook with every hit as if the platform would fall apart. The twig-thickets, the catapult, even the sky trembled. His bones groaned and his teeth rattled in his jaw. He had not understood why the enemy shot made so much noise until he saw the first explosion. One moment he was staring at the docking port on the spur, the next it had evaporated, leaving nothing but a glowing crater on the shortened tip of the branch. The Argosian ships were firing blast-poison, battering the promontory with round after round of explosive shot. Nothing and no one could stand in their way.

The Freeholders put up a staunch resistance but their static catapults were useless in the face of the new Argosian firepower. No one had ever heard of blast-poison being used in such a manner before, as a projectile weapon. There were no catapults to be seen on board the Argosian greatships that flanked the promontory, but the dirigibles were fitted with snub-nosed engines, black snouts that poked through portholes and spat out the devastating shot by some unseen mechanism. The *Hornet* and the *Wasp*, the *Flea*'s larger siblings, barely had time to take down one enemy ship in a concerted rain of bark-shot before they were both blown out of the Tree in smithereens.

After that first, gaping loss there had been a moment of mad hope when the *Lyla* materialised over the fleet, drawing a glorious arc of black smoke through the air. It flew like a stinging insect between the greatships, releasing a volley of fiery arrows. One of the Argosian vessels went down in a blaze while another lost its port sacks, and had to withdraw. The youths around Tymon cheered until they were hoarse. At one point the air-chariot flew close to the *Flea*, its complement of four archers waving merrily to the boys on their platform. Tymon saw Samiha leaning out of a porthole with the rest. Her bright hair was caught up under a hardwood helmet and she held her bow triumphantly aloft, shouting a rallying cry that made his heart beat and his spirit soar, though he did not understand the words. The sight of her out there, risking all, left him both proud and terrified. What use was his post on the front lines, he thought, irrationally, if she died before him?

For it soon became obvious that the air-chariot was simply too small to take on the entire Argosian fleet. Some of the stubby engines turned their snouts to the sky and the *Lyla* was chased away, beaten down every time it emerged from the protective cover of the thickets. At length it disappeared completely and the dirigibles resumed their task of pummelling the village and the promontory to ash. After that, the battle was over with bewildering rapidity. It did not seem to Tymon as if he had stood there for more than an hour, loading the dull grey gum-balls into the catapult as fast as they could be aimed and fired — hardly seemed any time at all before the slow boom of the arena drums told them to withdraw, to fall back to the Tree-caves. The resistance had ended. The Freeholders were in retreat.

The explosion came just as the boys had turned their backs on the platform, silent and dispirited, and begun descending the ladder to the western spur. The thickets sheltering the *Flea* took a direct hit. Suddenly the platform was gone, vaporised, and with it the catapult. The ladder sprang out of Tymon's hands; he was briefly aware of his companions frozen on the rungs, teetering in mid-air, before he fell, spun, plummeted through broken twig-ends and flying planks into the abyss.

And then — miraculously — it stopped. Someone grabbed hold of his arm and arrested his fall. He dangled, gasping, about fifty feet above the surface of the spur, the yawning drop between his legs. He looked up to see Solis above him, clinging to the ladder. The young guard clutched Tymon's left elbow with one hand and strained to keep his own grip on the rungs with the other. The ladder had dropped perhaps twenty feet, snagging itself against an undamaged stand of twigs. It lay at a drunken angle, balanced precariously on the creaking stems. Solis puffed out his cheeks with exertion.

'Catch ladder with other hand, *Argosi!*' he called.

Tymon reached out desperately towards the rungs but they were too far away. He was aware that Solis was not strong enough to pull him up. The guard was already flagging under his weight, his fingers slipping on the ladder.

'Swing legs!' Solis ordered through gritted teeth.

'Let me go!' cried Tymon. 'I'll just pull you down with me!'

'Swing legs, fool *Argosi!*' shouted the Nurian furiously.

So Tymon did. He kicked and flailed like a netted bird, swung himself back and forth until he built up his momentum. Solis grimaced with pain as he struggled to keep his hold. One of the other guards on the ladder clambered down to the aid of his captain, bracing an arm about Solis' chest and allowing him to take Tymon's weight with both hands. One large swing, and Tymon's fingers brushed the side of the ladder; another and his right hand grasped the rungs. At last he half hauled himself, half scrambled over the bodies of the others to cling to the shaking wood.

'Thank you,' he breathed, as he faced Solis. 'You saved my life.'

'Not to mention,' grinned the guard, rubbing the feeling back into his hand. 'You eat well in Argos. We fat you up for slaughter, maybe.'

The boys' mirth faded as they descended to the spur, however. A sad sight greeted them there. The bodies of two young soldiers lay inert on the surface of the branch and two more rolled and groaned on the bark. It was a smaller group than before that crept back along the path to the arena. Their progress was slow, interrupted every time an explosion shook the village. They were obliged to use the short, anxious intervals between assaults to stumble from one makeshift shelter to another, supporting their injured comrades between them. The village itself was almost obliterated. The majority of the light, strawframe buildings had been blown away by the explosions or consumed in the subsequent fire. Whole sections had been gouged out of the twig-thickets; gigantic holes ringed with flame showed clear through to the lowering sky, as if some huge, burning beast had taken bites out of the Tree. Only the arena remained relatively untouched, the terraces strewn with hot ash.

They joined the last of the villagers disappearing through a hidden passageway at the back of a drum alcove. Tymon helped one of his injured companions through the opening, staggering down the steep spiral staircase beyond. The wounded boy stumbled and moaned, leaning heavily on his arm. A soldier slid a panel into place behind them. They wound on and on, down successive flights of steps, deep into the branch at the promontory's heart. At last they reached the torch-lit Tree-cavity about a hundred feet below the level of the arena, where the remaining Freeholders had gathered to organise a retreat. The walls of the cavity shuddered with the echoes of the bombardment above.

Tymon laid his charge on one of the woven straw pallets reserved for the wounded, and made certain that the village doctor was aware of his case. The preoccupied grunt with which the harried, white-haired woman answered him appeared to be all he could expect in the way of a response. After that, he sought Samiha. He was relieved to find her entirely unharmed and distributing packs of emergency rations to the people gathered in the centre of the hall. He watched her a moment from the background, not willing to interrupt. She had an encouraging word for every one of the soldiers, he noticed, a hopeful remark or a piece of quiet praise. No matter how despondent the Freeholders were, they held their heads a little higher, and walked a little straighter after she had spoken to them. When she saw him she hastened to his side with a cry of joy. To his surprise and pleasure she threw her arms about him and pressed her face to his neck.

'Tymon! I was almost beginning to think ... it's good to see you,' she stammered, her helmet smashed uncomfortably against his ear. Then she disentangled herself, a pink flush in her cheeks. 'You must be the last squadron to return. Was it bad up there?'

'It was bad,' he answered gravely. 'We lost two men. They just kept pounding us with that new shot. I didn't think it was possible. They never even stopped to breathe.'

She shook her head. 'The Council has outdone itself this time. To use blast-poison openly — to destroy the Tree so completely — it's unheard of! No one has committed such a crime before!'

'With respect, *shanti*, no one has committed such a crime for a very long time,' put in Jamil from nearby. He smiled softly at the two of them.

'It is said the Old Ones waged war in this manner. *Syor* Galliano is not the only one to be inventing, or perhaps reinventing mechanical abominations.'

'Speaking of which, where's the old man?' asked Tymon, glancing about him. He could not make out the scientist's bent form anywhere among the Freeholders gathered in the cavity.

Jamil frowned. 'He should be here,' he said. 'He was here, perhaps an hour ago. I left him here to wait before I helped *syor* Laska start up the *Lyla* ...'

A quick interrogation of the other members of the workshop team revealed that Galliano was not there, however, and indeed that he had left the Tree-cavity some time before, bound for the hangar in the company of one among their number, a youth named Shasta. Shasta was accordingly found and questioned. He was a slight lad of about twelve and trembled under the wrathful gaze of the workshop supervisor, his eyes as round as a Tree-hare's.

'Why didn't you tell me where you were going?' cried Jamil, beside himself.

Shasta gazed back at him in consternation.

'*Syor* said he already discussed it with you,' he chirruped. 'The secret weapon. He went to get the secret weapon. When the drums started he sent me back here just in case. He said he'd arranged for you to pick him up in the *Lyla*. Did I do wrong, *syor*?'

25

'Absolutely not. I won't hear of it.'

Samiha flung rations, blankets and a gourd of water into a shoulder pack. Tymon had to step around the bag to speak to her as she moved with quick, angry motions from one task to the next.

'I have to go, Samiha,' he insisted. 'You know that. Why not just help me?'

'I must stay here and organise the retreat. I'm the only judge left in Laska's absence, the others have already gone on ahead —'

'I mean, let's make an arrangement. I'll go now, alone. If I make it back to the Tree-caves with the old man, fine. If not, you were going to do a last flyover with Laska, looking for anyone who might be stranded, right? Come to the hangar — we'll be there.'

'Of course we'll go to the hangar,' she exclaimed. 'But that doesn't mean you need to rush off now, on foot, through a storm of blast-poison. When we meet up with Laska at the other end of the Tree-caves, we'll take the *Lyla* and search for Galliano together, I promise you.'

'By then it'll be too late,' argued Tymon. 'What if he's hurt? The Tree knows what he's planning out there with all this talk of a secret weapon. What if he has some notion of saving the Freehold and sacrificing himself in the process? That would be just his style. This isn't heroics, Samiha, it's necessity.' He peered into her furious, downcast face. 'You know I'm right.'

She was silent, wrestling with a stubborn knot on the bag. At last she threw up her hands.

'I can't stop you,' she said. 'You're an Argosian and an honorary Freeholder, not one of my subjects. But it would please me if once — just once — you took my advice. If you go out there again in that fire-storm, you will die.'

'You don't need to worry about the fire-storm, at least. The attack is over,' he replied. 'Listen.'

And it was true. The distant thunder of the explosions had ceased. The woody walls about them were no longer trembling.

Samiha glanced towards the line of soldiers quitting the cavity. There were several exits to the chamber, most of them natural chimneys that plunged down through the heart of the branch to emerge at different points in the lower canopy. The Freeholders were climbing a ladder into one such shaft, their whispers echoing up the narrow chute. The wounded soldiers, including Tymon's two comrades-in-arms, had been lowered down before them on slings or woven bark litters. Only a few people remained behind in the encroaching dark; they waited at the top of the shaft for the Kion to join them. She shouldered her pack, her mouth set.

'Do as you will, *Argosi*,' she observed, tersely.

'*Syora*.' Solis stepped up to her side with a deep bow. 'I beg allowance to go with.'

'You do?' she said, taken aback.

'I help look for *syor* Galliano.' The guard flashed his impish grin. 'I promise *Argosi* we die together. *Y maza Sav*, not able to keep promise before.'

'Solis saved my life out there once already,' put in Tymon. 'I'll go with him, if you're agreed, *shanti*. I can't think of a better teammate.'

'You don't seem to need my consent,' Samiha noted. 'Be that as it may — Solis, *beni*. You have my permission to go. Though I'd appreciate as little dying as possible, please.' She turned her back on the boys, heading towards the shaft.

'We'll see you at the hangar!' Tymon called after her.

She waved to him without looking back, a brief gesture of impatience. He did not observe her face as she strode away, or see her bite her lip with anguish.

Solis borrowed one of the last remaining torches on the cavity walls and the two youths set off up the stairs again towards the arena. Tymon plodded despondently behind his companion. The spiral flight seemed, if possible, longer than it had coming down, and he did not like how he had parted from Samiha. He wished that he had found the courage to say goodbye properly, even to try and kiss her one last time while he still had the chance. Despite his brave words, he was not at all sure he would make it up to the hangar, or out again, alive. The silence overhead was ominous rather than reassuring. He wondered whether they would find the arena overrun by the enemy. Not one hint or glimmering of the Sight came to him to warn him of what lay ahead. He might as well have never heard of the Grafters or their unreliable power.

'Do you think the village will be crawling with soldiers?' he asked Solis as they climbed.

'Maybe nothing left to crawl on, *nami*. Maybe village all gone. We soon see.'

Tymon digested this in silence. 'I didn't expect you to be such a good friend, Solis,' he admitted, after a while. 'I didn't think you'd ever accept the likes of me on the Freehold. And yet here you are again, risking your life for two *Argosis*. Thank you.'

The Nurian youth snorted with laughter. '*Beni*. You also surprise me.' He glanced over his shoulder at Tymon, his eyes gleaming in the fitful light of the torch. 'I saw what happened in duel,' he said softly. 'I saw you make Grafter fire. I tell others: Caro wrong. We all wrong. You are Sign of Sap, like *shanti* say.'

'For what that's worth,' muttered Tymon awkwardly.

Sign or not, the Grafter's power did not do him much good, he reflected. His talent had not turned out to be as practical as he had hoped. He could not reliably predict the future. He could not influence others as Lace did. Back on the catapult platform, in the madness of the bombardment, he had tried to set fire to a ball of shot with a whispered word as he had done to Caro's club. The outcome had been a resounding failure. The pendant about his neck had remained inert, the gum-ball as smugly smooth and cool as a black egg. Whether because of his lack of experience or some other flaw, he was unable to consciously use his ability.

'It doesn't always work,' he grumbled to Solis, trudging in the other boy's long shadow. 'The power, I mean. It's hit and miss for me. And I didn't predict the attack. That would have been more useful than setting fire to bits of wood.'

'A Grafter is only a channel, Tymon. The Sap works through you. And you did not set fire to bits of wood: you made a Seeming. It appeared real simply because Caro believed in it.'

'What did you say?' Tymon faltered on the steps, staring up at Solis.

For the dark youth's voice had suddenly changed. He had spoken Argosian like a native and like an adult. Even his tone had deepened. For an instant, Tymon could have sworn that it was the fifth Focal who walked ahead of him up the stairwell in the dancing shadows. And then there was only Solis, holding aloft the torch and peering down at him enquiringly.

'What I say about what?' he countered, with his usual merry inflections.

'Did you say something just now about the Grafting?' asked Tymon.

'I say nothing. I know nothing of Grafting. Why?'

'My mistake. Sorry, Solis.'

He continued on, nonplussed. The whimsical nature of his gift, the way it intruded on his

496

everyday life and used him, rather than the other way around, was unsettling. The reality of having the Sight contradicted everything he had been taught at the seminary about what it meant to be living or dead. The two states were more permeable than he had ever imagined, uncomfortably interchangeable. *Worlds made one*, he thought — and could not remember where he had heard the phrase before.

Far below the two boys, on the creaking ladder that led down the Tree-shaft, Samiha also stopped short. She leaned her head against the side of the well and pressed her cheek to the cool interior grain of the Tree. The torchlight from below threw eerie shadows up the sides of the shaft.

'Mother, help him,' she breathed. 'For he is weak.'

The arena was still there, even if nothing else was. They slid aside the panel behind the drum — the soldier guarding the entrance was long gone — and emerged into what at first appeared to be a shower of grey rain. It turned out to be falling ash, hot to the touch. It brushed their faces, settled on their hair and hands as they stole through the empty arena. Far off, lightning flashed on the horizon, visible through the gap in the eastern thickets. It was followed by the low rumble of thunder. The storm had yet to break over the Freehold.

The path that led up the slope of the southern branch was equally deserted, littered with smoking fragments of the Tree. The boys took long detours around chunks of bark and fallen twigs. Quick tongues of flame licked through the blackened and empty building frames in the thickets above and there was a suffocating pall of ash and smoke in the air. Tymon dropped further behind Solis, toiling up the slope, anxious and preoccupied. Had enemy soldiers reached the workshop? Was Galliano alive? His mind was on possibilities and probabilities, on rescue and escape, on everything but his immediate surroundings. As a result the ambush took him completely by surprise.

A soldier stepped out from the debris like a sudden wall before him, black. Tymon felt his arms being grasped and pinned to his sides. He kicked out uselessly with his feet; a gruff voice barked at him in Argosian, and for an instant he could not understand what it said.

'Sign up for the tithe and get a full pardon, Nurry.' The words coalesced at last to form some kind of meaning.

'I'd rather die!' he spat out bitterly.

'By the bells. Look at this, Ned. What d'you make of it?'

The Argosian was a huge man, almost a giant. He lifted Tymon up bodily, turning him about as if he were a toy, and thrust his face close to the boy's, ogling him curiously. Tymon was shocked at the whiteness of his features, partially hidden under his padded helmet and cheek-guards. Then he realised that ash had coated the man's skin, giving him a ghostly pallor, and that he probably looked the same himself.

'Half-caste?' muttered the soldier doubtfully, as he scrutinised Tymon.

'Not likely,' sneered another, meaner voice. 'I got one of those. Black lice can't talk proper.'

Tymon glanced down in dismay to see Solis pinioned in the second soldier's grasp. He had clamped a hand over the young Nurian's mouth; Solis glared over the edge of it in mute rage.

'Home-born?' mused the giant.

'One of us? Pah. What's it doing here?' laughed his companion.

'I'm not one of you. I'm a Freeholder,' cried Tymon vehemently.

The smaller soldier whistled, grinning through the caked ash. 'Eddicated, too.'

'Well, they're young. Roll 'em on back to cargo,' grunted the giant.

As he spoke, two events occurred simultaneously. In a fluid motion, Solis jerked free of his captor and sprang away from him, mounting a broken twig-stump beside the path. He bent down swiftly and drew a leaf-shaped knife from his boot. The small man leapt after him, snarling, then halted, an expression of frozen astonishment on his face. He slowly toppled over, Solis' hardwood blade buried in his neck. At the same time the giant hurled Tymon away from him with a shout and lunged towards Solis. Tymon sprawled onto the surface of the branch at an awkward angle, winded. An excruciating instant passed before he could stagger up to help his friend.

It was one instant too long. He stood up, panting and staring at the disaster before him in disbelief. Solis lay stretched out on the path, deathly still beneath the hulking form of the giant.

Any hope that he might only be unconscious was dashed by the red stain that spread across his chest, the red that welled through his clothes and smeared the long blade in the giant's hands. The red of Sacrifice, Tymon thought, distantly. He wrenched Solis' weapon from the neck of the fallen soldier and ran forward with a yell, his voice thin and faraway in his ears. At that point he could have killed the other Argosian, stuck the knife into his countryman's back without a qualm.

He was not given the chance. More shapes crowded around him through the drifting smoke and he was caught up and immobilised, the weapon plucked from his fingers. His enemies pushed him down onto his belly and twisted his arms behind his back, securing them with twine. They also tied his legs. Voices shouted at him incomprehensibly. He was hoisted up and carried like a sack on a man's shoulder for a while, then thrown down again onto the surface of the branch.

He lay where he had been thrown, his face in the ash, unable to stop the shameful tears from rolling down his cheeks. Weak. The word echoed and re-echoed in his mind. He was weak and pathetic, and had brought nothing but trouble to his friends. He had not only failed to See the ambush; he had been instrumental in allowing it to happen. A thousand bitter regrets flooded over him. He should not have insisted on the trip to the hangar. He should have been more wary on the path. He could have run to his friend's aid a moment sooner. He had lost Solis and would probably never find Galliano. Black despair welled up in his heart and for a while he could see, and hear, no more.

He was roused from his stupor by the sound of ether venting from a dirigible. He craned his head to look about him, blinking. He realised he was not lying on the branch, as he had supposed, but on the floor of Galliano's workshop. The hangar had changed beyond recognition. The hollow knot had been blown to pieces by a gigantic explosion, its cylindrical walls blasted away. The little covered shed where the scientist had kept his sketches was obliterated and the place strewn with broken shards and fallen sections of bark. Nothing remained of the half-completed second machine but a ruin of dislocated bars. There was no sign of Galliano. A group of Argosian soldiers sat crouched on the floor near Tymon, talking quietly among themselves. They paid him no heed. A shadow filled the sky above the hangar; the boy glanced up to see the smooth underbelly of a dirigible hanging over the hollow. It was with a sense of inevitability that he identified its sleek, all-too-familiar form.

The Envoy's ship descended until it hovered a few feet above the hangar floor, its sails stowed. Soldiers appeared on the deck and lowered a ramp over the side. Tymon was slung once more over the giant's shoulder and humped onto the ship. The soldier kicked him down the steps to the cargo hold like a cumbersome bale.

'Catch yer breath while you can, Nurry,' he shouted after the boy, before disappearing from the lighted square of the hatch.

Tymon rolled down the steps and lay still in the empty hold. Every bone in his body ached. His soul ached. He closed his eyes.

'Who's there?' whispered a voice.

He was not alone in the hold, after all. He pushed himself up as best he could and squinted into the gloom. Someone else lay in a corner of the cargo bay. A little figure was splayed out on a heap of rags like a broken doll. Its face was turned expectantly towards him. In the place of eyes it had two closed wounds.

'Apu!' Tymon muttered huskily. A gulp of laughter, half hysterical, escaped his lips. He had thought that the old man must surely be dead this time.

'Ah, so you came after me, my friend. I was afraid of that.'

Galliano's voice was racked with pain. The boy manoeuvred himself to his side, shunting awkwardly on his rear across the floor of the hold. The scientist was stretched out at an unnatural angle on his heap of rags.

'I was caught in the workshop blast,' he gasped. 'A big beam fell right on top of me. Thought I was done for. But no, here I am. Can't see, can't walk, can't do a damn thing to help anyone, but here I am. And I managed to get you into trouble on top of it.'

Tymon shook his head. 'I got myself into trouble. But why did you go back to the workshop, Apu? What were you hoping to do?'

'You'd think I'd learn,' Galliano sighed. 'I ... I was shocked by the attack. The Council was sworn by its own articles of law not to use blast-shot, though the device is an old one — ah, very old. Who knows what logic they concocted to get around that blasphemy? I'm well aware of how to make blast-poison: second degree in Applied Treeology, after all. I'd always held off giving it to the Freeholders. Principles, don't you know. But after I saw what the fleet was doing to the village, to the Tree, I changed my mind. I went back to get ingredients. I was going to beat the Council at their own game. I didn't tell Jamil because I knew he wouldn't agree.'

'I agree,' murmured Tymon grimly. 'I wish you'd had the chance to make your secret weapon, Apu.'

'No, no!' The old man strained up from his bed of rags. 'It was the best thing in the world that I didn't! If I had, we'd have been just like them, don't you see?'

Tymon sat in sullen silence. Before the attack, before Solis' death, he would probably have agreed with Galliano. Some things were sacred. It was a terrible crime to reduce the Mother of all things to ash and debris. But now he was not so sure. He had come to hate the Council so much that it seemed worth the loss of a branch or two to be rid of the murdering invaders. He could hear soldiers barking orders on the deck above, the renewed sigh of ether filling the dirigible's balloons. They were quitting the hangar. He wondered where they would be taken and what life of misery awaited them.

Galliano reached out and caught hold of his tunic. 'Believe me, you don't want that kind of power,' he rasped, urgent. 'You pay for it in other ways.'

They were interrupted as another soldier came clattering down the stairs into the hold. A hardwood blade flashed briefly in his hand as he bent over Tymon. The boy barely had time to flinch before his bonds were cut and he was pulled roughly to his feet.

'Up,' leered the soldier. 'You're going to see the boss.'

He gave Tymon a push towards the stairs and scooped up Galliano's thin, desiccated form in his arms. The scientist gave a faint groan. Tymon sprang back to his side with a cry of concern.

'I said "up",' snapped the sentry, with a well-aimed kick at his shins. 'Or don't you "speaky the *Argosi*", Nurry?'

He was thrust up the stairs to the deck without further ceremony. The ship had risen well above the twig-thickets already, leaving the smoke and afterglow of the fires behind. The wind carried stinging drops of water, grey and cold, rain and ash mixed together. He shivered as the soldier propped Galliano against the dirigible's main mast like a lifeless puppet. A few of the dirigible's sailors hung in the rigging, staring inquisitively at them, and two more Argosian sentries loitered on either side of a squat contraption to one side of the deck. Tymon gazed at the blast-cannon with distaste. It was mounted on wheels and seemed smaller than its counterparts on the greatships. But it had that same evil snout, that air of smug destruction. A long box with a lock lay at its foot.

'Well, well, if it isn't our two prodigal sons,' remarked a voice behind him, as cool and biting as the rain-filled wind. 'Welcome home, both of you.'

Tymon turned with heavy reluctance to find Lace standing on the deck. The Envoy grinned.

'Come here, acolyte,' he said, calling over his shoulder to someone just inside the door of the captain's cabin. 'This will be educational for you.'

Tymon fully expected Verlain to emerge from the doorway and was startled to see a thin, youthful figure step onto the deck. A boy approached the group by the mast.

'Study the lesson,' continued Lace. 'These are the wages of folly and pride. Consider this heretic, who persisted in his stubborn beliefs. See what he has come to. Consider also your former comrade, who chose to serve the wrong Master.'

'Wick?' Tymon gasped in amazement. 'Is that you?'

His classmate was almost unrecognisable. Wick's face had hardened before its time. His expression was aloof as he surveyed Tymon.

'Yes, it's me, old friend,' he replied, his tone bright and careless.

'So — old friend — are you enjoying yourself?' Tymon could not keep the bitterness from his voice. 'Are you happy now that you can lord it over me again?'

Wick shrugged. 'I'm not happy to see what's become of you, Tymon. You always choose the wrong side, then blame other people when things fall apart. Don't hold it against me if I've taken a wiser path.' He smiled coldly. 'While you were grubbing in the bark with rebels and heretics, I was learning about the real Power in the world — a secret you couldn't even begin to understand, poor Ty.'

'He understands more than you'll ever know,' interrupted Galliano, shifting himself against the mast with a grimace of pain. 'Tymon's way beyond you and always will be, young Master Wick. But I think you realise that.'

'Shut up, old man,' hissed Wick. His façade of calm gave way and he rounded on the scientist, quivering with rage. 'Shut up and eat your useless tongue! I don't want to hear you — no one wants to hear you!'

He fingered something around his neck as he spoke, and Tymon caught a bright flash, a drop of trapped sunlight inside his former schoolmate's collar. *Orah*, he thought, with a pang.

'Blind and dumb,' declared Wick, drawing himself up as if he were reciting a magic spell. 'Blind you were, so now be dumb.'

Galliano emitted a strange, strangled noise. His head fell forward on his chest and he fainted. Tymon rushed to him, aghast, catching the scientist in his arms as he lolled to one side. The sense of wrongness he had experienced on the catapult platform, of things *not as they should be*, gripped him again. His own pendant pulsed with heat, indignant.

'Study the lesson, acolyte,' Lace reiterated softly. 'It's useful to be able to control a person, certainly. But better to exploit his natural inclinations without him even realising it.'

'What have you done to him?' cried Tymon, when he was able to force the words out of his tight throat. 'What have you done, Wick? He's just a helpless old man!'

'Relax, it's only a Seeming.' Wick's face was dark with sweat, triumphant. 'It won't last. He's always giving out unwanted advice. Now he has to take some of mine.'

The scientist seemed to be plunged into a deep sleep. Tymon readjusted his head and propped him back against the mast, unable to do more. He eyed Wick askance.

'I don't know what you think you've been learning, Wick, but it's not Grafting,' he said quietly.

'I've been learning about Power.' His friend gave a hard laugh. 'Which is something you'll never have, Ty. Why, don't you know I'm a deputy of the Council? I'll be heading my own missions to Marak soon. With what the Fathers have taught me, no one will be able to stand in my way. I can do what I like.'

'What you seem to like is being a murdering bully.'

'Boys, boys!' admonished Lace. 'Play nicely!' He walked over to the dirigible's deck-rail, his white kerchief fluttering in the wind. 'My young colleague does have a point, Tymon,' he said. 'You have no control over your talents right now, sometimes with tragic consequences. Think: if you had been able to focus your ability, you would have easily avoided the ambush that killed your Nurian friend.'

Tymon glared at him, wordless. Somehow, it was more distasteful to hear the truth coming from the Envoy's lips than a lie.

'Look at the progress Wick has made,' continued Lace. He leaned over the rail, searching the canopy below. 'You'd do the same if you were taught to use the Sight properly. You might still come back with us and learn, you know.'

Wick wheeled about in surprise to face his mentor, and opened his mouth as if he were about to say something. Then he thought better of it and subsided with a scowl, his arms folded tightly across his chest.

'You can offer all you like,' muttered Tymon. 'I'll never serve the seminary again.'

'Well, I didn't really expect you to be reasonable,' yawned Lace. He glanced up at the soldiers waiting by the cannon. 'Ready the shot,' he ordered.

The two soldiers rolled the engine to the starboard side of the ship, some distance from where the Envoy was standing, and wedged it against a special gap in the deck-rail. The cannon looked heavy, as if it were carved of solid hardwood.

'What are you doing?' asked Tymon suspiciously.

They were very high over the promontory now, close under the threatening clouds. Thunder rolled, a warning rumble, and the spots of water on the wind had become gusts of freezing rain. There were no targets for the blast-cannons here.

'Finishing up our business on the Freehold,' answered Lace. 'Come and see for yourself.'

The boy walked cautiously to the deck-rail, keeping a healthy distance between himself and the Envoy. He peered over the swelling curve of the dirigible's belly to find the ruin of the Freehold spread out beneath him. They were high enough now, drifting about a hundred feet above the village and a little to the south, that he could see the extent of the damage done to the promontory. Smoke wreathed the base of the outcrop; its summit still burned like a torch. Tymon drew a sharp breath and clutched the rail, for he recognised that image, knew it intimately. There below him was the fiery vision he had experienced in Samiha's house. There was the glimpse of the burning city. *You think that you're a Grafter, but you cannot even understand what you have Seen*, the Envoy had taunted him in his dream. And so it was. He had Seen the attack on the Freehold after all, been warned of it by the Focals all the way back in Marak, and missed the point entirely.

Apart from providing him with that crushing insight, however, he could not understand why Lace had decided to bring them up here to such a height. The battle for the promontory was clearly won. The Freehold lay in smoking ruins. The rest of the Argosian fleet had abandoned the village and withdrawn to the lower canopy in preparation for the rainstorm. The last greatships were sinking into the thickets about half a mile westwards, their sails tightly stowed. What unfinished business could the Envoy have among the clouds?

'Downwards, and a little to the right,' said Lace casually.

And then Tymon noticed it. A tiny gap pierced the twig-thickets, a treacherous opening that showed clear through to the branches south of the promontory. The gap lay in a direct line two hundred feet beneath the dirigible. It would have been hidden from any other vantage point. Small, vulnerable, barely visible through the veil of smoke, figures marched like ants along a subsidiary limb before disappearing again under the sheltering thickets. *Your friends are all dead, or soon will be*, repeated the sneering dream-voice in Tymon's memory.

'No,' he exclaimed, horrified. 'No, you can't do that.' Samiha was down there.

'I can and I will, young fellow.'

Tymon faced the Envoy, wild-eyed. 'There are innocent women and children in that convoy. They're just refugees. Don't do it, sir!'

Lace sighed, as if explaining something simple to an idiot. 'There are no innocent Nurians, only insurgents. Who do you think prepares the sweet little rebels of tomorrow? They get a taste for it in their mother's milk. Best wipe out the problem in the bud.'

One of the Argosian soldiers opened the box at the foot of the cannon and took out a gleaming, black ball. His companion stoked the engine's nozzle.

'I'll do anything you want!' pleaded Tymon. 'I'll go back with you to Argos! I'll study Grafting! I'll do what you tell me to do!'

'Who do you think you are?' The Envoy's eyes glinted with cold humour. 'I already made that offer and you refused. I'm not interested any more, and even if I was, it wouldn't change a tactical decision during wartime.'

He turned his back on Tymon, intent on the view over the deck-rail. On the other side of the boy the soldiers loaded the blast-shot into the cannon. Gingerly, as if it were a live thing, they slid the black ball down the engine's gullet.

'No!' cried Tymon again, desperately.

He was between Lace and the cannon. He could not take on the two soldiers at once, so he threw himself at the Envoy in the vague hope of wrestling his enemy over the deck-rail. It would not save the Freeholders and would in all probability get him killed, but he could not bear to stand by and do nothing. Wick jumped forward to stop him with a warning cry, but Lace had already gestured briefly, almost negligently, in Tymon's direction.

'Down,' he drawled, without bothering to look behind him.

Tymon felt a grinding weight descend on his shoulders. He fell to his knees on the deck, unable to move. The sense of wrongness emanating from the Envoy was so strong that it made him nauseous. His mind seemed to go to pieces, as it had in the presence of the Dean. But this time it was impossible to resist, to hold out against despair. *Weak, weak, weak,* chanted the dream-voice in his mind. *You're weak, and deluded, and pathetic.* And he believed it. He was what the voice said he was. He had never been anything more. He lost all hope and crouched where he was on the deck, defeated.

As he sat there, staring dully ahead, one of the soldiers opened a small hatch at the back of the cannon and struck a fire-stick. Perhaps people would die, Tymon thought, distantly, but it didn't much matter. Nothing mattered any more. Part of him had dislocated, detached itself from what was happening, and the scene on the deck seemed unreal. Thunder echoed, a booming crack directly over the dirigible. In the flicker of lightning that followed, he saw with surprise that a man wearing a long travelling cloak stood beside him. His green gaze searched out Tymon's and held it steadily. He had not been there before, did not belong on the ship with the others, the boy thought. Who was he?

'Don't be afraid of weakness,' said the newcomer quietly. Tymon could not be sure if his lips moved. *'In weakness find strength.'*

The calm directive — it was more of an incantation, or a prayer, perhaps — was vaguely familiar to the boy. It required a supreme effort to dredge up the memory but he recalled that once, what felt like a very long time ago, he may have heard words like that, words that gave hope.

'In weakness find strength,' he whispered to himself. Even if the hope was only an illusion, it was a comforting one.

The soldier in charge of lighting the cannon was having some trouble coaxing his fire-stick alive in the driving wind. He bent over the resin-coated sticks, cursing. His fellow sentry came around the back of the engine to help him.

'Take out the pith and the Sap flows,' said the green-eyed man. He nodded encouragingly. '*In emptiness* —'

'*In emptiness, power*,' murmured Tymon.

There was no doubt about it: he knew the words. Slowly, haltingly, the pendant about his neck began to glow, warming his chest. They were Grafting words, he remembered. He had time to reflect that the pendant glowed because it was *orah*, and that *orah* focused a Grafter's power, protecting him from —

He glanced up in sudden, belated recognition at his companion on the deck. There stood the fifth Focal. There was the dead man. The apparition fixed him with bright eyes, summoning him back to himself. The sense of helplessness and blank indifference vanished. He knew again who he was and what he was capable of. How had he forgotten so quickly?

'*Worlds that were severed*,' prompted Ash with a smile.

'*Worlds that were severed, we now bind together*.' Tymon finished off the Grafters' song, his voice stronger. He smiled back at the fifth Focal.

'What?' snapped Wick, beside him. He did not appear to see the dead man. 'What are you mumbling about, Ty?'

Tymon ignored him and stood up. He felt light and joyful and gazed about him in happy astonishment. It was as if a veil had been lifted from his eyes. The world blazed with a marvellous fire as it had the night in the arena. The soldiers on the deck, the sailors climbing through the rigging, all were playful knots of shadow and flame. Beauty washed through everything. The figure of Wick, peering mistrustfully at him, was a guttering candle, fragile and needy. His own body was no different, made of liquid light. A glad heat brimmed up inside him. It was the Sap, he realised wonderingly. This was the Sap.

'Concentrate,' warned the Focal's voice, a soft breath in his ear.

Ash was no longer visible, but the knowledge of what he had to do coursed through Tymon like a wave. He was no longer afraid, no longer in doubt. *Events and people were connected.* There was no time to lose. The light under the clouds had turned almost green and thunder cracked resoundingly overhead. Lightning flashed on the deck immediately afterwards. He saw that the soldier by the cannon had made his fire-sticks work at last. A blue spark leapt in the man's cupped hands.

'Fire,' Tymon called out urgently as he strode towards the engine.

'What's all this nonsense?' Wick hurried after him. 'What do you think you're doing, Ty? You can't do anything —'

'Fire!' shouted the boy again, through his schoolmate's question. He sidestepped Wick and waved insistently to the soldiers. 'Watch out! It's on fire!'

The man at the cannon hatch looked up at him for a split second, frowning. As he did so, a blue sheet of flame burst out of the opening and engulfed his hand. He dropped his fire-sticks and sprang back with a bellow of pain and surprise.

'No, no!' cried Wick, clawing past Tymon. 'It's a trick! Ignore him!'

'Back to your posts, men!' snarled the Envoy from behind them. 'I'll throw anyone who disobeys me overboard!'

But it was too late. The soldier with the fire-sticks was already scrambling away from the blast-cannon, an expression of abject fear on his face. His companion shouted to the sailors in the rigging, warning them to get away, get back, it was all going to blow, everything was going to blow. Large wet drops began to spatter the deck. Flames licked out of the cannon's blunt nozzle, blue and treacherous.

A black shape leapt in front of Tymon, causing him to come to an abrupt standstill. For an instant, he thought that a wild animal had been let loose on the ship. But the thing before him was no beast of the Tree. He saw with a shock that it was the Envoy. Behind the mask-like human exterior lay another reality, visible to his Grafter's eye as a thing made up of twisting darkness, all shadow and no flame, untouched by the Sap. It fluctuated, pulsed, acquired and lost definition, forever changing shape. Sometimes it had two legs like a man, but possessed no head; at other times it grew four legs and stumpy wings to become a hideous, malformed monster. The thing-that-was-Lace bounded towards the cannon, vomiting darkness. But the net of quenching shadow it unleashed was useless. Tymon's Seeming had passed the point of no return. Too many people had seen the blue tongues darting from the engine's mouth. The sailors' voices erupted in a babble of panic: Grafter fire had become real fire.

As if it realised its mistake, the shadow thing skidded to a halt on the wet deck. Tymon could have sworn he heard the sound of scraping claws through the mounting patter of rain. The knotty shape wheeled around, turned its headless malevolence on him as he backed away. Though it had no eyes, the boy knew that it Saw him. The thing gathered itself for another, final leap.

And then the blast-shot ignited in the cannon, and everything did blow.

26

Tymon was thrown backwards against the main mast by the force of the explosion. He tumbled onto the deck not far from where Galliano lay, crumpled in a heap at the foot of the mast. Consciousness slipped away from him. When he came to his senses again it was to the sound of the dirigible's hull wrenching and groaning and a stab of pain in his legs. He shielded his eyes against the red glare of flame. The subtle visions of the Sap had disappeared; barely twenty feet in front of him crackled a wall of ordinary fire, greedy and perilous. Where the Envoy had been there was only a blazing hole in the side of the ship. Tymon shuddered at the thought of the unnatural thing he had Seen with his Grafter's sense, bounding across the deck boards. He recalled Laska's warning, his talk of Beings outside the pale of human law. Was the Council in league with demons, then? Or did they not realise what was lurking in their midst?

Whatever Lace's true nature, however, he was gone, vaporised in the fire unleashed by the blast. Wick was nowhere to be seen either, though whether his schoolmate had been close enough to the cannon to perish in the explosion, Tymon did not know. Gigantic flames licked up from the hole in the deck, sizzling incongruously through the pouring rain. The starboard ether sacks were ravaged by fire and the ship had already begun to list. He heard the sailors' voices, a dim echo of dismay somewhere behind him. Feet thudded on the deck and soldiers barked orders. He could not get up to see what was going on. He lay where he had fallen, trapped and groaning, and soaked to the skin.

Something was wrong with both of his legs. He was only mildly uncomfortable if he stayed still, but any movement was torture. Gradually the voices of the sailors grew faint, replaced by the roar and splutter of flames and the hiss of rain on hot wood. The ship was leaning at a precarious angle now, spinning in a slow arc southwards. They had lost a great deal of altitude. He glimpsed one red envelope of a life-vessel in the sky, and then another, drifting northwards. Some of the crew had escaped the disaster on the dirigible. And still the screech of ether filled the air as sack after sack succumbed to the blaze. He found he could inch his way across the deck if he favoured his left side and used his elbows to haul himself along the planks. He dragged his unresponsive body to where Galliano lay and eased himself down next to the old scientist. The wall of fire had spread to form a high arc along the right side of the ship, impervious to the rain and sizzling greedily through the ship's rigging.

'Goodbye, old man,' Tymon whispered over the motionless form of his friend. He could have wept with exhaustion. 'Sorry you didn't get to find your World Below.'

'You give up so quickly!' Galliano stirred and smiled faintly. 'Shame on you.'

'It really is over this time, Apu,' Tymon replied. 'I can't get us out of here and the ship's going down. It might have been better if you'd stayed out cold.',

'And miss the final journey? Never! I wish to take notes on dying, my friend. To my knowledge I have never done it before.'

At that moment the timbers of the dirigible groaned and cracked, and the whole aft section of the hull ripped away in a blinding shower of sparks. The ship tilted steeply, throwing them like helpless jetsam across the deck. They began to slip — slowly, inexorably — towards the fiery hole on the starboard side. Tymon could feel the heat of the inferno through the driving rain. The danger was immediate, physical. He knew instinctively that no subtle art of Grafting would help him now. No apparition would come to guide him. He must save himself or accept defeat. He bowed his head and set his shoulders against Galliano's back, doing his best to keep them both from sliding into the hungry flames.

Some distance above the ruin of the Envoy's dirigible, out of earshot of the two forlorn figures on the deck, a steady thrumming filled the air. The *Lyla* wheeled through the rainstorm, making as close an arc about the doomed ship as her captain dared.

'Nothing,' said Laska. 'If they didn't make it on the life-vessels, then the explosion must have taken them, Samiha.'

She did not look at him, locked rigid at her post by one of the *Lyla*'s windows. 'Just one more time,' she pleaded. 'Fly by just once more.'

It was hard to tell through the noise of the storm and the propellers, but the Kion's voice might have trembled. Laska stifled his own objections and brought the air-chariot round to the north for the third time. The beetled form of the *Lyla* dipped and soared through the clouds, almost invisible in the lashing rain. It passed to starboard of the Envoy's dirigible. The ship itself was a flaming hulk attached to its few remaining ether sacks. The aft had disintegrated; all that was left of the starboard side was a bright and gutted hole, belching smoke into the stormy sky. The whole vessel listed so badly that the masts were tilted towards the level. Everything on the steeply slanted deck would have slipped into the burning belly of the ship or been consigned to the Void.

But not everything had remained on the deck. The anxious watchers on the *Lyla* saw them at the same time: two huddled forms at the base of the skewed mast, clinging like rats to the drifting wreck. Samiha gave a gasp and Laska pulled hard on the air-chariot's brake rod, driving down through the smoke and the rain.

'They're not moving.' Samiha craned worriedly out of the window.

As she spoke, one of the figures looked upwards and waved, his dirty white novice's tunic visible under the grey Nurian cloak. She expelled a slow breath of relief. They dropped the *Lyla* as low as they could over the mast, killing the back propeller and hovering about thirty feet above where Tymon and Galliano lay. But when Samiha began unrolling the emergency rope ladder from the air-chariot's hatchway, the boy only shook his head emphatically and pointed to his legs.

'One of us will have to go down,' said Laska. 'It's the only way.'

Tymon had greeted the miraculous appearance of the *Lyla* with a numb, disbelieving joy. He had been sure they would not be sighted through the clouds of steam and smoke that encompassed the ship. He had run out of places to crawl to and been waiting for the inevitable, for the dirigible to crash into the canopy. His relief at the reprieve was soon coloured by exasperation, however. He could see Samiha's breeches wriggling backwards out of the hatch. She descended the ladder, calling something inaudible to him over the din of the storm. What did she think she was doing? She might be able to carry Galliano up to the machine, but he was twice as heavy as the old man.

'Why is she so stubborn?' he exclaimed in annoyance. 'Why didn't she let Laska come down?'

'You don't understand,' muttered Galliano. The scientist's condition had worsened in the past hour. He was delirious with fever, slumped against Tymon on their perch. 'Don't question the heavenly angel,' he urged. 'She appears only once in nine hundred years.'

Tymon shook his head at Samiha once more, gesturing towards his ears, and then with a worried frown to Galliano. When she had climbed down low enough to jump onto the mast, balancing effortlessly on the rounded beam, he cried, 'You should have let Laska come. I can't use my legs, and you certainly won't be able —'

'Wear this,' she broke in, handing him a long, belt-like contraption she had slung over one shoulder.

It was a harness attached to a rope, he realised, a sling like the ones he had seen used in the Tree-shaft to transport the wounded soldiers. The rope belayed all the way to the air-chariot. He could make out the winch now, just inside the hatchway. He slipped the belt over his shoulders and tightened the buckle around his waist, embarrassed more by his outburst than his mistake. He should have given her other, more important news first.

'Solis didn't make it,' he said awkwardly. 'I'm so sorry, Samiha.'

He could not tell what she was thinking. As she bent over him to check the knot on the harness the rain sluiced down with redoubled force, slicking the hair to her face.

'I know, Tymon. We found his body outside the hangar,' she replied as she pulled the knot taut. 'Solis knew the risks when he went with you. We all did.'

She flicked the drenched hair from her face and squatted down on the mast beside Galliano, gathering the tiny scientist into her arms. He made no sound; he had lost consciousness again.

'The old man's worse off than I am,' Tymon warned her. 'He's been in and out ever since the explosion. He's running a fever. I'm worried that he's hurt on the inside, something we can't see.'

Samiha nodded and used another, shorter harness to attach Galliano to her belt. She braced him as gently as she could over her shoulder, then climbed briskly up the trembling rope ladder. Tymon stared anxiously up through the rain until she had delivered Galliano to the *Lyla*'s hatch and scrambled inside herself. Rain was prevailing over fire. The blaze on the dirigible had retreated to glowing, red-hot cavities at the ship's core. Warmth radiated from the planks of the deck behind him, now a vertical wall. He wondered if the flames had reached the space within. Then the air-chariot's propellers changed register and the *Lyla* lifted, drawing the harness taut. He grimaced as he was pulled upright with a jerk.

They rose with dizzying speed towards the clouds. Soon he felt the harness jerk once more and the winch began pulling him up through the whistling emptiness, the rain and wind stinging his eyes. He glanced down a last time at the glowing hulk of the Envoy's ship. Only the front half on the port side remained unscathed, attached to its dismal collection of ether sacks and drifting dangerously close to the topmost branches of the canopy. Perhaps it was a trick of the flames inside the dirigible, but he thought he glimpsed an ashen face at one of the fore-cabin windows, gaping up at him with panic-stricken features. He strained to see through the smoke and rain. Was someone still there, trapped inside the burning vessel?

Samiha wound up the last few feet of rope, her shoulders aching from working the winch. But when she leaned out into the pelting rain to pull Tymon through the hatch, he was already talking, pointing frantically down towards the dirigible.

'Just one sweet green second,' she grumbled.

She hauled him in until he was able to roll through the opening, as wet as a newborn chick. He started to speak again, then yelped as he rolled too far on the floor of the *Lyla*'s cabin and knocked his legs against one of the benches.

'I have no idea what you're talking about,' she said. 'Let me get you comfortable before you begin chewing my ear off. What's wrong?'

'Back to the ship,' he groaned. 'We have to go back to the ship. I saw him. Wick's in there and he's still alive.'

They did go back in the end, despite Laska's misgivings and Samiha's deep lack of enthusiasm. Tymon's account of Wick's political clout, his ties with the Envoy, only served to strengthen his companions' initial resistance to the idea. But the boy would not let the matter go. He dragged himself to a sitting position on the air-chariot's bench, puffing with pain, and harangued them. He had failed Solis, he said. He had failed his friend; he did not wish to fail his enemy also. This announcement appeared to confound the other two. Samiha glanced at Laska and Laska shrugged his shoulders. The captain steered them back in a loop towards the wreck, and they came level with the hulk of the Envoy's ship as it skimmed with ghostly speed above the tips of the twig-thickets.

There indeed was Wick, a lonely speck on the upturned port side, waving desperately to them. The proud deputy of the Council had scrambled half out of a cabin window and clung to the listing hull like a bedraggled green moth, his robes sodden in the rain. Flames licked up from the window behind him. It seemed to Tymon that they would never get him out before the dirigible smashed into the canopy. Laska brought the *Lyla* down as low as he could over the flaming hulk, but there was a heart-stopping delay while Wick was cajoled into climbing the rope ladder alone. Samiha refused to go down to help him and Tymon was in no state to do so himself. Only when the young priest had crawled up the shuddering rungs and through the hatchway to collapse, trembling, on the bench opposite his old schoolmate, was the *Lyla* finally free to veer in a long arc southwards and depart the wreck forever. As they sped away, the Envoy's dirigible hit the canopy with a deafening crack, trailing a stream of fire and smoke.

Then there was only the grey light of the rainstorm outside and the thud of the propellers as the two boys sat opposite each other in the narrow cabin. Samiha had her back resolutely turned to them, crouching by Laska at the controls. To the aft of the machine Galliano lay stretched on the floor, moaning in his delirium.

'They'll pay you a reward for my safe return,' declared Wick in the uncomfortable pause that followed.

Tymon did not answer at once. He had expected to feel triumph now that he had presided over his schoolmate's humiliation. Instead, he was achingly tired, and uninterested in humiliating anyone.

'Who is authorised to negotiate treaties for the Council?' he asked.

'I am, with the approval of the Admiral of the fleet.' Even now, Wick's mouth twisted with arrogance. 'In his Excellency the Envoy's absence, my mark and seal carry absolute authority in the five Domains, from Spice City to Cherk Harbour —'

'Then you'll talk to the Admiral and mark and seal a treaty with the Freehold judges,' interrupted Tymon. 'Once that happens, you'll be transported back to the Argosian fleet.'

Wick stared. 'That's it?' he asked.

'That's it.' Tymon lay down to rest, with a fair amount of trouble, on the hard bench.

'You should have joined us, you know,' said his companion after a while, his tone half sneering, half respectful. 'You could have been something special. Lace told me so. I was even jealous about it.'

Tymon sighed as Oren's pendant pulsed softly inside his tunic collar. He shrugged off the tendrils of power emanating from Wick, the spidery will to dominate.

'Stop doing that,' he growled. 'It won't work.'

Wick gave a grunt of forced laughter through the din of the propellers. His hand had crept up to the cord at his throat. 'Doing what?' he smiled.

'Listen, Wick.' Tymon raised himself up painfully on one elbow, to stare fully in the face of his adversary. 'I know you have a piece of *orah* there. Don't try and use it against me or anyone else. You won't find me as easy to take in as before, and I warn you, you'll have absolutely no luck with the *shanti*. If you were half as powerful as you claim to be, you'd use your wits and get out of this with some kind of dignity.'

He lay down on the bench again. The noise of the air-chariot's engine and the silence of its occupants filled the cabin.

By the time they reached the rallying point south of the promontory, the rainstorm was easing and patches of washed-out afternoon sky showed through the clouds. They settled on a branch just under the twig-thickets, near the spot where the Freeholders' old trading dirigible had been moored to await the arrival of the villagers. They were met by Gardan with the good news that Caro's convoy was making excellent time on the branch-paths, and would arrive by evening. Laska left in the air-chariot to establish the position of the Argosian ships while Samiha set about organising the removal of Tymon and Galliano to the temporary hospice aboard the dirigible. Gardan took charge of Wick.

The prisoner immediately began making high-handed demands and complaining of ill treatment.

Gardan gazed at him steadily with her bright blue eyes for several moments and let him talk. Then she reached forward and, with a sharp movement, ripped the cord and pendant of *orah* from Wick's neck, as one might confiscate a toy from a child. Wick gasped in astonishment.

'Gag the Argosian sorcerer,' said the judge flatly, turning to the members of her personal guard. 'Take him to the brig and see that he remains in solitary confinement until he is called for. Do not remove the gag or engage in conversation with the prisoner. He will be seen in due time by the judges' quorum.'

To Tymon's amazement, she then approached the stretcher where he lay waiting to be taken to the hospice ship, and offered the pendant to him. It was a rod of pure *orah*, about the length and width of a finger bone, its hardwood setting carved with the seminary's seal. He did not reach out at once to take it from her. He felt an instinctive repugnance for the smooth, shining trinket, as if it were polluted.

'It has been abused, Tymon,' Samiha observed by his side. 'But you should accept. Keep it safe until we can give it to someone who will cure it.'

'I'm not so concerned with the religious aspects of the thing,' added Gardan with a wink. 'I do think this gives us a chance to negotiate with the Argosians, however. We'll need the seal to ratify any deal. There's no way I'm leaving it in the possession of that talkative deputy in the meantime. Can I rely on you to keep it?'

'I'll do my best, *syora*,' sighed the boy. He slipped the pendant into his belt pouch; he could feel Wick's gaze burning into him as he did so. His last glimpse of his schoolmate was of him trotting behind Gardan, his wrists bound and a length of grey cloth wrapped tightly about his scowling face.

Tymon would not rest easy until he had seen Galliano installed as comfortably as possible on the hospice ship, and closely questioned an apprentice nurse, the only healer as yet on board, about the old man's injuries.

'I not know why fever,' was the girl's less than satisfactory answer. She looked about thirteen, and presided over the makeshift infirmary in the ship's hold with much in the way of clattering activity and a rolling of eyes. 'Doctor come tonight, she say more.'

But she proved adept at setting bones and with Samiha's help bullied Tymon out of his wet clothes and into a cot of his own. He gritted his teeth to keep from crying out as the two women cleaned the long scraping wounds and bound stiff strips of bark about his legs. Both shinbones were fractured, he was informed by the young nurse through pursed lips, as if this were entirely his fault. She then curtained off the section of the hold where he lay and bustled away, leaving him alone with Samiha in sudden and welcome silence.

'So, here we are,' he said.

He was pleasantly warm in the cot and the Nurian healing herbs had taken the edge off his pain. There were outstanding issues to be concerned about, he knew: Galliano's health, the fate of his wounded companions among the refugees, and the ongoing problem of whether

Wick's capture would persuade the seminary to make peace with the Freeholders. But he was content to leave the worrying for later. It seemed a thousand years since his dawn appointment in the arena. He smiled tiredly at Samiha as she pulled a chair near the cot and sat down beside him.

'I hope you know that you're reckless, and stubborn, and almost drove me mad with worry today,' she said.

'I know,' he replied. 'I'm sorry.'

'Good. Because for a while there I thought I'd lost you forever.' She searched his face. 'I know you're tired, but this is important. I'd like you to tell me what happened on the Envoy's ship.'

Tymon turned away from her on the cot. He did not want to speak of his experience under the Envoy's gruelling influence. He remembered with unpleasant clarity the crippling loss of will he had suffered at a mere word from his enemy. It had been so easy to give up his humanity, to slip into indifference. The thought of the beast-that-was-Lace haunted him. He struggled with his own reticence and exhaustion, loath to answer in depth but aware that Samiha deserved his trust. She deserved to hear about his moment of weakness as well as his strengths.

'I got through it all by sheer luck,' he began, automatically — then frowned, exasperated with himself. 'No, not luck. It was terrible. Lace took me apart. I forgot who I was. But I had a Grafting vision. Ash helped me. If he hadn't, I'd be lost.' He shook his head. 'The Envoy wasn't just a sorcerer, Samiha. On the ship, I Saw his true shape. I couldn't believe it. I couldn't believe Wick would actually listen to someone — something like that. He was a monster, a creature out of a dream. He had no head, but he could See me. He had no mouth but I felt like he could have eaten me, too. I know that sounds impossible.'

To his surprise she took his hand in her own and squeezed it tightly.

'It's not impossible,' she answered, her smile warm. He realised with dawning pleasure that she was proud of him. 'We humans aren't the only ones with the Sight. I know you don't like to believe in such things, but just as there are helpful powers in the world there are others who don't have our best interests at heart. I wish it were not so. But if you're going to be a Grafter — and you are, a powerful one — then you will encounter them. You've heard of them, of course. Even the priests in Argos have not forgotten that there are demons in the Tree, as well as angels.'

'Well, whatever Lace was, he's gone,' murmured Tymon, closing his eyes. 'He was caught in the explosion: there's no way he could have survived.' He did not voice the swift doubt that accompanied this remark: What was survival to such as the Envoy? Was it dependent on the same factors as governed human life?

She frowned slightly, as if she had thought of something more to say on the subject of Lace and could not bring herself to trouble him with it. But she only said, 'We'll talk more tomorrow. I should let you rest.'

'No!'

His eyes flew open. He was not willing to let her go, though his body ached and fatigue rolled over him in waves. He held tightly to her hand. He felt as if he had just won her back against terrible odds. She peered into his face, a curious tension in her expression. Her hair, still bedraggled and damp from the rainstorm, stuck in strands to her cheek. He could not help it: he reached up to brush away the tresses, as he had on the morning of their escape from Marak city. This time he let his hand linger on her cheek, caressing her. She did not push him away. His heart beat faster. A glad warmth rose up inside him, and he remembered the joyful pulse of the Sap. He did not ask what had changed her mind with regard to him. He did not care what she might still have held back and not yet told him. She bent close, her breath sweet on his face, until their lips touched.

The rasp of the curtain-runners jolted them apart.

'Time to go, *shanti*.' The youthful nurse gave a sly smile. 'Even *Argosi* hero need to sleep.'

27

Poor Wick. Poor misused, misjudged Wick, abandoned and alone, left on a forsaken stump of this forsaken and barbaric corner of the Tree — may it rot and fall to Hell, and take its lice-like inhabitants with it! Poor lonely little Wick, deserted by his so-called friends and forced to wait here, on this derelict outpost, for the arrival of Admiral Greenly and the Argosian fleet. Or so the damned lice said before they flew off in that abomination of theirs and left him to die. Cursed Nurries. He gave them what they wanted, too: helped them negotiate a nice little treaty with the Admiral, saved their dirty white skins from total destruction. And now they abandon him on this stub of a branch in the middle of nowhere, where no one would ever find him ...

'Stop wallowing in self-pity, acolyte, and use your eyes. The Admiral's ship is already on the horizon.'

A shudder passed through Wick. A voice had spoken, interrupting his thoughts in unpleasantly recognisable tones. He did not search the skyline for a dirigible but turned instead to peer behind him on the bare and flattened top of the lookout branch. Beside the charred pit of the signal fire, where there had been nothing but whistling wind moments before, a figure now stood. A shadowy outline seemed to patch itself up out of thin air, to piece itself together from odds and ends and fragments rather than possess any real existence of its own. The fragments solidified, taking on the form of the Envoy.

'Why, aren't you happy to see me, Wick?' asked Lace.

'Excellency —' gulped the youth, sinking to his knees. 'I thought — I thought —'

'Make it a rule never to think, acolyte,' said Lace coolly. 'You're no good at it.'

'I'm sorry, Excellency,' gabbled Wick. 'I've had a terrible time since ... since you left. The Nurries treated me shamefully —'

'And yet here you are, ultimately unharmed and waiting for a ride home,' noted the Envoy. He shaded his eyes and surveyed the dirigible on the western horizon. It was drawing rapidly nearer, green sails billowing. 'Almost as if you had betrayed me and given our enemies something in exchange for your freedom.'

'Betrayed?' The colour drained from Wick's face. 'I would not ... not ever ...'

'Wouldn't you now?' said Lace softly. He cocked his head to one side, considering his acolyte. 'Would you not sign a truce, perhaps, in order to save your own precious skin?' His eye strayed to Wick's neck, shorn of its pendant.

'They took it,' breathed the miserable Wick. 'They took the seal. They forced me to talk to the Admiral. They threatened ... I had no choice.'

'Ah, the dictates of circumstance,' observed the Envoy dryly. 'But I remain curious. How did you manage to convince the Admiral, of all people, to negotiate?'

Wick hesitated, squirming where he knelt on the branch. 'Forgive me, Excellency,' he said. 'After reports of ... of your death, sir ... the stories the survivors brought back from the ship ...'

The Envoy's eyebrows shot up.

'Mistaken reports, of course,' Wick rushed on. 'The Admiral thought it best to seek a compromise.'

He squinted worriedly up at Lace. His mentor seemed unconcerned at the admission, however, scrutinising the horizon.

'No matter,' he said. He shrugged, his scarf flapping in the breeze. 'After all, it worked out quite well for us.'

'You're not angry about the peace, sir?'

'No, acolyte. If I were angry you would know about it, be assured.' The Envoy grinned cadaverously at him. 'I'm quite pleased, actually. Annihilating the Freehold would have given the enemy a reason to stick together. Now, they're divided for good. The Nurian militant won't stand for a negotiated peace. He'll form his own faction and split them to the core. Your dear schoolmate has seen to that.' He leered as Wick's face spoke his question. 'Oh yes, we are grateful to Tymon. He continues to do us great service.'

'I don't understand, sir,' muttered Wick, evidently displeased at the mention of Tymon. 'I thought he was of no use to us any more.'

'Quite the reverse,' chuckled Lace. 'The Sap moves through him unaided now. But he is young, and proud, and full of pith. A most potent combination for our purposes, and one that appears only once or twice in a generation.'

This comment seemed to infuriate Wick. He clenched his fists. 'Is that what your Masters say?' he blurted out. 'That Tymon's the one you're looking for?'

There was a moment of absolute silence. The Envoy regarded Wick, the black of his eyes fathomless. He did not smile. His acolyte withered under that frozen gaze.

'You will not speak of my Masters,' said Lace, after a while. His voice was soft but the sheer malice in it might have cut the air. 'You are not worthy to crawl in the dust beneath their feet, worm of the Tree.'

He continued to fix Wick, unblinking, until the unfortunate acolyte literally grovelled at his feet. At last he glanced away and flicked a speck of dust from his coat with a thumb and forefinger, as if to clean off the last shreds of shadow, the tendrils of unreality that gave away the game.

'We have some busy months ahead of us,' he said tersely. 'Some trusted associates must be found to help us in our task. Gowron, perhaps, or young Ferny. We could do with fresh manpower.' He turned to Wick, brisk. 'Now, acolyte. I have come a long way, and am in need of replenishment.'

Wick's shoulders tensed; he grew smaller, crouched on the surface of the branch, as if he wished to disappear into the bark.

'Yes, Excellency,' he mumbled, wretched.

'You know, I don't mind admitting that I sometimes despair of you,' said Lace. He strolled behind Wick and laid his hands upon the boy's shoulders, the square, axe-like thumbs meeting at the nape of the neck. 'I have chosen you among all the others for my special favour, lavished every attention on you. But you waste your time on trifles. You would advance much more quickly if you let go of this jealousy of yours, this unprofitable envy with regards to your old school chum. It doesn't help us and, frankly, distracts you. You pay the price. I am right, am I not?'

'Yes, sir,' gasped Wick.

Though the Envoy's touch appeared to be light, his acolyte's face had become grey and drawn. He trembled as if Lace had clapped his shoulders in a vice.

'Well, well. Nothing's free, I suppose,' the Envoy sighed.

He contemplated the approaching greatship a moment longer before removing his hands from Wick's shoulders. When he released him, the boy sagged, breathing heavily, his head bowed in fatigue.

'Nothing is free,' repeated Lace with satisfaction. A pink flush suffused his harsh, coarse features, and he signalled the ship with a jaunty wave of his arm.

EPİLOGUE

Tymon did not accompany the advance party that journeyed back to Sheb for the peace talks. He remained at the camp south of the promontory with the other frail or wounded villagers, recuperating on the hospice ship until his bones had set and he was able to hobble about with a cane. Had he been in good health he still would have stayed, for he wished to keep an eye on Galliano. The old man was dangerously weak, suffering from a bout of fly-fever that had complicated his injuries, and Tymon would not quit his cramped quarters in the ship until his friend had made a full recovery.

As a result, he saw little of Samiha in the days following the attack. Although the long, drawn-out process of negotiation took place primarily on the Argosian Admiral's dirigible, with only Laska and Gardan presiding, the Kion did not consent to remain idle. She travelled back with her colleagues to the devastated village to oversee the beginnings of the reconstruction work. For once, her absence did not trouble Tymon. The knowledge that she cared for him, wanted him, had been planted like a swift seed in his heart. It filled him with a sense of possibility. He was willing to wait for her to be ready to see him again.

True to his word, he kept Wick's pendant safe and unused. It was no chore to leave the rod of *orah* lying untouched in his belt-pouch, for the very sight of the slickly glittering thing set his teeth on edge with unpleasant memories. He thought that he would be rid of it the day the treaty was signed. On that rainy winter's afternoon, more than a month after the battle for the Freehold, the hospice ship set sail at last for Sheb. But Tymon did not make the journey with it. Before the old dirigible had even cleared the twig-thickets, Laska and Gardan swept in on the *Lyla*, setting down on the deck. The boy was to accompany them to a different destination.

The ratification of the peace treaty occurred on the Admiral's greatship, at the Argosian fleet's current position, twenty miles west of the promontory. Tymon was obliged to wait uncomfortably through the procedures that took place in the Admiral's cabin, the only person seated during the ceremonial signing. He was ogled at by a gaggle of his countrymen and scrutinised contemptuously by the Admiral himself, a broad-chested, mustachioed patrician. Wick was nowhere in evidence. It was up to Tymon to present the seminary's seal to the daunting Argosian commander, to be affixed on the treaty parchment. After the Admiral had pressed down the seal on the warm wax, he broke off the carved base in a brusque movement and handed the rod of *orah* back to the astonished boy.

'Take it,' murmured Gardan, as he hesitated, reluctant to accept the accursed trinket. 'It's in our agreement. They keep the seal — not the sorcerer's pendant.'

'It is my studied opinion that sorcerers do not exist,' rumbled the Admiral. He looked Tymon coldly up and down. 'Traitors, on the other hand, are ever-present.'

And that was the end of it — or rather the beginning, as Laska pointed out to him kindly, when they had re-embarked onto the air-chariot. He had lost one home and found another. It was almost a relief to have his expulsion from Argosian society spelled out so clearly. He turned his back on the Admiral's fleet with a sense of finality and let the *Lyla* propel him noisily eastwards. They caught up with the old hospice dirigible near the promontory, and brought the air-chariot down on board. They were met there by Samiha, who embarked on the ship at the base of the promontory.

Together they watched from the deck, Tymon propped up next to the Kion on a folding stool, as the ship drew level with what remained of the western spur. The joy of his reunion with her after days of separation, even the triumph of the completed treaty was mingled with sorrow, for this was no glorious homecoming. It was Kosta and Solis' funeral and a memorial gathering for all those who had given their lives defending the Freehold. Laska and Gardan stood at the rail by the young pair, their heads bowed. Fine droplets of water stung their faces and the violated mass of the promontory rose, black and burnt, before their eyes. The bodies of the fallen had been prepared in the Nurian way, spice-embalmed and wrapped in white. They were brought to the end of the spur on biers of woven bark, where the grieving families waited, huddled in the tugging breeze. The rest of the Freeholders had gathered a little further down the branch-path. The dirigible hovered almost directly opposite the two biers, above the charred and gouged remains of the spur.

For a while the only sound was the wind whistling over the promontory and the snap of the dirigible's ropes. Then Samiha's clear voice broke the stillness, ringing out beside Tymon. He shivered as he recognised the slow cadences of the Song of the Dead. He remembered the last occasion he had heard her sing it, after the riot in the Marak shrine, and recalled the verses he had learnt long ago in Argosian. The Song was the same in both languages, a keening, wailing chant, a series of questions and answers, inevitably sung by women.

'Who lies between the worlds?' the first voice would ask.

'A father, a brother and a son,' the second would reply.

A tall woman standing on the spur sang in response to Samiha. Their voices echoed backwards and forwards between the branch and the ship.

'Why does he come here, sister?'

'He departs on the long journey, sister.'

'He goes in peace then, with the love of many.'

'He goes in beauty, to join the Mother.'

'In the beauty.' Tymon breathed the familiar refrain as the Nurian words faded on the breeze.

There was nothing left to do but bid a final farewell to the old judge and the young guard. The biers were dragged to the brink of the gutted limb and tipped over into emptiness. They made no sound as they fell. Tymon thought of the tales of the World Below, the second Tree beneath the Storm. Perhaps his friend's journey would end there.

'*Sav vay*, Solis,' he murmured, his throat constricting.

He imagined it would be over then. But other villagers walked out to the edge of the branch, throwing garlands of white bean-flower and little straw effigies into the wind. There was nothing more of their loved ones to lay to rest. After a time nobody else came forward. But still the Freeholders stood on the spur, and waited in silence.

'Now what happens?' Tymon muttered in Samiha's ear.

He shifted uncomfortably in his seat. The cool air had chilled his bones, only recently knit, and he could not venture outside or walk for extended periods. The signature ceremony had already tired him out. Besides, he was anxious to return to the hold to check on Galliano's condition.

The Kion took a deep breath and tore her eyes from the mists. 'Now, we go home,' she said.

There was to be no checking on Galliano for the present. As Samiha spoke, two of the guards on the ship, young men from Solis' regiment, pushed the gangplank out onto the edge of the spur. Several other villagers secured the dirigible's moorings and the crowd on the branch parted, opening up the path to the heart of the promontory. Laska and Gardan descended the ramp.

Samiha held her hand out to Tymon.

'Can you do it?' she asked.

He understood that she wished him to accompany her down the spur. He stood up experimentally, taking her arm.

'I think so,' he said. 'If we go slowly.'

They shuffled down the ramp behind the two older judges. Before Tymon could set foot on the spur, an unexpected sound caused him to falter on the gangplank. The Freeholders were clapping. Slowly, rhythmically, they clapped their approval, their eyes fixed on him.

'Why are they doing that?' he hissed to Samiha. 'What's going on?'

'I believe,' her mouth twitched with sober amusement as she helped him down the last step, 'I believe they want to show their appreciation for what you've done. Someone must have told them the story of what happened on the Envoy's ship. The gist of it got about, in any case.'

Laska and Gardan moved to the rear, leaving the way open for them, and Tymon limped along with Samiha at the head of the procession, embarrassment flooding him in a tingling rush. The clapping grew louder and whistles and cheers followed them down the spur. *Syon!* cried the voices. *Syon o Sav!*

'What are they saying now?' he asked.

'"Sign of the Sap".' Samiha's whisper was exultant. 'Your coming here is a fulfilment of prophecy, Tymon, whether you like it or not. You are a prophet. Everyone sees that.'

He stopped so suddenly that she clutched his arm in consternation, fearing that he might fall.

'I'm no prophet,' he protested. 'I'm not anything. Not until I learn how to use my gift. I might as well call down lightning on this place for all the good I'll do you till then.' He searched her face intently. 'I'm an ignorant fool,' he reiterated. 'I don't know what's out there, but It knows me. You know better than I do things like the Envoy don't just die. Or if one dies, there's another somewhere, ready to take its place. I can't rely on ghosts and spirits to help me out. I need to learn more.'

She gazed at him in growing wonder as he spoke; he had humbled her for once, rather than the other way around.

'You're right,' she admitted. 'Now that it's clear to everyone you're a Grafter, I'm sure the judges will want you to start your studies as soon as possible.'

He allowed her to lead him on, through the ranks of cheering villagers, though a further, problematic thought had occurred to him.

'There's no one here who can teach me, is there?' he whispered to her.

She shook her head. 'Only a full-fledged Grafter is qualified to train new students. We lost most of ours when the five Focals were killed. There's only one left: the Oracle of Nur.'

'Where does he live?'

'She lives in Cherk Harbour, in the South Fringes.'

'It's just as I feared,' he sighed gloomily. 'I haven't come home at all. I'm stopping on my way to somewhere else. Again.'

'Don't worry,' she assured him, pulling him close as he leaned on her arm. 'We can make this a good, long stop. I'd like that.'

His heart leapt at the admission. 'I'd like it too. But then, you knew that already.'

He wanted more than anything else at that moment to stay and share her life in peace, on the Freehold. But he also understood that this could not happen. Not yet. Not before he had stepped up to the mark.

'It's odd, now I think of it,' she remarked after a pause. 'There was a death on board the tithe-ship when I arrived in Argos city all those months ago. A pilgrim. I didn't know him. They didn't give him any rites. They just threw him overboard before we docked. Now here we are, welcoming you with a proper funeral. We've come full circle, I suppose.'

Tymon grunted with horror. 'That's a terrible omen. A ship bringing a dead body to harbour without rites is bad luck for seven years, so they say.'

'I shall not weep for Argos,' she replied.

'Not many people do,' he observed thoughtfully.

They continued down the solitary path together, hand in hand.

GLOSSARY

Amu: 'mother' in the First Tongue, term commonly used in Argos.

Apu: as above for 'father'.

Argos city: capital of the Argosian state, seat of the Priests' Council and largest city in the Central Canopy.

Bark-brick: dense sections of high quality Tree bark cut to form building blocks and used for durable housing or roads.

Bark-fibre: low quality Tree bark pounded into long strips and used to make rough paper, clothing etc.

Barley-mushroom: mildly hallucinogenic fungus.

Barley-vine: grain crop used for bread.

Blast-poison: semi-mythical explosive substance said to unleash a ball of fire so destructive it can reduce buildings to rubble and gouge sections out of the World Tree. Outlawed for many generations, the secret formula is known to a handful of scholars.

Bound-boy: recipient of the seminary's charity. Typically a boy from the poorer sectors of Argosian society, officially adopted by the Priests' Council and expected to pay off his masters' investment over a period of indenture.

Bread-Giving: traditional charity event occurring before the spring festival in Argos. Intended to demonstrate seminary's generosity to the less fortunate.

Central Canopy: the largest agglomeration of twigs and branches in the World Tree. The Eastern Canopy is only slightly smaller, but the term reflects the mindset of the Argosian cartographers who changed the name from Western to Central Canopy about five hundred years ago. Physical canopy corresponds to the borders of the Argosian state.

Choir-rat: pejorative term for a novice at the seminary.

Clinker-built: built with a system of overlapping planks.

College [the]: a section of the seminary reserved for the higher education of those taking priestly orders. Also the seat of the Priests' Council, governing body of Argos.

Colonies: sections of the Eastern Canopy under the rule of two major imperialist powers, Argos and Lantria. The Argosian colonies are called the Eastern Domains.

Council [the, or Priests']: supreme governing body of Argos, an authority in all religious and secular matters. Father Fallow, Dean of the College, is currently head of the Council and its most influential member. In times past the Dean did not hold such a position of authority, but Fallow has gradually whittled away the political and religious safeguards that kept power in Argos from falling into the hands of one man.

Damned-to-root: oath. Hell according to Argosian religious doctrine is supposed to exist at the roots of the World Tree.

Demons: denizens of Hell, malevolent creatures said to torment the spirits of sinners. Sorcerers are thought to be in league with demons.

Dew-fields: method of farming in drought-ridden Eastern Canopy. Cloth sheets are stretched between twigs of the Tree and used to collect moisture from condensation. Some sheets are also filled with compost and sown with crops.

Dirigible: common means of transport in the Central Canopy. These flying craft are fitted with multiple floatation sacks filled with buoyant Tree-ether. They use sails to capture wind-currents and steer with poles, parachute-like cloth breaks, or directional streams of ether.

Divine Mother: name given by Argosians to the World Tree, which they consider to be both Creator and creation. According to legend, the Divine Mother gave birth to all the plants and animals in the Storm, including human beings. Seeing that they needed the sun to live she stretched her arms and head above the clouds, lifting her children to the light.

Divine Mouth: name of a deep cleft or 'Tree-rift' in the trunk above Argos city. The Mouth is the site of an annual spring sacrifice in which a man is driven into the hollow chasm as an offering to appease the wrath of the World Tree.

Eastern Canopy: agglomeration of twigs and branches piercing the clouds eastwards of the Central Canopy. The Eastern Canopy has suffered a long-term climactic catastrophe over centuries, gradually losing first its leaves, then its Tree-water and Treesap, and finally its rainfall. The chronic drought that followed was probably the single most important factor in the fall of the Nurian Empire and Nurian loss of independence.

Eastern Doctrine: religion practised by Nurians and considered a heresy by Argosians, particularly in its modern form. Though the two schools actually originate in the same ancient belief system, there have been radical departures in dogma on both sides. Nurians do not believe in the divinity of the World Tree. Instead, they maintain there is a divine and invisible Tree of Being, a source of the mystic Sap that gives life to all things. Nurians also believe that the art of Grafting, or prophecy, is still practised in the world today.

Eastern Domains: name given by Argosians to their colonies in the Eastern Canopy, former states of the defunct Nurian Empire.

Eaten: a term used when referring to someone who has or will meet their demise in the Mouth.

Elder: Nurian term of respect for older or wise person.

End Times: eschatological period of reckoning foretold by prophets from both the Nurian and Argosian traditions. There are various Signs the faithful will be able to discern pointing to the advent of the End Times. See also 'Year of Fire'.

Eternal Maelstrom: another name for Hell, the whirlwind that whips about the roots of the World Tree, in which the souls of the damned are forever tormented.

Ether: see Tree-ether.

Explorer Sect: faction of Argosian priests interested in exploration beneath the Storm. They were disbanded a hundred years ago after allegedly being found to worship demons. Their theories have been declared heretical by the Council.

Festival: there are three main holidays or festivals in the Argosian year, corresponding roughly to seasonal events. The first is a spring festival which sees the annual Sacrifice. This is also the time when Argosian boys in their fifteenth year celebrate their Green Rites, or official initiation into adulthood. The second is a harvest festival in late summer. The third is the Tree Festival, a mid-winter holiday celebrating the demise of the old year and the beginning of the new. It includes both religious and secular festivities.

Fireflax: vine plant with chafing thorns, used to perform self-mutilation as a form of penance. Also boiled and peeled to make scrubbing brushes for use in the bathhouse.

Fire-sticks: thin shards of wood coated with a flammable gum and rubbed together to provide a spark.

Fire-watch prayer: special ritual liturgy said to protect from the ravages of fire.

First Tongue: language which predated both Nurian and Argosian and gave rise to both. Names in Argos often have a root in First Tongue (such as 'timon' for 'Tymon', meaning navigator). The First Tongue is also used in some Nurian Grafting rituals.

Fly-fever: infectious sickness resulting in high fevers and death in infants or those who are physically weak.

Focals: name given to the five chief practitioners of Grafting in the Eastern Canopy.

Four Canopies: the habitable parts of the world, namely the Central, Eastern, Northern and Southern sections of the Tree.

Freehold: remnants of independent states in the Eastern Canopy. The Freeholds have treaties of non-violence with the Priests' Council, however, this does not stop the Argosians from conducting periodic raids, or some Nurians on the Freeholds from fomenting rebellion.

Friend [star]: bright star visible in the Argosian night sky for much of the year and used as a navigation marker. The Friend is traditionally associated with good luck.

Frogapple: vine-growing fruit and a bumper crop in Argos. Frogapples are oval with a pointed end, have thin green skin and a light, sweet flavour when ripe. They are used in a wide variety of Argosian dishes.

Gap [the]: the region of empty air between the Central and Eastern Canopies where no branches are visible and only the Storm clouds stretch to the horizon. Most Treeologists accept that the trunk uniting the canopies continues here under the clouds, though some maverick thinkers deny there is any connection at all between the East and West sides of the Tree.

Grafter: a seer or prophet supposedly able to foretell the future from visions gained in a trance. The Grafters of legend claimed to communicate with a mystic force known as the Sap, literally the will of God according to Argosian tradition. Nurian tradition holds that the Sap is a life-giving energy flowing through the Tree of Being.

Grafting: the practice of conducting a Grafter's trance.

Greatship: the largest dirigible vessels, equipped with three masts and multiple ether sacks. They are used as merchant ships to carry cargo over long distances (i.e. between the Central and Eastern Canopies) and to conduct large-scale military operations.

Green Lord: saviour figure actively awaited by Nurians who will appear during the 'End Times' and pass judgment on the inhabitants of the Four Canopies.

Green/Divine Mother: names given by Argosians to the World Tree.

Green Rites: initiation ceremony taking place during an Argosian boy's fifteenth year and conferring the rights and responsibilities of full citizenship. Those who have not been to their Rites in Argos may not hold high positions in government or in the trade and artisan guilds. All applicants for entry to the Priests' College must have completed their Rites. No women or foreigners are eligible. These ceremonies take place in the 'Divine Mouth' and witness the death of a Nurian tithe-pilgrim.

Green Year: period of an Argosian boy's fifteenth year.

Guild Fair: event organised by the various Argosian guilds in order to interest students at the seminary in an apprenticeship with their organisation. Entry to the Guild Fair is only available to those students completing their Green Rites, or those with families rich enough to buy them a ticket.

Hardwood: a type of very dense wood mined from the inner sections of the World Tree's trunk.

Hell: a mythical region at the foot of the World Tree, sometimes referred to as the Eternal Maelstrom. This whirlwind gives birth to the Storm clouds. The shrieking winds are said to be inhabited by demons who torment the souls of the damned with flaming broomsticks.

Hunter [the]: well-recognised star constellation appearing near the Friend.

Impure/Impurity: Argosian concept associated with spiritual worth. Some activities are ritually unclean and must be avoided while engaged in particularly holy activities, such as preparing for the Green Rites. Whole segments of society are considered Impure in Argos, including women, foreigners, homeless vagabonds and travelling entertainers called Jays. Even touching such a person might incur a penalty for someone preparing for their Green Rites, for example.

Jar-pipe: device used to smoke jar-weed.

Jar-weed: mildly stimulant, addictive herb cultivated in Argos both for medicinal and recreational purposes. Side-effects with long-term use include lung disease and various other ailments.

Jay: a travelling actor or entertainer, outcast from settled Argosian society. Jays often live in extended family groups with a strong sense of internal identity.

They travel the Central Canopy in dirigible convoys and generally convene once a year in Argos city during the Tree Festival, when rules of Impurity are relaxed.

Juno and Lyla: tale of star-crossed lovers. Lyla is a beautiful maiden and Juno her young suitor. Lyla's family refuses the match and forbids her to see Juno, shutting her away in a high tower. Driven mad by grief, Juno wanders the canopy.

Kingdom of Light: title of the Nurian Empire ('Nur' meaning 'light' in the First Tongue).

Kion: title of the Nurian monarch, once a constitutional ruler of the Nurian Empire. Though the monarchy still exists it has been outlawed by the Priests' Council, forcing members of the royal family into hiding.

Kush: strong liquor distilled from tubers and bark and found primarily in the Eastern Canopy.

Lantria: nation whose borders correspond roughly to the South Canopy. Lantria is the second most powerful state in the Tree, as economically influential if not more so than Argos. Lantrians specialise in ship-building, mining for hardwood and increasingly in the trade of captured Nurian slaves.

Leaf-forests: stands of twigs and leaves, often growing so densely out of the top of a branch that the space at their base becomes a knotty lump. In this way a pedestrian might cross parts of the canopy without the need of a dirigible, using roads that wind up and down the branches and through the stands, spanning gaps between the leaf-forests on suspended bridges.

Leaf-line: horizon as seen from the confines of the World Tree.

Leaf-Letters: mystic divinatory language associated with the Tree of Being and used by Nurian Grafters.

Argosian sources do not generally mention the Leaf Letters.

Letter of Dominion: one of the Leaf-Letters.

Lightwood: a less durable wood than hardwood, mined from outer reaches of the trunk or from certain branches.

Loss: one of the Leaf-Letters.

Marak: relatively new colonial city (established in the last fifty years) with a mixed population of Argosians and Nurians. Grave tensions persist between the local colonists, the natives, and their Argosian rulers in the Central Canopy. Marak colonials are mostly merchants dealing in 'Treespice', the one plentiful natural resource in the Eastern Canopy.

Margoose: flightless bird raised for eggs and meat in Argos. Margeese lack feathers on much of their bodies and have a scaly, leathery hide.

Mora: stifling season before the onset of the autumn rains in the Eastern Canopy. Temperatures soar and the weather is oppressive and overcast.

Nurry: pejorative term used by Argosians to refer to Nurians.

Old Empire: former Nurian Empire.

Old Ones: first humans to settle the Tree, said to be both great Grafters and prolific inventors. They were the first to use dirigible technology and mine for hardwood, as well as obtain the mysterious shining *orah*, which adorned their houses and became a hallmark of their civilisation.

Orah: a type of magical hardwood mined from the heart of the Tree. The secret of obtaining it has been lost along with much of the knowledge possessed by the Old Ones.

Path [of Sacrifice]: high ledge on the trunk-wall leading from the main road out of Argos city to the Divine Mouth.

Penta: Nurian for 'Fifth', specifically one of the five Focals.

Pesh and Amran: two Grafters and prophets in the Argosian tradition. Pesh and Amran were missionaries who sought to convert barbarian tribes a hundred years after Saint Loa crossed the Gap.

Pon: worthless paper currency printed by the Governor of Marak.

Priests' Quarter: area of Argos city given over to the seminary and Temple complex.

Putar: pejorative term used by Nurians to refer to Argosians.

Rain-well: hole drilled into a branch to harvest rainwater.

Rites-duties: series of tasks to be completed by a Green Year student in time for the spring festival.

Sacrifice: a ritual occurring during the spring festival, in which a Nurian tithe-pilgrim voluntarily gives up his life. In reality many Argosian citizens suspect that the priests use some underhand means to secure a willing victim every year. Tymon finds out from Galliano that the ritual did not always involve a human sacrifice.

Saint Loa: sometimes referred to as the Father of Argos, or the All-Father, Loa was a Nurian prophet who preached a renewal of doctrine and criticised the corrupt and decadent rulers of the 'Old Empire'. When his movement was banned in Nur he crossed the Gap with his followers to establish a new 'Kingdom of Light' in the then-Western Canopy. He went on to start the Priests' College in Argos city. All Argosians claim to be descended from one of Saint Loa's twelve wives, but it is more likely that they are a mix of local tribespeople already in the region and Nurian settlers. Nothing is now known of the culture or language of the original inhabitants of the Western Canopy.

Saint Usala the Green: a prophetess living about five hundred years after Saint Loa. Saint Usala defied many of the conventions of Argosian society, not least the tradition that Grafting had come to an end. She set up Focal groups and insisted on teaching young people her art. She was finally declared a heretic by the Council and put to death. About twenty years afterwards the Council was forced to retract its ruling when it was discovered that many of her predictions had come true. She is still, however, considered to be one of the last Grafters.

Sap: mystic force which Argosians claim is the will of God and Nurians characterise as the source of all life. Both traditions credit the Sap with independent intelligence. Grafters are said to commune with it.

Seeming: illusion called into being by a Grafter which acquires physical reality if people believe strongly enough in it.

Seven Hypocrites of Mung: Mung was a city in the Eastern Canopy. The Hyprocrites were followers of Saint Loa, who after swearing fealty to him in Argos regretted their decision and wished to return home.

Shanti: the person calling the faithful to prayer at a Nurian temple. The *shanti* also lead some rituals. Practitioners of the Eastern Doctrine have no formal priesthood and look to the Focals for spiritual guidance. However, some *shanti* (lit. 'temple singer') have been known to give sermons and exhort their fellow citizens like Argosian priests.

Shillee: herd-dwelling mammal with small cloven feet that allow it to climb steep areas of the Tree with relative ease. Shillees eat moss and other plants and are kept by herders for their meat, milk and pelts.

Shortwheat: a type of barley-vine grown in the Eastern Canopy, drought resistant.

Sight [the]: the raw capacity or talent to be a Grafter. Someone with the Sight may experience premonitory dreams or visions.

Silesian bellweed: a hallucinogenic plant found in the North Fringes, toxic in high doses.

Som: a sedative made from purified Tree-spice, smoked to produce a lethargic state and vivid dreams. Highly addictive.

Sorceress of Nur: a legendary character who opposed Saint Loa in the Eastern Canopy. Her name has not been preserved but her machinations are legendary. She appears in so many different stories and over such an extended period that some scholars maintain the character is a composite.

South Fringes: southern extremities of both the Central and Eastern Canopies.

Storm: cloud-cover shrouding the base of the Tree in mist. The Storm is a repository for legendary horrors. As well as demons and the souls of the damned, strange beasts are said to inhabit the clouds, nesting in the lower regions of the Tree. Dirigibles sailing near the Fringes have reported giant flying snakes and tribes of winged monkeys in the Storm.

Storm Ventures: expeditions organised by the Explorer Sect, who claimed that Hell had physical mass and wanted to map the area beneath the Storm. According to seminary history books no one ever returned from the Ventures.

Strawpaper: cheap and low quality paper made from straw pulp and mostly produced in the Eastern Canopy.

Talek: Argosian wood money carved from hardwood discs. A *talek* generally bears the image of a stylised Tree on one side and a depiction of Saint Loa on the other, although different, limited edition tenders are carved on special occasions.

Tithe-ship: dirigible bearing a consignment of tithe-pilgrims from the eastern colonies.

Tithe-pilgrims: Nurians who have signed on to fulfil the annual quota of workers from their area of the Eastern Canopy. The families of tithe-pilgrims are paid up-front in barrels of water. Tithe-pilgrims theoretically regain their freedom after a period of hard labour.

Tree of Being: the Eastern Doctrine posits the existence of a mystic Tree of Being containing and connecting all things. It can only be Seen by Grafters in a trance who step outside the physical universe. The Sap is the life-energy flowing through the Tree of Being.

Tree-rift: natural chasm or opening in the World Tree.

Tree-cat: a medium-sized feral feline.

Tree-ether: a gas naturally occurring in pockets in the World Tree, tapped and harvested for use in dirigibles.

Tree-face: large flat area of bark, generally a section of the trunk.

Tree-gall: dregs left behind when Treesap is distilled and purified.

Tree-mines: man-made shafts sunk into the World Tree in order to extract certain products such as hardwood. Work in the Tree-mines is notoriously difficult and dangerous, often accomplished by slave labour.

Treeology: a study of the layout, composition and characteristics of the World Tree, including climate, flora and fauna. Treeology courses for students at the seminary also include some navigation skills and a rudimentary understanding of astronomy. Professors in Applied Treeology focus on engineering, physics, chemistry and climatology.

Treesap: liquid running through the branches of the Central Canopy, tapped and used by humans for various purposes. In the Eastern Canopy the Treesap has largely dried up, leaving behind a powdery residue called Tree-spice.

Treesap wine: alcoholic beverage made from fermented Treesap.

Treescape: a vista of the World Tree.

Tree-spice: residue remaining after Treesap has dried within the arteries of the World Tree. Mined for medicinal and preservative purposes among other uses.

Tree-water: naturally occurring reservoirs of rainwater caught in the World Tree. Some originate in the ice and snow of the Upper Fringes, creating quasi-permanent torrents through hollow channels in the Tree.

Tree-worship: Nurian term for Argosian religious doctrine. Nurians practising the Eastern Doctrine maintain that Argosian priests have forgotten or twisted the original teachings of Saint Loa, substituting worship of the ordinary World Tree for the divine Tree of Being.

Twig-tongue: a hybrid language spoken in the Eastern Domains, a mix of Nurian and Argosian.

Upper Fringes: the summit of the Central Canopy, leafless and covered in ice and snow. There is little air to breathe in the extreme Upper Fringes and they are mostly unihabited.

Void [Circling, or the]: general name for all that lies beyond the confines of the World Tree, including the Storm.

Weather spirits: a remnant of animistic belief in invisible spirits controlling the wind and weather.

Well of Worlds: an area in the South Fringes of the Eastern Canopy where the Storm clouds are thin. According to reports it is possible to see another canopy beneath the clouds.

West Chasm: region of open air near Argos city. Unlike the Gap, branches are always visible on three sides of the Chasm. The Storm clouds are obscured by those below.

White-neck: Argosian born in the Eastern Domains.

Wind-wells: windmill-like devices used by ancient Nurians to extract Treesap from deep shafts. According to some sources, it was this technological over-exploitation of the Eastern Canopy that led to the sap-wells drying up and the loss of the canopy's leaves. Other (Argosian) sources claim that Nurians lost their Treesap through wrong belief.

Year of Fire: an eschatological marker roughly equivalent to the 'End Times'.his is the moment all Grafting prophecy has been leading up to: the period immediately preceding the appearance of the Green Lord. Five 'Signs of the Sap' herald the start of the Year of Fire, including events as diverse as the death of certain flora and fauna to the doomed reign of the twelfth Kion. Some Grafter sources describe the Year of Fire as being the permanent mystic birth and rebirth of the world, but that interpretation has largely been sidelined in favour of more apocalyptic prophecies.

Yosha: fragrant herb found in the Eastern Canopy and infused in hot water to form a refreshing drink.

Nurian terms and phrases

Argosi: Argosian
Askar: temple
Attar: Tree-spice
Bas: enough
Beni: blessed
Foy: fire
Las: alas
Maz: thank you
Mo dia: my god
Nami: friend
Nosra morti: we will die
Penta: fifth
Putar: son of a whore
Sav vay: may the Sap watch over you
Sav beni: may the Sap bless you
Shanti: singer
Syor/a: sir or madam
Syon o Sav: Sign of the Sap
Vaz: go on
Y maza Sav: … and thanks to the Sap

ACKNOWLEDGMENTS

I could not have written this book without the staunch support of a number of people. I am deeply grateful to my agent, Helenka Fuglewicz, for patiently nurturing this project to life from its earliest days and to my editor, Stephanie Smith, for shepherding it through to completion. I am indebted to my mother, Bahiyyih Nakhjavani, who acted as teacher, mentor, first reader and best critic throughout. Last but not least I could not have been free to devote myself to writing full time without the help and support of my husband, Frank Victoria. To all those who participated near and far in bringing my dream to life: thank you.